Also by Lila Shaara
Every Secret Thing

THE
FORTUNE
TELLER'S
DAUGHTER

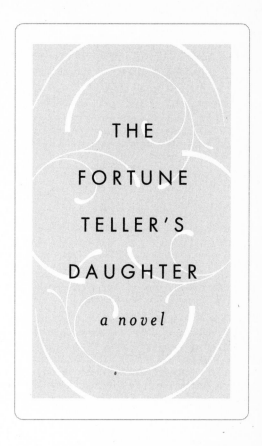

THE
FORTUNE
TELLER'S
DAUGHTER

a novel

Lila Shaara

BALLANTINE BOOKS NEW YORK

Copyright © 2008 by Lila Shaara

All rights reserved.

Published in the United States by Ballantine Books, an imprint of The Random House Publishing Group, a division of Random House, Inc., New York.

BALLANTINE and colophon are registered trademarks of Random House, Inc.

Illustrations from the Rider-Waite Tarot Deck®, known also as the Rider Tarot and the Waite Tarot, reproduced by permission of U.S. Games Systems, Inc., Stamford, CT 06902 USA. Copyright © 1971 by U.S. Games Systems, Inc. Further reproduction prohibited. The Rider-Waite Tarot Deck® is a registered trademark of U.S. Games Systems, Inc.

Library of Congress Cataloging-in-Publication Data
Shaara, Lila.
The fortune teller's daughter: a novel / Lila Shaara.
p.   cm.
ISBN 978-0-345-48567-0
1. Law teachers—Fiction.   2. Murder—Investigation—Fiction.   3. Florida—Fiction.
I. Title.

PS3619.H26F67 2008
813'.6—dc22
2008028782

Printed in the United States of America on acid-free paper

www.ballantinebooks.com

2 4 6 8 9 7 5 3 1

First Edition

Book design by Liz Cosgrove

For Michael, my father,
and Helen, my mother

Acknowledgments

One summer many years ago, my friend Sara Sturdevant sent me a postcard from a paleontological dig in Wyoming. The message was pithy. Camped out among the rocks and stars, she'd come to realize two things. "Nature is big," she wrote. "People are small." That was one inspiration for this book, along with countless other bits of information and images that have floated across my vision over the years: my father's interest in Nikola Tesla; my older son's blue eyes; my younger son's enormous heart; my husband's considerable unsung genius; the frustration, heartache, and great beauty of my oldest friends. One of these, Celeste Rosenau, deserves a special thank-you because of her army of book buyers across the country, ready to rally on behalf of a local girl long after I moved north. I was also inspired by the true stories of two women: Sarah Hoffman and Hedy Lamarr, whose accomplishments in biology and engineering, respectively, may never be fully appreciated by the public.

Dr. Martha Ann Terry of the Graduate School of Public Health at the University of Pittsburgh gave me essential information on the ownership of graduate students' research, and Bart Wise clued me in on a number of other pertinent intellectual property issues. Almost everything I know about bee allergies and epinephrine I owe to my longtime friend A. J. (Big Al) Caliendo. However, any mistakes made in this work about anything are mine.

I'm grateful for the priceless support of some new friends as well; many thanks to Nancy Martin, Rebecca Drake, Kathleen George, Kathryn Miller Haines, and Heather Terrell (buy their books!), along with the proprietors of Mystery Lovers Bookshop in Oakmont, Pennsylvania, and the members of the Mary Roberts Rinehart chapter of Sisters in Crime.

There was a real Purple Lady once upon a time, although to my regret I never spoke to her; she was not a southerner and bears little resemblance to Miss Tokay. The shrine and temple are only vaguely based on structures she actually built, although they were destroyed long ago by a dull-witted heir, and the details of the religion surrounding them differ considerably from what's presented here. I'll always remain grateful to William "Hungry Bill" Pelger and Edward Boytim for first showing me the shrine and letting me in on a local legend.

All Tarot interpretations are after Eden Gray, although I have taken a great deal of license with them.

My husband and sons are the primary inspirations for my life in general, and I try to thank them for that every chance I get. (Here goes: Thanks, guys!) Also, I extend vast gratitude to the Magnetic Fields, Robyn Hitchcock, Low, and Brian Eno, all of whom made music that was essential to my finishing the darn thing.

THE
FORTUNE
TELLER'S
DAUGHTER

The sun was almost warm, so she stood outside the idling car. She passed the time by watching the way the clouds moved with the air currents high in the atmosphere, the way the light reflected off them and scraped the sky. That light had torn through the dark space between the giant boiling furnace of the sun and the little blue earth that circled it, the journey taking only eight minutes. She imagined the sun's light bouncing off the clouds and careening back into space, out to the moon, to Mars and beyond. Years from now, she thought, some gelatinous creature on a rocky planet with a purple sky might see a tiny spark above the horizon that would be the very beam of light that was at this moment pinging off a cloud that looked like a white rose.

When her husband had finished saying his good-byes to the people gathered on the lawn, he came to the car, walking gracefully, athletically, his jacket flung over his shoulder. He had been raised in the Northeast and so didn't feel the chill the way she did. He wanted to make a few calls on the way home. She offered to drive, but the suggestion irritated him, and he shook his head at her as he threw his jacket over the seat to the back and got in. He was close to middle-aged but was well-tended and moved easily. She still felt a little flip in her chest at the way he moved.

In spite of his resistance to the cold, Charlie flipped the switch for the heat and left the windows closed. He turned on the radio, a classical station that made no money from commercials; it was supported by the rich families that populated the beautiful valleys in houses as large as state monuments. Something by Mozart, something too fast and ornate for her liking. She would have preferred Dvořák or Bruch, or maybe Aaron Copland. Charlie said her taste in classical music was that of a teenager or a precocious child.

They pulled out of the long driveway onto the narrow, well-paved road that girded the hills and led back to the town. Their house was not very far away, and while it wasn't as grand as the one they'd just visited, it was grand enough, with five bedrooms, a full bathroom in each, and a wine cellar. She was always grateful that it wasn't her job to clean it. The car moved quietly on the seamless pavement, and she looked out the window at the clouds and the sun. Charlie jarred her thoughts with a request that she get the phone from the pocket of his jacket on the backseat. She unfastened her seat belt and turned, lifted herself onto her knees and bent over, leaning between the seat backs to reach for the jacket. The angle made her stomach feel heavy. Through the rear windshield she could see a tractor trailer some distance behind them. It was gaining on them slowly, but she knew that as soon as Charlie caught sight of it growing larger in the mirror he would speed up. She suddenly felt vulnerable and light, imagining what it would be like to be hit by the semi or to enter free fall as the car flew off the embankment into the valley below.

The road took a turn, and she had to grab the seat back to keep from falling into the passenger door. She kept her left arm firmly around the headrest as she reached back again. Then she had the jacket by the arm; she tugged on it as it spread itself over the rear bench, and she had to pull and pull so that it came through the gap extended, as if she was doing a magic trick, the endless jacket. As the last of it popped through, she saw movement at the top of the exposed pocket, something golden and black. The wasp was silent. Later she was to think that that was not what you'd expect; you'd expect it to be buzzing with evil intent. But it simply walked up the face of the jacket, looking for sugar. She was calmer than she would have expected to be, even though they'd rehearsed what was to be done many times.

"Where's your EpiPen?" she said, keeping her voice low and serene.

"What?" Charlie looked at her with a face that suggested that she was playing a stupid game. "Why?"

"Where is it?" she said, knowing that if she said why she wanted it, there was a good chance he'd drive off the road in a panic.

"In the pocket," he said. "You know that."

She pulled the jacket toward her with great care and gentleness, trying not to disturb the wasp as it crept up the leather toward the collar. There was just enough room to reach into the pocket without touching the wasp. She eased her hand in and found a wad of fabric: a handkerchief wrapped around a chunk of something cold, the fabric slightly damp. She didn't dare pull the handkerchief out, fearing the disturbance might propel the wasp to flight. So she worked her fingers around the handkerchief, hoping to feel the thin plastic tube entangled with the cool cloth. A burning little mouth bit her fingertip and she almost jerked her hand back, but concern for Charlie overrode everything, including the safety of her own fingers. She pulled her hand out with care, surprised at the thought that there must be another wasp in the pocket; she got no satisfaction from the idea that the one who'd stung her was probably dead. Wait, she thought, it was the honeybee that died when it stung you; wasps can sting again and again. Good thing I'm not allergic, too.

Her fingertip was starting to burn, but she knew better than to react. She balanced herself carefully on her knees, twisted her body a little, and pushed her unstung hand under the jacket, trying to feel the lip of the pocket on the other side, trying to work her fingers into it without shifting the top. She found the pocket's edge after a few seconds, and her fingers wriggled in tiny movements as she explored the interior. She felt the phone and made a scissor of two of her fingers, gliding it out of the pocket and then laying it on the seat by her knees. Charlie's eyes darted to her hands every few seconds. When he saw that she'd produced the phone, he said, "Finally." That was when he saw the wasp.

He slowed the car, but there was nowhere to pull over. The semi behind them honked loudly, a huge sound that rattled her spine, and then Charlie gave the gas pedal a tap that caused the car to accelerate and decelerate so quickly that she was forced to grab the back of the seat again to keep her spine from crashing into the dashboard. After the ringing of the horn faded, she could hear Charlie's breathing. "Slow down," she said. "I'll get the pen. Just drive. It'll be all right."

The wasp miraculously hadn't been disturbed by the lurching of the car. It had reached the collar and was walking along it, smelling, tasting, exploring. She worked her hand again into the pocket on the underside of the jacket, expecting the pen to be there, but she could feel nothing else, just unfinished leather and grainy lint. She thought, Where the hell is it? She said, "It must be in your pants pocket. It's not in here."

"Yes it is," he said, his lips dry and pale. "I remember when we left the house. Cell phone in one, EpiPen in the other. I always do it that way."

"It's not there now. It must be in your pants."

"It's not in my goddamned pants, Emily." He used her name only when he was upset. Now his voice thinned as it got louder. "I never put it in my goddamned pants."

His eyes left the road again; he looked at the wasp as it lifted lazily off the leather and began its first loop up to the rearview mirror, then hovered for a moment by her face. She resisted the urge to bat it away. It landed on her shoulder, and she froze, still on her knees facing the backseat. Charlie stared at it, white-faced, and she said, "Just drive, Charlie. Look at the road. Maybe open the window."

He turned back, his lips slightly apart, and then the yellow and gold wasp lifted off her shoulder and circled again, perfect ellipses around her head, then around the dome light on the ceiling of the car, landing gently on Charlie's forehead before his hand had a chance to move to the window button. "Charlie," she said as he looked at her and the huge horn sounded again and they both knew that the world was about to explode. "I love you," she said. She never knew if he didn't say it back because he wouldn't have or because he never got the chance.

I

THE DEVIL

Depression;
experience without
understanding

Harry Sterling knew he was driving too fast. The narrow road was so black that the white stripe down the center was startling in the dark, bending and straightening as if it was belly dancing in the headlights. Harry had the steering wheel in a sweaty grip, matching the curves turn for turn, but he couldn't seem to get his right foot to lift up from the gas pedal. It seemed that no part of his body was responding to his wishes. His stomach threatened to eject its con-tents at any moment, which would be disastrous for both the interior of the car and his own survival. He was singing, loudly and atonally, "Carry On My Wayward Son," and nothing he could tell himself would make the singing stop. He was drunk, stinking, deadly drunk, and was horrifically aware of it with a tiny, sober part of himself, deep in his brain. It was the part that was trying to get his foot to lighten up on the gas, the part that was so very grateful for the independent intelligence of his hands.

Where am I going again? he asked that sober part for at least the third time. The sober part said, You're going to a fucking fortune teller. She's going to predict your future, you worthless, drunken bastard.

He didn't drink often, but when he did, terrible things happened. He couldn't stop at one, or even two. It always turned into six or eight or ten, no matter how hard that internal voice screamed at him, no matter how many sympathetic, disapproving looks he got from his companions, no matter how great his mortification from the waitress's rolling eyes or the contempt of other bar patrons. Most of the time he didn't even want liquor; he hated wine, and beer rarely called to him at all. But once in a while, something happened, some memory knocked him over or someone put a cocktail in his unresisting hand, bought a round, something, and then there he was, drowning in the pit of his own lack of self-control.

He had been to the Brew House only once before, at the beginning of the fall semester, his first at the university as a visiting professor. Most of the law students gathered there every Friday afternoon during the school year, along with a few of the younger professors. That Friday in September, he'd tried to keep it to one beer, but it turned into two, and then God knew how many. He'd managed to stagger out of the bar without doing anything too awful, although he'd woken up in his backyard wearing only his pants. He had felt as bad as it was possible to feel while still being alive, not only because of the hangover. The mosquitoes that lurked in the grass had feasted on him during the night. When he came to, his left eye refused to open, the numerous bites on his eyelid having caused it to swell to the size of a peach; the ones in his armpits prevented him from being able to fully lower his arms for two days.

That experience had been enough to keep him away from anything alcoholic for six months, until today, another Friday. His best student, a twenty-something second-year named Dan Polti, was going through an acrimonious divorce and wanted a sympathetic and divorced adult to talk to. Dan knew that Harry didn't usually drink, although he didn't know why. They'd sat for a while by themselves, Dan's head occasionally dropping into his hands as he talked while Harry sat helpless, trying to feel more sympathy than he actually did. Most of the other students were sitting at a long wooden table under one of the speakers that hung like huge tumors from the wall. The number of students at the long table had grown until privacy was no longer possible, and Dan had left. Harry had tried to leave as well, but Judd Lippman, another youngish law professor, had corralled Harry into joining the merriment at the long table, and Harry hadn't had sufficient energy to say no. Judd was one of those professors who preyed on the newest and most toothsome of the female students; he had his arm draped over one now, a slender twenty-four-year-old with the unfortunate name of Veronica Ho. Ronnie, as she was known, was shy and very pretty, a fact that Harry tried to find interesting but only succeeded in finding sad.

He'd tried to say no to the mug of beer that someone poured for him from a giant, sweaty pitcher in the center of the table, but the mug had stayed stubbornly in front of him, only an inch or so from his right hand.

"How's the book coming, Harry?" Judd hollered. Judd's hair was receding, and his forehead was shining under faux Tiffany lamps; these hung from what looked like fat, dark cables, but on closer inspection Harry could see they were in fact metal chains. The cobwebs coating them were so thick that they obscured the links. He took a drink. The beer tasted like soap.

"Fine," he said.

"What's fine?" said Judd. Judd was already drunk.

"The book," Harry said. "It's going fine."

Julie Canfield, a second-year who Harry had been told had a crush on him, opened soft brown eyes wide and said, "What's your book going to be about, Dr. Sterling?"

He took another swallow of beer. It still tasted lousy, but he took a third anyway. There was silence at the table. Oh, Jesus Christ, he thought, is every goddamned person here looking at me? Shit, shit, shit. *There is no book*, his brain screamed. Harry took another slug of beer, which emptied the mug. "Law. Media. Intellectual property." Sounds fascinating, he thought. Should have said it's about drying piss. Even more compelling. "Dust in the Wind" was playing through the pendulous speakers at a moderate volume. They would be cranked up when the band started playing, hours from now. Harry hoped he'd be home by then, snug in his bed, propped up by many pillows with the only Robertson Davies book he hadn't yet read, something cold and nonalcoholic on the nightstand.

"Hey, Harry," said Judd, his arm tightening around Ronnie Ho. He touches her in public, thought Harry, but he never looks at her. "You've been to the purple shrine thing south of town, haven't you? Crazy cult types. All right up your alley."

"You mean the Purple Lady's shrine?" said Julie. "I thought it was a witch coven. I went to the palm reader out there once."

One of the male students whose haircut and white shirt looked equally crisp said, "That's the scientist psychic, right?" A few people started laughing as he added, "Try saying that fast three times." Harry knew he should know the male student's name even though he hadn't had him in a class, but he couldn't think of it. "What are you talking about?" he said, appalled that he had some difficulty getting the sentence out clearly.

Judd said, "You haven't heard the story? It's pretty funny. It was Ronnie's roommate, right, Ronnie? The physics girl?" A rare glance at her face. The beautiful Ronnie nodded but said nothing. Judd went on for her. "This psychic tells her that she was buddies with a scientist who invented something big."

Ronnie spoke so softly it was hard to hear over the music from the sound system. A new song blared; Harry couldn't recall the title, but he knew that he hated it. "It was the Ziegart effect." She looked at Judd, who was looking at Harry, then said, "She said that Ziegart stole it."

"Didn't a lot of people say that about Watson and Crick and DNA?" asked the crisp young man.

"They were right, weren't they?" Julie said. "Allegedly?" she added, law school having taught her caution.

"What is it?" Harry said. The good thing about being drunk, he thought, is that you no longer care if people think you are smart or not.

Judd said, "Something about physics. Or gravity. I don't know. The witch doctor woman lives in a trailer, so I don't imagine she's hanging out with too many Einsteins."

"Her name is Madame Dupree. She told me that my mother was sick," said Ronnie. "It was true. She had diverticulitis."

There was some hooting at the psychic's name as the crisp boy said, "Anyone over forty probably has something that would show up on an MRI. These gypsy folks learn how to read people and tell them what they want to hear."

There was agreement and dissent at this comment, and Harry was too bleary to follow the conversation very well. He was only thirty-seven, but the idea of his impending middle age being littered with ailments depressed him so much that he drained his beer and waited patiently for someone to refill his mug.

"She's not a gypsy," said Ronnie. "I don't think so, anyway. And not all gypsies are criminals, you know."

Judd interrupted. "There's your book, Harry. It's got everything. Religious weirdos, science, and intellectual property." Yuk-yuk, thought Harry.

"Madame Dupree has helped my roommate a lot," said Ronnie, a little louder now, her reticence fading as the alcohol took hold. "I think she's for real." Ronnie stopped, looked around, regained her embarrassment, and looked at Judd again. Harry finished his new beer and poured another as someone asked where this psychic could be found. The name of the hated song flung itself at him from the bowels of his unconscious: "Pink Houses."

Now his sober self realized that he didn't know what time it was, didn't know how long it had been since he'd left the Brew House. Eerily, he knew exactly where he was; he had the directions to the psychic's home clearly in his mind, the mental map distinct and sharp. He'd spent a lot of his free time over the short north Florida winter driving around, getting to know the layout of most of Stowe County. When Ronnie had described the location of Madame Dupree's trailer, he'd seen the sign in his mind, dredged up from some Saturday ramble through the outskirts of town. A sign shaped like a saluting hand and covered with painted blue stars and the words *Psychic Readings* in large, curly letters. He had only a hazy recollection of the trailer itself, a double-wide, he thought, placed well back from the road. The hand-shaped sign would have been memorable enough, even if it hadn't been for the shrine that you passed first, a huge concrete edifice, terraced and topped with a giant purple heart surrounded by lights, some ten feet off the road. The Shrine of the Purple Lady. Given his past, he should have had more interest in it before now, but he hadn't wanted to ask anyone about it. He was outsider enough.

The road was straighter now, and Harry could see a bright light in the distance, notable because he had long passed all the normal lights of the town; he was out in the true country, where the black was so thick it had a texture, and then he could see the shrine itself, huge and brilliant. His foot finally rose off the accelerator as the thing took real form and he could see that there were spotlights in a semicircle on the ground, feeding it with light, and there were colors around the heart itself, Christmas lights strung insanely around and around the heart and the terraced platforms beneath it. Harry stopped singing.

But the car kept moving, slowly now, thank God, past the great gaudy shrine, and then he could see the hand, dim and small even in the high beams. As it grew, it was as clear to the drunken Harry as anything had ever been, the now-giant hand was signaling Halt.

2

THE TOWER

Unexpected disaster.
Old lifeways shattered

Josie Dupree laid out the cards as Maggie came in from the temple; she looked as tired as Josie had seen her. She went to take a shower; when she came back from the bathroom fifteen minutes later, Josie said, "You'd be pretty if you ever got any sleep."

"Thanks. What's there to eat?"

"Some spaghetti. Peanut butter and jelly. You forgot dinner again. I'm going to read for you."

"Not tonight."

"Can't help it. I have the urge."

"Busman's holiday," said Maggie, opening the refrigerator and peering inside.

"What?"

"It's an expression. It means that even when you're off work, you're still doing your job."

"Oh. You're looking mighty brown today."

"Dark brown or light?"

Josie paused, a large card in her hand, then said, "Light. Only flecks, though. Mostly you're blue."

"Hmm." Maggie shut the refrigerator door and walked to the breakfast bar that separated the kitchen from the combined living and dining area. "What do they say?"

Josie looked down at the eleven cards spread on the table, then gathered them together and put them on top of the deck, facedown. "Not too much."

"What was in the center?"

Josie paused, then shrugged. "The Tower. That's the main one."

Maggie stared at Josie and then said, "Big change."

"Yes. Soon." After a minute Josie added, "I went to a meeting tonight."

Maggie said, "Good. You stop going, you drink. I'm glad you're going again. I want you around forever."

"Nobody's around forever."

Harry staggered up the wooden steps and pushed through an unlatched screen door onto a wooden porch. The door slammed and bounced against its frame when he let go, unable to summon the coordination to close it more gracefully. In front of him was what appeared to be the main entrance into the double-wide, a narrow fiberglass door with a window, covered on the inside by a yellow curtain. There was light filtering through it; someone was up. He still didn't know what time it was, and the sober part of his mind seemed to have gone to sleep. He knocked on the door, hitting the frame beside the window with his fist. He was trying to be gentle but was afraid that being too gentle would mean no one would hear him, so he alternated the strength of his blows. Sometimes the door seemed to shake in its frame, making him guess that he was hitting too hard. Other times, he could hear no sound at all; too soft. He was pondering this, trying to calibrate the pressure to somewhere in the middle, when a light came on, hurting his eyes, and a short, dark woman opened the door. Her hair was curly and long, she was wearing a caftan covered with pink and purple flowers, and she was holding an enormous flashlight. She was speechless as he swayed before her, and his palsying pupils couldn't let in enough light for him to make out her face. He said, "Lawrence," then managed to turn to the side before he threw up.

He found himself sometime later in a small living room, sitting on a sofa with a coffee mug half-filled with ginger ale in his hand and a green blanket around his shoulders. The blanket was soft and smelled wonderful and he was trying to thank the two women in the room, but he couldn't seem to talk. His stomach felt trembly and vacant, so he was optimistic that he wasn't going to be sick again. He sipped the ginger ale, which tasted extraordinarily delicious. A thought struck him; fortune tellers expected to be paid, maybe even before services rendered, he didn't know. So he reached for his wallet, which stuck in his pants pocket alarmingly so that he had to tug and tug, and when it finally escaped from his pants, he rolled a little to the left from the momentum. Time was elongated; he felt he was moving through oil. He finally corrected, with his wallet in the hand not holding the mug. He couldn't make out what the women were saying till one of them took the flashlight out of the other's hand and said something about not needing it. Of course, he thought blearily. There's plenty of light in here. Way too much. It hurt his eyes.

"Here," he said, holding out his wallet.

The older woman took it, opened it, and pulled something out. He wondered if he should trust her with his credit card. He had only one, but it had a high limit. Maybe she was a gypsy, he thought; maybe she was a thief.

His mind went for a walk again, and he was only later to remember being led gently to the door and down the wooden steps to a car, not his, a smaller car with cracked leather seats that smelled of something like incense. A voice he liked, low and warm and slightly raspy, told him to get in, helped him to get the seat belt buckled, leaning over him with a smell of lemon mixing with the incense. Another blank, then he was being helped up the front steps to his porch by someone shorter than he was. The person unlocked his door, miraculously having his keys, then hands pushed him into his front hallway.

"Can you get yourself into bed?" the nice voice said.

"Uh," said Harry.

By the time Maggie got home, it was almost two a.m. Josie was still awake, not too worried but wide awake, not wanting to be as unguarded as she'd been when she'd let the drunken stranger into her home. Maggie came in the front door and said, "It's fine."

"Did he look green to you?" said Josie.

"Light green. Some black, though. Poor guy."

"Yes, I got that, too."

When Harry awoke, it wasn't quite morning. He didn't feel as terrible as he had when he'd found himself chewed by mosquitoes in his backyard, but he felt bad enough. His mouth tasted of vomit and sugar, and his head felt swollen and hot. He was on his couch, his shoes off, an afghan over his legs. "Jesus," he said out loud, then repeated, "Jesus." His voice sounded hollow, made out of paper.

After a trip to the bathroom, he made his way to the kitchen for coffee and a grapefruit; he saw the note on the kitchen table, his wallet and keys acting as paperweights. Small, neat printed letters said, "Your car is still at our place. You can come get it, or I can come get you." A phone number followed, and a name. Maggie Roth. Nothing was missing from the wallet.

3

THE FOOL

*The Seeker
has a choice.
Beware*

THE FOOL.

Harry called the number on the note. The phone was answered by a woman with a southern accent; it was not the pleasantly low voice of the person who'd given him a ride the previous evening. "Maggie isn't here," she said and made it clear that she wanted his car gone sooner rather than later.

There was silence in the car as the two men drove down Highway 21 until Harry's friend Serge asked why he had a yellow plastic bucket with a blue scrub brush and a bottle of Murphy oil soap rattling around inside it.

"No reason," Harry said.

When the purple-hearted tower loomed on the horizon, Harry asked Serge if he knew anything about it. Serge said, "Not much. I know they call it 'the Shrine of the Purple Lady.' " Serge slowed as they approached it, and at Harry's request, they pulled over. Neither man got out of the car; they gaped at it through the windows. In the daylight it looked shabbier than it had in the dark, the paint chipped and peeling, a few small chunks of concrete littering the ground in front of it. Now Harry could see that the Christmas lights weren't even hanging straight around the arch that encircled the big heart. But it was still impressive, the whole structure at least twelve feet tall, with cinder-block steps leading up on either side to the heart itself, a solid mass of concrete at least three feet across, painted a bright purple.

Harry said, "What does it mean? Who's the Purple Lady?"

"I think she's still alive. She's got some cult or something. I think it has to do with UFOs." Harry's eyebrows went up as Serge went on. "She used to have services out here. There's some kind of temple on the property, or at least that's what I heard. I've never investigated, myself." His voice dropped. "You know that Wiccan group on campus? They used to make pilgrimages out here a few years ago when they were more active, calling it a 'place of power.' I heard that they swore lightning bolts used to come out of the place." He smiled as his voice went up to a normal volume. "I don't think she liked the attention much. Just a crazy old hermit lady. The South is full of them."

The fortune teller's trailer was set farther back from the road than Harry remembered, which was good because his car had traveled a few yards into the front yard before stopping at an angle three feet from the front porch. He'd missed the oyster-shell driveway altogether and must have driven through the shallow storm ditch that lay between the grass and the highway. He didn't remember the bounce at all, though it must have been enough to whack his head against the ceiling of the car.

Age had turned the once-white aluminum walls of the doublewide a light gray. It looked clean and reasonably well-kept, with a sturdy screened porch attached to the front. The roof of the trailer looked new, covered with shiny green shingles with black borders, unlike any roof Harry had seen, although it wasn't something he paid much attention to in the normal course of things. The lot looked large, although maybe not so much by country standards. As he got out of the car, he could see that all the homes out this way were spaced widely apart. Across the highway was what looked like untended brush leading into deeper woods; a hundred feet or so south was another rusted trailer, this one a single-wide. The same distance in the opposite direction there was a small clapboard house, white with gray streaks of weather, which drew the eye downward, giving the impression the whole thing was slowly sinking into the ground. An old Ford truck whose wheels had long since been amputated sat in the yard on cinder blocks. There was no way to discern the truck's original color; the metal was oxidized from its tailgate to the rims of its missing headlights. The whole area was depressing, but woodsy and beautiful at the same time; even the squalid housing was somehow picturesque. Harry thought if you had to be poor, this was better than in a city; there was air, a little room, and no terrible winter cold. You could at least grow your own tomatoes.

A decorative windmill stood on one border of the fortune teller's property, wide silver fans turning grudgingly in the breeze. Nothing else separated her yard from that of her neighbors some fifty feet away; they lived in what Harry had heard called a "shotgun shack," painted yellow with green trim. It had the same unusual shingles on the roof and another overly cute windmill in the front yard. Beyond it was a small, disreputable-looking business standing alone amid the broken pavement of a minuscule parking lot. It was impossible to see what it was called from this angle, and Harry couldn't bring himself to care anyway.

"No flowers," said Serge after he'd gotten out of the driver's side of the car.

"What?"

"They've got a vegetable garden on the side." Harry looked to where Serge was pointing and saw a brown rectangle of tended earth by the side of the house. "This time of year, people are growing stuff. People out here usually pretty the place up with flowers. See next door? Those azalea bushes must be really old to get that big." Serge's wife was very proud of her flowers; Harry knew that his friend was far more knowledgeable about them than his interest would dictate.

Harry left Serge standing by the driver's door without answering. He walked to his own car, unsurprised to find it unlocked. He got in, turned the key, and was relieved that the engine started. He turned it off, got out, and walked around the car, inspecting the tires. None were flat, and he could see no other damage. "You can leave now," Harry said, taking the bucket and its contents out of his friend's car. "Thanks," he added.

The woman who opened the door was beautiful in a frowsy, middle-aged way. She was plump and curvy, wearing something drapey and colorful, reds and yellows in a swirling pattern, and she smelled like honeysuckle.

"Hi," he said. "I'm sorry." She nodded as he stood on the little screened porch tacked to the front of her home. The pool of vomit by the door was gone, although Harry could see its damp ghost on the wood and there was a lingering noxious scent in the morning air. He asked if she had a hose. She pointed to the side of the trailer, and after leaving the bucket on the porch, he found it curled behind the small vegetable garden. He uncoiled the hose, then turned on the spigot. He pointed the nozzle away from himself and held it so the spray hit only grass until he got up the wooden steps. Then he brought the business end of the hose quickly around so that it splashed through the screen and rested it on the planks. He poured some Murphy's into the bucket and picked the hose up again, filling the bucket with foamy, fragrant water. He got on his knees and began to scrub the dark patch on the wooden floor.

A tall black woman appeared from behind the trailer, walking with a wonderful loping rhythm toward the porch steps. She made a wide arc as she passed, avoiding the puddle he'd made with the hose. She clomped up the steps, and Harry could see that she was at least sixty, black hair threaded with white, pulled tight to the back of her head, ending in a bagel-size bun. Her face was wide, with cheekbones that spread like wings under large dark eyes with lashes that looked real, if improbably long. She was taller than Harry, which meant that she had to be over six feet, long-limbed and substantial, giving the impression of strength rather than softness. She was wearing a colorful, flowing, floor-length dress, big pink flowers mixed with green. It occurred to him to wonder if there was some sort of cult out here and big flowered dresses was its uniform.

"Are you the drunken white boy?" said the large woman.

"That would be me," said Harry.

"Are you drunk now?"

"Only on what's left in my bloodstream from last night."

"Good. You can do my porch next if you want." She smiled wide and drifted past him, then opened the front door. Apparently, she didn't have to knock.

He had rinsed the porch, cleaned out the bucket, and was coiling the hose, satisfied that the wood was now completely vomit-free, when the two women came out of the trailer. "You can have some coffee," said the fortune teller.

The coffee had far too much milk in it for his taste, but he said nothing. They were on the dry side of the porch, sitting on chairs of green resin; a huge wooden spool served as a table. Introductions had been made. The fortune teller's name was Josie Dupree, and the tall woman's name was Miss Baby. "Baby Thorpe. Before you ask, no, it's not my given name, but I'm the youngest of seven children and that's what everyone's called me since I can remember."

"So you're Madame Dupree," Harry said, looking at Josie. Her long curls were almost black, no doubt dyed that way, her face was coated with makeup, and her lashes were artificially thick.

She said, "Oh, Christ. Whatever. Those goddamned Wiccans."

Harry asked what had been gnawing at him ever since he regained consciousness that morning. "Why in hell did you let me in? I wouldn't have."

There was a moment of silence. Then Miss Baby said, "They can see auras, sweetheart. They knew you wouldn't hurt nobody."

"Oh?" said Harry. "Still kind of risky, don't you think?"

Josie Dupree snapped, "You don't know what the hell you're talking about, so you just keep quiet about it."

They sipped in silence again as Harry waited for the coffee to take effect. Then he said, "What's the deal with the Purple Lady's shrine?"

Miss Baby said, "That's Miss Tokay's place. She's a sweet old lady, and your kind need to leave her alone."

"My kind?"

"You uppity types. All of you folks over to the college."

"I wasn't going to bother her. I was just curious. She built the damn thing on a highway, for God's sake. It must be some sort of statement."

"I don't know about that," said Miss Baby. "She's got her ideas, same as everybody else. It's her land, she can do what she wants with it. Nothin' for you to be condescending about."

"I didn't mean to be condescending. Sorry."

Josie changed the subject. "Why'd you come see us? And who's Lawrence?"

"My dead brother. I thought you could channel him."

"I don't do that sort of thing. Sometimes people think I can, and I give 'em what they want if I think it'll help 'em. But I can't, really. Did you kill him?"

"Not directly."

"But lots of guilt."

"Yes," Harry said.

"Well," said Josie, "most of the people I love are dead, too. Everybody's got their load to carry."

Harry sat with this for a moment. Everyone drank more coffee. He said, "So you can't talk to dead people. What can you do? Besides reading auras?"

Josie looked at him, seeming to look around him, as if he was wearing something fuzzy. "You don't believe me, but I can see that you're not a happy man."

"By my aura?"

Josie nodded. "I'm a psychic. And I read cards, do charts."

"Don't you read palms?" He nodded toward the hand-shaped sign.

"My sister was a palmist. Not me so much," Josie said. "One of her men friends made that for her. I inherited it. I like the way it looks."

Harry was about to ask another question when two small figures burst onto the porch, causing the hinges of the door to squeal and the door to slap back when they were through. Harry hadn't seen them approaching from behind the trailer. Two little girls, one slightly taller than the other; Harry guessed their ages to be around eight and six. The taller girl was wearing a bright yellow sundress and was beautiful, with silky, coffee-colored skin and the largest brown eyes he'd ever seen. The younger girl was less attractive, mainly because her teeth were so prominent and misaligned that

Harry found it painful to look at her. The thought made him feel racist and mean, so he deliberately gave her a big smile and a wink.

"Where's my mamma?" said the taller girl.

Josie smiled and said, "She's at the restaurant, sweetheart, same as the last eight hundred Saturdays. She'll be back this afternoon."

"She was gonna show me a bird's nest she found in the woods."

Miss Baby said, "The two of you shoo now."

The pretty girl looked at Harry and said, "I'm Charlotte." She didn't bother introducing the homely girl. Harry was about to ask her name when the two of them clomped off in identical pairs of thick white sandals, disappearing around the back of the trailer, retracing Miss Baby's original trajectory.

Harry said, "Cute girls."

"Um," said Josie. Miss Baby said nothing.

"The note I got was from Maggie. Does she live here, too?"

"She's not here."

"Your daughter?"

"My niece."

Miss Baby said, "She works over to Crane's." At Harry's questioning look, she said, "That restaurant down the road, towards town?"

Charlotte's mother, he thought. "Is she a psychic, too?"

"Don't take that tone with me, boy," said Josie, sounding surly again.

"I didn't know I had a tone. She drove me home last night?"

Both women nodded.

"I'd just like to thank her. And to apologize. How long will she be there?"

After a moment, Josie said, "She gets off at one." She looked hard at him. "You're not gonna start nothing with her, are you? She don't need any shit from anyone from the college. I don't want you messing with her."

Miss Baby said, "It'll be all right. He's not what you'd call good-lookin'. You kinda soft. Need to lay off the doughnuts."

"Thanks for the tip. I have no intention of messing with any-body."

Miss Baby started to push herself off the chair. "I got to get back to my rat killin'."

Harry said, "Are you an exterminator?"

Both Josie and Miss Baby started laughing so hard that Harry could feel even his scalp turning red. He tried to smile back, but the blood rushing to his head made his hangover worse.

"It's just an expression, college boy. I got a salon over there," said Miss Baby once she could speak again, pointing with a long hand past the shotgun shack. "Bring your wife if she wants a shampoo and set."

"No wife, at least not anymore. But thanks."

"You could use some prettyin' up yourself. We don't do that many men, but we could try to work some magic on you." This set Miss Baby to cackling again.

Harry was about to walk off the porch with Miss Baby when a thought occurred to him. "Wait," he said, turning back to Josie. "Someone from the . . . college told me you said that you knew who'd really invented the Ziegart effect. What's that about?"

The women looked at each other. Josie said, "I say a lot of things when I drink. That's why I go to meetings now. I been sober for over a month. I heard about that effect thingamajig on some TV show." She added, "I don't say nothin' you can believe when I been drinking."

"You right about that," said Miss Baby.

It was twelve-thirty by the time Harry pulled up to Crane's. It was a squat, unprepossessing place, but the parking lot was almost full. Harry found a narrow spot next to a Dumpster. The first thing that struck him when he went inside was the quality of the light. Overhead were standard fluorescent fixtures, yet the light was yellower, warmer, nicer in general than he was used to in such places. Otherwise, the ambience felt familiar, like a thousand others of its kind, booths and tables, big glass salt and pepper shakers with metal screw-on tops, cutlery bundled into rolled white paper napkins. A fat man in khakis led him to a two-person booth, the only free spot in the place. He wasn't sure why he didn't ask about Maggie Roth; he wasn't sure why he was there at all. He didn't want to date a waitress, or even meet one. But he wanted to hear her voice again.

The woman who waited on him was in her fifties and had a voice that could peel varnish. As she filled his cup with coffee, he ordered eggs and bacon and toast, finding himself sickeningly hungry. There were three other waitresses, all in black slacks and white T-shirts and little white aprons. All but his were young, and two were fairly pretty, although one was black; if he could trust his soggy memory, his rescuer had been white. His eggs were fluffy and some of the best he'd ever eaten, which he put down to his hangover. When the nonpretty young waitress poured more coffee for him, he was able to rule her out, as her voice was high and squeaky. He decided he was being infantile, so he finally asked her if the other white waitress was Maggie Roth.

The poor girl had unfortunate teeth, and she showed the whole mess of them to him, laughing at his question as if it had been witty repartee. "Why'd you think Maggie was a waitress?" she said, snorting like a happy pig.

"I don't know," he said, sounding stupid to himself.

"She's kind of a retard, you know. She cain't do nothing with people."

As opposed to your superior social skills, thought Harry, but said nothing. Her gleeful cruelty suddenly made the remnants of egg on his plate look less appealing.

"She's in the back," said the bucktoothed girl. "Why you want her?"

It would be an hour before he realized that he could have told the nosy young woman it was none of her business. Instead, he said, "I've got a message from her mother." I hope Josie doesn't mind, he thought. What message can I say I'm bringing her? Oh God, that was stupid.

The bucktoothed girl, who Harry could see from her name tag was called Shawntelle, started laughing again, this time even harder. The pretty black waitress, a small woman named Dottie, joined them. "You okay?" she said to Shawntelle.

"He's got a message for Maggie from her mother." Snort, snort.

Dottie's eyes expanded. "What?" Shawntelle continued snorting. Dottie looked at her with tight lips. "It's not funny." She turned to Harry. "That's the meanest thing I heard in a long time."

Harry's stomach wasn't processing the eggs and bacon and toast at all well now. He suddenly remembered that Josie had corrected him. Not the fortune teller's daughter. Her niece. Oh, Jesus Christ, the mother was probably dead, and her aunt was a psychic. Oh *fuck*.

"I meant Josie. I guess that's her aunt then. I'm sorry. I thought that Josie was her mother. I didn't mean anything by it." *Double* fuck.

Shawntelle said, "He sees dead people." Her laughter was calmer now. "Don't worry, she prolly wouldn't be offended anyway. I told you, she's a 'tard." Dottie shooed Shawntelle away with a tug on her arm. Shawntelle moved off with a happy swagger.

He said to the anxious-looking Dottie, "I didn't mean to cause any trouble. I just wanted to thank her for a favor she did me. It was a stupid mistake."

After a second, the waitress said, "I'll tell Maggie you want to see her. You wait."

4

PAGE OF PENTACLES

*An introverted
young person*

Maggie Roth was too skinny and very pale, with a few freckles on the bridge of a small nose. Her hair was tied in a ponytail and was some sort of blond, dark streaks through it like little rivers of brown through yellow snow. She had on jeans that were too big and a white tank top that fit, so that he could see the stringy muscles on her slight, white arms. The first impression he had of her was that she looked tired. Then he looked into her eyes and was suddenly terrified of her.

He hadn't seen her coming. She slipped from the kitchen through the crowd silently, eel-like, until all at once she was there in the narrow booth across from him. Her eyes were wide, with shadows under the thin skin beneath, a person who didn't sleep much. But her eyes were also an explosive sort of blue, like a hundred little bright blue shards of glass were about to shoot out of them. She aimed them at him, and it was beyond uncomfortable, the feeling that she could hurt him with those sharp eyes. Eyes of blades. Then she said in a voice he recognized, "You're Harry."

"Yes," he said. "You're Maggie."

She nodded, rationing her voice. Her hands folded themselves on the tabletop, beautiful thin hands, strong, short, clean nails, no jewelry. Harry tried to speak but had to fight the remnants of his night's work first, coughed, cleared the passages; the second attempt was more successful. "Thanks for driving me home. And for getting me inside." And for not stealing anything, he thought.

"You're welcome. You get your car okay?"

"Yes. I met your aunt. And Miss Baby."

Her mouth flickered. Something was almost funny.

"And Charlotte," he added, remembering. "And another little girl. I didn't get her name."

The flicker was gone. She didn't seem remotely retarded to him. Maybe crazy. He wanted to ask her if she saw auras, too. Instead he asked, "You work in the kitchen?" even though he knew the answer, and wasn't interested in it anyway.

"I cook."

He had expected her to be a dishwasher after Shawntelle's contempt. He'd done a stint as one during college; he knew you could do the job and be crazy. He tried to focus through his hangover, tried to search for polite things to say. He had an inspiration. "The eggs were great. The best I ever had." This sounded unctuous and insincere, even though he meant it, so he added, "Really."

"Good."

He felt dumb and awkward and mildly queasy. He wanted to go home and never see this weird-eyed woman again. He had a moment of mild panic. Should he offer her money? A tip? He couldn't think of a way to do it that wouldn't be insulting but then wondered if not making the offer would be more insulting, and so he sat there looking at the saltshaker with his mouth slightly open, his sinuses still not working right. He thought, She's going to think I'm re-tarded, and this was almost funny, so he smiled, then looked at her, having no idea what to do next.

Her eyes smiled at him, although the rest of her face didn't. It was strange, he thought, how clear it was, that though her mouth moved only slightly, her eyes were clearly smiling. "I'm sorry," he said. "I don't know what to do. Or to say, except thank you, and I'm sorry for showing up drunk at your house in the middle of the night and throwing up on your porch." Her eyes smiled more. "But at least I washed it off this morning."

"Thank you," she said. "I'm going for a walk." And with that, she got up and left.

After Harry got home, he tried unsuccessfully to take a nap. He hated hangovers for many reasons, but this one was perhaps the most vicious, that alcohol prevented even rest, stopped him from being able to recuperate in the way that the rest of the world could. All he wanted was to lay his inflamed head on a soft, cool pillow and fall into a comfortable slumber, just for a few hours. He lay down on his bed, closed his eyes, and felt the first itch behind his right knee, not a terrible itch but enough that he couldn't put it out of his mind, he had to reach down and scratch, and as soon as that one was satisfied, another one began at the top of his left ear, then the bottom of his foot, then the small of his back, his right shoulder blade, and so on and on, till his whole body felt as if it was splattered with tiny electrodes. Synaptic torture, he thought. Shit.

He got up and went to the bathroom, looking at himself in the mirror, brightly lit by a crazed sun blasting through the window with such energy he had to squint. His hair looked comical, like a tiny version of the Rocky Mountains. He remembered someone say-ing recently that he wasn't much to look at, although it took him a little effort to remember who it had been. Miss Baby. The events of the previous evening and this morning seemed ridiculous, artificial, like something he'd watched on TV. He was deeply relieved that no one knew about his mortification other than Serge. His eyes adjusting, he looked more closely at his reflection. Gray hairs were winding their way through the brown ones. Only a few, but harbingers of things to come. He considered trying to go back to bed, then remembered all the terrible itching, his nervous system's determination to keep him awake and drive him insane. He decided instead to attempt to work. He turned on his computer, called up a search engine, and sat for a long time, looking at the bright screen and the empty white bar, waiting for his question. For no particular reason, he typed "Ziegart effect."

In the early afternoon, March already hot and heavy, Maggie came back to the trailer, glowing with sweat. Josie looked up as she walked in, the cards splayed on the table.

"Did that college man come to the restaurant?"

Maggie nodded. "Just to say thanks." She smiled at Josie. "You don't have to worry. He talked to Shawntelle."

"You don't listen to her. That trash. Did you talk to him?"

"Yeah." Maggie got a glass from a cabinet over the sink and filled it from the tap. "I think he was surprised that we didn't take his money." She started laughing, looking at the glass as though it was talking to her. Josie always found this startling shift in affect, this ability to find joy in water or a lightbulb or a cool breeze, disorienting, vaguely sinister. She looked at Maggie laughing and thought, He'd better never see her like this. But she knew he'd be back.

5

KING OF
PENTACLES

A slow man.
A mean man

Darcy Murphy was an unhappy man. He had hemorrhoids, and they bothered him on hot days, which in north Florida was three hundred days out of the year. With global warming coming, he figured it would soon be three hundred and sixty-five. The hemorrhoids didn't hurt, they itched, a burning, slow, relentless itch that made him long to rip his pants off so he could scratch his ass at the worst possible times, public times, sitting in his truck in traffic or while reading the  meter at a school during recess, with screaming kids and tired teachers staring at him, worrying that he might be a pervert. Sometimes he hoped global warming would just drown the whole goddamned boiling, itching state of Florida. The whole goddamned thing. A mercy killing.

It was Monday morning and he had an inspection. Just a drop-in, no appointment. He had a personal interest, but he had a professional one as well. People supposedly off the grid, as if that was likely. They had to be thieves, stealing electricity from their neighbors, therefore from the company. He imagined brightly lit parties with outdoor air-conditioning and speakers braying loud music from a four-hundred-watt music system, all powered by ill-gotten juice. His ass burned at the thought.

When he passed the shrine in the company van, Darcy said out loud, "Great God Almighty, what in the name of Jesus is *that?*" His van slowed, but a big pickup behind him blatted its horn, and he put his foot back down on the accelerator. When he saw the big wooden hand, he almost ran off the road. The truck was still behind him. As soon as Darcy saw the pickup move across the center line with the intention to pass, he pressed the pedal into the floor of the van. "Think you're such a goddamned hotshot, fucking asshole." The big white van rattled up to speed, then Darcy swore again when he saw a ramshackle beauty shop ahead with the street number painted squarely across the front glass window, telling him that he'd passed his target. He swerved left into the miniature parking lot of the Babyface Salon, his tires screaming and the van tipping up onto two of them, then landing back on all four with a metallic crunch. The pickup roared past with a burst of acceleration, a thick hand waving an uplifted middle finger out the driver's side window. Darcy tried to reciprocate, pushing the button to lower the window so hard that it made the top knuckle of his index finger ache, but by the time the window was down far enough to get his arm out, the truck was small on the receding road. Darcy swore again.

He made an awkward three-point turn and pulled back onto Highway 21; there was no one approaching from the south, so he could take his time with the numbers. "Shit," he said as he realized that the persons of interest lived behind the grotesque wooden hand. "It figures," he said, although upon seeing the double-wide, he revised his mental image of poolside parties.

·   ·   ·

Josie's first thought as she opened the door for the inspector from the electric company was that his aura looked poisonous. She didn't like him, not only for that reason. He smelled bad, the humidity making the sweat on him thick, its odor waving long, pungent flags. She was glad it wasn't really hot yet, or she imagined he'd smell like a dead cow. "Not again," she said. "You're the third one. We're not stealing anything. I wish you people would get that through your big fat heads."

Darcy Murphy liked the look of this one. A little on the heavy side but tasty, buttery all the same. Her looks took something out of him for a moment. But he reminded himself that she was a godless fake, taking the money of housewives with straying husbands and whiny teenage girls worried about whether or not their boyfriends would ever marry them. *Que será, será,* in his opinion. "I'll just have a look around," he said.

"Suit yourself," Josie said.

6

TEN OF PENTACLES

REVERSED

*Beware of embarking
on a risky journey*

On Monday, Harry taught a class on First Amendment law. It was half his teaching load, which he thought was embarrassingly light. He knew they expected his new book to be as successful as his previous ones. If there actually was a new book, he thought, and not just a huge, toilet-shaped hole in my brain. He got to his office, a small, unremarkable cube of beige textured wallpaper and scuffed green linoleum. At least it had a window; his office was underground, and a large rectangle looked out into a cement window well. Harry had wondered whether or not to be offended at where they'd placed him, but it didn't actually bother him. He had been mildly irritated that the window didn't open, but as soon as he'd gotten a sense of the local weather, his irritation had faded. He preferred the scent of the antiseptic air-conditioning to the lingering mildewy funk of the Florida air. He'd been told at his first faculty party that the Law School had been constructed on top of a dredged swamp; Harry believed it.

He looked at the half-filled shelves, the bare beige walls, and wondered as he had many times before how long he was going to stay here. He hadn't invested much in the place; no pictures hung on the walls, most of his books were at his house, which was still furnished largely with boxes. He'd been here eight months. The dean of the Law School seemed to like him. He could stay for two years, maybe even work his job into a permanent position. He couldn't decide if the prospect beckoned or sickened.

The door was open, but Serge knocked on it anyway as he peeked in. Tall, good-looking, and fit, Serge was his oldest friend. Harry had gotten him through law school and they both knew it. Serge was wearing a gray suit that looked expensive; Harry's was dark green and wasn't.

"You want to get some lunch?" Serge said.

It wasn't hard for Harry to persuade his friend to drive to a place twenty minutes away from campus, neither of them having another class until midafternoon. "I've seen this place," Serge said, "but never once thought of stopping to eat here." Harry wasn't surprised. It wasn't the kind of place Serge's wife would ever set foot in.

"The eggs are to die for," Harry said. "I don't know if anything else is good." He was happy to see that Shawntelle of the bad teeth didn't seem to be working that day. The fat man showed them to a table with a nod of recognition at Harry. Dottie gave them menus without a word. The selections were unsurprising, sandwiches and hot meals of the normal variety. "Nothing with portobello mushrooms, I gather," Serge said. They ordered sandwiches and coffee while Dottie wrote on a small pad with no expression, gathered their menus, and walked away. He added, "She doesn't seem to like us."

He hadn't mentioned Harry's drunken foray into this part of town after delivering him to his car two days before, and Harry saw no reason to bring it up now. Instead, he said, "Do you know anyone in the physics department?"

"Yes." Serge said. "You do, too. Frank Milford. You met him at our Christmas party. Big fellow. Quiet wife."

"Oh," Harry said, having no memory of having met such a person at any party at the Olnikoffs' house.

"Why do you need a physicist? Planning a trip to Mars?"

"Funny. Research. Does the name Charles Ziegart mean anything to you?"

"The discoverer of the Ziegart effect?"

"You've heard of it?"

"Yes." Serge shifted in his seat, trying to keep the green vinyl from permanently wrinkling his trousers. "We get *Popular Science*. It has something to do with electricity. That's all I can remember."

Harry said, "I looked it up on the Internet. There were over a hundred and sixty entries, articles, a lot of academic websites, even a few physics blogs."

"What an age we live in. Not long ago, blogs were all about porn and family photos. Now even Judd Lippman has one."

"Keep up, Sergei. Ziegart was a big name in superconductors." At Serge's expression, Harry added, "When you supercool certain metals, they conduct electricity with virtually no resistance."

"I'm trying to remember my high school physics. That's good, right?"

"Bet your ass it is. It increases the efficiency of the transmission of electric current geometrically. The science is beyond me, but the point is, it's extremely profitable for the university where he developed it, and presumably for him as well."

"Okay," said Serge. "I can see why this might interest you from an intellectual property perspective. I imagine a Nobel laureate gets more of the royalties from his work than more plebeian instructors."

"Ziegart never won a Nobel Prize, but that's not the point," Harry said. "I heard a rumor that Ziegart didn't invent it, or discover it or whatever. I don't know why, but it's got my insides prickling."

"You're way out of my depth." Serge paused as Dottie slapped an oval plate full of food in front of each of the men, then walked away without asking if they wanted anything else. "Is the source credible?"

"I doubt it. But for the moment I can't let it go. Don't ask me why."

Serge took a bite. He chewed for a minute, then said, "The sandwich is fine, but it's no better than half a dozen places near campus serve." He chewed some more. "Why are we here?"

Harry ate some of his roast beef sandwich and said, "Like I said, the eggs were great."

Serge waited, then said, "Where is Ziegart? Which university?"

"Cantwell. In central Pennsylvania."

"Can you call him directly? Get started that way?"

"I'd like to, but he's dead. That makes the subject a little delicate. I could be slandering the name of a Great Man."

"You love slandering the names of people."

"It's not slander if it's true. His widow's still on the faculty at Cantwell. I'll talk to her eventually if I keep at this, but I thought I'd better be more certain of my footing before I dump all over the presumably beloved deceased."

"Talk to Frank," Serge said. "He's the department chair. If he doesn't know Ziegart, he'll know someone at Cantwell besides the wife, or know someone who knows someone. He's also a nice guy, and likes gossip as much as anyone."

"Thanks," Harry said. "I will." Dottie came back to ask if they wanted anything else. Harry debated for only a second, then decided it didn't matter what Serge thought. "Is Maggie here today?" he asked.

"No," said Dottie, laying the check on the table, then walking away again.

"Oh," said Serge. "Who's Maggie?"

"Stop it," said Harry. "Get that smirk off your face. It's not like that at all."

"Like what?"

"Stop it," Harry said again.

Darcy Murphy couldn't find anything amiss, no misplaced cables, no untoward connections. The windmills were so dainty and stupid they made him want to spit on the ground, but his mouth was too dry. He got an extension ladder from his truck, dragging it with difficulty to the double-wide. He levered it awkwardly when he was close enough so that the top of the heavy ladder swung through the air and hit the roof with a loud clank. The fortune teller opened her door and leaned out. "What the hell are you doing to my house?" she yelled.

It ain't a house, he thought, it's a goddamned glorified tin can. "Just puttin' up a ladder. Gonna take a look at what you got on the roof."

She gave him a disgusted look and said, "You break it, you bought it," before slamming the door.

He tried to spit again, with the same result as before. He was more concerned with not breaking something of his own but managed to make it up to the roof without doing anything worse than scraping the skin off two knuckles. "Shit," he muttered and stepped carefully onto the edge of the roof. Good thing about trailers, the roofs had almost no pitch to them, so taking a look wasn't as death-defying as it was on real houses. He looked over the surface of the roof, not having to take another frightening step to do so. You never knew on these cheap-shit tin cans where the weak spots were. The mortification of falling into the fortune teller's lap through her cardboard ceiling was almost worse to contemplate than the injuries he'd sustain. Almost.

No way, he thought, looking at the green and black shingles. No way. They can't make me believe that those would do it.

7

QUEEN OF
CUPS

REVERSED

*An intelligent woman
of dubious integrity*

He got to see his son only one weekend a month, occasionally two, and on alternating holidays. He hated it so much that thinking about it made him sweat with anger and made his stomach hurt. So he did his best not to think of it, an effort that was only occasionally successful. The last visit had been canceled because of a trip to Cancún with his former in-laws for his son's spring break. Harry had spent the week trying not to miss his boy, teaching his classes, and reading a number of articles he found online about the Ziegart effect and its author. His research was interrupted by frequent evening phone calls from Dan Polti. The younger man was miserable and chatty, and Harry hadn't had the energy to put him off altogether, although he'd managed to avoid joining him at the Brew House. He'd let Dan crash on his couch twice that week after long conversations fueled by coffee and soda. By the weekend, Harry had decided that he never wanted to speak to another human being again. But Serge had demanded that Harry help him finish the patio on his beautiful house, and Harry again hadn't been able to find the strength to let his friend down. By Saturday night, he was exhausted.

Harry woke up at nine a.m. on Sunday, having fallen asleep about four hours before. He'd been awakened by a horrific dream in which he had been captured by someone he couldn't see and been unable to get out of the tub of water where his faceless assailant had imprisoned him. The tub had a sheet of Plexiglas stretched over its entire length, and there was only an inch or so of air between it and the water's surface. He had pushed his lips and nose into the tiny sliver of air, gasping and holding his breath, terrified that every breath sucked the volume of oxygen out of the small space, the shrinking of the air bubble making the Plexiglas bend toward the meniscus of the water, killing him slowly and cruelly. He awoke to sweat and panic and lay in damp sheets, grateful for the dusty light streaming through the window above the bed. He slept only a few hours a night these days, and he deeply resented any of it being tainted by nightmares.

He gave up on sleep, got up, emptied his bladder, and washed his face. He made himself a cup of instant coffee, which he loathed, but he didn't have the patience to load the coffeemaker. Cup in hand, he went to the phone and dialed the number of his ex-wife.

"What is it now?"

"Just a Sunday morning call. To Dusty. Can I talk to him?"

"He's getting dressed. We're on our way out the door to church."

"Can I talk to him for just a minute? And since when do you go to church?"

Ann sighed. In his mind he could see her nostrils pinching in irritation. "A lot of my friends go to this place. It's Unitarian. Even you shouldn't have a problem with that."

"How does Dusty feel about it? Better yet, let me ask him my-self."

"We're going to be late as it is. Call back later."

Harry wasn't sure why he went back to Crane's. The breakfast he'd had the week before had been excellent, and at first he thought that was what he wanted. Stoweville wasn't that big, and even though the restaurant was to the south, in the poor part of town, far away from Shively Street and Fairford Avenue, the streets where professors and lawyers and doctors had their stately historic homes, on a Sunday it still took less than twenty minutes to go across town for the best breakfast he'd ever had. He was almost there before he remembered the objectionable Shawntelle and hoped that he wasn't put in her section. He wondered if there was a diplomatic way to make sure of it.

The restaurant was crowded, full of large people speaking in boisterous southern accents, the women in bright dresses with wide hats and the men in suits. He mentally slapped his forehead as he realized it was just after noon on a Sunday, which in this part of the world meant just after church. Worship, he gathered, made a lot of people hungry.

He waited in a long line, undecided. He didn't want to be in a crowd, he just wanted some nice, fluffy eggs, some crisp toast, some quiet. The place was roaring, and he could feel a small pain begin-ning at the base of his skull, radiating up the left side, tenderly ca-ressing his temple. When the fat man who had seated him before got to him, a clipboard in his thick fingers, and asked in a wheezy voice for his name and the number in his party, Harry said, "Is Mag-gie working today?"

The fat man wheezed some more. "No," he said. "She's got Sun-days off." Harry mumbled, "Sorry. Never mind," and left.

.   .   .

He drove farther south on Highway 21 toward the giant hand, stopping at the massive concrete shrine. He pulled over, made sure the car was far enough off the road that a passing semi wouldn't pulverize it, and got out. There was no other car as far as the eye could see, so he walked casually across the two narrow lanes of asphalt. He climbed one of the cinder-block staircases that flanked the great purple heart, rising on either side like a small pyramid, and for the first time noticed there was a woman sitting on a pink lawn chair perched on the platform at the top of the inverted V made by the stairs. She was very old and very small, short gray curls atop a tiny bobbing head, a vast purple shawl around her shoulders, making her blend into the painted stone behind her.

"Hello," he said. "I was just admiring your handiwork. You must be Miss Tokay."

"Hello," she said in a voice that sounded as though the wind could carry it away in wisps. "I'm glad you like it. No more services, I'm afraid."

"Oh?" said Harry. "I didn't know you had services."

"The temple's closed now. Closed for repairs."

"Oh," said Harry. "What kind of services?"

"To get dictations from the Ascended Masters. Didn't you come for the services? People used to." She looked away from him now, out across the road to rows of pine trees. "It's a beautiful day."

"Yes," said Harry. "Where's the temple?"

"Which one?"

"There's more than one?" asked Harry.

"There's the old one and the new one. The old one was lovely. I miss it. The newer one is serviceable enough." Harry imagined she had no idea she'd just made a pun. "But it was never as nice. You can't see the old one from here. The new one is back behind, over there." She said "hee-uh" and "they-uh" in the Old South way of gentlewomen. She pointed a shaking, child-size hand with bent knuckles to a spot somewhere behind them. "Can you see it?"

Harry peered over the back wall of the shrine, through the pine and live oak trees of the lot beyond, and could see a wooden building, his view fragmented by branches; the building was painted white, although the blue-green wood underneath peeked out in occasional blotches. It looked as if it had originally been a two-car garage with a second story. Closer to the road and to the right was a large house, big white columns and tall, thin windows. It had once been stately; it was now forlorn and shabby, with gutters hanging atilt from the eaves and ivy suffocating the side windows. The roof of the front porch sagged in the middle like a giant, insane smile. The roof was dotted with green squares. A shingle salesman made a killing in this neighborhood, he thought. He hadn't noticed before the narrow dirt driveway next to the shrine that served the big house and the temple.

"Who are the Ascended Masters? I'm sorry, ma'am"—he was proud he'd remembered this southernism in time to avoid offending her—"but I'm new to town, and I don't know what you're talking about."

"I could tell you weren't local, honey," she said and winked. "No more services, I'm afraid. And it's too bad, because I'm going to ascend myself in just a little while. I still take dictations, and they've said they're getting ready for me."

Harry pictured celestial CEOs requiring dotty old ladies to "take a letter" for them; questions filled his mind, but he hadn't gotten a satisfactory answer to his earlier one. "What's the temple for? What do you do in it?"

Her face didn't change in any obvious way, but there was a subtle shift, a little tightening, some nervousness. Harry had been a reporter far too long not see such minute changes in expression and know they meant something. She looked away and said, "I see my ride to the stow-uh."

A car slowed, the first that had come along since Harry had stopped. A giant old Buick pulled onto the narrow verge, aimed toward town. Miss Baby was driving it. There was no one in the passenger seat, but two small girls sat in the back. Harry recognized Charlotte and her friend, sister, or whoever she was with the unfortunate teeth; both girls were in pink dresses and braids. The front passenger window rolled down by itself; the car was obviously not too old to have power windows. Miss Baby leaned over and said, "Why are you here?" She turned her gaze to the old woman. "Miss Tokay, he botherin' you?"

Miss Tokay didn't answer, just started wending her rickety way down the steps. Harry scuttled to her side, half expecting her to shoo him away, but she took his arm as he walked her down. When they got to the car, her arm dropped and he opened the door for her.

"We were just chatting," he said to Miss Baby.

"Pooh," she said.

After getting Miss Tokay situated in the car and closing the door for her, Harry leaned in the window and asked Miss Baby, "Are Josie and Maggie home?"

"Maggie's working," said the girl with the bad teeth from the backseat.

Harry was about to correct her when Miss Baby said, "No, they're not home. You leave them alone." She pressed the button to roll up the window and drove away, giving Harry just enough time to step back from the door.

He watched the car shrink as it went on down the road. There were no other cars. In the silence, he could hear something. Music. It was very soft, almost indistinguishable from the breeze through the pines. But it was there, unless he was starting to hallucinate. It was so faint that he couldn't make out anything specific, no melody, no rhythm, just something, some notes, a trilling, possibly a voice singing. He looked back at the shrine and thought, It's singing to me.

Miss Baby had lied, although he couldn't understand why. He wished no one ill in this scrabbly part of town. He saw two cars in the driveway of the double-wide: a battered blue Chevy Nova and a white Toyota Celica, both more than a few years old. Josie Dupree opened the door after the third knock, dressed only, as far as Harry could tell, in a robe of rose satin. Her face was a palette of thick, smeared makeup, and she had on earrings dangling halfway to her shoulders with clusters of what looked like little rubies. He thought of Mae West with everything dyed dark brown instead of blond. She plainly wasn't going to let him in.

"Is Maggie here?" he asked.

"She's at work."

"No, she's not. I was just there."

"You leave her alone. What the hell do you want with her?"

A male voice came from somewhere behind her. "Who the hell is that?" it said.

"Nobody," said Josie. "He wants Maggie."

"She's not working. Is she supposed to be at work?" Harry said. Then he realized that was probably her car in the yard. He had a misty memory of the white Toyota bringing him home. "Isn't that her car?"

"Go away," said Josie and closed the door.

EIGHT OF SWORDS

Someone with
a straitened life

Harry had no classes on Tuesday, so he decided to work at home. He still marveled at this, the wide-openness of academia, the trust placed in faculty by the administration that they would actually do something productive with all that free time. Of course, he told himself, he should be used to it, since being a journalist was much the same. Similar, too, in that not producing anything bore dire consequences. It wasn't really trust, it was simply the knowledge that the powers that be could squash you like a bug if you didn't do something to add to their prestige.

In the past, he had been a hard worker, tirelessly crossing the city, the country, even the world, to complete a story. He'd written two books in addition to his regular newspaper work, and each one had taken him months of globe-trotting before he could really start writing. He liked the traveling, the searching and questioning and digging. He wasn't wild about deadlines, but he used to be good at meeting them. Now he hadn't turned in even an outline; his agent had nurtured interest in a third book because of the success of the last two, but his editor was tapping his smartly clad toe, waiting for Harry to at least suggest a topic. Harry had been a journalism major as an undergraduate, and so, before he graduated from Georgetown Law School, he'd written a series of articles for the school paper on the homeless. It had gotten a lot of attention; this in turn had led to an internship at *The Washington Post*, while his classmates had gone on to law firms around the country. He'd found his calling, and his rapid rise at the *Post* from intern to senior reporter had been admired by some, envied by more, and resented by most of his co-workers. He knew that his fall, or at least tumble, wasn't unwelcome to a lot of people. If those folks could read my mind, he thought, if they could see how little is really going on in there, they'd piss themselves with delight.

Now, sitting at the oak desk at which he'd written two well-received books, all he wanted to do was sleep. But he knew that wasn't going to happen anyway, so he got himself a cup of coffee and opened his laptop and began looking for anything else he could find on Charles Ziegart. After two hours he stood, massaged his neck, and dug through his briefcase for the number that Serge had given him. He left a message on Frank Milford's campus voice mail and massaged his neck again.

He went back online and looked up the main number of the *Lucasta Mirror*. He asked to speak to Todd Greenleaf. The woman spoke with a Pennsylvania accent that he recognized with some discomfort. "He's retahred," she said.

"Does he still live locally?"

"No. Moved to Florida. I can't give out more information than that."

"I'm interested in the articles he wrote about the death of Charles Ziegart in the *Mirror*. Would anyone else have his notes, or any information about those stories?"

"No. He took all his files (fahls) with him."

He thanked her and hung up, wondering where in Florida Todd Greenleaf lived. Probably not close by; it was a big state, and people who left cold climates tended to go farther south than Stoweville. Harry looked at the clock. He'd find out more about the old reporter later. It was lunchtime.

She was working this time, as was Shawntelle, who waited on him. He didn't want to provoke the waitress's toothy amusement by asking after Maggie again, so he took his time over his soup and chicken salad sandwich, checking his watch every few minutes, trying to remember exactly what time it had been when she'd left the restaurant the first time he'd come here. Around one o'clock, he thought, and sure enough, a few minutes after the hour, she pushed through the swinging kitchen doors behind the cash register. He was embarrassed at how glad this made him, that he'd finally tracked her down. She was wearing what looked like the same jeans and top that she'd had on three days before, with the addition of a fanny pack of lined brown leather circling her hips. She was prettier than he'd remembered, in a nondescript, even-featured sort of way, though still so white she was almost transparent. She looked ghostly. Then the thought struck him from nowhere. This is what sadness looks like after it's been sitting on someone for a while. He wondered if he ever looked like that.

He was even more pleased when she made a slight gesture of recognition after she saw him, her hand moving up in a tiny, almost surreptitious wave. She spoke to the fat man behind the register, something quick, possibly a single word, and even as the fat man nodded in acknowledgment, she began walking toward where Harry sat.

"Hey," she said as soon as she was close enough to be heard over the roar of the lunch crowd.

Harry suddenly remembered his kindergarten teacher correcting another child in his class, saying, "Hay is for horses," and he resisted an urge to pass this on. "Hello," he said. He hadn't thought ahead about any possible topic of conversation, so he fell back on the one thing he knew they had in common. He looked down at his plate, then up at her again. "Did you make the soup?"

She shook her head, making the ponytail bob. "Just the sandwich."

"Good chicken salad."

"Thanks." She looked at him, then at her clean, short fingernails. "I'm going for a walk. Bye."

As she turned to leave, Harry said, "I was going to do the same thing myself, right after I was done here." He looked again at his empty plate. "Which I am now." He worked his hand into his pocket to retrieve his wallet. "Where do you go? To walk?"

She didn't say anything for a moment, just stared at him with those eyes of broken blue glass, while he pulled the lining out of his pants pocket along with his wallet. His keys tumbled with a clatter onto the vinyl seat of the booth. She said, "There's a place I go. The cemetery. But there's a park, too." She stared at the keys, then at his hand as he tried to push the fabric back into place. Then she looked back at his face. "It's shady."

Harry finally got himself put together enough that he felt he could stand up without looking even more ridiculous. "Would you mind some company?" He fished some dollar bills out of his wallet to put on the table as she said, "If you want."

Harry followed her car as they drove away from Crane's, down Highway 21 south toward the shrine. The cemetery was only a mile or so away, halfway between the restaurant and Maggie's house. You could see it from the road, but not the vastness of it, rolling away under live oak and pine trees, random concrete markers lacing the grass between the trees and the occasional azalea bush. At the far end of the cemetery was a small stream that crooked its way through the headstones into the trees that bordered the north end. He parked his truck next to her Toyota in the small parking lot near the road. She had a big straw hat in her hands, limp and soft with age, which she put on her head, tying a brown ribbon under her chin. Harry couldn't stop himself from commenting. Maggie said, "Miss Baby makes me wear it. To keep the sun off me. I wear sunblock, but she says it's not always enough. I burn pretty bad. She says it gives you wrinkles before you need them."

"Who needs wrinkles?"

"Anybody who wants to be taken serious, I guess."

"You don't want to be taken seriously?"

She shrugged.

They walked among the headstones at first, through the shady parts that spilled across the grass and islands of concrete. The dates started in the fifties; the cemetery wasn't as old as Harry had first thought. He was used to northern graveyards, the deaths starting as early as before the Revolutionary War. Here, anything before the twentieth century was considered impossibly old; Stoweville had been nothing more than a crossroads during the Civil War, with only a single battlefield. It had been an insignificant skirmish, now inflated to a fake grandeur by the local chamber of commerce. The gravestones were small and sad, cheap cement worn down quickly by the torrential thunderstorms that peppered the summer days with astonishing regularity. Poor-looking graves, he thought. No grand monuments to wealth and immortality, though many of them wore epitaphs of a flowery religiosity. Harry looked at the names: Smith, Townsend, DeLisle, Camden. All Anglo names, or French.

No interesting ethnicities, not even Spanish, which would have been all over the place if the graveyard had been situated even a hundred miles to the south.

They didn't talk at first, just walked at an easy pace on the pine-needle-covered path. He was grateful he had running shoes on, as did she, he noticed, an old pair, creased and stained; comfortable shoes for someone who had to work on her feet all day. The path paralleled the stream and wound between the graves, then broke through a hedge of azalea bushes into a pine wood. Harry was grateful for the extra shade. The thick stand of trees made the path dark enough that he debated whether or not to remove his sunglasses.

"Is this still part of the cemetery?" he asked.

"No. It borders on Gunhill Park. That's where we are now."

He had a notion that a number of acres of woodland had long ago been donated to the county by an eccentric paper magnate. The path wound through the trees, breaking after a hundred feet or so into an open area, a round garden with tiers of flowers in full bloom in concentric circles around a fountain, poured concrete in the shape of a horse in full gallop. The horse's head was pointed up to the sky, and a thick jet of water spewed from its open mouth, projecting forward in a clear arc. It reminded Harry of puking. He managed to keep the thought to himself. Instead he said, "Kind of upsetting."

This got a glance from Maggie but nothing more. Harry didn't know why her silence didn't bother him, nor did he understand why it felt so important to be with her at all. She was attractive, but not overwhelmingly so, and he didn't feel that kind of pull toward her. She was too young anyway; he figured she couldn't be much over twenty-five, and his initial gratitude should have been eaten away by mortification. It wasn't gratitude, he thought; it was something else. Curiosity, he guessed, but why she should excite this in him was a mystery. He could read her life in the circumstances that he knew.

Poor, semirural, relatively uneducated, single motherhood too young, a life that fit the definition of the word *straitened*. Maybe *strangled* would be a better word. But it wasn't as if he could fix anything for her. He wasn't Henry Higgins, had no power to make her affluent or enlightened. Yet here he was, unable to resist knowing more about her strangled life.

She walked more rapidly now, like a woman who had somewhere to go, and Harry found himself panting a little as he worked to keep up. They passed the fountain, making their way to where the path continued into trees on the other side. Harry asked a question that bobbed to the surface of his mind. "Why are you letting me do this?" At her glance, he said, "I'm not anybody bad to know, but you don't know that. I could be a serial killer."

She kept walking, but now with the tiniest, most ghostly of smiles on her face. "I know you're okay."

"How? The aura thing? I'd watch depending too much on that if I were you. Get some independent confirmation before you let drunken strangers into your house in the middle of the night."

She gave that ghost smile again. "It doesn't come up much. We know most of the drunks that show up on our porch."

He followed her along a mile-long trail through more pine woods and several more gardens of gardenia and crepe myrtle, then over a small wooden footbridge that spanned a cypress swamp. The heat wasn't too bad yet this early in the spring, but the shade was still welcome. She stopped for a moment on the bridge. The floppy hat gave her a comic silliness, a contrast to her customary gravity. She turned to look out over the black water, dotted with islands of green algae and water lilies. It was quiet, far enough from the highway that you could hear the *plop* of frogs into the water and the cheeping of the crickets. Harry was startled by a sudden hammering sound, loud and harsh; he thought there must be some construction going on nearby. Maggie watched his face as he strained to see something mechanical through the trees. She gave that almost-smile again and said, "Woodpecker. See?" She pointed upward and to the left, and then he saw it, a huge bird not fifty feet from them, halfway up a dying pine, its head jackhammering so fast you couldn't see the movement, could only hear the *rat-a-tat-tat* of its beak tearing at the bark to strip it of termites. Its head was topped by a bright red crest, and it looked to be at least as big as a crow, maybe bigger.

"I've never seen one like that," he said. "My God, it's huge."

"It's a pileated woodpecker. You don't see them much. They're shy."

Harry wondered why anyone who would know a pileated woodpecker from any other bird would be considered retarded by her co-workers. They started walking again, then Maggie said, "Why'd you say 'Lawrence' like that, on our porch?"

"Lawrence is my brother," he said.

"Josie told me," she said. "Why did you say his name like that?"

"He's dead," Harry said.

He expected the usual response—oh, how terrible, how did it happen, I'm so sorry—but all she said was "I know."

"He was murdered," he said. He hadn't meant to be dramatic, but there was no way not to make it sound that way. "Being drunk, I think I was going to ask Josie to channel him."

"She doesn't do that."

"So she said." He panted a bit, then went on. "I did a story for my paper." He didn't know whether if he said that it had been *The Washington Post* she would see him as name-dropping, or whether she wouldn't be familiar with it. "I was a reporter. Am a reporter." She was looking at the trees, so he couldn't judge her reaction. "The story was about a federal judge who was taking bribes. It was kind of a big deal." He glanced at her again. This time she looked back, still expressionless. "The story killed his career. He was prosecuted and disbarred and went to jail. He's out now, but he did eighteen months. I got a raise." They came to a section of the path where the sun broke through the canopy, blinding him, then the trees blocked the light as they kept moving, and he was blinded again for a moment by the sudden return to darkness. "The judge had a crazy son. The crazy son came to our house to kill me. I wasn't there, but my brother was, and the crazy son didn't know him from me. We looked a little alike. Not that much, but enough. He shot Lawrence in the face when he opened the front door."

He expected her condolences, something about how it wasn't his fault. Instead she continued her silence, but a sadness had spread over her face that looked at home there. He added, "I never had a drinking problem till after his funeral. Now I usually don't drink at all because, when I do, I can't seem to stop."

They broke into another small garden area, this one also circular, although in the center was a boxwood carved into the shape of a giant teardrop. The flowers surrounding it were well-tended and beautiful, purples and whites, and Harry stopped for a moment to look at them. Maggie stopped, too, then jumped back as a bee rose from a snapdragon blossom, gently approaching her with a soft buzz. She watched it with great attention as it swooped and rolled in slow curls through the air, then dropped down again into the snowy flower bed. She moved back to the path, which was now almost perpendicular to where they'd emerged from the trees. Harry followed her.

He was startled when she spoke. "This winds back to the cemetery eventually. What was your brother like?" Conversational bumper cars, thought Harry. I never know when I'm going to get whacked by a question.

"He was younger than me by three years. Athletic, handsome. We didn't look *that* much alike." He tried a smile, but he suspected it came out wrong. "He was the popular one. You know, the one good at sports, better with girls, that sort of thing. Our parents named him Lawrence because they thought it would be funny to have sons called Harry and Larry. But he was never called that, for some reason. It was always Lawrence. My wife saw him get shot." He made a point of not looking at Maggie now. "We got divorced not too much later."

"She thought it was your fault?"

Harry said, "She never said so."

"Any children?"

"I have a son. Dustin. He lives with her now. In Orlando. He's fourteen."

She seemed to be done with questions, so he decided to turn the conversational tide. "How old is Charlotte?"

A pause. "She's eight." Then, silence. She obviously wasn't interested in reciprocating life stories. Harry thought, God, she must have been a teenager when she had Charlotte, and remembered what it was like to have an infant around. He felt sadder still; a straitened life indeed. All he said was "Is the other little girl her sister? I don't know her name."

"Tamara. No, she's Charlotte's cousin."

"Ah." He couldn't think of a way to talk about the poor girl's teeth without sounding mean, and he couldn't think of anything more noticeable about her than that, so all he said was "She seems like a sweet kid."

There was no answer, and Harry realized that he hadn't actually asked a question. When Maggie did speak, it had nothing to do with Charlotte. "Why are you here?"

"You mean in Stoweville?" At her nod, he went on. "I quit my job a little while after Lawrence was killed and was at loose ends. My wife, my ex-wife, Ann, moved to Orlando for a job and to be nearer to her parents, and a friend of mine is on the law school faculty here, and pulled some strings and got me a position. I have a law degree. The job's temporary. Visiting professorship. This year and next year.

After that, I don't know. It's possible I could stay. Or I could move further south, to be closer to Dusty. I don't know. Teaching's okay. I'm trying to write a book."

"What about?"

"That's a good question. I have no idea." He debated how much to say for just a second, then said, "I've written two others."

"What about?" she repeated.

"One was about how pharmaceutical companies are dictating medical treatment, not only in this country but in lots of the world. I compared a few companies to robber barons of the early twentieth century. It upset some people. But that's good for book sales."

She didn't return his smile. "What about the second one?"

"It was about a few historical doomsday cults. I compared *them* to modern mainstream Christian fundamentalism. That one bugged a lot of people, too."

She looked at him from under the hat. Her face was speckled with the light that came through the holes in the straw. She asked the titles. When he told her, she nodded. He didn't know if that meant she'd heard of either of them or not.

He could see now that they were heading south again in a round-about way. Maggie said, "What's your son like?"

"The greatest kid who's ever lived." Then he smiled, and she gave her ghost-smile back. "Ann had hopes that he'd be like Lawrence, or like her. But unfortunately for him, he takes after me. The biggest thing he gets in trouble for is reading during class." His smile went away. "Ann loves him, but she gets frustrated with him, for the wrong reasons. Well, I would say that." He tried another smile but failed. "I wanted him with me, but the schools there are better, and she has more money. He needed to spend more time with her any-way. I wish I liked Orlando better." Then he added, "I don't want to move there."

"The schools here aren't that bad," she said, surprising him again.

"Especially in your part of town. People with money always get good schools."

"I don't have that much money," Harry said, embarrassed that she might see him as some smug fat cat. "Of course, it's not like I'm below the poverty line." He gave a jokey smile, meeting her plain crystal gaze under the bizarre straw hat, and had an uncomfortable thrill as he thought, She might actually live under that line and it might not be so hilarious to her. He looked away, thankful for the sudden flight of an energetic blue jay across the path.

The moan of cars from the highway had been slowly growing, and now the path broke into the cemetery again, ending in a swath of grass through headstones. Harry said, "I guess I should let you get on with your day." He waited for her reply, but there wasn't one. "Thanks for letting me join you. Sorry for talking so much, but thanks for letting me tell you my troubles, and about my son." He tried smiling at her again, but she didn't smile back.

Then she said, "You know, just because you wanted your brother dead doesn't mean you killed him." She got into the Celica and started the engine, leaving Harry standing by his car, his hand over his mouth. Then he got into his own car, and soon they turned in separate directions onto Highway 21.

9

KING OF
CUPS

*A man of power,
but with two faces*

It was after four o'clock by the time Harry got back to his house, and he had a message on his voice mail from Frank Milford. Milford was in his office on campus and was willing to discuss Charles Ziegart over coffee. By four-forty-five Harry was in the campus coffee shop talking to the head of the physics department at North Florida University.

Milford was tall and heavy, with thick fingers and a straining belt, a bald head the size of a basketball. Imposing, but not the least like anyone's stereotype of an egghead. Maybe the egg of a pterodactyl, thought Harry, though he had no idea how large a pterodactyl egg was. Harry assumed Milford was some sort of genius, since as far as he could tell, all physicists were. At least he figured their average IQ was above that of journalists or attorneys, or the government lackeys he'd met in Washington who called themselves scientists. Here, thought Harry, is the real thing, even if he looks like a sumo wrestler.

"Call me Frank," said the enormous physicist.

· · ·

Harry bought a small bowl of greasy vegetable soup and a cup of black coffee. He carried both to a table on a tray shaped like a stealth bomber. Milford had a salad along with a tall glass of iced tea. The salad was piled high with strips of cheese and ham, chickpeas, peanuts, olives, and croutons. There was a small plastic bowl on the side of the plate containing a lumpy white paste that Harry assumed was salad dressing. "Ziegart was a brilliant guy, there's no doubt about it," Milford said as he poured the dressing onto the salad. It fell in greasy clumps. Harry couldn't look away.

"I'm not surprised," he said, letting the department chair in on his theory about the intellectual superiority of physicists.

Milford laughed. "Well, there are all kinds of intelligence. All my colleagues are pretty good at calculus, but a few of them have a hard time putting their pants on right."

"Was there anything to the rumor that Charles Ziegart stole the idea of the Ziegart effect?"

Milford pulled a packet of sugar from a little basket of condiments in the center of the table. "I don't know. It could have been the work of one of his students." He opened the packet and poured sugar into his tea.

"But wouldn't everyone around him know that? It seems like a big risk to his reputation," Harry said.

Milford poured in a second pack of sugar. "You've worked in the private sector until now, right?"

"Yes," Harry said.

"Well, in most universities, graduate students do research under the guidance of a professor, usually responsible for a section of a larger research project. Basically, all the data belong to that professor. Dissertations get written about that student's piece of the puzzle, but it doesn't belong to him." He was now on his fourth packet of sugar.

"That doesn't seem terribly fair. Or legal."

"Oh, it's perfectly legal." Milford leaned back in the cheap plastic chair, causing it to give small screams of pain. "As to fair, it depends on your point of view. Figure the student wouldn't have access to lab facilities or other resources without his adviser. Usually the student is carrying out experiments thought up by the professor in the first place, so it's perfectly appropriate that the main credit go to the senior researcher. And the student often does get the credit, sometimes even first author on the published results."

"If his boss is generous enough."

"Well, yes. On the other hand, working for someone with a big name can get you pretty far by itself, so the student benefits a great deal by doing his mentor's scut work. The more well-known and well-thought-of your adviser, the better the job you're likely to get offered after graduation. Even if you're a tiny cog in a big, prestigious research project, you still get that reflected glory."

"So it's worth it."

"Most of the time. And most of the time, it's fair." He caused the chair to emit distress calls again. "Some people in our department think we should institute a policy where our students can control some of the data they produce. If we do, it will be pretty unusual; only a few other programs have anything like it, and no whole universities that I know of."

Harry said, "So, if Ziegart poached an idea, it was probably from a student. But no one would consider that unusual or unethical. So the rumor is spurious."

Milford sipped his tea, stalling, then said, "Well, I don't know about that." Harry felt himself moving back into old work habits. The "train-crossing" method of interviewing: stop, look, listen, let your subject fill an uncomfortable silence. Maggie Roth, he thought, was a natural at it. Milford finally said, "I don't know any particulars, remember, but I imagine that Ziegart, being such a big deal in electromechanics, probably had a lot of projects going on at any given time. But that means that he was probably spread pretty thin, so he may not have been doing much work himself. He was a bit of a celebrity, you know, good-looking and articulate, and was kept busy with interviews, PBS documentaries, even a few TV talk shows. His students probably were doing most of the actual work. Maybe even all of it. So the likelihood of there being some real unfairness was greater in his case than most." He shifted in his squeaking chair again. "I'm just speculating."

"I understand," said Harry. "I'm not going to publish any speculations. I just want to get a sense of how such a thing might have happened. If it did, of course."

"You know," said Milford, adding salt to a salad already overburdened with roadblocks to arterial health, "Ziegart was working in a combined physics and engineering department. An awful lot of what he was involved in had commercial applications. Most of his grants were probably funded by the government or by private industry. So what was at stake with a lot of his work wasn't just academic respect and fame."

"Money."

"Yes, from grants and royalties from patents." Milford ate a bite of his salad. "He did have a reputation as a bit of an egomaniac. I don't want you quoting me on any of this. I don't know any details, most of it is rumor, and I'm not comfortable saying anything nasty in print about someone who can't defend himself."

Harry reiterated his assurances that he was taking nothing as fact as yet. The big man went on. "When the Ziegart effect paper was being reviewed for publication, there were three names on it. I know because a friend of mine was asked to review it. One of the authors was a student of Ziegart's named Doug McNeill. McNeill died before the paper was published, which a lot of folks thought was convenient, because there was a patent issued soon after and the royalties were probably considerable. *Are* probably consider-able. You know anything about this?"

"Not really. Superconductivity."

"Yes. Some metals can conduct electricity with almost no re-sistance at all if they're supercooled close to absolute zero. But applications of this process are somewhat limited because of the difficulty in maintaining your conductor at those temperatures. But Ziegart developed an alloy that would retain superconductivity at close to normal temperatures. The process involved placing super-cooled tungsten in a superdense magnetic field. Very tricky, but he got it to work."

"That's the Ziegart effect?"

"Yes. The applications have been huge, and the military is all over it."

"In other words," Harry said, "lots of money."

"Yes, for Ziegart and for the university."

"But not for the other authors of the original paper?"

"Well, as I said, Doug died before the paper came out. When the final version was published, the only name on it was Ziegart's."

"Hence the name, the Ziegart effect, not the Ziegart-McNeill-Whoever effect."

"Well, the irony of that was that the first author on the original paper was named Ziegart, but it wasn't Charles. It was his wife. She was also his student." Milford took the last bite of his salad, wiping his mouth daintily with a napkin.

"He married a graduate student? How original," Harry said, try-ing to imagine marrying Julie Canfield, and perhaps stealing her work. The thought was actually chilling. He thought, Good thing I have no sex drive left.

Milford nodded. "It's the primary pool that many of us select our wives from, I'm afraid." He washed his salad down with a slug of tea. "Not me. My wife and I were in college together. But she's an M.D., so we don't talk shop that much." He shifted in the menaced chair and said, "Serge tells me you met your wife in college, too."

"Ex-wife, and we met in law school," said Harry, circling his hand around a cup of coffee, now cold. He could see Milford creeping up on an apology, but he waved it aside and said, "Did Ziegart's widow get the royalties after he died?"

"I don't know," said Milford. "The university usually gets the better part of royalties anyway. It's possible that she wasn't entitled to any credit. Maybe her name on the paper was his wedding present to her and for some reason he changed his mind. I never met her; in fact, I only met Charlie Ziegart himself once and that was twenty years ago, long before he married Emily."

"She's still on the faculty there, according to the university website, only I don't think the name was Emily. No. It was Pamela."

"I'm pretty sure there was a starter wife before Emily. I'd guess that's your Pamela. Emily died not long after Charlie."

"So all three authors of the original work are dead? That can't be a coincidence. I know that Charlie Ziegart died in a car accident. His wife was with him, but I'm pretty sure she survived."

"Suicide," Milford said, wiping salad dressing off his mouth with a cheap paper napkin.

"Oh," Harry said. "Are you sure?"

"Of course not." Milford sipped iced tea with the first trace of impatience Harry had seen in him. "I wasn't there. I'm only reporting gossip. But it's reliable gossip, from a number of Charlie's colleagues who knew them both. But it was something like five or six years ago now, and it wasn't anything interesting like murder." He laughed, a deep, nice, liquid sound, his good humor restored. "If there had been anything suspicious about her death, believe me, everyone would have been talking about it." He balled up his napkin and put it on the tray. "I don't know anyone at Cantwell personally anymore, but I know people who do. I'll contact them and get you a name and number soon so you can get some information right from the source."

Harry thanked him and stood up, not having touched his soup. He and Milford took their plates and cups to the conveyor belt by the kitchen that carried the dirty dishes away and made them disappear. Harry imagined busy elves touching each item with a wand, making it clean with a flash of light. It's been too long, he thought, since Dusty and I have shared a good book. He missed them reading the latest J. K. Rowling or Nancy Farmer novel to each other. And of course, the reality beyond the conveyor belt was banal; there were probably a number of poor undergraduates manning industrial-size dishwashers for minimum wage.

As Harry and Frank Milford said a cordial good-bye, Harry knew he wasn't about to let go of the Ziegart effect story. Not yet anyway. It sounded like a soap opera, and drama was always good, even in books about something as dry as intellectual property law. Maybe, he thought with an internal smirk, I'll get some of my students to do the research for me.

10

TWO OF CUPS

REVERSED

Misunderstandings,
imbalance.
Love doesn't help

Josie had a client when Maggie got home, so she slipped through the living room without a word to take a shower. Josie finished with the young woman a few minutes later. The client was a local, not from the university, a housewife who thought her husband might be cheating on her with the receptionist in his office. She had three children and a fourth on the way, and Josie had tried to be kind, but it was obvious to her that the woman had good reason to be suspicious. The King of Pentacles, reversed and in the central position of the layout. He was cheating all right, and almost certainly not for the first time. Josie had a sense that the woman knew it anyway; most of them did. It was Josie's unfortunate job on these occasions to try to make something good of it, to try to give the woman advice other than "Leave the lousy bastard and go home to your mother." With four kids, that wasn't likely to improve the woman's situation much. "Take his paycheck," Josie had said. "Put as much away as you can.

Get your own bank account. Plan ahead. Find your inner strength."
As though the woman had any.

The client wasn't as grateful as she should have been, and Josie
was glad of her policy for payment up front, before the reading. She
was pretty sure she wouldn't have gotten paid for this one, and
she was pretty sure the woman wasn't coming back. Josie thought,
not for the first time, that the woman had gotten top value for her
dollar and should listen, take the message of the cards to heart, and
be grateful that she had some warning of the nasty choice that
awaited her. But Josie had been doing this for long enough to know
that the truth usually just pissed people off. She often soft-pedaled
bad readings, sometimes even lying outright. After all, most of her
clients were paying her for dreams, for the hope of a glorious future.
But everyone's future is shit, she thought. Well, maybe not shit all
the time. But she knew of no good dreams that had come true; only
nightmares.

Maggie came out of the hallway to the bathroom with wet hair
pulled back from her face. She was dressed in fresh jeans, her
scuffed walking shoes, and a black T-shirt. Josie said, "You look like
you're fifteen years old. Marlene always looked like a baby. I know
you didn't get it from your daddy. He looked like a prune." She shuffled the big cards, then said, "Kate Mayhew called. Her dryer's not
working again."

Maggie shrugged. "I'll go over there directly. Miss Baby said she'd
come over and give me a haircut today."

"You go over to the salon, okay? After you go to Kate's?"

Maggie looked at Josie, drops falling from blond strings of hair.
"Roy's coming over? Or is it Calvin?"

"Roy. Get that look off your face."

"You don't have to do that, Josie. I can make do."

"I'm not doing it for you." Josie did something she rarely did; she blushed. "I didn't mean that the way it sounded. I like him, actually." Maggie's left eyebrow cocked. "Really, hon, it's true. I'm having the time of my life."

"At least Roy takes a shower between work and here."

"Don't you go being all uppity on me. Just because he runs a junkyard doesn't mean he's a slob."

"You're right. I just wish we didn't get so many favors from your men friends."

Josie felt her hackles rise. "Don't you go thinking like that."

"I'm sorry. I didn't mean it the way it came out." Maggie looked stressed. "That isn't how I see you at all."

Josie's hackles lowered. "You spend almost all your free time doing favors for everyone we know."

Maggie opened her mouth, then closed it, and Josie knew she'd been about to argue that somehow it was different. It was, of course. For one thing, Maggie wasn't sleeping with anybody. When Maggie opened her mouth again, she said, "I'd be happier if you stuck to one."

Josie slapped the big deck on the table. "You sure didn't get your tight little ass from your mamma, and you know enough about your daddy to know that he wasn't one for staying with only one woman, married, single, or whatever. If Dunc were still alive, I'd be the saintliest women alive. Quit pursing your lips at me like you just ate a rotten kumquat and come let me read for you."

"No thanks. I don't want to know right now." Maggie passed the breakfast bar into the small kitchen, opened the refrigerator, and pulled out a large pitcher of water. She got a glass from the cabinet and poured water into it, then replaced the pitcher. Watching Maggie's hands at work pushed away Josie's irritation. Her fingers were long and pretty, and she was so graceful with them, as if they could do a ballet all on their own. Josie thought she would have made a great puppeteer. Maggie didn't lay the cards out often; when she did, it was like watching a beautiful magic trick. Poetry.

Maggie took a long drink from the glass, then said, "Harry Sterling came to see me today. He took a walk with me."

Josie's stomach clenched. "What do you think he wants?"

Maggie almost smiled. "Someone to talk to. A stranger."

"You sure? You got to watch divorced men."

Maggie's smile blossomed. "I don't think he has designs on me. Anyway, I'm a tight ass. If he asks me into the backseat of his car, I'll say no."

"Don't be fresh. What did you talk about?"

"He just wanted to tell me about himself."

"Typical man. Especially those college boys. Think every thought they have is so wonderful you'll just drop your drawers at the second breath."

"Don't worry. I'm not going to drop anything."

That evening, Harry watched the news without much interest. Local TV news shows seemed to be about less and less these days, and the network newscasts were worse; the death of the son of a minor celebrity was the lead story, although there were earthquakes and wars that killed thousands in other countries. Land of the free, he thought. Home of the brave. For the first time in a while, he wanted a drink.

He hadn't spoken to his son for several days. Each time he'd called, Ann had told him that Dusty was sleeping or "out." Dusty had had his own cell phone for a while, so Harry tried to call him on it to bypass Ann, now a bizarre gatekeeper. But that number was disconnected, so he had to dial Ann's home phone. This time, Harry was determined to actually speak to his son.

Ann said, "I've just bought him a second iPod. He's also lost his second cell phone. The last one he lost cost me three hundred dollars. Whoever found it or stole it or whatever used it to call all over before we got the contract canceled."

"Don't buy him another one then. I wouldn't have gotten him the second iPod either."

"Well, they all have them. He needs to fit in somehow." She added, "There's hope for him, though. He has a girlfriend."

"He does?" Oh God, thought Harry. It could be worse; I could have a daughter. He remembered a colleague in law school who'd congratulated him when Dusty was born, saying, "With a boy, you only have to worry about one penis. A girl, you have to worry about all of them."

Harry wanted to ask more about this girl, but Ann was done talking with him. She said a brisk good-bye and left the phone to get Dusty from his room to talk to his father.

"What the hell, buddy?"

"Hi, Dad."

"How was Cancún?"

"Okay, I guess."

"Only okay?"

"I guess."

The most enduring fashion statement of the teenage boy was a mask of eternal expressionlessness, Harry thought. Dusty should meet Maggie; they could face off, see who cracked a smile first, or even a frown. Harry fisted his hands to keep from asking about the girlfriend, the surest way to get his son to shut down altogether.

"Dad, can I come back to live with you? I mean, like now? I know it would mean changing schools and all that, but you know, kids do it all the time."

Harry spent the next moment beating down his initial shock and joyful assent to this question; all he wanted was to say "I'll be there tonight—have your stuff packed." Instead he took a steadying breath and asked, "What's going on there, buddy? I thought we agreed we'd give it the whole school year at least. New school, new place, new friends. We knew it would be an adjustment and would take a while to get used to the change."

"It's not just that stuff." Silence. Harry could imagine his solemn son, struggling with his words, aiming them as carefully as if each was a bullet to be fired at a distant target.

"What's wrong?"

"Nothing. Nothing. Never mind."

"Don't blow me off like that. Do you need me to come down there? I will, you know. I can leave right now, and be there in three hours."

"I'm not going to off myself, Dad. You don't have to come here. It's nothing that dramatic. I just hate school, but I'd probably hate any school. I'm not doing drugs, I'm not cutting myself, I'm not doing any crimes. You can relax."

Harry hated the fact that he'd missed so much of this year of his son's life, especially since it seemed to involve so many changes, such a great shift from sweetness to bitter sarcasm. Dusty said, "On second thought, don't count on our next weekend. I've got some stuff coming up, and I'll be kind of busy. Maybe the one after that. Didn't Mom tell you I'm in a play? I've got rehearsals and sh— stuff. I'll catch you next time around."

Dusty hung up before Harry could respond. He considered calling back but didn't think that his son would speak to him again that night, and the thought of trying to work around all of Ann's defenses was too exhausting to be borne. He decided instead to take a walk in the neighborhood.

Darcy Murphy said to his wife, "You haven't been to that psychic bitch again, have you?"

She was peeling the cover off a packet of frozen macaroni and cheese. This stopped her in mid-pull. "I told you I wouldn't, didn't I?"

"That's not an answer."

She went back to her task. "No, babe, I haven't. I won't. I told you."

"You better not. I've seen her place. Something's off there. Gave me the creeps. Gris-gris and all that shit."

She knew better than to argue. "Dinner will be ready in"—she peered at the directions on the empty box—"eight to twelve minutes."

II

THE
HIEROPHANT

*Excessive worry about
social approval.
Peer pressure*

Harry hated formal parties, yet here he
was in a rented tux. Professor Edwin
Thorpe was retiring from twenty-five
years at the Law School to take a position as a state appeals court judge.
Goody for him, Harry thought, his internal voice sounding twelve years old. The
whole Law School, along with many
local dignitaries, had gathered for a formal farewell dinner in the Grand Hall of
North Florida University. Harry didn't
know most of the glittery people, which

spared him from having to talk to them. Serge looked like David
Niven in a tux that probably wasn't rented, flanked by his fashion-
able and slender wife, Amelia. She'd decided to nag Harry like a
pseudo-wife, messing with his collar and telling him that his cum-
merbund wasn't tight enough. A group of students, some of whom
had seen him humiliatingly under the influence, greeted him at his
entrance as if they expected him to be the life of the party.

Serge said quietly, "Julie Canfield is awfully pretty. She's smart,
too."

"Leave me alone."

In spite of his surliness toward his friend, Harry clung to Serge and Amelia, not wanting to stand alone and risk having to make small talk to any strangers. He was about to ask Serge how close he was to the revered new judge when his friend muttered, "Oh God, no, no." Bearing down on them was a thin man with no hair and a baggy pin-striped suit. The newcomer had a mustache that was two colors, red and white, mixed together in an unwholesome pattern that made Harry wish he had a razor in his pocket so he could whisk the scrawny man to the nearest bathroom for a shave. His face was jowly, even though he didn't look much over fifty otherwise; Harry guessed that in recent years he'd lost a lot of weight but his outer self hadn't caught up yet.

"Hi, Sheriff," said Serge.

"Professor Olnikoff. My favorite Rooskie. Hahaha. How the hell's it hangin'?"

Serge turned to Harry. "Harry Sterling, this is our sheriff. Melvin Kimble."

Sheriff Kimble turned to Harry and stuck out a hand whose skin looked like it had once covered a turkey, lined and loose. "Elected fair and square, no matter what anyone tells you. Hahahaha."

Our chief law enforcement executive is Woody Woodpecker, thought Harry. Makes you proud. "Hello," he said.

"You're the writer fellow. I heard about you."

Harry noticed that the sheriff didn't pretend to have read either of his books. "Hope what you heard was good." Hahahaha, thought Harry.

"I don't know. Heard you're a bit of a rabble-rouser," said the sheriff.

"Well, I always think the rabble is better off a little roused."

Harry felt his arm grabbed from behind and repressed the urge to whip around and kick his assailant in the crotch, the presence of the sheriff be damned, when he heard Judd Lippman's nasal voice say, "So, Harry, did you meet the fortune teller? Are you going to put her in your next book?"

Judd still held his arm, so Harry dragged him around, almost ramming Lippman into the sheriff.

"Let go of me, Judd. This tux is rented and your hands are greasy."

Serge's smile was hearty and false as he introduced Judd to the sheriff, who didn't seem to find anything offensive in the former's boisterous behavior.

"Hi, Sheriff," Judd said. "The dean of the Law School is mighty proud of himself for landing Harry. He's a famous writer. The good news for you is that he's not a real attorney, so he won't be in the courthouse much, nagging you about how you treat your prisoners."

"That's good to hear," said Kimble. Thank God he didn't laugh, Harry thought.

Lippman couldn't seem to stop acting like Harry's publicist. "He's discovered our local landmark, you know, the Purple Lady's shrine."

The sheriff smiled. His teeth had broad gaps between canines and subincisors. "I hope you don't judge us all by that Tokay woman's idea of beautiful architecture. If I could lock her up for building a public eyesore, I would. But the ordinances outside the city limits are pretty loose. And her family's old, so none of the pussies on the county board will do anything."

Judd said, "Did you meet her, Harry? Did you get your fortune told?" He smiled at the sheriff. "Harry's gonna put the fortune teller in his next book." He turned back. "Right, Harry?"

"I'm not sure yet. She told me that a colleague of mine, one that had a weakness for little girls, was going to meet a grisly and unexpected death very soon. I'll have to see if her prediction pans out."

Judd guffawed, mysteriously unoffended, and went off to find

Ronnie Ho; she was talking to another professor by the punch and had a hunted look when Judd greeted her with a large smooch on the cheek.

"That true?" said Sheriff Kimble to Harry. "You gonna write about some of our local crazies?"

"Not very likely, Sheriff. I'm interested in intellectual property now. So unless the Tokay woman stole the idea of a purple shrine from someone else, I'm not sure there's much there of interest."

"Her nephew can't wait for her to die or to go into a home so he can get his hands on her property. He's already got a lot of money, but then, some people can't seem to get enough." Kimble continued to look at Harry with no change of expression, but Harry could see all at once that the impression of a jolly and harmless good ole boy was, if not an act exactly, probably overplayed, and probably useful. After a pause, the sheriff said, "You must be interested in the First Amendment, being a newsman and all that. We don't have enough going on around here to get any reporters in trouble, so I doubt we'll see you around the courthouse nagging us about that either."

"You're probably right," Harry said.

Kimble seemed to be finished with him; he turned to Serge, singing the praises of the new judge. Harry was suddenly possessed with a powerful urge to ask if Judge Thorpe was related to a Miss Baby Thorpe, proprietor of the Babyface Beauty Salon. The fact that the judge was as white as milk only made it more irresistible. Amelia caught his eye and seemed not to like what she saw there. She asked the sheriff if his daughter had accompanied him; apparently she had, and Amelia tactfully led the man away.

"Amelia went to school with her," Serge explained.

"Amelia doesn't trust me," said Harry.

"Of course not. She's not an idiot," said Serge.

"I'm guessing he's smarter than he looks."

"For years, Stoweville's been notorious throughout the state for lousy sheriffs. Our last two have been terrible drunks. At least Mel isn't an alcoholic, he isn't an idiot, and as far as I know, he isn't a crook."

"Good to know." Harry looked at the crowd around the punch bowl, relieved he didn't feel the urge to fight his way through it to get a drink. He was also grateful to Serge for not trying to tactfully steer him away from alcohol.

Serge added, "Some of his people are idiots, though. I don't think it's Kimble's fault; he just doesn't have that much to choose from."

"I don't envy him," Harry said. "I just pray that the competence of his staff, or lack of it, is never my concern, or yours." He felt in his pockets, making sure he could locate his wallet and keys. "Give my regards to the new judge and my respects to Amelia. I'm going home." At least, he thought, I won't be hungover tomorrow.

12

THE EMPRESS

REVERSED

*Unstable mind;
the possibility
of insanity*

After his Thursday morning class, Harry sat in his office and stared at his blank computer screen. He went online to an address database to search for the whereabouts of Todd Greenleaf, the retired reporter. The only cells other than "name" that he filled in were "state" and "age range." He didn't know the latter, but guessed that "60–75" was probably about right. There were twenty-eight hits, and fifty-three for "T. Greenleaf." It was also possible, he thought, that Greenleaf was unlisted, although there were ways around that. He held an internal debate that lasted two or three minutes, then called one of his former co-workers at the *Post*, a woman who covered the Senate. Her desk had been next to his for four years. He wondered if she'd gotten too uppity in the two and a half since he'd seen her to talk to him.

For once he got who he was calling, not voice mail; to his relief she sounded pleased to hear from him, although she didn't ask much about his current circumstances. The fact that he had become so uninteresting and nonthreatening was depressing and liberating at the same time.

However, she was willing to make a phone call to the editor in chief of the *Lucasta Mirror* to get a number for Todd Greenleaf, or at least the city in which he currently lived. She promised to call back with whatever she could learn in a day or two.

Harry could see Maggie Roth walking through the cemetery, heading for the opening in the trees for the path to Gunhill Park. He got out of his car quickly and followed her at a trot. He called out her name. She turned, saw him, and stood waiting until he caught up with her a few feet from the trees. Her hair was different, shorter and puffier. It looked golden in the light, like a curly halo. She put the hat over it.

"Hi," he said, panting a little. "Do you mind company again?"

"It's fine," she said.

"You know anyone named Emily?" he asked as the shade cooled him, even causing a little chill as the sweat on his arms evaporated. "Any friends or relatives? Any old client of Josie's?"

"No," she said. Her look was curious.

"Did Josie know anyone named Doug? Even from a long time ago?"

Maggie shook her head. "Why?"

Harry had been debating how much to tell her of his research. "I told you that I'm working on a book. It's going to be about the theft of intellectual property. Well, maybe. I'm not sure yet." Her brows knit, so he went on. "Some ideas can be owned. Or at least, owned in a way. Like if you write a book, or a song or an opera, it's yours. You can sell it."

She nodded. He said, "There are a lot of ideas in science, too, that can generate a lot of money. But who owns the ideas can be pretty complicated from a legal point of view."

"Who's Emily?" she said.

"I heard a story about a woman named Emily who might have had her ideas stolen, someone that Josie knew. An old client, maybe. Same thing with Doug McNeill."

"I've never heard any rumors like that. Where did you hear this story?"

"From one of my students. Josie said something at a reading that she did for the student's roommate."

"Ah," said Maggie. "Was Josie drunk at the time?"

"She admitted as much to me."

"She fell off the wagon for a while. She's back on it now."

Harry shrugged. "I thought it was unlikely, but it got me looking at this particular scientist." His eyes moved up to the tree canopy. "I doubt that it will turn out to lead to anything worthwhile." He suddenly felt embarrassed by his aimlessness, following a ridiculous idea, trying to find an injustice that didn't exist rather than spending his time doing anything productive. And the perpetrator was a dead man, if he'd actually perpetrated anything. He found himself wanting to change the subject.

"So," he said, "how did you come to live together?"

"My mother died a few years ago. Then Josie's daughter and husband died within a few months of each other. We're all the family each of us has left."

"That's rotten, losing so many people so fast."

"Yes." They came out into a rose garden, a breeze making the flowers look as if they were waving to them. Maggie moved past the flowers with some speed, and Harry followed. Once they were back on the shaded path, she asked, "Will your students find what you teach them useful when they become lawyers?"

"I have no idea."

They walked onto the wooden bridge over the stream where Harry had had his first encounter with a pileated woodpecker. Maggie stopped, placed her elbows on the railing, and rested her chin in her hands. Harry joined her, expecting silence, but after a moment she said, "Do they let you do math in prison?"

"That may be the weirdest question anyone's ever asked me." Maggie looked back at him with an unreadable expression. "As far as I know, you can cipher your way to the electric chair. Why do you ask that?"

"Just curious." Then she said, "I used to listen to music when I walked."

He waited, then asked, "Why did you stop?"

She shrugged one shoulder. "My Discman broke."

"You could get another one."

"The ones that don't skip when you jostle 'em cost thirty dollars." She was looking at a frog as it leapt from the muddy bank into the water, making a small popping sound as it hit. Harry thought, That's a lot of money to her. She added, "I like the sounds of the woods anyway. Quiet is good."

Harry became aware of the heat as his body started to dampen. It wasn't bad, but later in the spring it would be. He said, "You ever consider walking in the mall? For the air-conditioning?"

She was examining the wood grain on the bridge railing with great attention. "I can't."

"Why not?"

"Fluorescent lights."

"What about 'em?"

"They make me sick." She stared out at the black water, the non-fluorescent light making blinding puddles on its surface. "Do you see dots?"

"What?"

She opened her mouth, then closed it. "Never mind," she said.

"No, really, what are you talking about?"

She hesitated, obviously unwilling to continue. Harry waited, and she said, "Little points of light. They move so fast, you can't really see them. Just a sort of gleaming of everything."

"Don't they get in the way of what you're looking at?" Harry remembered thinking she might be insane.

"It's not like that. Everything's made up of them. They're not in the way of anything. Like I said, never mind." She looked at him. "I'm not crazy," she said.

"I never thought you were," he lied. "Is it the same thing as seeing auras?"

"Oh no. Auras are made up of dots, just like everything else."

"Oh," Harry said. "Don't auras get in the way then? Or can you see through them or something?"

He could feel her gathering her patience as she said, "Do the colors of flowers get in the way of your seeing them?"

"Oh," Harry said. "I guess not."

They walked by a stand of dogwood trees that flanked the path, just starting to bloom white, a few pink. Harry said, "Speaking of crazy people, I met Miss Tokay."

Maggie didn't smile and he was afraid that he'd offended her, but she said, "I think she's just unhappy with what she sees every day. She suffered a disappointment, you know."

"Disappointment in what?"

"Love. That's what they call it, when you have a suitor, and you think it's going to work out forever and it doesn't." Harry almost asked if Maggie herself had had her heart broken yet but caught himself, remembering that she had a daughter. She was saying, "A long time ago a man lived with her, which was talked about quite a bit." She stopped and reached up to examine a dogwood blossom more closely.

"The story is that he was taken up one night by people who came from lights in the sky. Well, in the ground, actually, but they came from the sky originally. No one ever saw him again. After that she went to bed for forty days and forty nights, praying and meditating. Then she got out of her bed and started writing about the Sky People."

"Well, Judd Lippman would certainly think I'd come to the right place."

"Who?"

"Another person you don't know. Sorry. So what were these Sky People supposed to be like?"

"Miss Tokay says that they are like us, only better, and that from time to time they take people away in their ships. She calls that 'ascending.' "

"Like going to Heaven or something?"

Maggie nodded. "Something like that." She shrugged. "She published a few articles in some fringe sorts of magazines and eventually got a following. People used to come stay with her all the time. They helped her build the shrine. They held services a few times a week. Some of them lived with her." Maggie looked up at the sun leaking through the tree canopy. "But she got old, and they went away, or died."

"Or got taken up by the Sky People," Harry said.

Maggie smiled and looked at him. It was the first real smile of hers he'd seen, and it was enchanting, dimples and lit-up eyes. He suddenly thought, I could fall in love with that smile if she were ten years older and had a college degree. His snobbishness depressed him. She said, "Maybe. Most of that happened a long time ago."

"She said there's a temple, too. I guess that's where they held these services. Did her followers help her build that as well?"

The smile vanished. "Yes. There are two of them, actually. The first one was quite grand. Velvet curtains on huge French windows, a beautiful carved wood altar, that sort of thing. About twenty years ago, a sinkhole opened up underneath it and the floor fell in. Most of it, anyway. The walls and roof are still standing, so it doesn't look too different from the outside. The neighbors wanted her to tear the place down, but she wouldn't. She says it's a monument to Warner. Her suitor," she added at Harry's questioning look. "She's got it locked up to keep kids and trespassers from going in and falling to their deaths. By the time it collapsed, she didn't have so many followers anyway. But the ones she had left helped her to convert her garage into a new temple." Something had changed in Maggie's demeanor, but Harry couldn't figure out what.

"Have you been inside either of them?" he asked.

She shrugged. "I peeked inside the old one a few times, with Miss Tokay's permission. It's mighty creepy, the huge hole in the floor leading down to blackness." She looked up at him. "There's nothing to see in the new one. Just old stuff in storage."

Harry said, "I bet there are a few geologists at the university who'd love to take a look at that sinkhole."

"There's another one on her land, too. It's been there forever. I used to swim in it when I was a little kid. The water's real cold, and nice and clear. She's had a few scientist-types poking around for years, but she won't have any of it. It's her land; there's not much they can do without her letting them. But sinkholes are pretty common around here. It's all limestone, and there are lots of underground caves. Sometimes the ground gives way and what's on top just disappears."

"A good metaphor for life," said Harry.

"Ummm." She seemed to think about this for a minute. "Miss Tokay lives alone now. We try to help her out as much as we can. Miss Baby, too. Some other neighbors."

"Doesn't she have any family?"

"Just a niece in town, with a husband." She emphasized *husband* as though it should be in quotation marks. At Harry's look, she said, "He's a developer."

"So I heard," said Harry. In this part of the world, he thought, you were either with developers or "agin 'em." He told her about what the sheriff had said, about some people needing more money no matter what.

"Some people would be happy with any at all," she said. "Since no one wants to live out here, there's no call to build a subdivision or strip mall yet. That'll change one day; the town's growing."

"I can't believe the developer nephew would build houses where there are sinkholes. That's got to be illegal."

Maggie smiled a little. "This is Florida. You can build anywhere you want if you've got money. The niece's husband can't wait for Miss Tokay to die so his wife can inherit her land."

"Simon Legree." He paused, then added, "The bad guy."

"There wouldn't be that type of bad guy if so many Yankees didn't want to move down here and avoid paying any income tax." She shrugged again. "They don't care if the schools are broke and shitty, or if their condos pollute all the salt marshes. They've got theirs." It was the first bitter thing he'd heard her say. She was slightly ahead of him, and turned to give him a look over her shoulder. "We need lawyers to fight the developers. We need journalists, too." She smiled again.

13

TEN OF
SWORDS

*High rank and wealth
lead only to ruin*

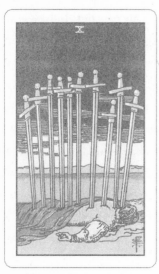

On Friday, Harry got a call from his contact at the *Post*. She had a phone number. "He lives in Winter Park. It's near Orlando," she said.

He dialed the number immediately and got an answering machine. He left a message, then decided to go for a walk in Gunhill Park.

She was looking up at tree branches that met fifty or more feet above her. "Hi," he said.

She said nothing at first, just made that hand gesture he'd seen before, a sort of wave, her hand lifted, palm out, then down again as though no one had ever taken the time to show her how it was done properly. Or maybe, he thought, she doesn't want to waste any effort on the petty give-and-take of human interaction.

"You're divorced," she said.

"Yes." Here we go again, he thought. Let the conversational Tilt-A-Whirl begin.

"She divorced you?"

"Yes."

"But didn't she love you?"

Jesus, thought Harry, just get a gun and finish it quick. "She did once. Then she didn't."

"How did you know she loved you?"

What a weird question, he thought. He was dismayed by how much distress it caused him. "I guess because she told me."

"You believed her?"

He started to get miffed. "Do you think I was foolish to?"

Her face shifted subtly, flattening out. "I'm sorry. Does this make you sad? That wasn't what I meant to do." She hugged herself and Harry realized that she was upset, too, although he couldn't have explained what it was in her body language that expressed it. "I'm sorry," she said again.

"It's okay." He ran a hand through his hair, feeling a slight dampness in his scalp, sweat from the unaccustomed exertion of brisk walking. "I don't know why I believed her, but I did. I'm a pretty good judge of people's honesty, usually. It's one of my strengths as a reporter." Her face remained wooden, her mouth a straight line. He went on. "I remember pretty much to the moment when she said it and didn't mean it anymore." Their pace slowed down, and he caught his breath. "Why are you asking me this? You sound like a sociologist doing a survey on the mating habits of the middle class."

She quit hugging herself and let her arms move with the rhythm of her steps. "There are just so many things I don't know," she said. "Especially about how people deal with each other. Did you love her?"

He shrugged. "Of course. Once I thought she was the love of my life."

"But not now?"

He turned his head to look at her. "What's this about exactly?"

She shook her head. "It's just something I've never understood, how you know. I thought it would be useful to ask a man about it, but I guess I was insensitive. I'm sorry."

"The subject is delicate. You could be misunderstood."

She nodded in agreement. "I'm not interested because I want anything from anybody, but it doesn't usually come out right."

Harry felt oddly hurt by this comment, which a distant part of him found amusing. Make up your mind, it said.

Harry called at the beginning of the week to insist on Dusty's visit. He tried to make the call while walking back to his house from the university after his last class of the day. He lived only a mile and a half away but hadn't ever considered walking back and forth till recently. The ground was level, and there were shaded sidewalks most of the way. He wasn't sure he'd want to make the trip on foot when the real heat set in, but the dogwoods and redbud trees were in bloom and he was surprised at how beautiful this part of town was. Its beauty was of a far more manicured variety than that of Gunhill Park, but it still was pleasant to take a little time to enjoy it. After all, he thought, I have the time.

But his cell phone didn't work, putting a dent in his pastoral mood. After pushing a few nonresponsive buttons, he concluded that the battery was no longer holding a charge. He swore at it, making a mental note to replace it as soon as possible. When he was back at home, he dialed Ann's number on his desk phone. After a few mild threats, he got her to agree to meet him at a halfway point the following Saturday morning, delivering their son to him as though it was a hostage exchange. Dusty would take the bus home on Sunday evening. He wouldn't mind as long as he had a book and his new iPod.

.   .   .

Harry had gotten a copy of the Ziegart effect paper from Frank Milford through campus mail on Tuesday. He read the whole thing through, understanding one word in five. The version that Milford had given him had been published in the *Northeastern Journal of Physics and Engineering.* The only author listed was Charles Ziegart.

He went online and found the website of Cantwell University in Lucasta, Pennsylvania. From it he obtained the main office number of the Charles Ziegart School of Physics and Engineering. He loved how much easier the Internet made doing research, although he'd found that most things you learned online were at best partial truths; there was no substitute for interviewing people in person. It was remarkable how often people lied, even about inconsequential things; but it was also remarkable how easy it was to tell most of the time, at least for him. The more fiercely earnest people looked, the more likely it was that something they were telling him was fabricated, constructed, or at least massaged. Harry was gifted in smelling falsehood, but even his powers diminished over the phone, and they disappeared altogether when looking at a computer screen. He could get started with the Internet and a few phone interviews; if anything interesting turned up, he would have to travel to Pennsylvania. He wasn't sure he was up to it. He didn't want to be farther away from Dusty than he already was. He almost hoped his initial inquiries would amount to nothing.

He left a message at Cantwell University with a secretary who sounded as though she'd been smoking since cigarettes were invented. His call was returned a few hours later by a woman named Gillian DeGraff, whose accent suggested northeastern prep schools and vacation houses on Cape Cod. Dr. DeGraff identified herself as Cantwell's dean of arts and sciences. "The director of the Ziegart School is out of town for a conference. He's only been with the university for three years, and didn't know Charles Ziegart. So Louise called my office." Harry gathered that Louise was the smoky-voiced secretary. "We're gratified to come to the attention of *The Washington Post*."

"I'm formerly with the *Post*. I'm teaching law at the moment. I'm also working on a book, which is why I called in the first place."

"I gathered that from what Louise said. What can I help you with?"

"I was interested in the Ziegart effect. More specifically, I want to know whatever you can tell me about Charles Ziegart himself. Did you know him personally?"

"Oh yes. He and I were quite close. My husband is Cantwell's chancellor, and Charlie was one of his best friends. I still have lunch with his wife almost every week."

He wondered if her casual use of "Charlie" was meant to impress him. "You mean his first wife?"

"He was married to Pamela for almost twenty years before he did the thing that so many academics do, I'm afraid. They get a midlife itch, especially with younger, adoring students around them. Men of Charlie's fame and ability often need a lot of ego support, you know. I'm sure you've seen such things yourself." She gave a laugh. Harry didn't laugh in turn. At his silence, she added, "Or maybe you haven't. I don't know how many journalists have that kind of giant intellect. I know some do, of course. Edward R. Murrow. Walter Cronkite and so forth. But you don't see so much gravitas in the media now."

Harry ignored the bait. "I understand he died in a car accident?"

"Yes, over seven years ago. It was one of the worst things that's happened to this university. Charlie was very beloved, and was a brilliant lecturer as well as a scientist and scholar. Wesley, my husband, actually closed the university for two days, something that rarely happens unless you've got a huge natural disaster or something."

"I assume the school was named after him later?"

"Yes. Several well-situated alumnae helped raise the funds."

"A nice bit of immortality."

"For a great man. Besides, he'll be remembered for generations for the work he did. I take it you're familiar with it?"

"Only what I've gotten off the Internet and from talking to the chair of the physics department here, Frank Milford."

"I don't believe I know him. Where did you say you were teaching?"

"I didn't. North Florida University."

"Oh." The syllable said enough. "Well, we can't all be Charlie Ziegarts, obviously." She paused, maybe quelling an urge to say anything more insulting about Frank Milford, then went on. "Have you done a lot of biographies? Do you specialize in scientists?"

"I'm not a biographer. I'm an investigative journalist." For someone in her position, Harry thought, she didn't seem very astute. He assumed she'd looked him up before calling him, checking out his bona fides. He certainly would have in her position. But merely invoking the name of *The Washington Post* was often enough to get into people's personal business. "I've written several books. Now I've turned my attention to intellectual property law. I'm doing a new book on the use of research funded by public monies for profit, as happens a lot now with pharmaceuticals." The lie came out of his mouth fluidly, making Harry remember how good at his job he used to be. He supposed he should feel worse about being such a good liar. Well, he thought, that *may* turn out to be the topic of the book. He waited for her reaction. It was pretty much what he expected.

"What does any of that have to do with Charles Ziegart?"

So it wasn't Charlie anymore. "I'm not sure, to be honest. But I understand that his work brought some military contracts to Cantwell, and I was curious about how that worked. I thought it might make a good contrasting case, if the government actually pays well for university research, as opposed to the outright theft of it that some companies in the private sector do. Or"—he gave a polite laugh—"allegedly do."

"Oh," she repeated. He could feel the chill descending on the conversation. "Well, I can't really disclose much about that," she said. "You understand."

"What can you disclose?"

"If you've read any of his papers, I'm sure you can imagine that there are many applications for his work. Universities always need money. We get only a small percentage of our budget from tuition and donations. An awful lot of grant money has evaporated in recent years for just about everything except medical research. And as you say, academic data get into the public domain pretty much imme-diately. So anytime a facility like ours can reap royalties from the work of our faculty, it's a great boon. It provides labs and equipment and helps fund the development of the next generation of scien-tists."

"Graduate students."

"Exactly."

"How much do the graduate students contribute?"

"What do you mean?"

"I mean, are they mostly free labor for the faculty, or do they do their own research?"

"For one thing, Mr. Sterling, graduate students are hardly free. At Cantwell, most of them are supported by the university. The re-search fellows get their tuition, benefits, and a generous stipend. And the work they do here is under the supervision of a world-class scholar, and that experience sets them on a professional road that they benefit from the rest of their lives."

"What happened to Doug McNeill?"

"What? Who?"

"Doug McNeill. The third author on the original Ziegart effect paper."

"He wasn't on the published version."

"I'm aware of that. Why not?"

"I'm not sure. He passed away, as I assume you know. Natural causes. I don't remember the details. He never took very good care of himself. What does that have to do with the topic of your book, Mr. Sterling?"

"Probably nothing. But sometimes it's helpful to get a whole picture of a subject, to know who he worked with. In this case, who his closest students were. Did you know the second wife, Emily Ziegart, well?"

Gillian DeGraff took some time to answer. "Not that well. As I said, I never really could accept her as Charlie's wife. She wasn't very friendly, especially once she got Charlie to marry her."

"She was his graduate student?"

"Yes. Not a very promising one, I'm afraid. She saw her opportunity to get ahead the quickest way possible, by marrying one of the preeminent scientists of our day. Poor Charlie did have a weakness for youth and flattery, and she was smart enough to know how to flatter him up and down. And of course, they spent long hours together in the lab."

"She was on the original paper, too, I understand."

DeGraff made a noise of disgust. "No doubt a reward for other services rendered, if you'll forgive my crudeness. I think the hardest thing for Pamela to accept was that, although Emily was young, she wasn't even all that pretty. Kind of chunky and graceless."

There was a sound of paper rustling, and Harry knew that she was winding up the interview. He said, "Why were their names removed before the paper was published?"

"Presumably because they didn't deserve to be on it in the first place. Charles Ziegart was a generous mentor." She rustled more paper and said, "If I may ask, how did you come to be interested in Charlie's work in particular, Mr. Sterling?"

Harry didn't see any reason not to tell her. "A graduate student here went to a fortune teller. The fortune teller claimed that someone she knew really invented the Ziegart effect."

"What?"

"I checked it out on a whim. The fortune teller is an alcoholic who occasionally watches the Discovery Channel. She has a niece who is a short-order cook. There aren't any physicists among her clientele or friends as far as I can tell."

"*This* is what got you interested in Charlie Ziegart?"

He didn't want to ask her yet about the likelihood of "Charlie" stealing the work of his graduate students. "It was brought to my attention partly as a joke, but partly because people knew of my interests. And Charles Ziegart is inherently interesting."

"True." More rustling paper.

"Do you know how Emily Ziegart died?"

"She killed herself. It didn't have anything to do with us." Harry was about to ask for more details when Gillian DeGraff said, "I'm afraid I'm already late for a meeting, Mr. Sterling. Good luck with your research," and hung up. Harry sat looking at the phone for several minutes, thinking.

TEN OF
WANDS

He still hadn't heard back from Todd
Greenleaf, so the next morning Harry
tried the number again from his office on
campus. He didn't expect to gain anything of interest from speaking to the old
reporter, but he didn't want to leave such
an obvious stone unturned. Virtually all
of the news stories on Ziegart's death
had been rewrites of Greenleaf's com-
prehensive article in the Lucasta paper.
He tsk-tsked such laziness but knew
from experience how little firsthand

news gathering went on. Budget cuts, shrinking subscription lists,
and a loosening of standards: more celebrity news and political spin.
He thought, I'm turning into a grumpy old man, pining for the good
old days.

When he got Greenleaf on the phone, he had to hold the receiver a few inches from his ear as the older man spoke in a piercing
voice. It was obvious that he was somewhat deaf, given how many
times he made Harry repeat every question.

"Married a hot young wife after dumping the old one," Greenleaf said. "Lucky SOB."

"Ziegart's accident was caused by a bee sting while driving? Sounds unlikely."

"Bugs cause car crashes all the time. I got a friend who eats through a tube now because he rammed a bulldozer when a cock-a-roach ran up his leg." His laughter was like ripping paper.

Harry pushed past his dislike and said, "I came upon a rumor that he stole his research, especially for the Ziegart effect."

"Really? Whaddya know."

"You never heard anything like that?"

"Nah. He was like an Einstein or something. Who would he steal from?"

"Maybe his students."

"You kiddin'? They're all there to learn from *him*. What the hell?"

"You never reported anything on Emily's suicide, either."

"Love does strange things to women, doesn't it? I sorta remember something about that, but there wasn't any interest in it at the paper. My editor, he didn't think it was newsworthy, you know what I mean?"

"Not newsworthy?"

"Oh, I think the old widow, ex-wife, whatever, put a word in the publisher's ear or something. Don't give the new wife any more ink, if you know what I mean."

"That didn't bother you?" Harry felt his skin tingle with something like anger.

"Nah. Happens all the time. And we had other stuff goin' on, if I remember. It was right around 9/11 and the Shanksville crash. All the Pennsylvania papers were busy with that. Mrs. Z number two offing herself just wasn't a big enough story to squeeze in. Not enough grease, you know what I mean?"

"Did you have any information on it? Stuff that you didn't use?"

"Nah. Didn't bother. I had me the carpal tunnel then, too. Didn't want to do anything that I didn't need to."

Harry wasn't sure how having carpal tunnel syndrome made one unable to place a few phone calls, but before he could ask anything else, Greenleaf said, "Look, all the facts I had were in print. I got a beer gettin' hot on the lanai, you know what I mean? Have a nice life." He hung up.

Darcy Murphy hated his supervisor, a man who'd had the money and the time to go to college. His boss was an electrical engineer, and Darcy always drew the syllables out—"eeelectrickahl ennnginnneeerr," like it was a clownish title, something fake. He knew his supervisor didn't like him much either, which hurt Darcy's feelings, although even he knew that made no sense.

Darcy hated being stuck in the office even more than he hated his supervisor, and even more than the Florida heat. The air-conditioned air made his sinuses dry up and crack, giving him headaches that made his eyeballs feel like they were going to pop from their sockets. He was nursing a bad one now, worse than a hangover, which was unfair since he hadn't tied one on for a long while. So many of his friends had joined AA, he thought the whole world was in some sort of goddamned 12-step program, talking about higher powers instead of Jesus or God or anything real. It made him think of that pagan stretch of Highway 21, with its blasphemous shrine and the fortune teller. His skin crawled at the thought. Something should be done, he thought. There ought to be a law.

His supervisor was younger than Darcy, which rankled even more than the degree. The Little Shit, as Darcy called him in private, was sitting behind a desk the size of an old Chevy; he looked like a snotty child in a school too big for him.

"Darcy," said the Little Shit, "I've reviewed your latest report."

He looked up at the scrawny man, swaying angrily above him. "You can sit down if you want."

Darcy considered scratching his ass in front of his boss but was afraid it might backfire, no pun intended, his gesture seen not as a mark of his contempt for the privileged child before him but as a sign of his own commonness. He tried to think of a way to do it while making it clear that he really knew how to behave in company and just didn't think the Little Shit was worth putting on any manners for, but he knew he couldn't pull it off. So he sat down, his rear end sending his brain a protest.

The supervisor said, "You found everything on the premises in order?"

"Seems so," said Darcy.

"Yet you added a comment that you think they 'bear watching' and recommended monthly inspections. We don't have enough manpower to be constantly checking on people who aren't doing anything wrong. Unless you have some other grounds for your suggestion?"

"Just a feelin'," Darcy said. "A hunch. Something's up out there."

"Something's up?" the supervisor said. The younger man waited, and Darcy read a sneer in the comment and the silence.

"I been in this job fourteen years," Darcy said, his teeth barely parting for each syllable. "I got me a nose for sh— stuff. They been looked at by a few folk before me. They knew something was up, too. Just because we ain't found nothin' don't mean there ain't nothin'."

The supervisor looked at Darcy while nervously chewing a large wad of gum. Darcy had always thought gum chewing was filthy. It made people look like cows. "Look, Darcy, I respect your nose. But I need a concrete reason to take men off other jobs to go bothering people. If you think there's something really wrong out there, we should make it a law enforcement matter. But if it's just your gut or, rather, your nose, well, we may need to move on, at least until something substantive turns up."

"Move on?"

"Yes." Chew.

Darcy got up, walked to the door without responding, then turned back. "You can learn two-dollar words, but you cain't get a nose in school. Boss." He didn't spit on the floor before leaving the room, but it was a close thing.

Harry was waiting for her in the cemetery parking lot, not wanting to brave the remarks of the staff at Crane's. For all he knew, she didn't want their remarks any more than he did. She gave him one of those smiles that didn't reach her mouth but lit her eyes up like blue kaleidoscopes. Harry wondered if she liked the Beatles or if she'd ever taken LSD.

They headed for the path through the trees. She spoke first, which pleased him. "I have a question for you."

"What's that?" he said, mentally bracing himself.

"I read some of your articles at the library. From when you worked at *The Washington Post*."

He could feel his entire body flush. It was weird, he thought, how much her interest and good opinion mattered to him. "So what's the question?"

"Did what you do help many people?"

Harry was startled. "Sometimes," he said. "A few. I found out about bad things that people were doing, and tried to expose them. Sometimes that helped stop them."

"Then why did you quit?"

Harry couldn't speak. She slowed her pace, so that he could catch up. When he did, she went on. "I don't understand why you'd stop doing your job even after something as terrible as your brother's death." She waited for a moment, but Harry remained speechless. "It's not like anyone threatened your son or held you in chains. Why would you just stop? Why wouldn't it make you try harder?" She spoke with the first sign of heat he'd seen in her, and it made him giddy, charged with a breath of fear. He was getting defensive, so he stopped himself from answering, not trusting himself not to be hostile.

She looked at him directly, her bright eyes hard. "You could go on. You're choosing not to." She looked away, and Harry could think of nothing to say. They finished the walk more quickly than before and said a stilted good-bye in the parking lot. As she drove away, he remembered that he'd wanted to talk to her about Dusty and was ashamed of himself.

15

TWO OF
PENTACLES

*False sociality. The situation is
more than the Seeker can handle*

Harry didn't pick his son up till Saturday
morning since there was a rehearsal of
the high school play on Friday night. This
made the visit extremely short, but it
was preferable to not seeing him for another week. Dusty wanted to stop at
the Law School before they went home,
mainly because he had found the snacks
in the vending machines in the faculty
lounge to be of high quality. As luck
would have it, the place seemed to be
teeming with students, and Harry had to

introduce the boy to everyone. The worst moment was when Julie
Canfield made a point of coming into his office to meet his son. "So
you're Dusty," she said unnecessarily, looking like a flight attendant
in a smooth blue suit. Why she felt it necessary to dress this way on
a Saturday eluded him until she explained that a new candidate was
in town to interview for an open faculty position. Harry had forgotten, not feeling enough a part of the establishment of the place to
have such matters concern him. The candidate was giving a lecture
that evening as part of his ordeal of being looked over by everyone

in the school; Harry silently gave thanks that he'd been spared a similar rite of passage.

Julie made small talk with Dusty for what seemed like hours. They were wrapping it up finally, with Dusty giving her a desultory description of his role in the upcoming production of *Guys and Dolls*, when Dan Polti appeared in the office doorway, Serge not far behind. Serge seemed delighted to see Dusty, who revived a little upon seeing someone he knew. Serge introduced Dan and renewed what Harry was starting to see as a conversational vortex. Dusty hadn't said much in the car, having been more interested in napping and listening to his iPod than in talking to his father. Now Dan made the suggestion that they all get some lunch together. Serge echoed the sentiment with enthusiasm, and Julie had to be included. Harry was miserable.

The only worthwhile eatery on campus was closed on weekends, so they had to go elsewhere. Serge had the largest car, so it was decided that they would all ride together. "How about Crane's?" said Serge. "We can show Dusty the local color." Harry tried to change the destination, but when Dan heard where the restaurant was and realized that it was near the Purple Lady's shrine, he declared that it was something Dusty had to see if he was to truly appreciate Stoweville culture. Harry was overruled.

He didn't know whether or not to be relieved at the hour when they arrived; it was well after one o'clock, so Maggie was already off work. He didn't see her among the diners and recognized only Dottie and the fat man with menus, who he'd learned was Calvin Crane, the owner. Fat Calvin nodded at Harry, and to Harry's dismay, Dottie waited on them, saying a nicer hello than he'd gotten so far at the restaurant. The waitress made much over Dusty, saying that it was hard to tell whether or not he looked like his father. "Maybe," she said to Dusty, "if you grow a beard, too." She looked at Harry and said, "Maggie's gone for the day. Do you want me to tell her that you were here?"

"No, thanks." He felt everyone else at the table looking at him and began reading his menu as though it contained the formula for happiness. He told himself that he was being ridiculous, but he couldn't get rid of the sensation of having a dirty secret exposed. He didn't have much of an appetite, especially after Dan said, "A waitress, eh? Cool."

Serge said, "You never told me how your talk with Frank Milford went."

"Fine," Harry said, trying to psychically will Serge to shut up.

"Is that the physics chair?" Dan said. "Does this have something to do with your book?"

"The Ziegart effect," Serge blurted, and Harry wanted to throw the saltshaker at him.

"Oh," Julie said, eyes big and soft and brown. "Are you investigating the rumor that Ronnie told you about?"

"Is that where you heard it?" Serge asked.

"What rumor?" Dusty said, and Julie explained Ronnie's contention that a famous physicist had stolen his most famous discovery.

Dan said, "Tell him the source, though. A drunken fortune teller."

"She lives near here," Julie said.

Harry said, "I doubt I'll be able to dig up much. There were three authors on the original paper, and they're all dead."

"Just as well for them," Dan said. "Physicists burn out really young. They all do their best work before they're thirty. It's a known fact."

Serge said, "Don't tell that to Frank Milford. It might make him mad, and he could squish you like a grape."

When they were finished eating, Julie made a point of saying how wonderful the food had been, even though she'd had a salad that wasn't anything extraordinary as far as Harry could see. It was as though she thought he had a personal stake in the quality of the place and wanted to please him. The notion made him even more anxious to get rid of all these extra people, so he and Dusty could be alone and go for a walk or see a movie or go home to talk.

Dan and Julie made sure Serge didn't forget to go a mile or so out of their way to drive by the shrine. Harry was grateful that Miss Tokay wasn't sitting on its summit, fearing having to explain any more chumminess with the locals. When Serge mentioned a UFO cult, Harry squelched a desire to fill him in on what details he now knew.

Dan pointed at the hand-shaped sign on the horizon and said, "What do you think, Professor Sterling? Would Dusty like his fortune told?"

"Call me Harry," Harry said automatically for at least the fourth time. "I think you probably need an appointment."

Dusty said, "Why don't we all go to the beach? We could stay at the house."

At the questioning looks of the law students, Harry explained. "We have a small house at Delacroix Beach. We can't go, Dusty. It's rented this weekend. I reserved it for a few weeks from now so you and I could go. What do you think?"

Dusty just shrugged, but Harry could see Julie Canfield's brown cow eyes light up with interest. "I love the beach," she said. Oy, he thought.

On the way back down Highway 21, they came to a small strip mall just past Crane's. "Can I get a Coke, Dad?" Dusty asked, spying a convenience store on the far end of the row of shops. Serge proclaimed that it would be on him, slowed the car, and pulled into the parking lot. There were no spots directly in front of the store they wanted; instead, Serge parked by a pizza place that didn't look too clean. They unpacked themselves from the car, and as Harry straightened in the heat, the asphalt dancing and shimmering, he saw a dusty white Celica two cars away from Serge's copper-colored Element. It was parked in front of the business neighboring the pizza parlor, a Laundromat with large glass windows. Harry couldn't stop himself from taking the few steps over to look in. She was sitting beside an empty white laundry basket, talking to a little black girl, the one with the bad teeth. Charlotte was sitting down next to Maggie, and the girls were laughing and Maggie was smiling and Harry couldn't breathe for a moment. Ten feet away, Dusty said, "Dad?" and Harry woke up and followed his son, his students, and his best friend into the convenience store for cold drinks and ice cream. The transaction didn't take long, and when they came out, Harry felt the Celica at his back as he got into the car. He felt like yelling or crying or hitting something, but managed to do nothing at all.

They made it home by late afternoon. Dusty was hungry again, so Harry ordered a pizza, not having been sure what food to stock for his son's brief visit. There had been a time when he could have gone into a grocery store and pointed with confidence at everything on the shelves that Dusty loved, liked, hated, or hadn't ever tried. Now, he felt as unsure about his son's food preferences as he did about everything else.

Dusty emerged from his room after the pizza arrived, earbuds firmly in place. His hair was parted unevenly down the middle, brown like Harry's but straighter, his only obvious genetic gift from Ann. His skin was starting to rebel under a light tan. At least he gets outside once in a while, Harry thought. His shoulders were broadening, although there was little meat on them as yet; there had been a time when Harry might have teased him about having a coat hanger left in his shirt, but not now; not with this person he no longer knew at all, who was so raw and so closed off, so easily bruised.

"What music are you listening to?" Harry said.

"Just a band. You know."

"No, I don't. There are a lot of bands."

"Logroller."

"Oh," said Harry.

"Just one of their songs. I have all different people on it. I've got maybe forty bands on here."

"Oh," Harry repeated, as the memory of a similar thin face, marvelous cheekbones, and soft eyes like Hershey's Kisses came to him with force. My God, he thought, he looks like Mom.

Dusty said around a mouthful of cheese and sauce and dough, "So are you, like, dating a waitress?"

"No," Harry said, still thinking about his mother. "Don't talk with your mouth full. It's gross."

Dusty swallowed. "What about Julie? She seems nice. She's pretty and all."

"No. She's a student. Not even a friend, really. She's too young anyway."

"Uncle Serge married someone younger than him."

Harry said, "She wasn't his student. She worked at the university. Some sort of administrative something or other. That's how they met. It's different."

"How?" To Harry's relief, his son was between bites when he spoke the word.

"Serge didn't have any power over her."

"He's a professor, right?" Dusty took another bite.

"Yes."

"Well, if he said to someone high up, 'That girl's got to go. She annoys me,' they'd probably fire her, right?"

Harry stared at Dusty. "Swallow *before* you speak. And no, they probably wouldn't. Professors don't have as much clout as you think. I doubt I could get anybody fired. Serge probably couldn't either. Unless they were doing something illegal."

"Well, the bigwigs would be a lot more likely to believe you than a secretary or something, wouldn't they? If you said they'd stolen something or whatever, they'd listen, right?"

"Oh, God, I don't know. How the hell did we get on this?" Harry looked for another topic. "What the hell keeps happening to your iPods and cell phones? Your mother says that you keep losing them."

The animation in Dusty's face withdrew like low tide. In its place was the affect-free mask. He shrugged, took another bite of pizza. "I don't know," he said. At least he was trying to keep his mouth closed around the wad of food. "I guess I'm just forgetful."

"Forgetful my ass," said Harry. "And your mom said you have a girlfriend. She's in the play, too, right? What's she like?"

Expression rushed back in the form of uneven red patches on Dusty's face, making him look not quite ripe. He continued chewing while looking at the table. Harry thought, Uh-oh. When Dusty was done with his mouthful, he took another piece from the box and said, "Mom was wrong."

"Oh," Harry said. "Talk to me."

"I am talking," said Dusty, his mouth full again. "It wasn't anything. Mom exaggerates stuff, okay? She wants me to be normal. I'm not, okay?" He looked up, the blank face imperfectly back in place. "I'm a geek. Like you, right? Ha ha. She tells me that sometimes. I'm a fucking geek, okay?" His eyes dropped in embarrassment for his reckless language.

"Don't swear," Harry said automatically, then, "I hate that I don't know this stuff. I hate that you're not with me." Shut up, he thought. "What's her name?"

Dusty's hands had moved to the pizza box, restless and ungraceful; they started in on the corners, tearing each one open in turn with a tiny jerk. He finally answered. "Michelle."

"Who ended it?"

"She did, obviously." The redness had evened out across Dusty's face, and now included ears and neck and what Harry could see of his son's scalp at the part.

"I'm sorry. But believe it or not, you'll feel better in a month or so. It seems like a long time to wait, but you'll be better off in the end." Harry was appalled by what was coming out of his mouth.

"She called me *gay*."

"Oh." Harry's mind churned.

"I'm *not* gay, Dad. You don't have to freak out about that." His hands were now removing the top of the box entirely from its moorings. "I didn't tell Mom because I knew the first thing she'd think was that it was true and then she'd have to send me to counseling and try to fix me and shit, and I'm *fine*. I'm just freaking *fine*."

Harry wanted to hug his son so fiercely that he could feel his arms tingle. But he didn't want to propel him back into his bedroom, into the solitude of his iPod. He sat for a moment. Then he said, "I didn't think you were gay. But even if you were, you wouldn't need to be fixed. Do you even know what being gay means?"

"God, Dad, of course. Oh God, leave me alone."

Harry grabbed his son's wrist to prevent flight. "Some guys like guys. And some girls like girls. Instead of boys." *I'm screwing this up. Oh fuck it*, Harry thought. "It doesn't make them broken, or sick or stupid or whatever this girl meant."

"Thanks, Dad. That helps a lot."

At least he had his son's eyes on him now, even if the pain in them was enough to send Harry running for a bottle. "Do you remember your mother's cousin, Rudy?"

"Sure."

"He's gay."

Dusty's eyes opened, and for the first time in their conversation, Harry could see a gleam of interest in them. He relaxed the hand on his son's wrist, and Dusty didn't flee. "No way," Dusty said.

"Way," said Harry. "He's a really nice guy. You remember his friend Blake?"

"Yeah," said Dusty, his eyes looking away at a memory. "Whoa. No way."

"Yes way. In high school it's a bad thing to be called, but think about what people actually mean. Remember our 'nerd' discussion?"

Dusty closed his eyes. His hands were now balled into fists and were resting on the table. "Yeah. Nerds are just smart people, and lots of folks don't like it when people are smarter than they are." He breathed in and opened his eyes.

Harry ignored his son's irritation. "Right, so they call them names and try to make them feel bad."

"Yeah. And beat them up. There's a kid in my class who's probably really gay, Dad. He got beat up after school by a bunch of kids. He had to change schools."

"That sucks. I hope his parents sued the shit out of the school." Harry rubbed the back of his neck and regarded his son. "So why did she call *you* gay?"

Dusty took a third piece of pizza and looked away while he bit into it.

Harry said, "It's because you're quiet? Smart?" He silently swore to his son that he'd never utter the word *sensitive*.

After a moment, Dusty said, "Yeah." He seemed calmer now, anger replaced by sadness. "I'm doing the scenery. I'm good at art. And I was stupid enough to say I liked it."

"Ah," said Harry. He thought, If I could, I'd slap each kid till he or she bowed down to you like a king; or better yet, I'd slap all their parents. He said only, "Teenagers are the most vicious bunch of con-formists you'll ever meet. No offense. So you have an excuse for worrying about what others think of you." He took a second slice of pizza. "I don't know what my excuse is."

"For what?"

"The waitress," Harry said. "Her name's Maggie. She's perfectly nice, but I'm not dating her. She's too young, too, like Julie. But still, I don't know why I'm so jumpy about letting people know that she's my friend."

"What name are you afraid that people will call you?" said Dusty.

"Egomaniac," Harry said. "Like I have to go slumming to find someone who'll think I'm hot shit because I'm who I am and she's a lowly waitress. I mean, cook. She's not actually a waitress."

"Is it true? Does she make you feel like you're hot sh— hot stuff?"

"No. Actually, she's a lot smarter than me, at least about some things." Harry looked at the table, embarrassed to meet his son's cynical gaze. "But maybe I'm just telling myself that because it makes me feel better. You don't always know your own motives for things, you know."

"Maybe you just like her," Dusty said. Harry looked up and saw that his son's gaze wasn't cynical at all.

16

THE HERMIT

Warnings and wisdom.
The Seeker finds
a spiritual guide

Harry delivered Dusty to the Orlando-bound bus on Sunday afternoon. The first thing he did after he got back home was shave off his beard. Dusty had told him that "a lot of girls don't like dudes to be all hairy and sh— stuff." He thought of it as a sort of sacrifice, an irrational form of atonement for Maggie's disappointment in him. The thought that she might no longer want his company on her walks bothered him enough to keep sleep even further away than usual. He was aware that part of his worry was nonsensical; she didn't know he'd essentially denied her when she was in the Laundromat with the two girls. Still, it ate at him; friends didn't pretend not to know each other.

He called her house after shaving to find out when she was going for a walk the following day. Josie answered the phone. When he asked for Maggie, she hesitated; Harry had the impression that she was about to tell him Maggie wasn't home. But in a second, Maggie's voice replaced Josie's.

"Are you mad at me?" Harry said.

There was a pause. "No."

"Good. Dusty was here this weekend and I couldn't get out for a walk. Are you going tomorrow?"

"She's not here," Josie said as she let him in the door the next afternoon, and Harry could tell at once that she was drunk. She didn't stink of it, exactly, but there was an odor, and he imagined that, if he could see her aura, it would be syrupy and brown, the color of bourbon.

"Can I wait for her?" he said, trying to psychically push his way in. "I told her I'd pick her up. Where is she?"

Josie looked confused and moved back from the door, which Harry took to be a gesture of welcome. She shook her head and said, "She's just out somewhere. Errand. She'll be back. Nobody is as good as their word as Maggie." Her bleary gaze focused on him. "You're not as ugly without all that hair on your face."

"Thanks," Harry said. He looked around for a glass or a bottle but saw nothing. She has it hidden, he thought. She's been taking sips and putting it back each time, in case Maggie comes home. As if Maggie wouldn't be able to tell that she'd been drinking. Poor Josie. Poor Maggie. Then Harry thought, Maybe I should go to an AA meeting, just once. Check it out.

Josie collapsed onto the sofa, making old springs chirp as her body caused them to bounce slightly. He sat down in a spindly chair opposite her, wanting to keep his distance because she seemed so hypersexual. He didn't know why he found her slightly repulsive, but he had an idea that she felt the same way about him. The phone rang, and Josie answered it as though he wasn't there. The conversation was brief, Josie telling someone else that Maggie wasn't available. She didn't reassure the caller that she'd be back soon.

As soon as the call was over, Josie burped and then said, "You pay someone to do your taxes?"

"What? Er, yes. Why? Do you need me to recommend a good CPA?"

Josie waved an irritated hand. "No. I was afraid you'd make Maggie do 'em for you. Everyone around here, they get Maggie to do their taxes. I keep telling her, she should charge. How much do you pay?"

"I don't remember. Sorry. I could find out, if you really want to know."

She looked mad at him, as if he'd said something stupid. "It won't matter. She won't charge anything. Everyone wants to know their lottery numbers, too. Maggie hates it. Calls it the poverty tax. So I don't give 'em out. If they don't hit, people get awful mad anyway. It's like Baby. She doesn't charge enough at the salon either. Doesn't charge some folks at all. Miss Tokay. Maggie, of course. At least she's smart enough to do her own taxes. Sometimes she even helps Maggie out. When there's too many forms to do. Poor Baby hates that salon. But she's stuck with it. Two granddaughters to raise. What the hell's she gonna do? We're all stuck, one way or another." She burped again and said, "I take care of her."

"Maggie or Miss Baby?"

She snorted with irritation. "Maggie, of course. She's not real savvy, as you folks would say." Harry wasn't sure which group of folks she was referring to this time: academics or Yankees or something else. "I watch out for her. Always have. I was more of a mom to her than Marlene. Except for when Marlene lived next to the farm. With that man. Can't remember his name now. Wait. Jimmy, Maggie's daddy. That was only for a couple of years. Then she came back to me." The phone rang again, and Josie was just as brisk with this caller as she'd been with the last one. "She can't do it now. She's working. You know." A pause. "I'll tell her."

She hung up and then leaned over, opening a shallow drawer in the coffee table. She pulled out a pad of paper with lines; Harry realized that it was the kind waiters use in restaurants to record and add up a bill. Then she picked up a chewed-looking paperback book from the end table and used it as a lap desk. She wrote something on the pad; Harry tried to read Josie's curly handwriting upside down with no luck. She tore the paper off and put it on the end table. She replaced the pad and pen in the drawer.

"Maggie's popular," said Harry.

Josie's eyes squinted at him; her mouth squinted as well. "Don't you go thinking like that."

No, that kind of thinking fits you better, he thought. Harry figured that Maggie had to earn more than Josie did, even if it wasn't much. He'd seen her doing the laundry, and he suspected that she did more of the housekeeping. He said, "It seems to me that she takes care of you."

Josie threw the book at him, the front cover peeling off and fluttering to the floor as it became airborne. He was so surprised he didn't have time to duck, and it hit him in the middle of the chest. It didn't hurt much, but his heart was pounding with shock.

"Hey!"

"You're not listening," she said. "It's a responsibility. Sacred, even."

It was Harry's turn to want to throw something. He said, more loudly than he liked, "You act like you care so much about her, but you talk like she's retarded, just like Shawntelle does. There's nothing wrong with her at all."

"I know there's nothing *wrong* with her. She's my baby, and she's so beautiful. I know you're going to break her heart, and I'll have to kill you, and then I'll go to jail, and there will be no one to take care of her anymore, because Baby has enough to deal with, and Miss

Tokay isn't up to taking care of anybody, and you're not going to do it because all you want to do is break her heart."

Harry told himself that Josie had had patience with him when he'd shown up drunk at her home in the middle of the night, so he was bound by karmic law to return the favor. He picked up the book, whose pages were orange with age. It was a copy of the *I Ching*, and it was heavy. "It's not like that."

Josie looked at him with so much anger that he feared another projectile, but nothing seemed to be close enough to her hand. He tightened his grip on the fat book.

"You are such an idiot, as well as an asshole," she said. "Asshole," she repeated, looking at the floor, and Harry had an idea that she wasn't drunk enough to suit herself, and she started crying.

The door opened and Maggie walked in, dressed the way she always was, in jeans and a T-shirt, although the T-shirt had brown and black smudges on it. He'd never seen her anything but clean. She took in the situation in a moment, and Harry was embarrassed at his relief. She sat down next to Josie and put an arm around her shoulder. Josie was sobbing, her hands over her face, making soft glugging sounds. Harry's pity was mixed with an embarrassment that made him feel as if his whole body was being rubbed raw. Maggie gave Josie a small shake, saying in her ear, "Come on, let's get you to bed. Come on now, come on." She worked Josie up and off the sofa, and alternately pushed and guided the older woman to the hallway. Harry stood and shifted from foot to foot, thinking, What do I do now? He sat down again and waited.

It was only about ten minutes, though it seemed longer to Harry, alternating between standing and looking out the living room window and sitting on the lumpy couch or on the rickety chair. Once he got up and got himself a glass of water, almost knocking a plate loose from the stack of dirty dishes on the counter. It was heading for the floor; Harry tried to catch it but succeeded only in knocking it into the sink. It didn't break, for which he was grateful, but the noise had been fearsome. He really didn't want to wake Josie up, if she had passed out. He had just placed the plate carefully back on the pile when Maggie emerged from the hallway. She'd changed her clothes; the jeans were slightly darker, and her T-shirt was a different color and free from stains. She sighed as she saw Harry, the dark patches of skin under her eyes darker than usual. "Sit down," she said. "I'll take care of this mess. You want something to eat?"

She washed the dishes in silence, her movements fast and beautiful. Harry thought her hands looked like they were painting something in the water, or making a sculpture of the clean dishes in the dish drainer. Like a dance, he thought. Like theater. She was done in a few minutes and then made them each an omelet. Harry thought he could watch her work all night.

"Do you read cards as well?" He was halfway through the omelet. He was deliberately taking his time. It was very good.

"Of course. Palms, too. Horoscopes. I learned at my mother's knee. And at Josie's."

"I remember now. Josie told me. Your mother was a fortune teller, too."

"It's the family business."

"Do you believe in any of it?"

She took another bite of her omelet, which was noticeably smaller than his. "That's not an easy question to answer."

"Not a yes or no?"

"If I have to do that, I'd say yes. But with the cards, you're not exactly predicting the future. It's more like you're looking at probabilities." She ate a last bite and looked up. "You want a reading?"

Harry thought about it. He wasn't sure he wanted to know anything about the future, then was amused at himself for even that small moment of belief. "Sure," he said. "What's the charge?"

She smiled a little, looking so weary that Harry regretted letting her cook for him, letting her clean up the kitchen and put her sodden relative to bed all by herself. He was about to tell her that he'd changed his mind, that she didn't have to do anything else for him tonight, but she said, "No charge." Her eyes sharpened on him, and she added, "Sorry, I was so preoccupied, I didn't notice at once. You shaved off your beard." Harry had to force himself not to pull back, uncomfortable that she was looking so closely at his face. She said, "You have a good chin," and the urge to pull away left him.

She got up, went to the desk in the corner of the living room, opened a drawer, and pulled out a carved wooden box. She opened the lid and lifted a small bundle wrapped in black cloth. She brought the bundle to the table and sat down. Harry sat opposite her. She unfolded the fabric, revealing a large deck of cards.

"I have my own spread," she said, folding the square of fabric and putting it aside. She picked up the deck with her right hand. "The way I lay out the cards."

"I know what a spread is," Harry said. "Until I was eleven years old, I lived in a series of communes with my hippie parents."

"Oh, my. What happened when you were eleven?"

"Social Services cracked down on weirdos that year, and Lawrence and I went into foster care. There was some concern in the 'community' that my parents and their friends were doing drugs and having too much sex. They were certainly having a good time, but I'm not sure we suffered much from it."

Maggie placed the oversize deck of cards on the table. "How long before they got you back?"

"They didn't."

"What?"

"They visited every few months. Once our foster parents realized that they weren't going to spirit us away, they even let us visit their camp a few times, until we came back once smelling of pot. We hadn't been given any, but it was all around. My foster mother threw away the clothes we were wearing." Harry pointed at the fat Tarot deck. "Our foster parents were fundamentalists. Lawrence and I went to church twice a week for six years. We went to Bible camps and tent meetings and miracle services. I send the Wileys a card every Christmas, but I haven't been back in their house since I went to college, nor did I set foot in a church again till I did research for my last book. Exorcising some demons, although Bernie and May Wiley would hate for me to put it that way." He pointed at the cards again. "They called those the 'Devil's Picture Book.' All divination is satanic to them." Maggie picked up the big deck. Harry continued, "They weren't badly intentioned, just terrified of everything they didn't already know."

He realized he had no idea how she was going to react to any of his story—offended, angry, sympathetic. All she said was "The universe is big. People are small." She broke the deck into two roughly equal halves. "Some people want their god to be as little as they are." She started shuffling. Her handling of the cards was flawless, and he told her she could have a career in Las Vegas. She said, "Uncle Dunc told me never to gamble. He said the house always wins."

"Uncle Dunk?"

"Duncan Dupree. Josie's late husband." She cut the deck again and said, "Where are your parents now? Your flesh-and-blood ones?"

"Dead." At her look, he went on. "They took too many quaaludes and camped out in the Rockies in December. They died of exposure." He smiled, feeling his dry lips catch on his teeth; not enough spit. "They died happy, in their sleep."

"Oh, Harry." Her face was so sweet he thought he might have to look anywhere else. "How old were you?"

"Fourteen."

"Dusty's age," she said, then shuffled the deck again.

Harry was never to remember the reading with any precision, although he tried to re-create it several times. It was dreamlike, as were the images on the cards. Their names meant nothing to him: the four of cups, the Hanged Man, the ten of wands. His childhood should have prepared him for some of this, he thought. He knew all the key words of astrology, which Maggie assured him was related to these cards, and a woman who'd lived in the commune with his parents had read palms. His life line, he remembered, was supposed to be long and jagged, and he remembered her telling him that he would die twice, although not literally.

Maggie told him he needed to ask a question, something that could be resolved in a few weeks and that didn't require a simple yes or no answer. Harry couldn't think of a specific question, so she suggested that he ask about the future in a general way. She shuffled the deck, the cards flowing between her fingers like a bright, colorful liquid, and he was thankful that she hadn't made him do it, as they were much larger than normal playing cards and he imagined them spurting awkwardly from his hands and spraying all over the living room. She laid the shuffled deck in front of him. "Think your question into the cards as you cut the deck. Keep the time frame manageable, a few weeks or months."

He actually tried to do it, to think about his anxieties about the near future, and the separate, caretaker part of his mind found this funny. She made him cut the deck, then picked it up and started taking cards from the top, laying them one by one in a line in front of her. There were a few with terrible imagery: a red demon holding a man and woman on leashes, beggars freezing to death outside a stained-glass window, a giant roulette wheel with hapless angels falling to their deaths. Although maybe these weren't the actual meanings; maybe there was a Rorschach quality to them, and the reading told him more about Maggie's psyche than his own. Likely, he thought. But still, he couldn't help the intensity of his attention.

"Lots of loss in the past," she said.

"Uh-huh."

"Deception, too. Violence. Bad luck."

Harry was silent.

"See this card?" She pointed to an image of a caped figure hunched with sorrow over three spilled goblets.

"He looks pretty depressed."

"Yes, and he's looking at the spilled cups, but notice he's ignoring the ones behind him that aren't spilled. That's you. You've suffered a lot, but you haven't paid enough attention to the good things that are still there. Love, other things of beauty in your life."

"Huh," Harry said. He pointed to someone hanging upside down from a cross. "That looks bad."

"Actually, it isn't. That's you now. You're learning something, waiting. Allowing things to unfold instead of forcing them."

"I got the Death card. That can't be good. And it's upside down. Yippee."

"It's hard to make it a happy card, but it's usually not literal. Reversed it tends to mean you're stuck repeating the same mistakes over and over. But these are your fears, not necessarily what's going to happen. You have a lot more control over your life than you think." She looked over the spread, her chin in her cupped palm. "You're resisting a number of changes and making certain decisions. But you've got lots of choices." She pointed at a number of the cards as though Harry could interpret these as choices. He tried to look intelligent but had already forgotten what she'd said most of them meant. "Some kind of trip. Possible success, but you've got to make some decisions first. There are some people around you who aren't truthful, and some are abusing their power. Something in your professional life is going to surprise you."

"Who's this?" Harry pointed to a card in the center of the spread labeled "The Magician." "Is that me?"

She stared at the card for a moment before saying, "I don't think so, given where it is. I can't tell if it's supposed to be an actual person, or something that's going to happen. It's powerful, and central to everything, but I'm not sure how. Maybe you'll have a big surge of creativity." She looked up at the clock and massaged the back of her neck. "I'm pretty rusty at this. If you want a real reading, you should get Josie to do it. I've forgotten most of what I used to know, and I'm too sleepy to concentrate properly." She gathered the cards together and wrapped them in the black cloth, then stood up. "I'm too tired to take a walk today. Maybe you should go." She closed her mouth and then opened it again. "Was that rude? I'm sorry."

"No," said Harry. "I shouldn't have made you cook for me." He got up, feeling suddenly awkward and unsettled. "Thanks. For the reading, too." He glanced at the hallway, beyond which lay her inebriated aunt. "Will you be all right?"

"I've done it before, Harry. We'll be fine, but thanks for asking."

She closed the door behind him, and he could hear the lock engage. The images from the cards stuck in his head like scenes from a disturbing film. He wondered what mistakes he was repeating. This, he thought, is the height of stupidity. She can't see the future in a deck of cards any more than you can. But he knew he was going to be looking at people in the Law School with a bit more suspicion than usual for the next few days.

17

FIVE OF PENTACLES

Misery loves company

On Friday, Harry went to Orlando in time to see Dusty's play. He checked into a motel and got to the high school just before curtain time. Ann saw him come into the auditorium and waved, patting the seat beside her, so he had no choice but to join her. Sitting so close to her felt strange and off-putting, like spending time with someone who you knew was a neo-Nazi or a Klansman but who was socially presentable and polite. You wanted to point and yell and denounce them, but it was difficult if they didn't give you an opportunity by doing anything heinous. In fact, Ann was unusually pleasant to him. The play itself was nothing out of the ordinary, and Dusty wasn't even onstage, so Harry stored up in his mind complimentary things to say about the scenery. During the intermission, Ann said, "You're looking good, Harry."

"Oh? Thanks." He couldn't remember ever getting positive comments from her about his appearance before. It only made his discomfort worse, especially when he thought he might be expected to return the favor. She looked good, too, of course, and it occurred to him that maybe that was the whole point of her comment, to get him to say as much. He felt childish withholding it, but she never looked bad anyway, so she could probably stand one evening of not being told how gorgeous she was.

"How's the book coming?"

Harry surprised himself by being honest with her. "Not well. I don't have anything. I'm aimless."

"But I thought you said you were doing research."

"It's not really going anywhere. I could attempt to destroy the name of a much-respected deceased scientist. I suspect there's a sordid little story in his home life, but what's the point? I'm not sure how that would illuminate the human condition."

Ann stared at him, a puzzled expression on her face. All she said was "You've lost weight."

On Monday night Harry called Maggie, but a drunken Josie told him that she was out; Josie didn't know when she'd be back. Harry had no confidence in Josie relaying a message, so the next afternoon he drove to the cemetery parking lot ten minutes before she usually arrived after work, hoping that Maggie wasn't going to change her routine that day. When her car pulled into the lot a few minutes later, his relief embarrassed him.

He described the high school version of *Guys and Dolls* and Dusty's artwork. She nodded as though it was interesting to her, which Harry found doubtful. She said, "You don't have to work on Fridays?"

He explained about his schedule. "I work a full week. More, usually. It just isn't within set hours, except for when I'm teaching."

"A lot of that time you're working on your book."

"Yes."

"I still don't understand what it's about."

"Well, that's because I haven't figured that out yet. When I heard the rumor about Charlie Ziegart stealing work from someone else, I thought there might be something there. But now I doubt it."

"Charlie Ziegart?"

"He was a scientist who invented something called the Ziegart effect, which has something to do with electricity. That's who supposedly stole the work of Josie's friend or whatever that I asked you about. You haven't remembered anything more, have you?"

"Nothing new has occurred to me. I haven't asked her either. Sorry."

"Just as well. I think the guy just had a turbulent love life. Not very newsworthy."

"I read your book about cults."

"Really? What did you think of it?"

"I thought it was good," she said. Harry felt happy, though he wasn't sure he believed that she'd actually read it. She added, "I liked that you didn't paint all southerners as racist fundamentalists."

Maybe she *did* read it, he thought. "A lot of them are," he said.

"So are a lot of northerners."

"True," said Harry. "I was raised by a pair of Pennsylvania evangelicals, after all. Ignorant as dirt. Racist as all hell, although they don't think of themselves as such."

They were in a garden that he'd been in only once before, with the giant teardrop boxwood in the center. The air smelled of camellias, a scent he was proud he now recognized. "They live in Downesport, Pennsylvania. Lawrence and I made a joke of it. Anytime anyone was having a good time or making too much noise, someone would say, 'Down, Sport.' " For no obvious reason, his mother's face appeared again in his mind's eye. It was time to change the subject.

"What about your parents? You said your mother was a soothsayer, like Josie."

She smiled. "I like that. Yes, she was a soothsayer."

"She died?"

"Yes."

"How?"

"A hit-and-run. She was taking a walk."

"Jesus. Did they ever catch who did it?"

She turned away from him as she moved a branch that had broken and was now dangling in their way, hanging only by a thin bit of soggy bark. He was behind her, and she held it aside for him as she answered, "No. They never did."

"What about your dad?" He could hear the woodpecker again and followed the rapid *dat-dat-dat* sound until he saw the bird on a tall pine, six or seven trees away from the path.

Her gaze moved to the woodpecker as well. "He worked for the telephone company. He fixed downed phone lines. They met after a hurricane." Harry waited for more as they navigated the large, tangled roots of a wizened southern pine that crossed the path like a stile. Harry thought it wasn't long for this world; just looking at the tortured branches made him ache with imagined arthritis. He said, "His name was Roth?"

Maggie nodded and said, "He was Jewish. Mom thought that meant that he'd have a lot of money. When it turned out he didn't, she ditched him. Although he had another family anyway, so I guess the ditching was mutual."

"Yikes. I guess you didn't get to know him very well."

"There were a few years where I saw him quite a lot, before he went back to his 'real' family. Then he and Mom got together again for a while when I was about twelve. He'd gotten a better-paying job. It was always nice when he was around, although I suppose he must have been pretty rotten to be married to, since he obviously couldn't be faithful to anyone for long. Including my mother."

"Well, at least you had a father around when you were a teenager," Harry said, thinking about Dusty.

She said, "How is he?" Harry started, realizing she'd been reading his thoughts.

"Okay, I guess. Sullen. He won't talk to me much. I know on some level that he needs me, but it's hard to get him to admit it, and if he doesn't, I'm not sure what I can do," Harry said as they moved on to where the path continued to the wooden bridge.

The shade hit her face before she said, "My dad thought I was crazy," then she stopped, and Harry saw with surprise that she was embarrassed.

Harry said, "He was obviously wrong."

They reached the bridge, and she stopped and looked at him for a moment, then said, "You're not sure. I know what you were thinking when I asked you if you saw dots." Harry protested, horrified again that she could read him so well. "It's okay," she said. "But he had me tested for everything you can imagine: ADD, learning disabilities, Asperger's syndrome, schizophrenia, other stuff."

"My God. For one thing, that's expensive."

"He'd had a good year."

"Why all the tests?"

She shrugged. "He was worried."

He couldn't help asking, "So, what was the outcome?"

It was a few seconds before she answered. "They said I was 'highly sensitive.' Also shy. My dad told me that at least they'd ruled out the possibility that I was a sociopath; I guess that was a concern since I was so lousy at dealing with other people."

Harry knew he looked appalled.

"The point is," she said, "sometimes it's not the best thing to show your kid how worried you are."

Harry nodded. "It sounds like he loved you, in his way."

"I loved him," she said. "I don't know if he loved me or not." She moved again, leaving the bridge to go along the trail where the trees were deeper. Harry followed, saying to her back, "Do you know anything about your father's other family?"

They rounded a few clumps of pine saplings before she said, "I looked them up online at the library. They all still live in Atlanta."

"You ever think about contacting them? They're your siblings, after all."

She stopped suddenly, startling him, and kneeled down and pointed to a small, pretty plant on the side of the path with furry leaves and tiny white flowers. "Be careful of these. Stinging nettles. If your skin touches one, it feels like you've gotten an electric shock." Harry regarded the harmless looking little weed, impressed, storing the information to give to Dusty later.

"I'm not even sure they know about me. It would probably be a nasty surprise if I came knocking on their door." She stood up and, still not looking at him, said, "One son's an airplane mechanic. The other's a cardiologist. They'd think I just wanted money." She turned to him and gave him one of her breathtaking smiles. "I'm the disappointment of the family." He didn't smile back. She began walking again, and he followed; as soon as he came abreast of her, she said, "One time my dad took me to the beach without my mom. I still have some of the shells we collected. He had a board with a rope attached to it, and he'd pull me through the waves. It was the most fun I'd ever had. I love the ocean."

"I have a beach house," Harry said before he could stop himself. "Well, Ann and I own it together. Just south of Jacksonville, Delacroix Beach. Only about an hour and a half from here. We rent it out most weekends, but sometimes I go, usually with Dusty. It's a nice place to write, but we need the rent money to pay off the mortgage and taxes. We bought it before the divorce." He stopped, took a minute to think before he spoke, then said carefully, "Maybe you could borrow it sometime."

She was staring at him, the meaning of her expression a complete mystery to him. "That's nice of you. Maybe sometime," she said, and Harry realized she never expected the offer to materialize, and she was letting him off the hook.

18

TEN OF
CUPS

He hated when his mother invited Gillian over. He no longer lived at home, but he spent at least one night a week there to get a good dinner and updates on the gossip that circulated around the campus like blood through a body. Gillian didn't like him, although he wasn't sure why. He didn't like her either, but he hid it well, his manners oiling her up whenever he saw her. Still, she seemed wary around him. He wondered if it was because he looked so much like his father; he sus-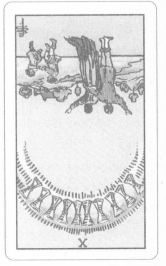pected that Gillian had had a crush on Charlie at one time. Not a serious one, nothing like an affair. More like the feelings a tenth grader might have toward her math teacher, safely in the realm of fantasy. It was exhausting, though, having to act so pleased to see her.

She had joined them for dinner. "Wesley has so many meetings, and I hate to eat alone. I haven't seen you in a few months, Jon. You're looking very handsome. Have you made any decision about graduate school? You know you wouldn't have any problems getting into any program here. I know Pamela wants to keep you close by."

She smiled at him, but he could see the dislike behind it, and thought, Back at you, you lying old bitch. He said, "I haven't decided yet. There's plenty of time."

She turned back to Pamela. "I have some news. I don't know how you're going to feel about it, but you have a right to know. A reporter from *The Washington Post* is asking questions about Charlie. I should say, a former reporter. He teaches at some redneck college in Florida now and writes books."

Pamela put down her wineglass and wiped her mouth with a linen napkin. "It doesn't bother me. I'm glad that there's interest in Charlie again. What's the reporter's name? Would I have heard of him?"

"Harry Sterling. He's written two books. I haven't read either of them, but they were published by Teller's, in New York. I thought you might be upset because he asked a lot of questions about Emily. I didn't like his tone. He might be out to make a name for himself, and you know how that is. It's always easier to make headlines by saying something nasty than by saying the truth."

Gillian had the attention of both people at the table now. "Why would he be interested in Emily?" Pamela asked, her brow wrinkled, her hand tightening on the stem of the wineglass.

"A fortune teller told him that she knew someone who really invented the Ziegart effect. Even he admitted it was a bizarre story, and didn't seem to give it a lot of credit. But he said that's what got him interested in Charlie."

"Do you believe him?" Jonathan said.

She turned to him in surprise. "Shouldn't I have? He's got a professional reputation, after all. You'd think he'd check his facts and wouldn't just print a bunch of garbage."

Pamela said, "Oh God. People publish garbage all the time."

Jonathan said, "Which redneck college?"

. . .

Harry walked with Maggie at least three times a week. Each meeting lasted only an hour or so, and he was surprised at the extent of Gunhill Park, how many paths there were through the pines and the oak trees, how many little gardens were tucked away amid the woods. They seldom met anyone else, since their visits to the park were usually on weekday afternoons, and only the occasional retiree or dedicated jogger took to the paths during the heat of the day. Maggie didn't work on Sundays or Mondays, and by tacit agreement he no longer tried to find her on those days, only met her at the parking lot shortly after one o'clock, when her shift was over. Sometimes he had lunch at Crane's and followed her car afterward, but he found himself less interested in the food there now that the smirking waitresses knew him.

Her car wasn't in the lot yet when he arrived that Friday. It was a hot and heavy afternoon, the sky thick with gray clouds that only let the sun peek its boiling face through every few minutes. He was getting used to the dense air of Florida, finding it only marginally worse than the sticky climate of Washington. Here the stickiness just lasted longer, although he remembered when he'd first moved to Stoweville last August, he had thought he might go mad with the constant weight of the outside air, with the blistering heat, with the fog of angry mosquitoes every evening. He had fought potential madness by staying inside too much, or by driving everywhere instead of walking, safe and cool inside his car, the windows tightly shut against the vicious nature of the place. He had driven down country road after country road, obsessively drawing a vast mental map of his surroundings. He'd been past the cemetery and Gunhill Park several times and had never felt the slightest pull to leave the comfort of his car and explore any of it on foot. Now he felt as though he'd been allowed through some previously hidden door that opened into a secret place of shade and birds and flowers. Not to mention a blond woman who was possibly insane but who was

connected to him now in a way he couldn't figure out, even in his
dreams.

He got out of his car and leaned against the closed door, determined not to take so much shelter against the air. It smelled of flowers he couldn't identify, of dying blossoms, wilting in the heat. He
could feel sweat starting to prickle in his armpits and down his back,
but for the first time since he'd arrived in the Deep South, he didn't
mind.

He had to wait for only a few minutes before the Celica purred
its way into the parking lot, and he had a moment to think what a
quiet old car it was, no smoke billowing from the tailpipe, no sput-
tering or clanking in the motor. Another preconception shot, he
thought. She got out and gave him a cautious smile. Her eyes were
so blue, they almost didn't look real. He wondered if they qualified
as "cornflower blue," a phrase he'd read many times, but to his
knowledge he'd never seen a cornflower. He thought, I'll have to ask
Amelia. Then the thought occurred to him that he could probably
ask Maggie, but he was afraid it would sound like he was trying to
flirt with her.

"Where do you go? When you're not at home, and you're not at
Crane's, and everyone says you're working? They're very cagey, Josie
and Miss Baby. They're never going to tell me."

She didn't look at him. Instead, she stopped on the path under a
clematis-choked trellis that arched over them, acting as a doorway
into one of the gardens, the one with the galloping horse fountain.
She kneeled on the path where the dirt and pine needles gave way
to the brick of the path around the fountain and pointed to a clus-
ter of ivy. "Do you see it?" she asked.

"What? No." He bent down, squinting, trying to see what was so
interesting about the clump of green leaves. She reached a slow,

careful hand into the ivy and took something between her thumb and forefinger, then pulled it out, bringing it toward him. It looked like a twig at first until he saw that it had legs no more substantial than thread, waving around in buggy alarm.

"What the hell is that?" said Harry.

"It's called a walking stick."

To Harry, her ability to distinguish the insect from the foliage was nothing short of miraculous, and he said so. She gently put the walking stick back in the vines. "If you know they're there, it's not so hard." She stood up, then moved toward the fountain. Harry followed her.

"I don't know why I can talk to you," she said, pausing for a moment to look at the fountain, water droplets landing on her face and on Harry's arms, cool and fragrant. "Mostly I know that what's going to come out of my mouth will be all wrong, so I just don't bother."

"That's me," Harry said. "Everyone's kindly uncle Harry." Her smile was so beautiful that he bent over to pick up a twig and quickly dropped it as though it had bitten him, pretending it was alive, just to make her smile again.

"Thanks for your advice before about Dusty. Living apart is hard. I don't feel necessary to him."

"It's not his job to make you feel necessary. Or real."

"You're right," he said, looking up through the canopy to where the sun was poking through in slender gold shafts, almost hot enough to melt the ground below. "Wait till you get to the teenage years. I hear girls are worse. Where's Charlotte's father?"

She looked up as well, stopping again when the sound of a woodpecker battered the air. "I don't know. I never knew him."

"How could you not know him?" The images this conjured up in his mind were so lurid he grimaced.

Her face was puzzled under the straw hat. "Charlotte is Miss Baby's granddaughter." Her face cleared in understanding. "You must have heard her call me her mamma."

"Sorry, I assumed she was yours." You shouldn't feel so relieved, he thought. You should just feel stupid.

"It's a joke we share because we're so much alike. Her own mother's long gone."

"Dead?"

"I don't know."

"Oh. You seem close to her and Tamara. You want kids of your own?"

She shrugged, walking faster. She opened her mouth, closed it, then said, "Josie's kind of like my kid anyway. She's lost everybody else, so she kind of hangs on to me hard. She was only fifty-two when Uncle Dunc died."

"Was he a fortune teller too?"

She smiled. "No. He was a plumber. That trailer may not look like much to you, but he worked nights, weekends, and holidays to save up enough to buy the land and then a double-wide. One of the things I'm most proud of is that I helped him add that porch on." She stopped and picked up a pinecone the size of a football. "You know," she said, peering into the big cone as though there was a story inside of it, "you can eat parts of these."

"No thanks," said Harry. "I'm picky about any brown foods. I only eat the finest grained hardwoods."

Maggie smiled and tossed the pinecone to the side of the path.

Harry said, "Josie lost her daughter, too?"

She nodded, the hat brim bobbing. "Dunc had pancreatic cancer. Got him fast. No chance for any medical 'intervention.' " She said the word as though it were a bad joke. "Dee was gone less than a year later."

"What happened?"

"Her last boyfriend drove in the demolition derby, so she followed him around the country. One night, she had a bad pain." She stopped again, lifted a leaf to look at a caterpillar that was vigorously destroying another, little black mandibles moving back and forth with great speed, reminding Harry of a paper shredder. "He had somewhere to go, so he dropped her at a Baton Rouge emergency room." Maggie put the leaf back down and continued walking. "It was an ovarian cyst that had ruptured. If they'd gotten to her sooner, she'd still be alive."

Harry said, "Dee was short for what?"

"Delores."

"Margaret and Delores. So you were close, growing up."

Maggie gave another small smile. "Magdalene. Not Margaret." She fanned away a mosquito. "Dee was named after sadness. Me, after a sainted whore."

They were approaching their cars, the heat making the asphalt of the parking lot shimmer. Harry said, "You never answered my question. About where you go when you're not working."

"Sometimes I'm at the Laundromat."

"Uh-huh. You don't want to tell me."

She dug her hand in her jeans pocket for her car keys.

"What's his name?" said Harry.

She looked up, startled, then smiled wide and, for the first time since Harry had known her, started to laugh. The sound was wild and indescribably beautiful. Her face was lit with the closest thing to joy he'd seen in her, and he couldn't do anything but stare at her as she said through her laughter, "You think I'm somebody's mistress, maybe a geisha?" She laughed some more, leaning over a little, supporting herself with her hands on her bent knees. When she looked up, she said, "If I were, I'd have my own washer and dryer." Her laughter stopped and her smile faded, and she reached her hand up and patted his cheek. "Poor Harry. I'm sorry if I embarrassed you." She looked at her keys in her other hand and separated the car key from the others on the ring. "I'm not that interesting." Harry was surprised to see that she was blushing. "I'll see you later," she said as she got into the Celica. As she drove away, Harry got into his own ferociously hot car, thinking, I still don't know where she goes.

19

TEMPERANCE

REVERSED

A bad combination.
Competition

"He's lost his second iPod," Ann said. It was Saturday morning. Harry had been awake for hours, preparing his final exam for one class and grading papers for the other. It was the last week of the term.

"Don't buy him another one," Harry said.

"Oh, never mind," she said, sounding angry. Harry didn't have any idea what response she'd wanted from him.

That afternoon he was back online, reading about Charles Ziegart's receiving the Presnell Award for Achievements in Applied Physics. Harry wondered how much of the work had actually been done by Ziegart. His eyes were starting to water from reading on the screen when his doorbell rang. He looked at the clock; it was three p.m.

He peered through the window on his front door. Lawrence had died at 9:47 in the evening; Harry knew the exact time from the police report. A neighbor had been working on her computer and had glanced at the clock at the bottom of her screen when she heard the shots. Harry wasn't really worried that anyone was going to shoot him in his doorway, but he no longer opened his door to anyone in haste, even though, in this neighborhood, home invasions were unlikely. He spared a thought for Maggie and Josie and hoped that his visitor didn't throw up on his porch.

It turned out to be a young man, mid-twenties, in jeans, blue cotton shirt, and a tweed sports coat. He was good-looking, high cheekbones and dark curls extending a little too far down over the back of his collar. "Can I help you?" Harry said through the screen door, still securely latched.

"Am I addressing Harry Sterling?" said the young man. His voice was that of a singer, strong and confident with full tenor undertones. His hands were in his pockets, which made Harry uncomfortable.

"Who are you?" Harry said.

"I'm Jonathan Ziegart. Charles Ziegart's son."

It was an embarrassment that he asked Ziegart Junior to flash his driver's license before he was allowed in the house, but he did it anyway.

Harry Sterling was not what Jonathan Ziegart had expected. He'd thought he would be short and round, someone who wrote his books on an old manual typewriter with a glass of scotch on one side, no coaster, and an overflowing ashtray on the other. He'd imagined someone unshaven and bent, a squinty eye with thick glasses and a harsh voice. Instead, he saw a tall man, light brown hair short and badly cut, clean-shaven, no glasses, wearing worn khakis and a short-sleeved NFU football jersey. He looked like he'd been strongly built at one time but had gone slightly soft, almost blurry. He didn't look at all dangerous.

He complimented Sterling's house, which got a shrug and a nod. The latter said, "This is quite a surprise. You're on my list of people to contact, actually, so this saves me a phone call. What brings you here? It's a long way to come to be interviewed."

"Believe it or not, I was in the area." Harry motioned him into the living room and to a sofa across from the front window as Jonathan went on. "I was on my way to Gainesville. There's a conference at the University of Florida and I'm giving a paper. I hate to fly, so I drove down. Gillian DeGraff told me you were writing a book on my father. Stoweville is more or less on the way, so I thought I'd stop and see if you wanted to talk to me. Sorry I didn't call first. My cell phone battery died during the last leg. I found a motel room outside of town and figured I'd just drop in and try my luck. I found your address online."

Harry asked if he'd like something to drink. Jonathan said, "Got any beer?"

"Sorry. I've got some ginger ale and iced tea. Water. You're welcome to any of it, but that's all there is."

Jonathan looked at him for a moment. "In recovery?" he said.

"No." Harry looked as though the question irritated him.

Aha, Jonathan thought. "Iced tea would be great."

Harry got them both drinks from the kitchen, handing one to his guest. He put his own down on the coffee table. Jonathan noticed with some disapproval that he didn't use coasters; pale rings on the wood attested to the fact that it probably never occurred to him to protect his furniture. Not that it was particularly nice furniture, but it still said something about the man.

Harry sat in a chair across the room in front of the window. Too late, Jonathan realized that Harry was largely in silhouette but could see his face clearly. Harry said, "I wasn't sure a trip to Pennsylvania was going to be necessary anyway, but I appreciate your taking the time to see me."

"I knew you'd talk to me sooner or later, so as I said, I thought I'd save you the trouble of coming to Lucasta."

Jonathan had the impression that Harry didn't believe him, which was galling since he was speaking the truth.

Harry said, "Was there anything in particular that you think I should know?"

"Whatever." Jonathan opened his hands wide. "I'm an open book."

"Why don't you tell me about yourself? I know very little, other than that you're Charles Ziegart's son."

"I'm also a scientist."

"Oh? Are you continuing your father's work?"

"I shouldn't say it myself, of course, but I have to admit that I've been called a chip off the old block more than once."

"Well, good for you, Encyclopedia Brown." Harry paused, and Jonathan got the impression that the reporter was reining himself in. "Tell me about your father. Was he a good dad? Play catch with you, tuck you in at night, that sort of thing?"

Jonathan felt himself getting angry; he tamped the feeling down and bolstered the smile on his face. "It might surprise you to know that he took quite a bit of time out of his incredibly busy schedule to be with me. He took me to the lab all the time. I was kind of a pet of everyone in the department."

"You were close."

"Unusually so, I think."

"Were you close to your stepmother as well?"

Jonathan leaned back in the chair and waved the words away as though they were gnats. "Emily wasn't my stepmother."

"She was married to your father."

"Briefly. But even my father realized it was a mistake before long. I'm sure you've heard this from others. She was a bit rapacious, and went after him the moment she got to Cantwell. I try not to speak ill of her, but she caused my mother a great deal of pain."

"It sounds like your father helped."

Jonathan could feel the anger flicker up again, biting him like a small but fierce bug. His opinion of Harry Sterling was deteriorating. "He was busy, and didn't always pay attention to what was going on with the people around him. Emily was very good at manipulating him, and eventually she manipulated him into marriage. She had his interests in common. My mother is an academic, but she's not a scientist. Well, she thinks she is. She's a sociologist." He couldn't stop himself from laughing.

"Did you know Doug McNeill?"

Jonathan thought, Where did that come from? "Why do you want to know about him?"

"He was on the Ziegart effect paper initially. Then he was taken off. Why?"

"Poor Doug. He was horribly fat. That sounds terrible, but it was such an overwhelming fact about him, so it's the main thing I remember. He didn't have very good social skills either, unfortunately." An image came to Jonathan's mind, so powerful that it threatened to overwhelm his attention. One of the worst days of his life, and one of the best. He pushed the memory out again and closed his hands around his glass to keep them from shaking.

Harry was saying, "He was taken off the paper because he wasn't attractive?"

Jonathan's heart was still hammering; he collected himself. "No, of course not. I think it was a mistake that he was on there in the first place. His name was removed as a correction."

"It didn't have anything to do with his death?"

"Of course not," Jonathan repeated. "He choked to death on a piece of cheese."

This seemed to surprise Harry, but he recovered quickly. He said, "What about Emily's name? Same issue; she was on in the first place, then she wasn't."

"Like you said, same issue. Or sort of the same. She wanted

credit for my father's work. But she didn't deserve any. At most, she did some grunt work for him, like a lot of his students. It was fair that her name didn't wind up on the final version."

"Which was published posthumously?"

"Yes, unfortunately."

Harry shifted in his chair, leaning his head forward a little. Like a prosecutor, Jonathan thought, and knew his agitation was starting to show in his face. He deliberately relaxed it, letting his cheeks go soft, his forehead smooth out. This man's an asshole, he told himself. He knows nothing but thinks he knows so much. Well, that's why you're here, to give him the real skinny. He was about to add that Doug was an opportunist, and that his father was impossibly kind-hearted, easily victimized by those less attuned to academic courtesy, but before he could speak Harry said, "How do you know this? You weren't very old at the time, surely?"

"I was seventeen. I was exposed to my father's work every day, Harry. I grew up knowing practically everyone at Cantwell. I certainly knew who'd helped him, and how." He thought for a moment, then thought, No point in holding anything back. He leaned forward. "I'm not sorry that Emily killed herself. You see, Harry," he said, "she murdered my father."

Harry put down his glass, but he showed no other reaction. All he said was "That's the first I've heard of this."

Jonathan didn't believe him. "It was kept quiet. There wasn't any proof that could be used in court. But she might as well have shot him with a gun."

"I thought your father died in a car accident."

"He didn't die from the crash itself. I'll tell you the whole story in exchange for a refill." When Harry returned from the kitchen with a full glass, Jonathan was relieved that his hands were under control and settled back in his seat. "They were at one of the faculty teas that the DeGraffs have at the beginning of every term. Gillian's husband, Wesley DeGraff, is Cantwell's chancellor, and they have the teas outdoors at their house. My father and Emily left early because Dad had an interview to do that evening. She claimed later that yellow jackets somehow found their way into the car. My father was allergic to bee and wasp venom. He'd almost died from a sting a few years before, so he always carried a disposable syringe of epinephrine. But Emily said she couldn't find his EpiPen anywhere. He was driving, and she said he panicked and got stung, and then they ran off the road. They were both banged up pretty badly, but she managed to call 911 on the cell phone. He wasn't breathing by the time the paramedics got there." Again, Jonathan's breath shortened and his heart raced; he told himself to calm down. His eyes had adjusted somewhat, so he could make out Harry's face. The latter seemed almost bored by the story, which Jonathan found puzzling.

"Did they ever find the missing EpiPen?"

"They didn't find it in the car. Turns out it was in some bushes on the grounds of the DeGraff house."

"Were Emily's fingerprints on it?"

Jonathan laughed again, and then Harry's shadowed face flickered with a quick something, an expression gone so fast that Jonathan didn't have time to decipher it. He said, "No one checked, Harry. The police never treated it as suspicious. They ruled it an accident, and that was that."

Harry paused, then said, doubt flowing from him, "You think Emily tossed his EpiPen in the bushes and somehow planted yellow jackets in their car?"

"Not as hard as it sounds, Harry. Turns out he had a handkerchief with a slice of honeydew melon wrapped in it, and they found another dead wasp in that same pocket."

"But no one else thought that was suspicious?"

Jonathan smiled. "Sure, a lot of us did. But Dad liked his fruit. He did that sometimes, wrapped a piece in a hankie for later. It was one of his more eccentric habits. Lots of people knew about it. And the EpiPen could have fallen from his pocket at the party. So that's what the police concluded."

Harry smiled back, but he didn't look friendly. Jonathan didn't know what he'd done to produce such contentiousness in the reporter. "But that was a pretty big risk, surely. She could have been killed in the crash herself."

Jonathan shrugged. "I always assumed that she expected to have more control over the situation. They were run off the road by an impatient truck driver. I'm sure she didn't plan that. I figured she was going to get him to pull over first, then pull the handkerchief out."

"Why?"

"What?"

"Why would she want him dead?"

Jonathan was surprised by the question. "To get his money, of course. To keep everything for herself."

"But from what I understand, she didn't profit from his death at all."

Jonathan nodded, relieved that he understood what the problem was. "That's only because my mother made sure of it. She told Emily that if she didn't give up her claim to everything of my father's, we'd get the police to look at her more closely, for both my father's murder and other things. I was there for the conversation. My mother was very persuasive."

"What other things?"

"I shouldn't say. I can't prove anything." Harry raised his brows at Jonathan, but he went on. "We were partly bluffing." He smiled again. "We had suspicions of certain improprieties, with grant money and so on. But no proof. But Emily took my mother's warnings to heart." He leaned back in his seat and shrugged. "My mother has a lot of clout in Lucasta. And Emily knew that Mother's word would carry a lot more weight than hers."

"Even," Harry said, "without any actual evidence of wrongdoing."

"Oh, yes," Jonathan said. "I'm sorry that none of this can be corroborated, which I know you need as a reporter, but I thought you might want to know why everyone is so hostile to Emily's memory." I can't understand why you're not more hostile to it, thought Jonathan. You should be. He added, "My mother doesn't need any more pain, Harry."

Harry nodded. "I can understand that."

Harry got Charles Ziegart's son out of his house before dinnertime; he had no interest in prolonging the interview. The younger man's affect had been the most interesting aspect of the story so far. Against his will, his interest was piqued again, although, he suspected, not for the reasons that Jonathan Ziegart probably intended.

20

JUSTICE

REVERSED

Injustice,
inequality

Harry taught his last First Amendment class of the term on Tuesday, giving back papers with grudging praise. "You folks may make it as attorneys yet," he said, shocked by how happy the cliché made most of his students. He gave a final exam in his Media and Law class on Thursday, and realized that all he had left to do was mark them and enter his course grades online. He commented on this to Serge, whom he met in the hall-way outside their offices waltzing with the head administrative assistant of the Law School. Serge said, "My favorite time of year," and waltzed some more. Harry returned to his office, plopping the pile of exams on his desk.

He had just sat down when Julie Canfield came through the door. Fortunately, she wasn't in either of his classes this term, but since they'd had lunch together and she'd met his son, she'd been hovering around him more than ever. Harry didn't know how to discourage her without being mean; when they met in the hall he tried to adopt a stoic, emotionless façade, but he usually wound up making ridiculous jokes. She always laughed way too hard at them, which Harry found more annoying than if she'd kicked him. She'd made a point of telling him that she was going to be in Stoweville all summer. Thank God I wasn't waltzing when she came this way, he thought. She might have cut in, and then he chided himself for being an egomaniac, even as she said, "Professor Sterling, remember that I'm available to help with any research you need done for your book." Her ability to call him Harry had evaporated after that Saturday afternoon, and he'd decided that the formality wasn't a bad idea. She smiled, her teeth smooth and so white they were like ice. "I'm a good typist, too, although I know I'm not supposed to be willing to admit that."

"I'll let you know," Harry said, shuffling papers busily until she left.

An hour later, he'd read six essays, finding each one more boring than the last. He decided to take a break, getting himself a cup of coffee after making sure no one else was in the lounge. When he got back to his desk, he thought about Doug McNeill, obese and unliked and unrespected. He hadn't done much research on "Poor Doug," so instead of reading more beastly essays, he turned to his computer and typed "Douglas McNeill" in the search bar. It wasn't long before he was staring at the screen in surprise.

On Friday morning Harry went to the campus to enter his grades on his office computer. Frank Milford had e-mailed him the name and number of a secondhand contact at Cantwell named Ed Sanderson. He punched the appropriate numbers while looking out his window at the mixture of bricks and cinder blocks that made up the wall of the window well. The phone rang twice, then was answered by a voice that sounded like that of a man with pebbles in his throat, low and bumpy. "Sanderson," he said. He didn't sound anywhere near as round and friendly as Frank Milford.

Harry introduced himself and his subject, emphasizing his past tie to *The Washington Post*. Sanderson seemed unaware of Harry's conversation with DeGraff and sounded generally unimpressed.

"There's information on Charlie all over the place. What do you want from me?"

"You knew him personally?"

"I've been here for almost thirty years. I was on the committee that hired him. I was junior faculty then; I'd only been here about five years at that point."

"He would have been how old?"

"Mid-twenties. Right out of grad school at MIT."

"He'd already made a name for himself by then?"

"He was a rising star. His dissertation involved equations to define surface features of light-deflecting materials."

"You mean stuff that's invisible?"

"Exactly."

"I've read about this," Harry said. "Right out of Harry Potter."

"I wouldn't know." Harry could picture the man's nose rising. Sanderson went on, "Other people, at Duke and elsewhere, have reached the experimental stage. Charlie never got that far."

"So, what did Ziegart do once he was at Cantwell?"

There was a brief laugh from the phone, dry, like a little cough. "He liked playing with guns."

"He worked on military projects?"

"He wanted to. I thought at the time that it was because the money was so good. But now, I don't know. That was part of it. But I think he just liked the idea of laser beams in outer space. In real life, he mostly worked on increasing the efficiency of energy transmission. He had great success with superconductivity, although the problems involved with making it practicable were always there."

"Did he make much money off this research?"

"The more patents he filed, the greater his percentage of the return on them. The military was interested in the Ziegart effect research, so I imagine the money involved by then was serious. But those figures are not at my fingertips, and I'm not sure I should divulge them anyway."

"What can you tell me about Emily Ziegart?"

There was a short silence before Sanderson answered. "What exactly do you want to know?"

"She was Ziegart's student before she was his wife?"

"Yes."

"What was her specialty? The same as his?"

"Well, of course there was some overlap, or she wouldn't have been his student in the first place."

"Did you know her very well?"

"No. Charlie and I weren't close, not on a social basis, you understand. I'm a workhorse. Charlie was more of a player, schmoozing the local money people, society folks and so on. He was handsome and from that world to begin with. He knew his way around the hunt club, if you know what I mean, and he looked good in a tux."

"What about Doug McNeill?"

"Oh God. Poor Doug." Here we go again, Harry thought. "I was afraid you were going to ask about him. He was kind of a mess. Bad health problems."

"But as a student?"

Another silence. "He was okay. He followed Charlie around as though he were God. But a lot of people did that." Sanderson gave a sigh. "Look, poor Doug was close to three hundred pounds. Not terribly presentable. He had skin problems. He was always sweaty.

He had a squeaky voice, he wheezed, he smelled funny. In a profession of nerds, geeks, and misfits, he was at the bottom of the social barrel. I hate saying all this since the poor fellow's dead. I wish I'd liked him more. I felt that way when he was alive. Most people felt sorry for him and found him annoying at the same time. A bad combination. He had an eating disorder, and to see him put away any food was not a pretty thing."

"Were he and Emily friends?"

"Not that I know of. They were both Charlie's students, of course, and so were in a pretty small social universe. Neither of them was exactly popular, so it's possible they had bonded in some way."

"Why wasn't Emily more popular?"

"Charlie started seeing her almost as soon as she got here." Harry was interested that Sanderson put the active verb on Ziegart. "They were married by the end of her first year. As his wife, she was kind of above the other students. Or outside them, I should say. I doubt anyone here could claim to have known her very well."

"Did Charles Ziegart steal her work, or Doug McNeill's?"

"Of course not." There was an indignant pause. "Graduate students' work belongs to their professor by definition. Charlie didn't steal anything."

"What I don't understand," Harry said, checking his notes, "is why Charles Ziegart took Doug's and Emily's names off the paper before it was published. They were both on the original draft. Why would he do that?"

"I don't know for sure. There are lots of possible reasons. I never understood why Doug was on in the first place, to be honest. He worked on optics, and as far as I know, wasn't involved in the work on the Ziegart effect at all."

"But Emily was?"

"Well, yes. She was the project leader. Under Charlie, of course.

Her suicide was such a waste. There are so few women in the sciences. As far as I know, she never finished her Ph.D."

"Why not?"

"I have no idea. I assume it had to do with the trauma of Charlie's death. There were even rumors that she was responsible for it."

"Do you believe them?"

"No, they were ridiculous." Harry thought, Then why bring them up? Sanderson went on. "She was in the car with him, and she was pretty badly hurt herself. But the article came out not long after, with Charlie getting sole credit for the Ziegart effect, so after the fact it looked like she might have had a reason to be pissed at him. After his funeral, she just left. That didn't help stop the rumors."

Harry let that sit for a minute, then said, "So was she a scientific gold digger? Stealing Ziegart away from his happy family to bask in his reflected glory?"

"I wouldn't say that. Just, you know, an ambitious student. Not that unusual. And Charlie and Pamela had gotten divorced just before Emily came to Cantwell."

"That wasn't the impression I'd gotten. Why?"

"I have no idea. I wasn't privy to the internal details of their marriage."

"It wasn't considered improper when Charlie and Emily started seeing each other? What was her maiden name, by the way?"

"I can't remember. Something unremarkable. Unmemorable." Harry could hear Sanderson blowing air at the mouthpiece of the receiver. "When faculty date graduate students, it isn't exactly comfortable for everyone, but there's nothing illegal about it. With undergraduates, the rules are stricter. And Charlie was the kind of guy that everyone forgave. Charming." This didn't sound like a compliment.

Harry said, "One last question. Was Emily a better student than Doug McNeill?" There was silence. "Dr. Sanderson?"

"How the hell am I supposed to remember that?"

"I've only been teaching one year, and without referring to a single test score, I could rank groups of students pretty easily. I'm not talking about anyone's worth as a human being or the respect or happiness in life that they're entitled to. Strictly from an academic perspective, you can't tell me which one of them was stronger?"

"Okay, Emily was probably stronger academically. I don't know how this could possibly be important to anyone now."

"Because the school started a scholarship in the name of poor Doug McNeill, who no one apparently liked or respected, no matter how unjust that may have been. There's no scholarship in Emily Ziegart's name. Her only offense seems to have been that she was young and attracted Charles Ziegart. No one seems to be mourning her at all. That doesn't seem right."

Sanderson was silent; Harry imagined he had taken a mechanical pencil from a pocket protector and was doodling swearwords on a blotter in front of him. He liked the image. He waited until Sanderson finally said, "It's not a big scholarship."

"No, but I was able to find out that it's funded by one of Charles Ziegart's patents."

"Not one of his major ones."

"True. But why? I can understand why a suicide might not get that kind of honor. But why did Doug? It wasn't his family who insisted. He apparently didn't have any."

"I don't know. I don't make decisions like that." Sanderson sounded irritated.

"Who does?"

"Ask Gillian."

"She started the scholarship?"

"I didn't say that. I don't know anything about it. But I assume she would." Sanderson cleared his throat. "The department got a letter about Emily's death five or six years ago. I remember Louise Glade, our administrative assistant, putting it on the bulletin board. It was sent by a relative, a sister I think. So someone somewhere is probably mourning her. Now I've got things to do." Then he hung up.

21

QUEEN
OF CUPS

A woman who lives in
her dreams; at times she sees
things that may not be there

Maggie had called before he'd left to meet her at the cemetery. As soon as he heard her voice on his answering machine, he picked up, thinking about the things he'd told her, things he hadn't even told Serge. Well, he thought, I've been slowly going crazy myself for the last couple of years, so I guess it's fitting that I have a friend like her.

She said, "Would you mind a short visit with Miss Tokay? I asked her if we could walk on her property today, and she said that would be fine." Speaking of crazies, Harry thought cheerfully.

He met her at the end of the dirt drive tucked next to the shrine. The house was about fifty feet down the narrow road, which was crossed by a chain with a sign attached that said "Private Drive." Maggie unhooked it before they took their cars in next to the house. It looked even more decrepit close up than it did from a distance. One of the pillars holding up the roof of the front porch was missing; in its place was a tower of cinder blocks piled one on top of the other; they met the edge of the roof a few inches lower than the pillar would have done, hence the roof's smiling sag. The green and black shingles above were the only things about the place that looked sound. The porch floor was wood, and Harry wondered how long it would hold the weight of the cement blocks. The rest of the place looked as though termites feasted there regularly; there was no reason the porch planks would be an exception.

They parked in front, where the driveway disintegrated into a yard of hard-packed clay with intermittent patches of flattened grass. Maggie led Harry to the front door, the steps giving slightly, as though they were made of canvas. The door frame was peeling, but the door itself looked new and expensive, enameled steel painted a bright violet, with a heavy brass knob and a dead bolt.

"They mean it when they call her the Purple Lady, don't they?" said Harry.

"Yes," said Maggie, knocking on the door, then turning the massive knob. The door was unlocked and opened easily. She leaned her head in and said loudly, "Miss Tokay? It's Maggie. I've brought Harry."

They walked in, the cool dark of the hallway making Harry's irises ache with the effort of widening enough to see. The space was almost as large as Maggie's living room. After a few seconds he got the impression of an ornate fixture hanging from the ceiling and a grandfather clock that was taller than he was, flanked by a pair of heavy chairs. Through the shadows, he heard Miss Tokay's gentle little voice say, "Maggie? Come on in, honey."

Maggie led Harry from the front foyer into a large room, lightened by sunlight shining through tall, slender windows. A heavy, impossibly old ceiling fan turned sluggishly, making a soft, rhythmic buzzing sound, like bees doing a tango. The room was furnished with pieces that were all at least as old as their owner: an oak roll-top desk in a corner, a beautiful Persian rug that edged up to a fire-place with a brass screen, two wing chairs in rose-colored velvet, a few small tables, and a Tiffany floor lamp beside a Victorian sofa under the trio of windows in the far wall. Miss Tokay sat in its center, wrapped in the same purple shawl she'd worn the day Harry met her; she was backlit by the window, so her features were in shadow and her hair wisped around her head, glowing like a halo. Harry was willing to wager that her attitude in the light was intentional. She looked up at them with a smile, her teeth the brightest part of her face, and she extended her tiny hand in greeting. Maggie approached her and took it, leaning down and giving the old woman a kiss on the cheek. Then Maggie stood up and waved toward where Harry stood at the entrance to the room, as though Miss Tokay needed to be shown that he was there.

Miss Tokay beamed at Harry and held out her hand again, so he had no choice but to walk over to her and give her his. He hoped he wasn't required to kiss her as well. Miss Tokay's hand was cold and felt like little twigs encased in skin, and she didn't let go until after she'd said, "So nice to see you again." She asked him to sit, indicating one of the wing chairs. Maggie left the room, and Harry hoped she was coming back.

Miss Tokay said, "I like you."

Harry waited, but she appeared to want a response of some kind. "Thank you," he said. He thought he should probably tell her he liked her, too, but it seemed premature.

Miss Tokay seemed satisfied with his thanks and went on. "Maggie wanted to take you for a walk on my grounds. I thought it would be nice to talk first. I don't let many people on my property. You understand."

"Do you get pestered a lot?"

"Oh, yes."

Maggie came in then with a tray holding a stained thermal coffee carafe, spoons, and china cups in a purple floral pattern. She set the tray down on a small wooden table in front of the sofa and poured coffee into the cups, handing one to Harry. Miss Tokay accepted another from Maggie, thanking her. To Harry, she said, "Josie's a nice enough neighbor, but when Maggie came to live with her, it was really a blessing." Maggie smiled, took the third cup off the tray, and sat down in the remaining chair.

Harry said, "When was that?" He was appalled at the things he still didn't know about her, and hadn't thought to ask.

"When she came back from school. That was how many years ago, Maggie? Right after Dunc died, right? Or was it your mother?"

Maggie said, "Mom died first, then Dunc, a couple of years later. It was right around then."

"That's right. Poor Dee was still with us."

Harry said to Maggie, careful not to sound shocked, "You went to college?"

"I never finished."

"What did you major in?"

She smiled, but there was no heat behind it. "Getting away from Stoweville."

Miss Tokay added, "It's so nice that she doesn't go anywhere now. Unlike Dee, before she left us, of course."

Harry wondered if the old woman had any idea how that remark could be taken as a cruelty. She seemed not to have heard Maggie's comment about wanting to get away, and her gaze at her young neighbor was nothing but beatific and happy. Maggie smiled back at Miss Tokay, but at the same time she looked heartbroken, too, and he remembered his first impression of her, that she had buried a crushing heartache. He hadn't noticed it in her for a while, and he felt ashamed again, as though he'd been using her as a crutch without seeing how she bent under his weight. Then he looked back at Miss Tokay, wondering how he'd wandered so far from the society of his neighborhood and his university to get mixed up with all these eccentric country folk.

"Have you ever seen ball lightning, Mr. Sterling?" said Miss Tokay.

"No," Harry said. "I've heard of it. I didn't think it was a real thing." He had been about to add "like UFOs" and was relieved to have caught himself in time.

"We have a lot of it here. Tell him your story, Maggie."

Maggie looked a little uncomfortable at being put on the spot, but she said, "When I lived with my mother and father, the house was next to a farm. I was out on the porch one afternoon watching the heat lightning on the horizon. The sky was a funny greenish color, like it gets before there's a tornado." She said this as though it was common knowledge, though Harry had never heard of any such thing. "It came out of the sky and down to the ground, bouncing like a basketball made out of light. It bounced one, two, three times." She put her cup down on the tray and moved her hands up and down to show him. "Then it flew into the barn next door. I ran after it. The vet was coming that afternoon to give the cows some shots, so they weren't out in the field. As I came into the barn, I saw the ball of light fly out through the back wall. There were six cows in the barn. Three of them were standing, three were lying down. Cows don't usually do that." Harry nodded; *that* he knew. "I ran back outside, but the ball was gone. I went to tell my mother, who didn't believe me, but later our neighbor found the three lying down were dead. The others were fine." She shifted in her seat, animated. "The lightning bounced off every other cow. There was a little patch of burned straw between the last one standing and the wall where the light had disappeared. There were four scorch marks on the ground outside where I'd seen it bounce, each one perfectly round. The dead cows had them, too. I cried over them for two days."

Miss Tokay said, "We get a lot of ball lightning here. The scientists at the university think it's all silliness we ignoramuses made up, but they think that about lots of things."

Harry said, "Like the Sky People."

Miss Tokay smiled. "Maggie told you about them? Well, they're related, you know. Ball lightning is the residue from the light ships. When you see it, that means that they've been traveling around somewhere nearby."

"Do they travel around here a lot?"

Miss Tokay looked at him, assessing. He willed his face to blandness, not knowing how sensitive she was to the scorn of strangers. She must have decided that he passed whatever muster she considered important, because she said, "Not so much nowadays. They came here a long time ago and buried their ships deep underground. They came to observe us and to help keep us from destroying ourselves. These are critical times. The Sky People are very disappointed in us. The way we're raping the earth without thought of tomorrow or our children or our responsibilities to the planet. And each other." She stopped and looked at Maggie, who smiled at her. "It's distressing, but there's still hope." She seemed to be shrinking slightly, and Harry realized that her speech had tired her. "You understand now why I don't let just anybody walk all over my land? Lots of nosy folks want to see into the sinks, get a look at them. But the Sky People only come out when they think best. And they don't want to be seen by just anyone. When they show themselves, they mean business. Usually, it's for an ascension, and those Wickers, or whatever, have no idea what they're dealing with."

"Wiccans," Maggie said absently, pouring herself another cup of coffee from the carafe on the tray.

"Yes, well, the earth is alive and precious, and they do seem to understand that, at least. But I don't want people trampling the edges of the sinks, get themselves drowned, get me a lawsuit."

Harry could feel his head swimming, getting itself drowned.

"What 'sinks' are you talking about?" He imagined women in black hoods crowding into Miss Tokay's laundry room, each trying to dive into the washbasin.

"Sinkholes," said Maggie. "I told you, Miss Tokay's got two big sinks right on her property."

"Oh, sink*holes,*" Harry said. "What's an ascension?"

Miss Tokay smiled; Maggie's face was unreadable. "When you leave this plane, the Sky People have to choose you. Not just anyone gets to ascend." She took a dainty sip of coffee. "Those who've ascended pass wisdom to us on this plane."

"How?" he said, vastly intrigued.

"Some of us have been granted the ability to communicate with them. We take dictations and pass them on to interested parties." She looked at Maggie. "I've thought for years that Maggie would be perfect as my successor, but she keeps putting me off."

"Maybe someday, ma'am, when I have the time to give it the proper attention."

Harry was surprised at Maggie's diplomacy given her fear of always saying the wrong thing. Miss Tokay said, "The Sky People and the Ascended Masters choose you, honey. If they want, you'll wind up listening to them whether you have the time or not." She looked away at the walls, at the table. "Warner hasn't been giving me as many dictations lately, since we don't have services in the temple anymore. He's not very happy about that."

Harry was grateful he remembered that Warner was the name of Miss Tokay's disappeared beau. He was trying to think of a tactful way to ask more about him when Maggie said, "Do you want to see the sinks?" She looked at the tired old woman on the sofa. "May I show him, Miss Tokay?"

22

THE DEVIL

*The Seeker comes closer to
getting the point but is too
afraid to take any real action*

Miss Tokay's property was dense with
pine trees and scrub oak. Maggie told
Harry that the Tokay estate stretched out
over nine hundred acres. He was so impressed that he whistled. Then she told
him to keep an eye out for rattlesnakes
and he stopped whistling. They walked
on a flat, sandy path dotted with pine
needles and cones for a while without
saying anything more. Harry wanted des-
perately to know what Maggie thought
about the Sky People but was afraid to

ask; he also didn't want to seem to be making fun of Miss Tokay the
moment she'd graciously let them take a walk on her land. But after
many minutes of silent walking, Maggie said, "I've never seen them.
I don't want to hurt her feelings, but I don't have any intention of
starting a dialogue with the Sky People or anybody who's died. Or
ascended." She smiled. "In case you thought a cult was operating out
in this neck of the woods."

He was a little ashamed at his relief. "Shucks, and I thought I had
a great topic for my book. UFO cults are very marketable these

days." He breathed in the air, a deep smell of pine and something tangy, the pleasant funk of brackish water. "Spiritualist groups have a long history in the U.S. Mostly out west, though. You don't see so many in the South. They have roots in the late nineteenth century. UFOs are a twentieth-century wrinkle, of course."

Maggie nodded noncommittally, and he wondered if he was boring her. She said, "Speaking of topics for your book, how is that going? You haven't mentioned it in a while."

Harry said, "I was stalled for a bit, but I talked to a family member of the scientist I told you about, Charles Ziegart. I'm interested again, although I still don't know if there's anything there that would make a worthwhile book."

"A family member?"

"His son." Harry was about to tell her about Jonathan Ziegart's visit when the brush to the right of the trail seemed to explode. It was a moment before he recognized the source of the commotion; two white-tailed deer burst onto the path about twenty feet ahead of them and dashed across and away through the trees to their left. Harry said, "Jesus H. Roosevelt Christ," in surprise.

Maggie had stopped dead in front of him, and Harry came up beside her. "I haven't seen deer that close in the wild since my foster father took Lawrence and me hunting when I was fourteen. I'm glad he wasn't here or he'd be grinding out venison sausage by now." Her hand was on her chest, and he realized that she'd been more startled than he was by the deer. "Hey," he said, "I thought you were Nature Girl. Let's hope there aren't any gators or panthers in these woods or we'll both have strokes." She didn't smile, and he added, "Are you all right?"

She nodded a little jerkily, then took a deep breath. "I get a little twitchy sometimes when I don't sleep, and I startle easily."

"Me too," said Harry. "And it's really hot. Do you have water?"

She nodded again and pulled a bottle out of her fanny pack. She drank some, then offered the bottle to him. He took it and drank as well, pouring it into his mouth so as not to get his spit on the spout. He handed it back to her and said, "You sure you're okay?"

"I'm fine," she said. "Let's keep going." The trail was wide enough for two people to walk abreast now, so Harry stayed next to her. "So you were saying?" she said.

"I can't remember. Oh yeah, the Ziegarts. Sounds like regular family dysfunction with a few twists. The son is from a first marriage. Ziegart married one of his graduate students, who nobody liked apparently. The son, Jonathan, told me that she murdered his father. All very high drama."

"You don't sound impressed." She took another drink and put the bottle back into her pack.

"It doesn't make a lot of sense. It seemed to me she lost everything when he died. And she was in the car accident that killed him."

"How was she supposed to have murdered him? Did she shoot him or something while he was driving?"

"No, it's more baroque than that. He was allergic to bee venom, so he always carried an auto-injector syringe of epinephrine." At her blank face he explained, "Severe allergies can make some people's immune systems go into overdrive. They go into what's called anaphylactic shock. They can suffocate if they don't get an antihistamine in them right away. That's what epinephrine is. Anyway, Emily allegedly tossed his syringe and somehow smuggled some wasps into the car."

"Sounds unlikely, and pretty dangerous for her."

"Exactly. Everyone I've talked to seems perfectly willing to trash her good name, so you'd think if there was an obvious motive, adultery or gambling addictions or whatever, someone would have suggested it by now. Jonathan was vague but hinted that she wanted money."

"Did she get any?"

"Not as far as I can tell. And the ex-wife didn't seem to have to work very hard to make her give it up. I feel sorry for her. But maybe I won't when I learn more."

"Where is she now?"

"Dead. Suicide."

"So she can't defend herself."

"No," said Harry. "Maybe that'll turn out to be my job. Or maybe to sully her name further. Or neither."

And that's when it occurred to him how much graceless young Emily Ziegart had come to mean to him. He remembered the movie *Laura*, in which the gruff detective had fallen in love with a beautiful murdered girl. Well, he thought, no one has called Emily beautiful. But something about her spoke to him and said "Help me." In his mind she sometimes had Maggie's face, sometimes a feminized version of Dusty's. Irrational, probably stupid, and almost certainly unhealthy. Maybe Emily Ziegart had in fact been a murderer, or at least a manipulative opportunist. But he couldn't make himself believe it. For the first time, he really felt it, that he was going to write this book. Whether it would get published was another matter. But, he thought, so what? I have a job.

The trees broke open, and the ground ended in a ragged circle about thirty feet across. Maggie said, "Welcome to Tokay Sink."

Someone had built a low wooden barrier around the rim of the sinkhole. Maggie walked up to it and looked over, so Harry assumed the banks were sound. He joined her and peered into the giant hole. The sides were made of small jutting rock ledges covered with weeds and lichen. A live oak grew about ten feet down out of one of the cuts in the rock, curling upward in search of sunlight. The sink was filled to a few feet below the tree with dark green water, covered in spots with lily pads and sheets of yellow pollen. It looked to Harry like the mouth of an ogre-size shark, open and hungry.

"You used to swim in there?" he said.

"The water was higher then. Dee and I were too stupid to know how dangerous it was. The main problem is that there's no bottom, not for sixty feet down anyway, so you get tired treading water. If you can't get a good grip on something growing out of the side, you can drown pretty easily." She smiled at him and said, "We were young and strong. And light. The weeds didn't just pull out when we grabbed them." She looked back at the water. "It's nice and cold, but I wouldn't advise it now, no matter how hot it gets."

Harry was about to comment how a nice, shallow swimming pool would be a much better idea before realizing that Maggie and Dee probably hadn't had access to one. Certainly not the Olympic-size outdoor pool at the university. You couldn't get in there without a university ID. He doubted Maggie had known anyone who had one.

"The good old days," he said. "Does anything live in there?"

She shrugged. "Frogs. Turtles. Some snakes. Cave fish. It connects to miles of underground caverns that spread all over north Florida. Some people like to scuba dive in them, but that's pretty dangerous, too."

"I'll bet," said Harry. "Good place to hide a body, though."

"Temple Sink would be better," said Maggie.

"Oh, that's right. There's another big hole like that."

"Yes. They all have names."

"Go ahead," Harry said. "Scare me to death."

She led the way down another trail perpendicular to the one that had brought them to the monstrous hole.

"Jesus, what the hell is that?" he said as the trees abruptly thinned and he could make out something enormous and dark ahead. It was the size of a large two-story house, but it was hexagonal, made of rough unpainted wood, and on one of the flat walls that he could see was a double window over ten feet tall. The finish of the building was gray and weathered, and as they got closer, he could see that the window rims weren't joined properly; all the edges of the place had a fun-house, tilted quality that made him a little queasy. He stopped and stared, his hands on his hips. "I guess this is the temple."

He moved again when Maggie did, following her to the other side of the weird building. The giant hexagon had similar pairs of tall crooked windows on three of the six sides. On the far side of the temple, in a wall between the windows, was a heavy wooden door with an odd, bumpy texture. As Harry got closer, he could see that there were small pictures carved into the wood, all different from one another. He could make out an eye, a coiled snake, a pyramid, an ankh symbol, a peace sign, and the head of what looked like a dog. Each picture was in deep relief, approximately three inches across, ten to a row across the door. There were rows and rows of them up and down both panels; the thought of how much work went into the construction of the door itself made him tired. It was clear that the carvings hadn't been done by professional, or even particularly talented, artists. The door itself must have been several inches thick, although it was difficult to tell since it was shut tight, another formidable brass doorknob and dead bolt gleaming on its right edge. Each of the tall windows had been covered with plywood. Harry now noticed that there were poles topped with spotlights at five-foot intervals around the circumference of the place. Each light pole had a green roofing shingle mounted at an angle below the light fixture.

Harry smacked his forehead with his fist. "They aren't shingles; they're solar panels. If it's as dangerous as you've said, it makes sense that there are good lights around the temple. But everyone around here seems to have the same thing on their roof." He looked at Maggie. "How did that happen?"

She had stiffened, looking at him now as though he was a state trooper and she was a drug runner. "They're practical. You know. It's cheaper in the long run. The power goes out a lot around here because of all the thunderstorms. This way, it doesn't."

"But they're expensive. How come everyone around here has them? You can't afford a washer-dryer, but you can afford to cover your roof with solar panels?"

"They were all a gift. Miss Tokay wants to save the planet. She says the Sky People are all about getting rid of pollution, okay? It was a gift to everyone who's helped her out."

"She has that kind of money?"

"Well, not anymore. Don't mention this to her, all right? She gets embarrassed. Do you want to see inside or not?"

"God, yes."

She pulled her keys out of her pocket. "Do you have keys to everything of hers?" he asked. She ignored him and unlocked the door. It made a loud, spine-skittering screech as she pushed it slowly open.

"It's only safe to go in about two feet. Then the floor starts sloping, and it's only a couple more feet before it's gone altogether. So you can take one step in if you want a better look. But that's it. We haven't had to fish anybody out yet, so please don't be the first."

"I'm not that eager to meet the Sky People, believe me."

Maggie stepped through the door, making Harry's heart beat a little faster at the thought that maybe she wouldn't come out again. He followed, taking one careful step over the threshold, his foot coming down onto solid planks. The darkness was thick and hot, but the light from the doorway, mixed with the occasional strand leaking in from around the plywood on the windows, helped his eyes to make out details after a moment. The smell of dampness was almost overwhelming, and there was a soft rushing sound, along with the drips and trickles of nearby water.

It appeared to be one very large round room, although Harry assumed it was actually six-sided. There were long, thick curtains hanging in shreds off the windows. In the dim light they looked black. Maggie was little more than a silhouette in the darkness, and she reached out a hand. "Don't go any further than this," she said. Harry almost took her hand; maybe because it was dark and danger-ous and he could pretend that he needed her to guide him away from the edge, even though he had no intention of taking the slight-est risk. If he were Judd Lippman, he thought, he would talk her into doing it right here, inches from death. Judd probably got off on that sort of thing. Harry found it depressing for God knew which time that he wasn't more like someone else, maybe not the objection-able Judd Lippman but someone else. I'm like goddamned Hamlet, he thought. And not in a good way.

He could see more details now that his eyes were adjusting. He took a sideways step closer to Maggie, feeling the need to keep his voice low even though he knew it made no sense. "It looks like all the people fell in," he said; there were benches by the far wall, but he could see some of them tilted at insane angles, half of them dan-gling down, their legs caught on the wood floor where it simply stopped, raggedly black and gone, like a cartoon image of a black hole in outer space. The room was mostly empty because there wasn't much floor left to hold anything.

Maggie pointed at the windows. "All the curtains are purple vel-vet. Or they were. I'm not sure what color they are now."

"I'll take your word for it," he said, watching the hand he hadn't taken as she carefully turned around and eased it under his elbow, saying, "We should get out of here."

Out in the shaded heat, Maggie's hand left his arm. "What did you think?" she said.

"Creepy as hell," he said. "Very H. P. Lovecraft. Does anyone read him anymore? This struck me as exactly the kind of place that he'd have huge alien monsters spurting from."

She smiled. "I never knew how you pronounced any of the places they came from, but they scared the crap out of me anyway."

He returned her smile with great approval. As they walked away, he looked back for a moment and said, "It must have been hard giving that up. You said they moved the services to the garage after it fell apart?"

"Yes," she said. She was walking fast in front of him, so he double-timed to catch up.

"I'd be interested in seeing that one, too. Do you think she'd mind?"

"There's nothing in it. I told you, just old furniture and stuff stored there. All the temple stuff is gone."

"Huh. Okay." He couldn't imagine why she was lying. He figured something in there must be illegal, although he was slightly hurt that she thought he'd tell on her. But then, it might not be her secret; it might be that someone else, even Miss Tokay herself, was harboring something in the garage that it was best no one knew about who was supposed to be an officer of the court. He almost laughed at the image of Miss Tokay brewing white lightning or methamphetamine next to a Model T. Then he thought about the solar panels. He was pretty sure Maggie had been lying then, too. They're not supposed to have them, he thought. They're being hidden in plain sight. Maybe someone stole them.

They said good-bye once again at their cars, parked in front of Miss Tokay's house. Harry was about to ask Maggie if she wanted to go somewhere and get some coffee, or better yet, something cold, but before he could say anything, she said, "I have to go check on Miss Tokay. I'll see you later." He wondered if she was reading his mind again.

23

DEATH

REVERSED

Catastrophe.
Everything changes.
The old rules are swept away

Darcy Murphy dreamed of Josie Dupree. She had fangs and a great black cape, but she looked good, like Morticia Addams or some other vampish creature, dark and sexy and possibly lethal. In the dream her head grew wide till it looked like that of a beautiful, wild-eyed cobra; it bit him and he screamed, but he woke up aroused and sweating. When his wife asked what the problem was, he told her he'd dreamed of beating the Little Shit to death.

He thought that the sky was starting to gray up as he rang the doorbell. Josie opened the door, not as surprised to see him as she should have been.

"What do you want now?" she said.

"Another look around," he said. "I missed a few details in my report. My boss is on my ass."

"Okay," Josie said. She gave a dramatic sigh and opened the door. He walked in, taking in the cheap green carpet, the stained flowered sofa, the scratched coffee table. Then he saw the cards laid out on the small dining set in the corner of the main room. Big cards, bright colors. They didn't look like normal playing cards.

"What are those?" he said.

"Tarot cards," she said.

"What the hell's that?"

"They're cards for doing readings. About people's lives."

"Fortune-telling cards?"

"Sort of. I can't really claim to predict the future. Just what's likely, given current circumstances. My niece says it's like when they use radar and such to predict the weather. The predictions are only good for a little while ahead, and only for conditions as they are right now."

Darcy couldn't take his eyes from the bright colors of the cards on the table. "Devil worship bullshit."

"Don't be an ass. Isn't anything devilish about it."

"You wanna tell my future?" he said.

"If you got fifty bucks."

His attention turned to her. His eyes slitted as he looked at her cleavage, her messy hair, her loud lipstick, her heavy earrings. "Girl, I got your future in my hands. You want me to like you."

Her hands went to her hips. "But I don't."

Darcy felt anger flaring in his chest and in his groin. His wife could have told Josie that anger was a tonic to him. "I don't care if you like me, girl. It don't matter if you think I stink like dog shit. You just better act nice, that's all." He looked around the shabby room. "Where's that blond girl? She your daughter or what? You got different last names."

"She's my niece. She got off work a half hour ago. She'll be home any minute." Darcy could smell the lie on her; the stink of it and of her growing fear spread through the sad little room.

Darcy Murphy had never raped anyone, unless you counted the times he'd talked his wife into sex when she really didn't want to and he'd pushed, even shoved a little, until she gave in, or at least didn't push back. He'd been unfaithful more than once, mostly back when he was a meter reader; he was still amazed by what easy pickings some women were, alone in the daytime with nothing on but nighties and boredom, even for a raggedy straw man with hemorrhoids. But now this woman with her hair and her incense and all that color, he'd asked around; she knew what was what. There was no point in her being all prissy; he'd wager she'd been around more than he had. Some women liked to fan the flames with a little nonsense here and there. That was okay with him, but only to a point.

Josie said, "I think you should leave."

"Do you now?"

She looked around him as though he were fuzzy somehow, as if she was looking at something just over his shoulder. He turned involuntarily to see if there was something there.

"My niece will be back in just a few minutes." She was lying, he could tell, and nervous, too, which made him happy. Nervous was good, she had been so cocky and bitchy. He felt the shift in power like a dial turning in his chest.

"No, she won't. No need to be scared, honey. Just be nice. I'm a nice man, you'll see, honey, you'll see." Darcy was crooning at Josie now, moving toward her as if she was beloved, as if all he wanted to offer was comfort and sweetness. Josie backed up, the coffee table and couch behind her. Darcy walked toward her again, arms out to enfold her. The rain was coming down now outside, hard, in thick sheets, and there was a crash of thunder that shook the double-wide so hard it seemed it might skitter off the cement blocks that held it off the ground. Darcy expected the lights to flicker, maybe go out altogether, but they didn't so much as wink at him, not the slightest hum, and part of his mind remembered the solar panels and the windmills at the same time as he expected the lights to blink off. When Josie picked something up off the coffee table that looked like a flashlight, he wasn't alarmed or even mildly curious what she was up to. When she pressed the button on its side and brought the front of the flashlight toward him, he was about to tell her that the lights weren't flickering so there was no need; it made no sense to him at all when she pressed the flashlight against his outstretched arm, and while he expected to feel some warmth from the bulb, he had only a second to realize that it wasn't warm at all. He was never to remember exactly what happened next, but in his nightmares for some time to come, he dreamed that his hair exploded away from his scalp, taking his ears and eyeballs with it while lightning cut the sky and thunder crushed the ground. He usually woke up screaming. Somewhere the irony was dancing in the very bottom of his mind; now he finally believed that they weren't stealing anything.

24

DEATH

REVERSED

Catastrophe.
Everything changes.
The old rules are swept away

They had just passed the rose garden, approaching Maggie's favorite spot, the little wooden bridge, when the rain started. There'd been some warning; the clouds had been slowly darkening for the last fifteen minutes, with red and yellow flashes on the horizon, a few closer, but it hadn't seemed particularly sinister until the last few minutes, when the sky had grown a dark blue-gray and Harry had tried to get Maggie to head back to where their cars were parked. But she had ignored him and instead run back to where the path opened onto the cemetery. She was standing next to a small headstone, looking up with a strange expression, waiting, almost hopeful. He wondered again if she were quite sane, if her shyness and eccentricities were symptoms of something deeper and more desperate. Then he saw what she did, a floating blue sphere, like a glowing sapphire the size of a soccer ball. It was falling from the sky in a gentle arc, landing and then balancing for a moment on the top of a headstone. It floated up again, leaving a silver and blue trail in the air; a small part of Harry's mind reckoned that the trail was on his retina, not in the air itself. Then the sphere arced back down to the ground, bounced and flew again, and disappeared into the trees of Gunhill Park.

Then the rain hit, beginning with a great wind sweeping through the trees, making it look as though they were consciously forming a huge wave, fans in a forest stadium, up and down and sideways, with a great whooshing sound that was as loud as a jet engine, loud and grand. Maggie's hair blew in all directions, circling her head in a dancing display that didn't make her look any saner. Harry briefly wondered how that was physically possible, that nature could move the air around you and blow parts of you not in one direction but in all of them. Then he could feel wet drops on his shirt, fat ones, whole cupfuls in each drop, hitting first his shoulders, then his head, then pounding the ground and the leaves and the surface of the stream. Roaring blankets of water fell in long, graceful loops around them and on them; all Harry wanted in the world at that moment was to be in his car with the heater on high, maybe already in his driveway so he didn't have to navigate the torrents on the roads.

Maggie's arms went out to her sides, her head lifted, and Harry saw that she was smiling. Not a ghost-smile, nothing sad or halfway about it. Her face was turned into the rain, being beaten by the great washes of water from the sky, and her eyes seemed to be asking a question of the clouds and she was laughing and grinning in the bellowing, blowing wind. He'd only caught glimpses of her real smile before, a smile that made him think of Marilyn Monroe, not because that was who Maggie looked like but because her smile was the same, young and pure and sweet, utterly joyful. Her clothes were pressed to her, her slight frame and perfect breasts as visible as if she were naked. She was the most beautiful woman Harry had ever seen in his life. He thought she might be singing, and he was terrified.

He had his hands on either side of her face before he had a chance to think about anything else. He kissed her mouth with such ferocity that the sane, dry part of him, the part that always stayed sober no matter how much he drank, that part of him was worried that he might be hurting her or that she might slap assault charges on him later, after the rain. But even the sober part of Harry went silent when her arms found his waist, wrapped around him, and she kissed him back.

He would have taken her on the nearest headstone if that internal judge hadn't piped up again. They were outside, anyone could see, they'd catch pneumonia, she'd hate him later, he had no condoms. But he kept kissing her and she kept kissing him back, through rain so thick it seemed that white-water rapids were pummeling them from the sky. Harry stopped breathing for too long, and then he and Maggie were both gasping for air, faces dripping and slick, and he thought for just a moment of dragging her to his car, maybe doing it in the backseat, but the judge wagged a mental finger at him. Their eyes caught, and she started laughing again, and this time his fear of her didn't stop him from laughing back until the rain stopped.

25

ACE OF
SWORDS

REVERSED

*Winning at
a terrible price*

By the time Maggie came in, Josie had been sitting on the couch for a half hour with an unconscious man on their living room floor. Maggie was so wet that her clothes were wrinkled and clinging; she was shivering with cold even though the rain had stopped a quarter of an hour before. Josie assumed she was intent on getting to the bathroom, to a warm shower and dry clothes, but the body on the floor stopped her. Josie had seldom seen Maggie nonplussed; a faraway place in her mind found some gratification in Maggie's frozen surprise.

"I actually had to use it," Josie said. "He was trying to rape me."

"Oh God," said Maggie.

"Exactly," said Josie. "We've got to park him somewhere."

"Okay," said Maggie, looking around the room as though there was an answer to be found lying on an end table. "Oh God," she repeated.

Josie took a moment through her panic to look more closely at Maggie's face, seeing the reddened skin around her mouth and her stunned expression. It didn't take Josie more than a heartbeat to understand the situation, possibly better than Maggie did. But she filed it away for later and said, "Where are we going to put him?"

Maggie chewed her lower lip, her hands in her wet denim pockets. "Downtown, maybe. Somewhere near the university?"

"As good as anywhere. Minnesota might be better, but it would take too long." Josie moved to the phone. "Calvin Crane is coming over in a half hour. I'll call him and put him off."

"What if his wife answers?"

Josie gave Maggie a look. "I'll tell her I almost killed a man today. It's all in a day's work for a heathen fortune teller."

"Are you all right? Did he hurt you?"

"No. He didn't get the chance, fortunately."

Maggie changed clothes while Josie made the call. When her niece came back into the living room, she kneeled down next to the man on the floor and looked through his pockets until she found his keys. She went outside with them and came back in a few minutes later. "There's a clipboard in his truck with his assignments for the day. We're not on it."

"Thank God," said Josie. She looked down. "How are we going to get him in the truck?"

"We have to hoist him."

Their first effort was a failure. "We need a third set of hands," Maggie said, and Josie could read her thoughts as clearly as if they were printed in the air above her head.

"No," Josie said. "We're not calling him. I think you and I can do it if we put our minds to it. But if not, we'll call Baby. She's strong."

Maggie was the stronger of the two of them, so she lifted from under his arms while Josie took the legs. Josie grimaced when the dirty soles of his work boots knocked against her dress. I'll never wear it again, she thought. They got him out to the porch; Josie lost her grip on his ankles only once, dropping them with a loud, one-two thud on the porch floor.

The storm started again as they rode back from a parking garage off Shively Street, having left Darcy Murphy lying behind the front seat in the extended cab of his truck. Maggie drove the Celica slowly since the rain was coming down so thickly against the windshield that light was having difficulty penetrating the glass.

Josie said, "Do you think they'll check for fingerprints?"

"Only if he reports it, and they take him seriously."

"Will they?"

"I have no idea, Josie. But since he tried to attack you, he's not very likely to want the cops involved. I doubt he'll remember much. I wiped down the steering wheel. We can't do better than that."

"God, that man is terrible. You should have seen what was coming off him. A shade of black with purple streaks in it that were so sickly it made me ill to look at him. He hates me something awful."

"Why?"

"I don't know. It seems to really stick in his craw that we don't pay his company anything. Hope he's not a racist, or he'll be worse at the Thorpes'."

There was silence as Maggie had to slow down even further, the rain coating the car in an almost opaque bubble of silver. Josie studied her, looking around her and through her, and said, "You were on a walk when the rain started?"

"Yes."

"By yourself?"

"No."

"What happened?"

Maggie sighed. Josie knew that Maggie would have liked to keep more to herself. It wasn't so much that Maggie was secretive, Josie thought, as that she didn't want anyone worrying about her. She'd rather no one thought about her at all.

"I'm not sure. It rained. I got a little out of control, like I do sometimes. He kissed me. Then he didn't want to come near me, all of a sudden." Maggie swallowed, peered hard through the windshield. "I haven't been able to read him for a few weeks now."

"You know what that means."

"I know. But after today, I don't expect to see him for a while. Maybe ever."

Josie waited for Maggie to start crying like a normal girl in love, but she didn't; she just blinked and drove and then said, "I'm so stupid sometimes."

And Josie knew that was the closest Maggie would come to admitting that she'd come to care for him. She felt a pain stabbing through her, a pain of love and pity so sharp and strong she squirmed in the seat with it. Poor girl, poor doomed girl, she thought as a craving for a tall glass of Southern Comfort hit her. Then to her surprise, Maggie added, "Better to lay low, anyway." The rain had eased, and Maggie risked a quick look at Josie. "Is Calvin staying away long enough for us to get you to a meeting?"

26

THE LOVERS

REVERSED

Mistakes in love

Harry had planned a trip to the beach house with Dusty for the coming weekend, but Ann called him on Tuesday night; her father had suffered a heart attack and Dusty wanted to stay in Orlando and make sure the old man was all right. "I told him he didn't need to, but you know how attached he is to my parents."

He asked for details; he'd never been close to his former in-laws but harbored no hostility toward them. Ann assured him that the heart attack had been a mild one. Nevertheless, Dusty wanted to stay close.

"Do you want me to come?" he said.

"No, it's not necessary. But thanks anyway. Maybe next weekend, if you're free."

Dusty got on the phone while Harry was processing the unusual invitation. After his son's brief greeting, Harry said, "How are you, pal?"

"Okay. Granddad isn't doing so hot, though. I'd rather be at the beach, you know, but, like, I think Grandma needs me, you know?"

"Sure. Your mom says I shouldn't come. Is that all right with you?"

"It's okay. Mom says you'll be around more this summer anyway."

Harry thought, She did? He said, "I may take a trip up to Pennsylvania in a few weeks to do a little research. You were a big help to me on the last book when we went to the Smithsonian and the Library of Congress. I was hoping you'd come with me again, be my assistant. We could go fishing, maybe. What do you think?"

"That sounds okay, I guess. I gotta go."

Harry had a dream that night about Maggie. It was the first one of its kind that he'd had, and the fact that it was erotic didn't help him get back to sleep after he'd woken up at three a.m., sweating and calling out as he kicked the sheets. He got up, made a cup of warm milk, which he'd been told by a pharmacist friend back in Washington really did have soporific qualities. It didn't work, so he sat up and read a book about the politics of academia that he'd gotten from the university library till the sun came up.

He didn't go to Crane's that Wednesday for lunch, nor did he go south of town to meet Maggie for a walk in the cemetery. Instead, he took a walk around the campus. There wasn't enough shade, so after one long circuit, he was afraid he'd pass out from heatstroke. He went into the university gym. It had a weight room and an indoor track, both of which he used. The track was elevated, and as he trotted along he could see tall young men and a few women playing basketball below him. The sounds of the balls and the soles of their athletic shoes hitting the shiny wooden floor were echoey and dreamlike, and he missed the woodpeckers and the buzzing grasshoppers, but he didn't go back to the cemetery.

.   .   .

The only good thing to come out of Tuesday's rainstorm, as far as Darcy Murphy was concerned, was the fact that his hemorrhoids seemed to have been cured. He figured it was some witchy side effect of whatever hoodoo the Dupree woman had put on him. He'd woken up in his car in the middle of downtown, the rain screaming so loud on the roof of his truck that it amazed him he'd slept through any of it. If it was sleep, which wasn't likely. She'd done something to him, although he couldn't remember what. He'd never been so confused in his life, and when he got home that night and his wife asked him about his day, he opened his mouth and couldn't speak for a full five minutes till she asked him if he was drunk. The woman had no idea how lucky she was that he didn't take a swing at her, he thought. If she'd looked at all like Josie Dupree, he might have killed her where she stood. He was never to pester her for sex again, although at that point, neither of them knew it.

He called in sick to work the next day. He felt awful, like he had a terrible hangover, although he'd quit drinking months before, as his wife well knew. But she still hovered over him and worried that he might fall off the wagon and become a useless bum like her useless bum of a father. He knew that a psychiatrist might say she'd married him because he was just such a useless bum himself, but he had a good job and had quit drinking, neither of which could be said of her father.

Harry was angry and discombobulated, looking at the screen of his laptop and not seeing it, reading and rereading his notes, forgetting what he'd read the moment he was done with a page. His whole body ached, partly because he'd punished it at the gym the day before. On Thursday afternoon, he gave up and called Maggie. "Where is she?" he asked Josie.

"What do you care?"

"Josie, I'm getting tired of this. You're not her social secretary."

"She's not here. What do you want with her, anyway?"

Harry sighed. "I don't suppose you'd give her a message, would you?"

"Maybe."

"I have a beach house. It's not much, but it's only an hour and a half from here. It's empty this weekend, and I thought that if she wanted, she could spend a day or two there." Silence. Harry sighed again, although silently. "You could go, too. If you wanted."

"*On* the beach? Not back behind where you sit on the porch and stare at other people's trash cans?"

"On the beach. You can sit on the porch and stare at the Atlantic Ocean. It's small, but the beach itself isn't too built up yet. It's still pretty private."

"You're not going?"

"No." Even as Harry said it, he thought that maybe he was lying, that he'd been hoping they'd go on Friday, and he'd find his way to the house a little later, saying he'd been in the mood for a drive and he thought he'd just check on them. He wouldn't even need to stay the night; he could drive back in the dark, after having spent just a little time in the familiar old house. With Maggie. And probably Josie. This made it less appealing, but still worth the trip. Maybe he could get Josie to drive back early. He knew it wasn't likely.

"Maggie works on Saturday."

"Oh. That's right." His mind tried to rearrange his plans. "But she's done by one. You could be there by midafternoon."

"Why are you doing this? She's not going to sleep with you for it."

"God, Josie. I know you don't think much of me, but come on."

"I'll think about it."

"You have to ask her. It's not up to you."

"Okay. I'll talk to her tonight."

Harry hung up, feeling uncomfortable and conflicted. He wasn't sure why he felt he owed Maggie anything. He hadn't walked with her for two days, but it wasn't as though she needed him in any way, on the walks or anywhere else. He wasn't entirely sure that she even liked him. He felt guilty for ditching her without a word, even though she probably wasn't concerned at all. She'd kissed him back, but he'd half convinced himself that she was just being passive. But he had to face the fact of his physical desire for her, a burning, rolling, sloppy ache in his belly and in his groin. He wasn't sure which filled him with more guilt, the desire itself or his denial of it.

"Mr. Radley's oven isn't working," said Josie over her cards as Maggie walked in. "I told him you'd probably have time today."

"Okay," Maggie said. "I guess I could do it now and shower afterward. You think he'll mind that I'm all sweaty?"

"Since you're not charging him, I think he wouldn't mind if you smelled like a squashed skunk." She turned over another card. "Harry called."

Maggie looked up from the bill she was examining. "What did he want?"

"He offered us his beach house this weekend."

"What? He wants us to go with him?"

"No. He said since he's not going, we could use it if we wanted." Josie felt bad about the feathers of brown disappointment that plumed around Maggie, but she knew she'd better kill that little hope in the girl's heart before the hope ate a hole in it.

"Why's he doing that?" said Maggie, still clutching the forgotten bill.

"Guilt, I imagine."

"Because he hasn't been around, you mean."

"Yes. He was dripping with it so thick I could almost smell it over the phone."

Maggie's eyes were wide and blue and hurt. "What should I do?"

Josie shrugged. "It's up to you. But I don't see why we can't take him up on it. We won't trash the place. We could even leave it cleaner than we find it or do something else nice for him, if it would make you feel better. You could bake him a pie."

After leaving to brush her teeth, Maggie came back into the living room. Josie was at the small table, reading cards. Maggie glanced at the cards but then deliberately moved her eyes to Josie's face, avoiding seeing which cards were lying there. "Will you call him, Josie? You know I'd make a mess of it."

Josie heaved a heavy sigh. "No, you wouldn't. But of course I'll talk to him, honey. I'll do anything you want. Always."

After Maggie left to go fix Mr. Radley's oven, Josie called Harry. He said he'd bring the key and directions to them the next day. Josie knew that he planned to come in the afternoon, hoping to see Maggie, and she was equally certain that Maggie wouldn't be at home. She went back to the table and spent a long time on the reading, shaking her head at the outcome. This beach trip wasn't going to be a disaster; no one would die, no terrible injuries or horrible sunburns. But it wasn't going to be the break that Maggie needed, and Josie thought Maggie needed a break more than anything in the world. She wasn't surprised that the King of Swords and the Queen of Cups appeared, both reversed and emerging as influences in the near future. Bad news, she thought; a hostile woman and a man you can't trust. That had to be Harry. She wondered if he'd renege on the offer of the beach house at the last minute.

She put the cards away in the wooden box and put it in the cupboard under the window nearest the table. She walked into the kitchen and pulled a small bottle out of the cabinet over the refrigerator, tucked so far back behind the rubber bowls and mismatched wineglasses that she had to use the step stool to reach it. She left the stool in place so that she could return the bottle in a hurry if she needed to. She didn't bother with a glass.

27

THE SUN

REVERSED

Homelessness;
plans disintegrate.
Marital disharmony

Maggie was gone when Harry showed up at the double-wide on Friday afternoon. He wanted to see her but didn't at the same time, and it made him feel young and stupid. So he'd waited until well after lunch, about the time he expected her to come home after her usual walk, and when he saw her Toyota in the driveway behind Josie's Chevy, his stomach tightened up and he felt things moving through him that had been still a moment before. You're thirty-seven years old, he told himself. Divorced. Seasoned. Well, perhaps more than that. Maybe overripe. In any case, you're not sixteen. Even though she practically is, and that makes you a drooling, dirty old man.

He parked the car behind Maggie's and got out with a great mental effort. He made sure the key and the folded paper on which he'd printed out directions to the beach house were both in his pocket and walked up the wooden steps to the front door. The vomit stain, he noticed with some relief, was now entirely gone.

· · ·

Josie said, "You can come in, but she's not here."

Harry walked in, so disappointed his stomach hurt. He fished the key ring and paper from his pocket and handed both to Josie, explaining unnecessarily what they were.

"I'm not an idiot," she said.

"You're welcome," he said. "It's okay to use anything that's there. I don't think that there's much food, but there are towels and beach balls and all that sort of stuff. This is to the pantry." He held up the smaller of the two keys. "You can eat anything you find in it, although I'd be careful. Those chickens have been in the freezer for years."

"Good to know," said Josie, showing him to the door.

There was a storm that night, but it had blown over by the next afternoon, so the drive to the beach was clear and easy on a rain-damp highway, dark clouds of mosquitoes hovering above puddles in the culverts. "Glad your air-conditioning works," said Josie. "We need to keep the windows closed." They were in Maggie's Toyota, Josie in the passenger's seat and Tamara and Charlotte in the back. Miss Baby had been invited but was so grateful at the thought of having some time alone in her house she'd waved her arms to the heavens in gratitude. Her granddaughters were singing "Kung Fu Fighting," and Josie had told them three times to be quiet. Maggie smiled and put a CD in the player in the car's dashboard. It was a British singer named Robyn Hitchcock, and Maggie started singing along loudly to a song about trains. She asked Josie only once if Harry had said anything about joining them at his beach house.

"No, honey. Nothing at all," Josie said, seeing Maggie's happy, singing face fall into disappointment and wishing that she were going to have a better time. She couldn't help adding, "You always did prefer Yankee boys to our homegrown variety. I remember you had a big crush on that Drew Stebbins in high school, the one who moved here from New Jersey."

Maggie's smile returned a little bit. "He never even knew my name." She didn't take her eyes off the road. "Do you think we'll ever be together?"

Josie said, "You won't let me do a reading for you, so I can't say for sure. But between what he does and what you do, I don't know, honey. I don't see how it's going to work. I'm sorry."

There was a moment of silence before Maggie said, "You know, I would never abandon you, Josie. Even if I left." Josie didn't speak again for a long time, and when she did, it was to tell the girls not to sing so loud because it gave her a headache.

The house was old and rustic but didn't sag the way Miss Tokay's did, so it seemed all right to Josie, who'd been half afraid that it would either be so nice and shiny that they'd have to spend the whole two days worrying about getting sand or salt water on expensive rugs or furniture, or so run-down it might topple onto their heads if the storm returned. The door facing the driveway led to an enclosed porch that ran the length of the house, with a bathroom at one end and a kitchen off the other. Maggie brought in plastic bags of groceries and clothes along with a small Styrofoam cooler. Josie helped her unpack them and found that one of the keys on the silver ring Harry had given them opened a small, mostly empty room. "I found the pantry," she said. There were shelves on the walls half filled with bags of chips and boxes of cereal. Inside was also a chest freezer, which contained two frozen chickens, three steaks, and a tub of chocolate ice cream. Maggie said, "We'd better leave all that alone."

Josie said, "He said use anything and eat anything. But we've got enough. And he was right about one thing. Those chickens look like they were frozen before World War Two."

The enclosed porch contained only a daybed and two bookcases under jalousie windows filled with children's board books, paperback thrillers, and romance novels. There were only three other rooms, the living room through the kitchen and two small bedrooms. Both the living room and the largest bedroom had sliding glass doors leading out to a screened porch on the ocean side. The walls were decorated with beach art, paintings of lighthouses and sea oats, a few stuffed fish, and a fishing seine laced with crab shells and conchs. The doors and windows were closed and the house was stuffy, so after putting their few belongings in the larger bedroom, Maggie opened the sliding doors to the sea air. The wind immediately picked up her hair, blew her T-shirt against her chest, and she smiled her big smile. "My God," she said. "Oh, my God, this is the best thing."

"Yes," said Josie. "We've earned ourselves a little vacation."

The girls wanted to go out to the beach at once, so Maggie helped them find their bathing suits. Josie took note of the wooden rocking chairs on the screened porch. "I'll watch you all from here," she said.

There was a dirty beach umbrella on the porch along with a half-deflated beach ball and some colorful plastic pails and shovels. The girls took the latter and Maggie took the umbrella, an armful of towels that they'd brought, and a bottle of sunblock. She put on her floppy straw hat and followed the girls out to the sea. She had on cutoffs and a T-shirt, not owning a bathing suit. Josie watched them work their way across the hot sand to the water and rocked in the chair, wondering where she'd put her flask and what liquor these rich lawyers kept in their vacation house.

She'd fallen asleep in the chair and was dreaming of Duncan, slapping her gently between the shoulder blades, saying, "Josie Posey Puddin' and Pie," the way he'd always done. It was a gesture that was as familiar to her as the scent of her baby, taken now as Dunc had been, the loss fast and terrible. She didn't believe in God, something she tended to keep to herself since her clients had certain expectations of spiritual feeling from someone in her profession. She believed in what she did, believed that there were forces in the ether that shaped destinies and helped or hurt people, depending on the whims of Fate. But she didn't believe in a consciousness behind it all, or at least not a benign one. Sometimes she thought she did believe in a god but saw him as evil, or at least capricious. He hates us, she thought. Or just thinks we're interesting lab specimens. Or maybe there's more than one and they sit up there laughing, pulling off our wings for sport. That's sort of a quote from somewhere, she added to herself. Maggie would know.

She was so startled by the slam of the screen door and the wailing of a child that her legs jerked up and down before she was entirely awake. Maggie was carrying Charlotte, Tamara following close behind. There was blood dripping from the older girl's left foot, falling in fat splotches onto the painted wood planks of the porch floor. "She ran her foot into a horseshoe crab," said Maggie. "I hope they have something here, bandages or something." Josie got up, horrified to find herself irritated at the noise and the fact that she hadn't had an opportunity to grab a sip from her flask while they were on the beach.

Maggie took Charlotte into the small kitchen, hoisting her up onto the counter and putting the wounded foot into the sink so there wouldn't be more blood on the floor. Josie took Tamara into the living room and turned on the TV while Maggie found a bottle of peroxide and a box of Band-Aids in the bathroom.

.   .   .

Once the injured foot was cleaned and bandaged and the blood was wiped from the floor, Maggie got the girls comfortable on the couch in the living room. The house had satellite TV, so there were channels with perpetual cartoons, a treat so rare that Charlotte's tears reduced themselves at once to a soft snuffling. Maggie brought two bottles of ginger ale from the cooler, and soon the girls were sitting side by side on the couch, entranced by colorful characters bouncing off each other on the screen. Maggie got up from Charlotte's side, announced she was going to take a shower, and disappeared through the kitchen to the bathroom. She reappeared a moment later, a serious look on her face. "Did you bring any shampoo?" she asked Josie.

"No. I was going to use whatever they had. Harry said we could."

"I forgot mine. What's in the bathroom looks expensive. You sure it's all right?"

"He said so, Maggie. It's only shampoo."

The sound of a car in the short sandy driveway didn't surprise Josie, although she wouldn't have said earlier that she'd expected any such thing. She knew it wasn't Harry, although she couldn't have said how she knew, any more than she could have said how she knew that she loved her niece or that she was never going to be able to stop drinking. She left Charlotte and Tamara in the living room and walked slowly to the front door of the little beach house. She could hear the water running in the bathroom, could hear Maggie singing the way she always did when she began to relax. Josie also knew that Maggie wasn't going to get to relax for long.

The door was locked, and now the doorknob turned hard, back and forth as though it was angry. Josie pushed aside the white curtain that hid the window in the door and saw where the anger emanated from. A woman's face met her gaze through the glass, a beautiful face, but with a mouth that looked as though it could do nothing but bend down in a scowl. Josie and the woman stared at each other through the window for a moment; Josie could see the colors dancing around the woman's head, dark red spikes weaving through a cloud of dull yellow, expanding and contracting in a mass that looked like it had a life independent of the beautiful woman. She's scared of us, Josie thought, and angry, and we're about to piss her off a whole lot more.

Josie was reaching to turn the small latch on the doorknob when it turned by itself; the door opened, revealing that the woman had a key and had used it. She walked over the threshold and closed the door behind her with a bang. "Who the hell are you?" she said.

"I'm Josephine Dupree," said Josie calmly. "Who the hell are you?"

"I'm Ann Sterling," the woman said. "I own this house. What are you doing here?"

"I thought Harry Sterling owned the house. We're friends of his. He offered it to us for a day or two." The colors hadn't changed to anything less hostile. Josie went on, "We're not doing anything wrong," then was irritated with herself. That's the truth, she reminded herself. We have a right to be here.

Ann Sterling said, "Where is he?"

"He's not here. It's just us."

"Is he coming? I need to talk to him."

And then Josie saw it as clearly as if it had been acted out in front of her. His ex-wife had thought she would find Harry here alone. She wanted him back. Josie felt another stab of relieved sorrow on Maggie's behalf. A woman like the one in front of her always got what she wanted. Maggie never did. It seemed to be a law legislated by the capricious, psychopathic gods.

"Well, you can't," Josie said. "He's not coming."

Ann lowered her head, looking at Josie with speculation. "Who else is here?"

"My niece. Two children, our neighbor's granddaughters."

"Just the four of you?"

"Yes." Josie wasn't sure what to do next, thinking it probably wasn't a very good idea to suggest to this woman that she leave them alone in what was after all her house, even if it was perfectly legal and moral for them to be there. But Josie didn't want to have to entertain Ann Sterling, and she didn't want to leave the house just because the woman was intimidating and used to having her way in all things. Before she could decide what to say next, the bathroom door opened and Maggie came out in a cloud of steam like someone returning from another dimension; she wore a faded green chenille robe, pushing her hair up into dark blond spikes with a towel, looking like a teenager. As soon as Maggie saw Ann, she stopped and stared, her blue eyes crackling.

"Maggie, this is Ann Sterling," Josie said. "Harry's wife."

Josie could read Maggie's expression easily enough, guarded pain and a hint of resignation.

"Hey" was all she said.

Ann said nothing, staring at Maggie with dark, angry eyes. She sniffed the air; Josie thought she looked like a golden retriever after a hard rain. Then Ann said, "That's my shampoo. Camellias. It's made with essential oil. I buy it specially in Orlando. It's very expensive. I can't believe you thought it was all right to use it. It's mine." She said the last part as though Maggie wasn't bright enough to have gotten the idea from the rest of her speech.

"I'm sorry," Maggie said, lowering the towel, eyes widening, clearly at a loss.

Josie said, "It's not like she can give it back, you know. Harry said we could use anything here."

"Well," said Ann, "Harry was wrong. I guess you could use his things if he really did give you permission, but he doesn't have the right to give you carte blanche to use mine. We own the house jointly. I assume he told you as much. The right to use a property is called usufruct. You don't have it."

"You're a lawyer," Maggie said, the towel now clutched between hands with whitened knuckles.

"Yes. A good one." Her eyes moved to the scene beyond in the living room, where Tamara and Charlotte cackled with laughter at something bright and loud on the television. Ann's eyes widened, and Josie realized that she was registering that the children were black. Josie wasn't sure if that made things worse or not.

It wasn't easy prying the two girls from the television, harder still to make them understand that they weren't going to be spending the night in the beach house. But Josie and Maggie managed to get their possessions back into the grocery bags and the girls out of the door without making too much of a scene, and they were headed back to Stoweville by the time the sun had set.

The next morning, Harry got up early, having slept only about three hours. He put a few things in a small duffel bag, then drank some coffee as he sat at his kitchen table. The window faced east, and he could see the sun glaring orange only a small distance above the horizon. Fortunately, he thought, by the time he left it would be high enough not to blind him as he drove to the coast.

When he got to the beach house, neither the Celica nor Josie's dented Chevy was in the sandy driveway. He thought, Maybe they went for groceries, maybe they're out just driving around. He brought in his duffel, not sure if that was a good idea. Inside the house, there were signs that someone had been there as recently as an hour or two before: clean dishes drying on the dish rack, damp streaks and the scent of camellias in the shower. He tried using his cell phone to call Maggie's house, to see if for some reason they'd decided to leave early, but the battery gave a silent digital sputter and died, and he cursed his procrastination in not replacing it. There was a land line, but it had no long-distance service; renters tended to abuse the privilege, and they all had cell phones these days anyway. For the first time, he cursed his real estate agent's attention to detail.

He found a can of ginger ale in the pantry and took a clean cup from among the drying dishes on the counter. He was glad to find the ice trays full so he could drink it cold. He took it to the screened porch on the ocean side and sat for a while, watching the pulsing of the waves and thinking about Emily Ziegart. I need a picture of her, he thought. I need to see her face.

He had just put the cup in the sink when he heard a car's tires crunching the scrub and gravel on the driveway. He was stunned when it turned out to be Ann.

"Is something wrong with Dusty?" were his first words at the sight of her.

"No. He's fine. Well, he's not entirely fine, but nothing like what you're thinking. That's part of the reason I'm here." She was wearing white tailored pants and little gold sandals, beautifully pedicured nails peeking out from underneath little paper flowers on the straps. Her shirt was sleeveless and cool, mauve with green stripes and small pearl buttons, open at the neck, just barely hiding smooth tan cleavage. Her makeup was perfect, as was her hair, curled and brown and long. He'd thought she was the most beautiful woman he'd ever seen when he met her during his first year in law school, and she was still stunning. He felt a flip of amazement in his chest; he'd been married to her, had sex with her, been intimate with her in ways that he'd never imagined before meeting her. He still felt a vestigial electric zing of attraction, even though she'd tossed him aside like garbage as soon as Lawrence had been buried. Nothing had prepared him for how painful the death of his brother had been, and the subsequent disintegration of his marriage had sunk him so much further, he had never expected to feel anything like pleasure again. Only his son's need of him had kept him from killing himself, and he sometimes wondered if that had been merely an excuse, since Dusty rarely seemed to need him at all. Harry had to remind himself of what Maggie had said: it's not Dusty's job to make you feel real.

"I thought you'd be here yesterday. Some people were here. Not renters. They said that you'd let them use it." She saw the duffel on the couch. "Were they telling the truth?"

Harry's chest grew cold. "You came here before?"

"Yes. To find you. I got a shock, let me tell you."

"You talked to Maggie? Or Josie?"

"I guess so. I can't remember what names they gave. They looked so guilty about being here, I thought they might be squatters. Their clothes were in grocery bags, not anything like suitcases, so I wondered." She stopped, and Harry opened his mouth to ask what else had happened, what their reactions had been to her arrival. But she spoke before he could. "Is she the Waitress? The blonde?"

"How did you know about that?"

"I talk to Amelia, Harry." She walked into the kitchen. Harry followed three steps behind. She looked around, opened the cutlery drawer, then closed it, as though checking to see if anything was missing. Then she looked him full in the eyes for the first time.

Harry wanted to ask her again how Maggie had reacted to a stranger barging in on them, this particular stranger especially. But he found himself saying, "Why'd you come all this way? Is your father okay?"

"He's out of the woods. Back at home. Dusty's with them."

"Good." He moved to the table. "You could have called. You haven't let me talk to Dusty much the last few weeks. I don't like to be cut out this way. I worry all the time." He sat down, trying not to lose his temper, trying not to start yelling. He'd thought that he wasn't angry at her anymore.

"I'm not trying to cut you out, Harry." She sat down in the chair opposite him, the other end point of a diagonal line. "It's just that I thought maybe we could see you more this summer." A pause. "The two of us."

There was a heavy silence that lasted a minute or more. Then Harry said, "What do you mean?"

"Just what I said. Dusty has a lot of fantasies about us getting back together. I've been thinking, maybe he's not so far off the mark. I don't know about you, but as I get older, I think about real life more. About the kinds of things that matter. You and I were married for a long time. I know you better than I know anyone else in the world." At Harry's expression, she spoke faster. "I miss certain things, you know? I bet you miss them, too. Being a family. Being the kind of couple we used to be. We don't have to make any decisions now. But I thought maybe you could stay with us for a few days after you're done for the term. I have plenty of room. You're just renting in that town." She waved her hand as though his house was smoke she could propel away. "You could keep it, or not."

"I'm committed to teaching next year. I'll need somewhere to live." Harry didn't tell her that the term had already ended. He felt like someone else was speaking. He had no idea how he felt about what Ann was saying. He had no idea if he was understanding her at all.

"Okay. I just wanted to plant the idea. How about we talk in a week or so, and see what you think then?"

Harry's mind finally focused and he said, "Ann, what's going on with Dusty?"

She sighed. "Nothing really. I mean, I think it's normal teenage boy stuff. He's so flat affect and gloomy, it's hard to say what's going on in his head." She looked down and started scraping at a hardened crust of something on the surface of the table with her fingernail. "I don't think he's depressed. Not in the clinical sense, anyway." She looked up. "He needs you, but he needs me, too. That's why I thought it might be better if you come down and stay, rather than waiting till he's done in June and coming up here for a visit. You could spend, you know, 'quality time.'" Ann never used clichés. Harry felt completely unmoored. Who is this person? he thought. I've never met her before. A very small, almost microscopic part of his brain whispered, Yes you have, yes you have, but Harry couldn't hear it.

28

NINE OF
PENTACLES

*Be careful;
a friendship is at stake*

Harry felt the dead cell phone lying like a tiny corpse on the passenger's seat as he drove back into town. It was after ten o'clock; he didn't know when Maggie and Josie went to bed, but he cut over to Highway 21 anyway on the chance that he'd see lights in their window.

The shrine was brightly lit as usual, and he found it comforting, as if its message was meant for him. But recalling Miss Tokay's ideas about the Sky People and their choosiness, his comfort left him. He told himself that since he wasn't ready to ascend, maybe their disinterest was for the best. He drove farther, slowing down by the big signaling hand. The lights were out, and he kept on driving.

After he got home, he debated for fifteen minutes whether or not to call Maggie, worrying that he'd wake her up, or worse, get an awakened or drunken Josie on the phone. He decided he needed to be a man about it and made the call. The phone rang and rang but no one picked up, and he cursed the fact that they were either too poor or too cheap to have an answering machine.

. . .

He slept a little but was awake by six. He lay in bed, trying to return to sleep, but the sun was so strong that it seemed to have incorporated itself into the very walls of his bedroom, and the crows and mockingbirds and blue jays outside his window were screaming at one another. He thought, I hate the South, I hate the daytime, I hate nature. Then he remembered Maggie in the rain and the ball lightning, and thought, No, I hate insomnia. He kicked off the covers, knowing that he would not sleep again that day.

In the kitchen, he stared at the phone, he stared at the coffeemaker. He used the latter, wondering if he drank too much coffee, knowing that of course he did. He'd tried alcohol, but that didn't help at all, and not only because of the incessant need to urinate every hour on the hour after a binge. He'd tried sleeping pills after Lawrence had died, but the hangover they gave him was worse than that from beer, and the sleep somehow even more poisonous, making his waking hours so much more depressed that it scared him. His experience with antidepressants had been worse. At least chronic insomnia means that I probably won't die in my sleep, he thought, then realized that that was what most people wanted, to simply go to sleep and not have to think about what was happening to you as all systems shut down and your heart went *pitter-pat* and then still. He imagined gasping for his last breath while being wide awake, feeling every organ grind to a squishy, disgusting halt. Then he thought, I wonder how Emily Ziegart killed herself.

He went online and wasn't surprised when his search produced no results. He thought about how to try to find out but realized he didn't know her maiden name, didn't know which state she'd moved to and died in, much less what town. He didn't even know in what month or year she died. Death records were public, but you needed a place to start. The more he thought about it, the more he realized that it probably didn't matter anyway. Charlie Ziegart was certainly everywhere in the information world; you'd think his widow would be as well if she'd died in a way that the media found interesting.

Then he did an image search on Emily Ziegart. The results showed the same three pictures of Charlie that he'd come across before: the first and most common an improbably handsome head shot; the second, Charlie at a lectern, smiling and making a sweeping gesture with his right hand; and last, Charlie in a cap and gown, solemnly accepting the Presnell Award on a curtained stage. There were no pictures listed of wives, or of Charlie's son, Jonathan. Then Harry typed his own name into the white bar under "Image Search." He enlarged the first entry, a grainy head shot that made him look a lot less intelligent than Charlie Ziegart, still available in cached newspaper archives. There was another Harry Sterling in Miami who made a living selling real estate, and who had pictures of himself splattered all over the World Wide Web. But of himself, reporter and now professor Harry Sterling, there were no other images available online. There were none of Ann either, or of Dusty.

He waited until eight o'clock, then called Maggie. When he got no answer, he drove out to her house again. Both cars were in front of the double-wide, and Miss Baby and Josie were sitting on the porch, drinking coffee.

"Well, what in the name of the sons of the pioneers are you doin' here?" said Miss Baby, her face almost happy to see him. Josie's was not. She looked a good deal older this morning than she had the first time he'd talked to her on the porch. Miss Baby answered herself. "You've come to see Maggie, ain't you?" She laughed and laughed, but Josie didn't join in. Miss Baby added, "Josie's giving you the stink eye. You screwed up my mini-vacation, boy. The grandgirls were with 'em at that beach house of yours, and I had a date. I was pretty pissed at you, you know that? I haven't had the house to my-self in thirty years." She didn't look mad at him, but Josie did, star-ing at him with her big decorated eyes, the color of angry mud.

"I'm sorry, Josie," he said. "Miss Baby, my apologies to you as well. It was a misunderstanding."

"I know what kind of misunderstanding," Miss Baby said, appar-ently having been designated the mouthpiece for the morning. "A little inconvenience with the wife. It takes all kind of balls for you to be here this mornin'. But Maggie's gone, so you wasted your trip, unless you're here to kiss our ancient asses."

Harry suspected that Josie didn't like having her ass called an-cient, but all she did was stare at him. He wondered if she were sober. He opened his arms wide and said, "What can I do to make it up to you ladies?" He put his arms down and his hands into his pockets. "I checked the rental schedule for the house before I came. It's free three weekends from now. You want to try it again? I promise I'll make sure it's all yours." He looked at Miss Baby. "You can go on that date. Although you're making me jealous."

That always worked in fiction, he thought; a younger man flirt-ing with an older woman always made her feel good, a nice pleasant joke. Miss Baby curled her lip and said, "You ain't good-lookin' enough for me, white boy. If you think I'm gonna get all gooey and giggle at you for pretendin' to flirt with me, you're as stupid as you are ugly." Harry realized belatedly that Miss Baby was just as angry with him as Josie was.

"I told you to leave Maggie alone," said Josie in a terrible flat voice. "I told you. I know people, you know. I could have you killed." Her words were just the slightest bit slurry, but Harry still believed her. "All southern boys have shotguns. Accidents happen." She sat up straighter and said, "Like Baby told you, Maggie's not here and she won't be back for a while. She's got better things to do than wait around for some Yankee married boy to talk shit to her and try to get in her pants and then leave for his goddamned skinny wife-bitch."

Even Miss Baby looked a little uncomfortable at this unpleasant speech. Harry was openmouthed; nothing would come out. He turned, got back into his car, and left.

Miss Baby said, "Who do you know that kills people 'cause you want them to? It ain't your boyfriends. Pair of pussies."

"Nobody," said Josie, "but I hope it scared the shit out of him."

"That's always good," said Miss Baby.

Harry parked at the cemetery lot and stood among the graves, calling Maggie's name. He saw a pair of joggers heading for the trail into the park and an old woman with a small dog standing over a grave at the farthest line of headstones. He walked for a while in the cemetery, reading names and epitaphs. He came to one that he recognized: Duncan Dupree, beloved husband and father. He'd died at the age of fifty-three. The headstone was small and rounded, like an open clamshell, and there was a vase next to it filled with dead daisies. He tried to feel less hostile to Josie but didn't succeed.

He thought about walking farther, but his energy was flagging; he hadn't had any breakfast and he was hungry and it was very hot. He needed a shower and food. He stopped at Crane's, and Shawntelle barked her horsey laugh at him, telling him that the "crazy cook" wasn't there. Harry didn't know if it was better to be thought of as insane or retarded by the likes of Shawntelle.

He decided to go home, but as he neared the strip mall with the Laundromat, he slowed and pulled into a parking space in front of it. He got out of the car and peered through the glass window. She wasn't there either.

29

NINE OF WANDS

*Temporary cease-fire,
but the war isn't over*

Harry stewed at home for half an hour, then drove to the tiny store where he'd purchased his cell phone the year before. After waiting for forty-five minutes for a bored clerk to help him, he explained the problem with the phone's battery. The clerk stared at him with contempt and said, "It's over a year old. You can't get those batteries anymore." Harry didn't say anything, but something in his face must have alarmed the young man, because he added, "But we might have a recycled one in the back."

Harry gave a smile the clerk also didn't seem to like and said, "Why don't you check?"

After putting the semi-new battery in his phone, he spent the rest of the afternoon with Serge at the university swimming pool; he recognized that he was sulking, but he thought, I can't apologize to someone who won't let me. If I could talk to her, I'd invite her to come here, and I'd get to see her in a bathing suit, wet and happy and cool. It wasn't the beach, though, so maybe she wouldn't like the chlorine and the concrete. He thought, I should know that about her.

Serge asked him about his research, and Harry told him what he'd learned about Charles and Emily Ziegart. "I don't know why I can't let it go. I doubt there's anything to it that you could hang a book on. It keeps scraping around inside my head."

They were sitting in ribbed plastic chairs under a large green umbrella. The pool lay in shimmery blue splendor before them. The summer session had started, so there were a few students in the water, their young skin tan and taut. Harry thought, I was never that taut. But he could swim farther than he had when he was in his twenties, and had done laps today. His body felt better, even if his soul still felt heavy and loose.

Serge said, "Then keep going. Maybe your instincts are telling you something your conscious mind just doesn't know yet. You know"—Serge turned toward Harry; his sunglasses were dark, so it was impossible to tell for sure if he was looking Harry in the face—"Amelia says you're getting better looking as you get older. She's pissed, actually, since she says that's the way for men and not for women. You've lost weight. You're not sick, are you?"

"I love you, too, Sergei. So your wife thinks I'm handsome, eh?"

"No. Just less ugly than you used to be." Serge turned back to contemplating the pool and the young women around it. "Did you know that this Friday is Stoweville's sesquicentennial?"

"Its what?"

"It's been around for a hundred and fifty years. There are going to be fireworks."

"Yay."

"They launch them from Lake Austell."

"That's great."

"You can see them really well from our back patio."

"You're very fortunate."

"We're having a party."

"Yippee."

"You're invited."

"Oh, God, Sergei. I hate parties."

"You don't have to drink."

"Great. That makes the whole idea of a party so much more exciting."

"What about Maggie?" Serge said.

Harry was silent.

"I want to meet her."

"Why?"

"Because. Are you dating this woman?"

"No."

"Oh. I thought you were. You've been so squirrelly about the whole thing, I thought sex had to be involved."

"It's not."

"Oh. I see. She's just a waitress."

"She's not a waitress."

"She works at a restaurant."

"Yes. She cooks."

"Okay, well, that's what's important, I suppose." Serge drank from his water bottle. "How about Julie Canfield?"

"Jesus Christ, Serge, why are you being such a matchmaker? Are you really worried that I'm going to run off with Amelia?"

"No, I'm worried that you're going to run off with your ex-wife."

Harry felt the shock of this settle on him for a moment before he said, "I doubt that she's really interested."

"Are you?"

"No. But you know, there's something still there. Like a taste you can't get out of your mouth. Not even a good taste. But a familiar one."

"Lovely," said Serge. "Continuing with this disgusting metaphor, I had the impression that Maggie was being a sort of mouthwash. I'm done with this, by the way. Come up with some other image for me. Please."

"Serge, she's, like, twenty-five. I don't want to be in charge like that. You know what I mean; the big educated man taking on the unsophisticated woman and being her mentor into the big complicated world."

"My God, I had no idea you were such a snob. Egotistical, too."

"That's the whole point. I don't want to be Judd Lippman."

"I hope not. Judd Lippman is an arrested adolescent with power issues. I guess that leaves Julie Canfield out, too."

"Thank God."

"Come to the party anyway. Hey, you could bring Maggie, not as a date but as a way to introduce her to your terribly sophisticated friends."

"Hay is for horses. I don't have any sophisticated friends."

"Well then, according to you, she should fit right in."

Darcy Murphy hadn't been in to work in a week. The Little Shit had called him three times, pretending to be concerned for Darcy's health but really more worried about the backlog of work that was piling up on his desk. See, thought Darcy, I'm worth three of you, but that didn't help his headaches and his increasingly frequent panic attacks.

He got up at six, then at nine, and again at ten, trying to sleep, then trying not to when he dreamed of snakes and explosions. The Little Shit called him at eleven; at first Darcy thought he was going to whine again about trying to get him back on schedule. But instead, he told him that Darcy's cousin from up north had called the office and asked for his home number. The Little Shit hadn't given it to him but had taken the message because the cousin said the matter was urgent. Darcy was about to tell the Little Shit that he didn't have any such cousin when his supervisor said, "He said something about an inheritance and he had to talk to you right away. You need to tell him that work isn't the place to conduct personal business."

Darcy took the number down and was about to hang up on his boss when the younger man went on, "You're popular these days. I forgot to tell you that last week I got a call from a prospective buyer for one of your properties. Seems they'd heard there were some concerns about the power configuration of the place and they wanted to talk to the inspector in charge. I gave them your name but said they'd have to wait till you were in the office to talk to you. It was that place out on Highway 21. I guess the owners are moving." He laughed, something the Little Shit would never have done if Darcy had been standing in front of him. "I guess you'll sleep better after they're gone, eh?" Darcy slammed down the phone.

He looked at the number of his "cousin," assuming it was some sort of scam, but he was smart enough not to give anyone any money, and there was always the possibility of something real happening, one break in his sorry life. He dialed the number and was shocked to find himself talking to an agent of the Federal Bureau of Investigation.

On Tuesday morning, Harry waited until eight-thirty, then called Gillian DeGraff again. It took three times before he finally reached her.

"I thought we were done, Mr. Sterling. I've told you all I can about Charlie Ziegart. Anything else you need to know is a matter of public record."

"Actually, I was hoping that you could tell me more about Emily Ziegart."

"I believe I told you that I didn't know her very well."

"I was hoping you could give me some names of people who did."

"I don't have any names for you, Mr. Sterling. She kept to herself. She wasn't very interested in befriending anyone who couldn't help her career."

"It seems to me that there were lots of people there who could have helped her career. I don't know what good it would have done her to be standoffish with any of them, especially you."

"I couldn't tell you, Mr. Sterling. It wasn't so much that she was standoffish as it was that she was . . . a little off. She had a lot of crackpot ideas, most of which weren't practicable at all. Charlie indulged her, but he was just that kind of man. Maybe she had a personality disorder or some other problem, and just didn't know how to get along. I have no idea. But I've told you everything I—"

"What crackpot ideas?"

A long-suffering sigh. "Free electricity, for starters."

"Free? As in, you don't have to pay a utility company?"

"Yes. It isn't even an original idea. Some famous scientist from way back when was her idol. His name escapes me now."

"Not Edison?"

"No. Someone crazy."

"Nikola Tesla?"

"That's it. She claimed that he'd already done it, using the earth as a conductor or some such thing. It's all she ever talked about. It annoyed everyone."

"What was wrong with the idea?"

"Good Lord, isn't it obvious? It was totally impractical."

"Do you know how she killed herself, or where?"

"No, but I don't think I'd discuss that with you in any case."

Harry decided to swerve his line of questioning again. He liked flustering Gillian DeGraff. "What was her maiden name?"

A pause. "I don't remember. Isn't that funny, how things slip your mind?"

"You can't remember her name?"

"No, I'm sorry."

"Who wrote her letters?"

"What?"

"Her letters of recommendation. From her college."

"What?"

"You know. College. Where you go before you can go to grad school. She must have had letters, test scores, transcripts, all that kind of thing, with her application. I assume you keep files of previous students."

Silence, then, "Mr. Sterling, do you have any idea how many students have passed through this school?"

"I imagine you must store the records for a variety of reasons. It can't be that hard to find the file. Unless your record keeping is unbelievably sloppy."

He could almost hear the hissing sound of air through flared nostrils and pursed lips. "That information is confidential anyway."

"For someone who's deceased?"

"I don't see why we should flout confidentiality for somebody who appears to be interested in smearing Charlie Ziegart. His second wife wasn't worth the effort you're putting into her, Mr. Sterling. You'd be much better served talking to Pamela."

"I intend to. Since you won't let me see Emily's file, will you at least tell me where she did her undergraduate work?"

"I don't remember."

"Not Cantwell?"

"No."

"A state? A part of the country?"

"I have no recollection, if I ever knew."

"Do you know how old she was?"

"What?"

"Her age. You know. The number of years she'd been alive before she died. Was she a normal-aged student? Or was she inordinately young, a child prodigy or something?"

"Goodness, no. I believe she came to Cantwell directly after college, but she was the typical age, twenty-something, when she arrived. I can't be exact. I never threw her a birthday party." Before Harry could ask another question, she added, "We're done, Mr. Sterling. Good-bye, and don't call me again."

Harry hung up after she did and scribbled more on his pad, adding to his notes everything he hadn't had time to write while he was talking. Unbeknownst to Gillian DeGraff, he'd recorded the call, which was illegal but nonetheless helpful when he looked at his notes later, trying to recall tone of voice and other nuances that he might have missed while scribbling notes. For ten minutes he wrote, then paused, his hand over his mouth, his thumb supporting his chin as he looked out his dining room window at the backyard, a slender red maple bent in the middle as though it was leaning back to look at the sky. The phone rang, startling Harry; he picked it up, thinking it might be Dusty. It was a hoarse female voice that he didn't immediately recognize but knew given some time he would.

"Mr. Sterling?"

"Yes."

"Grenier."

"What?"

"Grenier. That was Emily's college."

Now he knew who the smoky voice belonged to: Louise Glade, the administrative assistant in Ziegart's department at Cantwell.

"Ms. Glade?"

"I'm not giving away state secrets, although you'd think I was. I'm calling from my cell phone. I'm in the bathroom. Gillian just came into the office screaming bloody murder about your nosiness.

You're supposed to protect the confidentiality of your sources, right? I don't want to lose my job."

"You mean Grenier University in Virginia?"

"Uh-huh." He heard the click of a cigarette lighter and a faint intake of breath. Smoking in the girls' room.

"Thank you for the information. Why are you telling me this?"

"Because Emily got screwed over. And now she's dead, and they've been slandering her ever since Charlie died, and she can't defend herself, and that's just wrong."

"Do you know anything else? Her maiden name? Where she was from?"

"She was Emily Timms. From some southern town."

"Not in Florida?" Harry had a little thrill down his spine.

"No. Alabama. I'm pretty sure. I'd have remembered Florida." The thrill went away. But he thought, I've got to grill Josie.

"Any family? Anybody I could talk to?"

"She had a sister, because that's who wrote to me to tell me that Emily had killed herself. The sister lived out west. Denver was where she wrote from."

"Do you remember her name or anything else about her?"

"No. I'm sorry. Emily didn't talk much about her home."

"What else can you tell me?"

"She was a truly kind person. I'm Jewish, and she got me Hanukkah cards and always remembered my birthday. She watched the phones for me a few times. Let me tell you, nobody else here would ever have done that. Pamela Ziegart is a bitch. You won't hear that from anyone but me, but it's true."

"Ms. Glade, do you have a photograph of Emily?"

"You want to know what she looked like?"

"Yes. Is there one?"

"This isn't a high school, Mr. Sterling. We don't have a yearbook." Breath blowing smoke. "I could send you a JPEG of the last group shot with Charlie at the DeGraffs'. She was in that one." Harry thanked her and gave her his e-mail address. She continued, "I probably won't call you again. Gillian's pretty mad at you and I don't want her mad at me." Before she said good-bye, Harry heard the cigarette lighter click again. Louise Glade was breaking more than one rule at Cantwell University.

30

KNIGHT OF
CUPS

REVERSED

*A young man who is
not what he seems*

Harry went for a long walk in his neighborhood again, the weather being fine, hot but clear; the dry air felt as if it was tightening and refreshing his skin. When he got back to his house, he poured himself a tall glass of iced tea and sat down at his computer. To his surprise, there was already a message from Louise Glade. The text was far shorter than the banner above it: "Found it. Emily's left of Charlie." He opened the attachment with a curious excitement, and as he waited for it to appear on the monitor, he imagined the smell of stale cigarettes traveling from Louise's undoubtedly tar-stained fingers through the wires and misting up at him around the keys.

The picture had been taken outdoors; the sun must have been behind the photographer, since almost everyone in the well-dressed group was wincing blindly. Charlie Ziegart was at the center of a group of fifteen people. Harry would have had no trouble finding Emily, even if Louise's directions had been ambiguous; to the right of Charlie was a grinning boy that Harry could see was the adolescent version of Jonathan. The grin was too wide, and Harry couldn't imagine Dusty ever giving the camera the gift of such open glee.

Emily Ziegart was a head shorter than her husband, and was the only member of the party not smiling. She was also the only one not directly facing the camera; instead, she was angled a quarter turn toward her husband, giving the impression of movement. Her eyes hadn't reached his face yet when the shutter had clicked. The couple weren't touching, but her hands were lifting, as though she was about to take his arm, but like her gaze, her hands hadn't yet made contact. Her face was small enough relative to the rest of the scene that he doubted he'd recognize her in another picture if he came across one, but it was enough to get a sense of her. She was altogether rounded and soft-looking, her hair long and straight, some vague light color. She was dressed in brown trousers that were too tight and a wrinkled matching jacket buttoned up to her breasts that sat too wide on her shoulders. Her posture was rounded, too, giving her an air of weakness mixed with anxiety that was hard to look at for long. He examined her face more closely. Round cheeks and a small mouth, dark eyes in shadow. Harry thought, She doesn't look like a genius.

His eyes wandered back to Jonathan, and it was only then that he noticed the boy's hands, clasped at crotch level. The left hand was underneath the right, and Harry rolled his chair back, then pulled himself closer to the desk again, staring at the screen from different angles. But after his eyes had recognized the images for what they were, there was no unseeing them; Jonathan's left hand was giving either his father, his stepmother, or both the finger.

Harry blessed the Internet when he found the main number for the physics department at Grenier University through the school's home page. His call was answered by another female administrative assistant, causing him to wonder at the persistence of certain gender roles in the labor market. He'd never once seen a male secretary at a university. There must be some, he figured, but it was apparently like male nurses or male bank tellers; they existed, but in such small numbers that encountering one was cause for raised eyebrows and bemused shrugs. He identified himself and asked if he could speak to the chair or some other senior member of the faculty. The phone went silent and he was about to hang up, assuming that he'd been cut off, when a man's voice broke the silence by saying, "I'm here."

"This is Harry Sterling. Who am I speaking to?"

"Did Samantha put you through without telling you who you were going to talk to? She always does that, and it's mighty annoying. She doesn't screen my incoming calls either, and if I could fire her, I would."

"It's okay," said Harry, worried that complaint on his part might result in Samantha's fourteen children going without food or health insurance. "And you are?"

"Cameron Jenner. I'm the chair. Harry Sterling? Name means nothing to me."

Harry went through his identification spiel again, explaining that he was doing a book on Charles Ziegart. "I understand that his second wife, Emily Timms, did her undergraduate work there. I was wondering if I could speak to someone who knew her or, better yet, worked with her."

"Ernie Thornburg was her adviser, but he died a couple of years ago. She took some classes from me. I wrote her a letter for grad school."

Eureka. "Would you mind telling me about her? Whatever you remember?"

"She was memorable. And of course, with all the tragedy that happened later, that made her even more so."

"You're referring to her suicide, I suppose?"

"That, and Charlie Ziegart's accident. And what happened to her career in general."

"Which was?"

"All I know is that, after she went to Cantwell, we never heard much about her again. I expected her to get her Ph.D. in four years and to be out winning Nobel Prizes in six. But she went to graduate school and fell into a black hole. She married Ziegart, but it didn't seem to do her any good. Shame."

"She was a good student?"

"She was the smartest student I've ever had. She had a fantastic intuitive grasp of theory, but she was more of an engineer than a theoretician. She could take one look at a problem and within a few days have a practical answer."

"Did you know that her name was on the original Ziegart effect paper?"

"I heard that. I expect his ego won out in the end, though. He wasn't a big one for sharing credit, from what I understand."

"You wrote a letter for her?"

"Yes. I couldn't say enough about her, since she was as promising a student as I'd ever seen, and had no money to speak of, so it was important that someone give her a full scholarship, stipend, and so on. She got offered a spot everywhere she applied. I expected her to go to MIT or Berkeley or to one of the Ivy Leagues. But Cantwell wanted her something fierce, and showered her with money and a chance to work with Charlie Ziegart. They wooed her in a way that even MIT didn't. So that's where she wound up."

"Do you think that was a bad idea? For her, I mean?"

"In hindsight, it sure seems that way. It's not easy for a woman in the hard sciences, even today. But if she takes the MRS track, that often makes it harder."

"The what?"

"You know. Getting married. MRS."

"Oh," said Harry as Jenner laughed. "What do you know about Ziegart's death?"

"Car accident. Something about a bee."

"Did she have any contact with you, or anyone else at Grenier, after she went to Cantwell? Or after she left there?"

"Not that I'm aware of. She just disappeared. She didn't seem particularly stuck up when she was here, but she shed us like an old snakeskin once she married Ziegart." Harry asked again about personal information, specifically a hometown. "I don't know. Somewhere further south. Georgia or Alabama."

"Would you be willing to fax me copies of some of the documents in Emily's file? High school transcripts, application, that sort of thing?"

"I don't know that that's strictly legal. If Samantha can find it, I guess you could look at it. But only in person."

Harry sighed. "I think I'll be making a trip up there soon. My next question is a little delicate, but I have to ask. I've heard a few rumors that Charlie Ziegart was known to use his graduate students' work and pass it off as his own. It sounds like that might have happened with Emily. Do you know anything about that?"

A pause. "You've probably been told that it's rarely that simple. I'm sure Charlie got his students to work on his projects; that's the whole point of graduate school. His students were using his grant money, his equipment, his expertise, his supervision, his general concepts, his suggestions for experiments. So the results should have been his by rights."

"No rumors of overdoing it?"

"I'm not comfortable with this conversation. There's nothing I can tell you that will help you, although I'm not clear what you're looking for anyway. I thought you said you were doing a biography on Charlie Ziegart. It sounds like you're after him, which is pretty shitty of you, if you don't mind my saying so."

"I'm not after anybody. I'm doing a book on intellectual property. Charlie Ziegart's name came up, and I got interested in his methods. And, to an extent, his wife."

"Well, I've told you all I know. If you want to pay us a visit, Samantha can help you out with the file."

"I've been told that Emily had some unpopular ideas about electricity."

Jenner laughed. "The Tesla stuff. That was something she came to her senior year. Undifferentiated transmission of electricity."

"What was wrong with the idea?"

"Well, she thought it should be free, like oxygen. But someone still had to pay for the infrastructure. Have you heard of Nikola Tesla?"

"Yes. He was the real inventor of AC power and radio. Edison and Marconi essentially stole all the credit."

"That's good. Not many people know about him, even though he invented most of the technology we use today before everyone else could catch up. Emily had a bit of an obsession with Tesla's work. He built an enormous tower whose purpose was to broadcast electricity to anyone who wanted it. He'd developed a cheap and efficient way to do it, too. But the infrastructure was gargantuan, and no one wanted to pay for it and get no profits."

"But Emily wanted to revive the idea?"

"She did revive it. A lot of Tesla's data was lost after he died, and how he managed to generate all that power isn't well understood. Emily figured out how he did it, or claimed she did. She'd talk about it with anyone who'd listen. But there was no point, really. No one was going to fund building anything like that."

"Poor doomed girl," Harry said before he could stop himself.

"Well, yes. I guess that's a poetic way of putting it. She was an oddball in all sorts of ways. When she first got here, she was interested in testing some psychic phenomena, a notion from which she was disabused pretty quickly. If her scores hadn't been through the roof, we'd have kicked her out, but it all worked out in the end."

Not for her, Harry thought. Psychic phenomena. Josie had to have known her. He thought, Maybe she doesn't remember. It's possible, it was years ago, and Josie's a drunk. Maybe she liked her and has blocked all memory of Emily because it's all so sad. But the fact that everyone in Josie's neighborhood had solar panels on their homes couldn't possibly be a coincidence. He had that prickling feeling again. He wrote on his pad "Talk to Josie" in large block letters. "What do you mean, it all worked out?"

"Her college career. It was remarkably successful. She was incredibly productive, published a number of papers. I don't remember how many, but on at least two of them, she was the sole author. That's pretty amazing for an undergraduate."

Josie was about to lie down for a nap when there was a knock at the front door. A handsome young man with a clipboard stood on the porch. He smiled when she asked him what he wanted and said, "Another inspector from the power company, I'm afraid."

She wondered why he was in a suit, then thought, This one's higher up than Darcy Murphy. Fear lanced through her. Not police? No, from the power company, he said. She wished she hadn't had so much to drink. She couldn't think properly, couldn't read him clearly, and knew that she needed to.

"Not again," she said, trying to adopt her usual annoyed tone. "What do we need to do to convince you folks that we're not stealing anything?"

He smiled wider. "I know it's a nuisance. But it's just a matter of paperwork. Do you mind if I have a look around? Inspector Murphy did a thorough job, I'm sure, but I'm one of his supervisors and he's up for review, and I need to double-check his work. Nothing to be alarmed about."

She could make out some colors, a sickly brownish orange shot through with streaks of dark red. His aura looks bloody, she thought. I'm glad I'm not his wife. She said, "I guess you can look around, but you're the fourth one to do that. I can't imagine what you're looking for that your other people haven't already seen."

The new inspector said, "Nice solar panels you have on your roof." He pointed upward with his pen. "How long have you had them?"

"It should be in your paperwork, honey. A few years, I don't remember exactly how long. Since you can see 'em so clearly, it should be obvious to you how we're getting our power. They call it the Sunshine State, remember?" Maggie was always telling her that she should be nicer to these men. After all, she thought, he's good-looking, even if he does look like he's fifteen years old.

"Yes, ma'am," he said. "That it is." At least he's more polite than the last one, she thought, then remembered why she should be afraid of that thought.

"Okay, then," she said. "Look around all you want. But then leave us alone." She shut the door on him, unplugged the phone, lay down on the couch, and closed her eyes, her heart pounding with fear.

31

THE
HIGH PRIESTESS

*The Seeker should
keep her mouth shut*

Harry spent the rest of the morning looking at whatever he could find under the
name Emily Timms on the Internet. He
ran a search of all the obituaries in newspaper archives in the greater Denver area
for the last eight years. No mention of
either Emily Ziegart or Emily Timms, but
that meant nothing. He didn't know that
she'd died there, only that that was where
her sister had lived. A general search
found seven papers in various bibliogra-
phies and collections with her name as
one of the authors. Two of them, as Cameron Jenner had said, had
her name alone. All this, Harry thought, before she was twenty-two.
The titles were meaningless to him, things like "Magnetic Field Cal-
culation in Laser Doppler Vibrometry," but he got the general idea.
Hers was a mind on fire. He looked at his note to himself: "Talk to
Josie." He called the trailer but, as usual, got no answer.

Harry went to lunch at Crane's. He arrived before one o'clock,
not wanting to be thwarted at the cemetery. Shawntelle waited on

him with a smirk, while Dottie gave him disapproving looks from across the restaurant. Harry wondered again what they thought of him, feeling old and embarrassed. But he lingered over his sandwich, waiting for her to emerge from the kitchen.

She came out on schedule, and he felt his stomach tighten as he waited for her to spot him. He couldn't decide on an appropriate expression; he tried smiling but had a feeling that it wasn't sitting right on his face, so he tried to make it blank, but that felt wrong as well. He wasn't sure what his face was doing when she turned and saw him, her own looking mostly surprised. No one had alerted her that he was there; he had no idea what that meant. She said a brief something to Calvin Crane, then walked to his booth.

"Hey," she said.

"Hey yourself," he said, smiling now for real, no longer caring what his face looked like. "Can you sit for a little while?"

"Sure." She sat down.

"Do you ever actually eat here? The food's pretty good. Can I treat you to lunch?"

"No thanks. I had something. I eat for free."

"Oh. I was pretty much done, so it's just as well. Not everyone likes to have people watch them eat anyway." Get to the point, the judge said, so Harry went on, "I'm sorry, Maggie. About the beach house and everything." Her face didn't change, and he said, "She wasn't supposed to be there. Are you angry? I can never tell with you."

She smiled then, so sweetly that he felt his stomach loosen and his breath shorten. He could see the smudges under her eyes, darker than they'd been the last time he'd seen her. She wasn't sleeping much either. "I'm not mad," she said.

"Thank God," he said and smiled back.

"I'm going for a walk," she said. "If you want to come."

.   .   .

"I've been kind of a schmuck. I have more to apologize for than for the beach house," he said.

"It's okay," she said, looking out from under the hat into the shadows under the live oaks.

"No, it's not okay. I got to see ball lightning. Or I think I did. I didn't behave very well after that, though."

"It's okay," she repeated, stopping and squatting on the ground. She was examining a pile of red sand on her side of the trail. "Fire ants. They're everywhere. People pour all sorts of chemicals on them to kill them. But they're just trying to find a safe place to keep their eggs."

Harry looked down at the top of her head, obscured by the broad hat. "Don't they sting?"

The hat spoke. "Yes, but it's not that bad. Little bumps that itch at lot. But they go away in a day or two." She stood up. "I left my foot in an anthill once for about five minutes, just to see how bad it would be. I didn't enjoy it, but it's not like it did anything permanent. People expect the world to only feel good. They'll burn anything up that discommodes them." She walked forward even as she turned to look at him. "Just don't kiss me unless you mean it," she said and then continued on toward the bridge. Harry followed her.

"Tell me about the solar panels," he said.

"What about them?"

"Don't be coy. Someone around here knew Emily Ziegart."

"I don't know anyone by that name."

"Emily Timms, then."

She shook her head. "No."

"Where did your cousin Dee die?"

"Baton Rouge. Four years ago."

Probably too recent, he thought, although the dates were unclear. He said, "She was an only child? No half sibs or anything like that?"

"No."

"What was her middle name?"

"Dee wasn't a scientist, Harry." She sounded impatient. "She was never married to a scientist either."

"What was her middle name?" he repeated.

"Jane. Delores Jane Dupree. From her birth to her death it was never anything else."

"You said Miss Tokay gave everyone the solar panels."

Maggie smiled. "Her first name is Edith. I don't know her middle name."

"She's too old anyway. She has a niece, the one married to the objectionable developer. What's her name?"

Maggie looked at him for a while, the smile blooming larger. "Gretchen." She started laughing, and Harry found himself joining her.

"I know I sound obsessed," he said. "I haven't had a lot of sleep. But I know she had something to do with the solar panels. I bet Miss Tokay knew her. Maybe she was a follower."

Maggie's smile drifted away with the hot breeze that carried a red-tailed hawk high above them, its wide wings not moving. She watched it as she said, "Miss Tokay hasn't had a follower in over twenty years."

"She never had kids? No grandchildren tucked away anywhere?"

Maggie's eyes shifted to his again. "Not that I know of."

"When did everyone get them? The panels, I mean."

Maggie looked for the hawk again, thinking. "A little bit before Dee died. Maybe five years ago. At least, that's when the first ones went up."

"I'll need to speak to Miss Tokay again."

"You won't find out anything. I told you, Harry, she'll consider it terrible manners if you ask her if she spent a lot of money on her neighbors."

"I don't care. I'm in the grip of this thing. I feel like the only defender of Emily Ziegart. Emily Timms. I have an image in my head of her dying alone and bereft. I've dreamed about her." He wished he hadn't admitted the last part.

" 'You become responsible, forever, for what you have tamed,' " Maggie said.

"What? Is that a quote?"

"Never mind," she said. "It doesn't really fit anyway." She turned away from him and walked toward the bridge. He followed her. Once on the bridge, they both stopped to look at the water. After a few minutes of comfortable silence, he asked her if she would go to Serge's party. "There'll be fireworks."

She turned from her contemplation of the lily pads and said, "You know I'm not very good with new people. I . . . Thanks, Harry, but I don't think it would go well."

"Please."

She looked at him for a long time, her eyes shielded by the brim of her hat.

"Please," he repeated. Sweat was running freely down his back now. After a minute she finally said, "Okay."

He drove behind her to the double-wide. He wanted to interrogate Josie, even though the idea obviously made Maggie unhappy. He walked with her into the trailer after their cars were parked in the oyster-shell driveway. Josie was asleep on the couch, her billowy dress in disarray around her, her mouth open. Her snores were regular and almost musical, and under other circumstances Harry would not have dreamed of waking her. Maggie stayed him with a movement of her hand, then gently shook her aunt's shoulder.

Josie woke with a loud snort, sitting up so rapidly that she almost fell to the floor. She saw Harry first, standing at the foot of the couch, and she recoiled as though he had a weapon. Maggie said, "It's all right, Josie. He just wants to talk to you. I'll make you some tea." The smell of rum hung in the air faintly, like flowers.

Maggie went to make tea, and Josie wiped her hand over her face as though there was a film on it. She said, "Do you want a reading, or what? I'm not in the mood. Even you need to make an appointment."

"No," he said. "I don't want a reading."

He waited while Maggie got mugs and tea bags ready in the kitchen. Josie sat on the couch, not moving, breathing a little heavily, staring beyond Harry in a way that he was getting used to. After a moment, the kettle whistled and Maggie brought Josie a mug of tea thick with milk. Maggie nodded at Harry, and he said, "I know you knew Emily Ziegart, Emily Timms. I know that's who put up the solar panels or at least who made them. I want you to tell me everything you know about her."

"Who?" Josie said, but Harry could tell she was pretending. She tried to meet his eyes, but hers kept moving to the carpet, to the desk that held the big cards, to something outside the window.

"You know who. What's the big secret? She wasn't a criminal, was she? Why hide the fact that you knew her?" He took a breath and waited.

Josie sagged a little then, sinking farther into the couch, as though she were going to fall into the springs. She said, "She was so sad, it broke your heart to look at her. She came to get a reading from me, only once. Just the one time. Emily." She moved on the couch, wiped her face again, drank some tea. Her hands were shaking. "Saddest girl you ever saw," she repeated. "I didn't know her. I never knew her." She started crying. "Those damn panels. Brought us nothing but trouble. An ill wind. But blew no good at all." She started crying harder. "Leave me alone. She's dead. Dead, dead, dead." Maggie was at her side, an arm around Josie's soft shoulders. Josie turned bloodshot eyes to her and said, "I'm so sorry I'm drunk, honey. I promise I'll stop, I promise. I'll promise you anything if you make him go away." Maggie continued to soothe her, a ritual that Harry thought was probably a familiar one to both of them.

Maggie put Josie to bed. When she returned to the living room, her face was so pale he was afraid she was going to faint. She said, "I've never heard any of that before. I don't know where it came from."

"Did Emily have something to do with Miss Tokay? She must have."

"Not that I know of."

"I'm going to talk to her, Maggie."

She nodded, then said, "I've got to stay here. I'm not going with you this time."

32

THE
HANGED MAN

*Taking time to
think things through.
A sage, a prophecy*

Frank Milford had introduced Jonathan Ziegart to the sheriff over the phone. "He's the son of a famous scientist. He was hoping you could give him a tour." Milford's wife was the sheriff's wife's gynecologist. The sheriff agreed, although without much enthusiasm.

Now Jonathan had come to collect on the promise. The sheriff showed him the holding cells and the desks of his deputies. The receptionist, a pretty woman of about thirty named Serena, offered to take over when the sheriff was called away to the demands of his office phone. Jonathan joked with her about the possibility of them "accidentally" being locked in a cell together for a few hours, making her blush and giggle annoyingly until he was rescued by the sheriff's lieutenant deputy. He was a man only a few years older than Jonathan himself named Faber, with sandy hair and a regulation mustache.

As Faber led him through the labs and evidence room, Jonathan told him that he was studying to be a forensic anthropologist. Faber said, "There's a fellow over to the college that we use when a hunter stumbles on some bones in the woods. Happened once a few years ago. There were only a few of 'em, and no one could tell if they were human or somethin' else."

"What else would they be?"

Faber shrugged. "Only had a few ribs and some bits. Turned out they were deer bones."

"Ah," Jonathan said.

"Once, over to the hospital, they found a baby in the laundry. Dried up. Parts missing. Couldn't tell that one either."

"The parents must have been upset."

"Well, no. Turned out to be a monkey. Some doctor had one pickled in a jar. The cleaning crew broke it and dint tell nobody. It was in the papers for weeks." Faber scratched his head. "The doctor was pretty bent out of shape, though." Faber regarded his fingernails and the detritus from his own scalp. "But bits of people are always found in the sinks."

"The what?"

Faber described sinkholes to Jonathan. "People are always dumpin' stuff in 'em. Car batteries, old tires, even appliances sometimes. Great place to dump a body. They're real deep. Most sinks are in the middle of nowhere. Bodies don't show up for years. And sometimes the corpses travel through the underground caves. Creepy as all hell."

"Interesting," Jonathan said. "It sounds like there's more of my kind of work here than I would have expected. You folks ever think about hiring one on full-time?"

"No, not enough call for that, I imagine. But the guy who we use, he's pretty old. You thinking of relocatin' down here?"

"Maybe. I had an internship with the FBI when I was an undergraduate, but government work is a little too political for me. A nice small town would suit me fine. I'm from one, so I understand the people." He offered to buy Faber dinner after work, knowing he was probably disappointing Serena. "I hope you'll tell me all about Stoweville," Jonathan said with a broad smile. "Where I'm from, there are any number of interesting eccentrics. How about here? Any local crazies?"

As Harry approached the purple door, he wondered how compos mentis Miss Tokay actually was and how many of her recollections could be trusted. He prepared himself for another lecture about the Sky People and lifted his hand to knock. Before his hand made contact, he was startled by a voice behind him. Miss Baby was coming out of the woods behind the house. "What you doin' here?" she said loudly, panting and imposing in cream-colored muslin, wide pants and a top that looked like a collection of pale scarves loosely sewn together.

"Wow. You look great," he said.

"Pooh," she said, coming up the steps, her long legs allowing her to take two at a time with no apparent effort. "You gettin' skinnier," she said. "You're not so ugly now."

"I'm here to see Miss Tokay." As soon as he said it, he braced himself for Miss Baby's scorn at being told the obvious. He wasn't disappointed.

"Well now, is that a fac'?" Her drawl had returned, and Harry realized that much of her broad accent had been exaggerated for his benefit. He thought, what a dumb-ass they must think I am. He turned to knock again, but Miss Baby stopped him with a "Leave her be, Harry." It was the first time she'd used his name. "Miss Tokay's been a little ill lately. Excuse me, I mean 'pohly.' " She smiled. "I came over to look in on her." She edged him aside and moved between him and the door. "What you doin' here anyway?"

"I just wanted to ask Miss Tokay about Emily Timms. She knew her. I want to find out how."

"Why?" She put her hand on the knob and appeared to consider something. "You know," she said, "you've never asked me anything. Evidently you're not as enlightened as you think you are. You figured I'm just an old black country woman. Why talk to me about anything big and important that you'd be interested in, right?"

Harry felt his surprise as a cold tickle across his shoulder blades. Then he got angry. "I didn't think to talk to Miss Tokay either until Maggie told me that she gave everybody solar panels."

Miss Baby regarded him for a moment, a smaller smile now resting on her magnificent mouth. "I'll let you off the hook for bein' a bigot this one time," she said. "Let's go in together."

Miss Baby made tea, a strange replay of the last time Harry was in the living room of the Tokay house. The Purple Lady was in her place on the sofa, but the light was softer, the sun going down off to the left of the tall, thin windows, sending peach rays across a purple sky. Fitting, Harry thought. "Why purple?" he said. "I keep forgetting to ask."

Miss Tokay thanked Miss Baby as the latter handed her a cup and smiled at Harry's question. "The Sky People send purple light to the ascended ones. It's the light of wisdom, the light of healing. Of love, of protection. The ascended ones send it on down to us in an attenuated form. The color itself has all these qualities, just to a lesser degree."

Harry said. "Miss Tokay, how well did you know Emily Timms?"

"Who?" Harry repeated the name. "Oh." She sent a look to Miss Baby. Both their expressions were cryptic. "Emily. A sweet girl. Very sad, though. She ascended some time ago. I hear from her often."

"How did you know her?"

Her smile was sweet, gentle and misty. She looked at him for so long that he thought she'd gone elsewhere in her mind, but finally she said, "I'm not sure how she came to be here. She was a visionary. She understood about the purple light of Kwan Yin."

Harry said, "Kwan Yin is a Buddhist deity. Chinese. A bodhisattva."

Miss Tokay beamed even more broadly. "I'm so impressed, Harry. Is it all right if I use your first name? Maggie refers to you by it. I was hoping we could be friends by extension."

"I'd be delighted, ma'am."

She nodded, still smiling. "The Sky People don't mark petty ideological boundaries the way we do, Harry." She might be crazy, he thought, but she wasn't simple. "Kwan Yin, Jesus, Buddha, Mohammed, they're all ascended and holy and sources of inspiration and protection for those of us who have yet to ascend. Once we do so, of course, we join them."

"If the Sky People say so."

"Of course."

"Miss Tokay, this is fascinating and I'd love to talk about it all night, but I'm burning with the question of Emily Timms at the moment."

Her smile softened. "I love burning questions." She seemed to wake herself up. "I couldn't tell you how she found herself here, Harry. But she became a good friend to me. I wondered at times if she was an avatar of Kwan Yin herself. So wise and so kind."

"But you say she ascended?"

"Yes. Years ago now."

"You communicate with her, though?"

"Yes."

Harry put his hands together in his lap to calm himself and give himself patience. "How did she kill herself, Miss Tokay?"

"How does anyone?" she said.

"Miss Tokay."

"She changed from one state to another. That's all I acknowledge, Harry. Metamorphosis. If you want sordid material details, I'll be honest with you. I don't know them."

"How did you hear about her death?"

"I heard about her ascension," Miss Tokay corrected. "And I heard about it from her."

Harry helped Miss Baby bring the teacups and tray back to the kitchen, which turned out to be large and pink and not particularly clean. There were broad swatches of paint cracked and ready to tumble off the ceiling, riverbeds of broken plaster down the walls. The floor was covered with a sheet of linoleum in a pattern of white and indigo squares. It had spidering lines lacing through it, concentrated in pale, scuffed patches that clustered around the appliances, each of which looked far older than Harry, maybe as old as Miss Tokay. "All right," he said to Miss Baby as he placed the tray on the broad wooden counter. Before he could say more, Miss Baby said, "She knew Dee. She was here for a little while, visiting. Miss Tokay took a shine to her. That's pretty much the whole story."

"Then why is everyone so skittish about telling me anything? What's the big secret?"

Miss Baby sighed. "She'd had a bad time. She had nothing to speak of, but was too proud to live off other people for long. And she was afraid that some folks with a lot of money and power up in Pennsylvania were going to figure out a way to frame her for the murder of her husband. She was convinced she was in terrible danger." She pointed to the bottle of dish soap and a rag perched on the inside edge of a wide, shallow porcelain sink. He started the water and poured a little soap on the rag.

"Was it true?"

"How'n hell would I know? She thought so."

Harry washed the cups, handing each one to Miss Baby after it was rinsed. "How long was she here? When did she leave?"

"I don't recollect either one. She stayed awhile. She left years ago."

"Were you surprised when you heard she'd killed herself?"

"Sad. Not surprised. She had a mess of troubles." She held up a hand as she saw his mouth open for another question. "Now don't ask me what they all were. I suspect you know as much as I do about that. Maybe more. So, Harry," she said, taking the last thin china cup from his hand, drying it, and restoring it to its mates on a shelf above the stove, "please leave Josie and Miss Tokay alone about this. It's a painful subject for both of them."

"I thought Josie didn't know her very well," he said, trying to wend his way through this new wrinkle in the story of Emily Timms.

Miss Baby spread the dish towel on the handle of the stove and flashed him a look. "She didn't help her much, did she? You and she don't mix well, like syrup and ketchup, two things I like but not on the same plate. But still, Josie helps people. She does it with a whole heart. Sometimes when she can't help, her heart breaks a little."

Miss Baby pushed him out of the kitchen into the hallway, now so dark it was hard to find the door. She flipped a switch, and the hall lit up with a warm yellow glow, although it was weighted down by the dusty violet paint on the walls and the heaviness of the grandfather clock on the wall facing the entrance.

"Shouldn't we say good-bye to her?" Harry asked, resisting Miss Baby's strong nudges toward the outside.

"She always takes dictations this time of night, or tries to. We can show ourselves out. She expects it." They were outside on the porch, and Miss Baby pulled the front door to as she said, "You might think about leaving Maggie alone, too." Her face didn't look so kindly anymore, so he only said thank you and good night and got into his car. She waited for him to back down the driveway before disappearing into the dense dark trees as if she'd never been there. He debated with himself whether or not to go back to Maggie's, but he remembered that she had to get up at five-thirty the following morning to go to work, and Miss Baby's parting words hung heavily on him. He drove home, feeling disappointed, although he didn't know why.

33

THE
HIGH PRIESTESS

*She is the woman
of the Seeker's dreams*

Jonathan looked forward to the party
more than he had any other in his memory. He spent a half hour combing his
hair to get it to look like his father's. He
could remember the old man saying,
"Good hair means good looks; good looks
mean getting lucky."

He was especially looking forward to
seeing Harry Sterling again. Frank Milford had introduced him to a number of
physics professors; Jonathan had asked
careful questions about Harry, and had

THE HIGH PRIESTESS

gotten some good gossip. You had to love small universities. The
new law professor was dating a waitress who was also a fortune
teller, if the department administrative assistant could be believed.
No one wanted to act disapproving. It would have been a much
more interesting item in the information pool if the liaison had been
adulterous. As it was, people's class notions were offended, but no
one wanted to admit it, so they clucked instead about "superstition."
Jonathan knew from his mother's work that everyone was superstitious if circumstances became sufficiently dangerous and uncertain.

He had carried the same linen handkerchief for seven years. It had been his father's, and aside from when it was laundered, he always had it in his pocket. "That's superstitious of me," Jonathan said aloud to the mirror. It was the first time he'd actually thought about it; having a scientific upbringing, he thought, I should know better. "I'll test it," he said aloud. He left it on the dresser, giving it a tense look as he closed the door behind him.

Josie had always thought Maggie was pretty, had always suspected that with a little help she could be beautiful. So she wasn't surprised at what Miss Baby, allowed free rein at last, could do with her. More than once Miss Baby had to tell Maggie to sit still, as if she was Charlotte's age, squirming and continually picking up Miss Baby's tools to look at them. Like she'd never seen anything like these before, eyelash curlers and curling irons and tweezers. Well, thought Josie, she hadn't dealt with them very much, even though Josie herself had an enormous cosmetic tool kit in her room. But Maggie had never pored over such implements like normal girls. Josie didn't like it much that Maggie was being dropped into normalcy in this way, fretted over the outcome, imagined Harry Sterling gaping at her as she walked into his house, thunderstruck by the new Maggie, proposing to her on the spot.

They were in the Babyface Salon; Miss Baby had cut Maggie's hair and was now blowing it dry while the curling iron heated. Maggie's face was already covered in makeup, chemicals that as far as Josie knew had never come into contact with her skin. Miss Baby had drafted her granddaughters; Tamara was assigned to Maggie's hands and Charlotte to her feet. At Maggie's protest, Miss Baby said, "I know you think Charlotte's going to be president someday, but it's never bad to learn a trade." Maggie looked quickly at Tamara; Josie knew she was always worried that the younger girl would feel lost and angry in Charlotte's beautiful shadow. Maggie said, "And Tammy's going to be a vet and take care of all the animals in the world." Tamara smiled her unfortunate smile, and Maggie smiled back with such tenderness that Josie felt her chest get fluttery and hollow. It's her and Dee again, she thought. I can't believe I never saw it till now. Dee had been pretty enough, thought Josie, and she had been sweet and reasonably bright, but her small fire had been quenched so easily next to Maggie's blaze. Poor Dee, poor baby, Josie thought, then looked at Maggie and thought, Poor Maggie; if there was a card just for her, Josie wasn't sure whether it would be called "Guilt" or "Shame."

Maggie put up with all the frilly attention she was getting until Miss Baby shook a giant can of hair spray, preparing to shellac her hair so that its effect couldn't be destroyed with an absentminded swipe; Maggie looked at the can, and even she knew what was coming. "No," she said. Miss Baby put it down reluctantly. She pulled off the plastic sheath that she'd wrapped around Maggie's shoulders to keep the hair and makeup from infiltrating her clothing and made Maggie look at her face in a hand mirror. She stared at herself for a moment and then said, "Do I look like a regular woman now?"

"You look like a million dollars, sweetheart," Miss Baby said. "You look like chocolate cake."

Josie hadn't been able to bear the thought of Maggie being humiliated in a public setting. Since her niece had seemed set on going to this party, Josie had tried to get her to buy a dress, had dragged her to Dillard's to try to find something, had forced her to look at racks of clothing under cold fluorescent lights. Maggie had hated every second of it, had winced and pulled away every time a saleswoman approached them. After a half hour she had started breathing heavily, like a cat hyperventilating in a fast-moving car. "I can't," she said to Josie. She grabbed a blue rayon blouse with white buttons. "Is this good enough? I have a new pair of jeans. Will that work?" When she looked at the price tag, her eyes grew huge. "Oh my God. I can't pay that for a shirt."

Josie had managed somehow to get her to do it, though she had had to shove her to the counter. When the woman behind the register had asked if Maggie wanted to try it on, Josie had wanted to scream at her. When they'd gotten back to the house with bag in hand, Josie had had to take a nap and had wanted a drink so bad her mouth tasted sweet with it. Now Maggie went to her room to change into the new jeans and the blouse. Josie thought about jewelry but knew it was hopeless; Maggie was going to wear her heavy man's watch and nothing else. But when she emerged in her new clothes, she looked so sweet, the jeans and the blouse actually fitting her properly for once, not hanging in folds that made her look like she weighed nothing at all. Now you could see she had breasts and a waist and a cute little fanny. She didn't look fancy, but by God, thought Josie, she looked mighty pretty.

Harry neither gaped nor proposed when Maggie arrived at his house an hour or so later, but he was impressed and said so, trying not to be too left-handed in his compliments. But Maggie didn't seem to like it, so he stopped after telling her how nice she looked, making a joke about it, acting hurt that she didn't return the compliment. He wanted to get her to smile, but she was too nervous. He told her to sit at the kitchen table while he made them some tea. The party had already started, but he wasn't in a hurry. "I got a call from Ann about an hour ago," he said. "Dusty got caught vandalizing his school."

"Oh, no. Vandalizing how?"

"He sprayed some obscenities on the outside walls of the gym. He was caught walking away. He had the can in his hand." He turned the heat on under the kettle. As the gas licked the copper bottom, he added, "They're not prosecuting, thank God, but they've suspended him for two weeks. It's near the end of the school year, and there are a lot of exams and assignments and so on. If he misses too much, he may have to repeat the ninth grade." He sat down across from her. "I have to go down there. I'd get there too late if I went tonight. I'm leaving first thing in the morning." He got up as the kettle began steaming, and got two cups and tea bags ready as he said, "I'm going to stay for a while. I haven't spent any real time with them, with Dusty, since Christmas."

He turned his back on the stove and looked at her, sitting carefully at the table with impeccable posture. He wondered what her lack of expression meant. He said, "She wants me back."

Maggie's face didn't change, but her hands moved slightly, closing into loose fists on the table. She said, "I know. What do you want?"

Harry poured the water. "Dusty wants us all to be together again. At least, that's what Ann says. Dusty hasn't said anything to me about it, and he wouldn't talk to me tonight." He put the tea in front of her. "I just want my son back. To live with him all the time, not just occasional weekends. I'm not sure what I'd be willing to do to have that." He sat down and drank some tea. Then he said, "There'll be buffalo wings at the party."

The Olnikoffs' house was spacious and gleaming; from the driveway it looked like a miniature Tara, although not that miniature, Harry thought as they walked the short distance between the houses. The entryway was larger than Harry's bedroom, and Serge led them into a living room with cathedral ceilings and a fireplace with a stone front that was at least fifteen feet high. It was wonderfully cool in the house after the thick heat outside, but Harry couldn't imagine a cold enough Florida winter for the blaze that would fill that fireplace.

He introduced Maggie to Amelia and to Dan Polti, the only familiar faces in the group of about fifteen people that dotted the room other than the neighbor between his house and Serge's, a fat man named Dinwiddie. It was a relief that Serge hadn't invited Judd Lippman. Amelia dragged Maggie off to "give her the tour," Amelia wearing a beautiful smile, while Maggie stayed enigmatic, her blue eyes grabbing his only once before she was led away.

Dan said, "So. The Waitress, eh?" Harry didn't bother correcting him. Dan watched her rear end as the two women moved into the distance. "Not bad," Dan added. He looked back at Harry. "So, you nailing her? Everyone's wondering."

Harry was as surprised at his own prissiness as he was at Dan's coarseness. "She's my friend," he said.

"Mind if I, you know? Take a shot?"

"God, Dan, we're not frat boys. No offense, but you're not exactly every young girl's dream right now. Get through your divorce first before trying to start something else."

"She's a waitress, Harry. I'm not going to marry her." Dan seemed to think this was funny, and that was when Harry realized that he was already drunk. He thought, No wonder your wife left you. You're an asshole.

Harry shook Dan off as Maggie and Amelia returned from the outside, where their hostess had no doubt been showing off her flower gardens. Amelia tried to press a glass of wine into Maggie's hands, but Maggie kept giving it back to her in a comic give-and-take that lasted several volleys. As he approached, Maggie had succeeded in getting a glass of club soda and was being regaled with a story about dogs by the obese Dinwiddie. Amelia was warning Dinwiddie not to let his Jack Russell terrier eat her gardenias when Harry's stomach grew tight; Dan had reappeared, leading Julie Canfield into the room. As soon as she saw Harry, Julie pried Dan's hand from her arm and walked toward the little group with a pleasant smile.

As Amelia made introductions, the two young women looked at each other with what Harry feared was complete understanding. Julie shook Maggie's hand; Maggie's face registered nothing as her unresisting hand was pumped up and down. Amelia complimented Julie on her shoes, which led to a discussion of women's footwear. Dinwiddie rolled his eyes at Harry behind Amelia's back. Julie looked down at Maggie's feet. She opened her mouth, then closed it again. Maggie said, "I don't give a lot of thought to my shoes."

Julie said, "I thought, being a waitress, that good shoes would be important."

To Harry's surprise, Maggie actually smiled. She said, "I'll have to bring it up at the next union meeting."

Julie looked confused. "You have a union?"

Dinwiddie added, "You're a waitress?"

Maggie said, "No, I'm a cook. I wasn't smart enough to be a waitress." Dinwiddie laughed so hard he spilled his drink on Maggie's blouse and was trying to wipe it off with a napkin when Harry pulled her away.

He headed for the French doors that led to the backyard, where the food had been set out on picnic tables. Everyone already seemed to be drunk, and as Harry worked his way around the furniture in the living room, he and Maggie were waylaid again, this time by Dan Polti and Serge, who were arguing about animal rights. He wasn't sure what twists and turns the argument had taken till that point, but Dan grabbed Maggie's arm, saying, "Tell this man that if you've got people dying of AIDS, you've got to weigh that against the deaths of a few monkeys. People are more important than animals."

Serge nodded as though reluctantly conceding the point, but Maggie turned to Dan and said, "Why?"

Dan said, "What? Well, you know. It's obvious."

"Not to me." She stared at him as he looked drunkenly back.

Then she turned and walked out the French doors by herself. Harry followed, not sure whether anyone was owed an apology.

It was dark now, and she was looking up at the stars, bright and distinct in the hot black sky. Harry saw his own motives clearly for the first time. He thought, You're not Henry Higgins. You're not even Dr. Dolittle.

"I should go before it gets any worse," Maggie said. Her voice was huskier than usual.

"You're doing fine, if that's what's bothering you." Too late Harry realized that might be insulting.

"This isn't my kind of thing, Harry. I tried to tell you. It's making my head hurt." She turned to look at him, and the light from the little paper Chinese lanterns draped around the patio reflected in her enormous, crystal eyes. She doesn't look real, thought Harry; or she looks like another species of human altogether. "I can't figure out why you wanted me to come here," she said, and Harry realized that her eyes were glistening so much because there were tears in them. She swallowed and blinked, and nothing overflowed, but Harry felt as if he'd done something terrible.

"Serge wanted to meet you," Harry said softly so that his voice wouldn't carry into the house. "I thought you'd like him. Dan's not usually such a jerk."

She opened her mouth to say something, but Amelia called them back in from the wide doorway into the house. "Frank Milford's here, Harry. He's got someone with him he wants you to meet."

Frank Milford stood next to a large, nervous woman who was introduced as his wife; Harry knew he should remember her from a previous meeting but didn't. Behind her stood Jonathan Ziegart.

"Look who I managed to snag," Milford said jovially to Harry as he and Maggie walked into the living room. "I got us a celebrity."

Harry hung back, Maggie at his side, while Milford introduced Ziegart to the other guests. The newcomers slowly approached them through the small crowd, stopping every minute or two while Amelia Olnikoff facilitated the introductions. When Ziegart saw Harry, he lifted his arm in a wave, a happy smile on his tan face. When he saw Maggie next to him, his smile widened.

When Jonathan Ziegart saw Maggie Roth, she took his breath away. She's luminous, he thought. I'll bet no one else here can see exactly how luminous she is. He had to bring himself to full mindfulness in order to break his gaze upon her and saw Harry Sterling looking at him with no friendliness whatsoever. Ah, Jonathan thought, at least one other person here really sees her. He made himself smile at Harry, saying, "We meet again. Nice to see you, Harry. Is this your date?"

Harry said, "This is a friend of mine. Maggie Roth. Maggie, this is Jonathan Ziegart."

Ziegart bowed and said, "Son of Charles. Have you heard of him?"

Maggie said nothing, just stared at him with a cold, blank expression. It was obvious that Harry didn't want to have to talk to him, which Jonathan found perplexing. He couldn't imagine what he had done to irritate the man.

Harry said, "Why are you here, Jonathan? I thought that you'd be back in Lucasta by now."

"I wound up meeting old friends and staying in Gainesville longer than I expected. I thought I'd drop in on the way back to check out the physics department here. Frank took me to lunch, and when he told me about this party, I was grateful for the invitation.

Fireworks are one of my favorite things." He laughed as he added, "I met your sheriff. Nice man."

Harry's eyes were still not friendly. "Why would you have met our sheriff?"

Jonathan said, more laughter in his voice, "Relax, Harry. It wasn't in the commission of a crime." He accepted the glass of wine that Amelia brought from the bar. Then he turned back to Harry. "I'm interested in law enforcement. Frank called him for me and set up a tour of the courthouse." He looked at Maggie. "I was glad to be invited to a party where there are people other than scientists. Our hostess tells me that you are a waitress?"

Maggie paused for a moment before saying, "I'm a cook."

"Ah," said Jonathan. "An honorable profession. Food is such a basic need. My mother would say that eating in company is the social glue that binds us all together." I'm so happy I could spit, he thought. "Someone also said that you were a fortune teller's daughter." I'd love to get you alone, with candles, have you tell my future, he thought, but knew that this wasn't someone to use flowery language with. She looked prickly, like a blond sea urchin. Go slow, Jon, he thought, take it easy.

It didn't appear as though Maggie was going to respond to him, so Harry stepped in. Jonathan found it interesting that Harry seemed worried about covering for the woman's possible rudeness. "Her mother passed away. But Maggie's aunt is a professional psychic."

"Ah," said Jonathan. "That's it. I heard that, too. I just got the details wrong."

Harry wasn't sure how the second drink had gotten into his hand. The first had been put there by Jonathan, who had said, "Hey, Harry, you're empty-handed. It's always better to be a little loosened up when you're on a date, right?" Harry had been watching

Maggie as she stared unbelievingly at Dan, swaying next to her, putting an unsteady hand on her arm. Harry wondered if he was trying to persuade her that people were more wonderful than pileated woodpeckers. Jonathan had leaned in close and said softly, "Is she yours, Harry?"

"Mine?"

"Your girl."

Harry hadn't expected the raw jealousy he would feel when others approached her. The magnitude of his mistake made him so nauseated that he had to sit down. The beer Ziegart handed him seemed like the only thing that would settle his stomach down from the mess he'd gotten it into.

He is good-looking and charming, he thought. Harry suspected he was like his father. But when Jonathan asked Maggie to show him where the food table was in the backyard, Harry was surprised that she went with him out the French doors. Harry went to the kitchen to find another beer.

Ziegart came back in alone ten minutes later. Harry was talking to Serge and an attractive couple, the man in a suit and the woman in peach chiffon. Serge had introduced them, after a whispered apology about Julie Canfield's presence. "Blame Amelia, although I may have forgotten to tell her that Maggie was coming." The couple was married and shared a last name; it was something like Parks or Banks, and Harry had lost it as soon as it was uttered. The discussion centered on finding a reliable contractor, and Harry's interest had long since waned to nothing. Jonathan disappeared for a moment, then reappeared with two bottles in his hands. He approached the little group; Serge and the pretty couple wafted away, leaving Jonathan and Harry alone. Harry couldn't think of a thing to say, but he took the bottle when Jonathan offered it to him. He wanted to ask Jonathan if he'd made a date with Maggie but knew that it would come out wrong. Jonathan said, "So, how's the book coming?"

"It's not. Not really. I don't know."

"Huh. A shame. Maybe I'll write a biography of my father if you don't. I'd be interested to know what you've uncovered. I assume you've talked to people other than the ones I know." He stretched his shoulders back and took a breath as though the air tasted good. "I like this town. I like this university and I like the people I've met. I'm thinking about where to relocate after I get my degree." He looked at Harry and smiled. "I'm getting a little tired of Pennsylvania winters. Florida sounds better and better."

"It'll all probably be underwater once global warming really hits," Harry said.

"We're inland here, Harry. Besides, I hear there's no income tax."

Maggie came in a moment later, and Harry pried himself from Jonathan's happy company to join her. She was hugging herself and looked miserable; Harry was about to tell her that they could leave when Amelia announced that the fireworks would be starting any minute. "I should go," Maggie said quietly, her whole body radiating tension. But Amelia was upon them and pulled on Harry's arm, talking beyond him to Maggie, saying that they had to come outside. Harry grabbed Maggie's hand with his free one. Amelia kept pulling on him and he kept pulling on Maggie till they were by the folding chairs in the backyard that were lined up to face the sky where the fireworks were about to be launched. He wondered how obvious it was that he was drunk. Maggie didn't struggle and didn't comment; they both wound up on a pair of canvas seats on the far right of the yard, Harry on the end. Julie Canfield sat on the other side of Maggie, smiling as she ate buffalo wings with long pink fingernails. Jonathan leaned forward as he sat down next to Julie, giving Harry a wink and a grin.

The fireworks started ten minutes late, but the view of them was perfect. Harry caught Maggie's eye and tried to smile at her, but she wouldn't return it. Dinwiddie made a comment about how the people who packed the explosive canisters had to know what they were doing. "Burn your ass to cinders," he said.

"How do they get things that explode to look like that?" Julie said, wiping the barbecue sauce off her mouth with a napkin. "It's like magic."

Serge said, "They ignite different chemicals to get different colors. All I know is copper, which makes blue."

Jonathan said, "Sodium is yellow and orange. Strontium makes red. I can't remember what makes green. You know, Maggie," he said, leaning forward again, "my father was a famous physicist. I learned all about fireworks from him," but she didn't look at him, or at anyone else.

34

NINE OF
WANDS

REVERSED

*Bending under
adversity*

"You're drunk," said Maggie. She'd never seemed angry at him before, and he was surprised at how erotic it was, her eyes hard and dark and shiny. She pulled on his arm, saying, "I'll get you home."

She led him to Amelia, to whom he made slurred thanks. Harry stopped short when they were halfway to his house, in front of the large brick home of the fat Dinwiddie, causing Maggie to be pulled back slightly as her grip on his arm forced her to stop as well.

Harry looked at her razor-sharp eyes and her tight mouth, and for once she didn't look that young, she looked like no age at all, just angry and tired. Harry said, "I love you," and put his hands on either side of her face, kissing her deeply, opening his mouth, then moving his hands to her back, around her shoulders, kissing her and kissing her and feeling almost sober for a moment, until she jerked away from him with a force that made him realize how drunk he was. Harry heard a whoop from the porch next door and saw Dan Polti bent over the railing, waving a beer bottle at him. "You the man, Harry!" he said before throwing up into Amelia's gardenias.

Maggie muttered, "Josie would tell me to let you get yourself home."

"She's one to talk," he said, regretting the words as soon as he said them. "Don't leave me, Maggie," he added, hating the gushy way his lips curled around the simple words. "I'm sorry. Please, coffee, you know, or something."

She walked in front of him, not waiting for him to follow, no longer touching him. I love her, he thought. I'm such an asshole, and I'm so fucking drunk, and I love her.

She waited on his front porch while he made his way carefully up the steps. The door wasn't locked, so she opened it as soon as he was at the top, and held it open for him. "Can you get yourself into bed?"

"Come with me," Harry said, hating himself again. That separate sober part of him was at it again, the part that peeled away whenever he got himself into such a predicament, that watched him and judged him and in a strange way, took care of things, making sure he didn't destroy his car or his house. Usually it kept him from saying anything too horrible, anything that would slap him later with mortification or with something worse. But that function of it seemed to have gotten drunk as well, and he could hear how inane and pathetic he sounded.

"I'll help you with your shoes," she said as soon as they were in his bedroom. Her face was white with anger. "I can practically hear Josie screaming at me that this is demeaning."

Harry lay down on his bed, and the world began to move in an unpleasant way. He fixed his eyes on Maggie's face as a sort of linchpin, to keep him from throwing up. A stable point in a moving universe. What Frank Milford or Charlie Ziegart or Emily Timms would call a frame of reference. "Get in with me," he heard himself saying. I wish I could stop making such an ass of myself, he thought.

She pulled off his other shoe and jerked the cover over his clothed body. "You're not in any shape to fuck anyone."

"Oh, man." Shock thrilled through him. "I've never heard you use language like that."

She leaned forward and said softly, "There are a lot of things you haven't heard." Then she straightened, looked toward the door as though she expected someone to walk through it. She said, "I'm getting something out of my car and then I'll stay in your kitchen for a while, just in case." She moved toward the door, then turned back and said, "I won't steal anything."

He must have passed out, although he didn't know for how long. He heard something in another part of the house, raised voices, a door slamming, voices again. He felt sober and drunk at the same time, and sore, as if all his bones had been rammed with something hard. He pushed his feet off the bed, wishing he didn't feel so drugged and dizzy. He got himself upright somehow and worked his way to the bedroom door, one foot in front of the other, hearing the voices, quieter now, Maggie's and someone else's. A man. Jealousy shook him, although his separate brain told him not to be an ass; Maggie was the last person who would be having a tryst in his house while he was sleeping in another room. Although, that part continued, this evening he'd seen something in her he'd never seen before, some sort of fire and anger that he both feared and found arousing.

His bedroom door was partly open, so it made no noise as he pushed through it. He was more graceful than he had a right to be, staggering a little but managing to stay on his feet and to move forward without knocking into the walls. He got to the end of the hall and stopped, seeing Maggie in a clinch with Jonathan Ziegart.

When his eyes refocused, he realized that that wasn't exactly true; Maggie was backed against the far wall of the living room, Jonathan inches from her, his arms on either side of her, hands pressed to the wall, boxing her in. He was saying something low and firm. Maggie's face was dark, her mouth compressed, her eyes sparkling with emotion. Harry was frozen in shock, and then he could hear Jonathan's words: "You think you're better than me."

Maggie said, as softly as Jonathan but crisp and clear, "Of course I'm better than you."

Jonathan gave a hiss of something, probably rage, and Maggie ducked under his arm and ran to a small table by the sofa. Jonathan grabbed her arm and spun her around, but not before she'd taken something from the table with her free hand that looked like a long flashlight, and then there was a bright flash of white light and a popping sound, like an exploding lightbulb. Harry's bleary brain couldn't make sense of what he was seeing; Jonathan's arms flew up and sideways and his head whipped back. He seemed to move backward without taking a step and then he was four or five feet away from her, propelled against the front door. He hit with a smack, the door rattling in its frame; then he collapsed and lay on the ground. He didn't move again. A smell filled the room, something between burning rubber and roasting chestnuts.

Harry told his legs to move, and after a second or two they did, jerking him forward into the room. Maggie looked up, a terrible expression on her face.

"Is he dead?" Harry asked.

"No," she said. "No, no."

He checked Jonathan's pulse. The beat was strong and regular, so Harry and Maggie hoisted his inert form onto the sofa. His face was slack, eyes halfway open, only whites showing, and a thick line of saliva threading from the side of his mouth down to his chin. "We have to call an ambulance," Harry said.

She nodded and said, "You do it. I'll make some coffee. Tell them he had a seizure."

"But he didn't. What the hell did you do to him? That flashlight is some kind of stun gun?"

She nodded again. "But he'll be okay. Don't worry, I didn't murder him." She wiped her hands on her jeans as though they were badly soiled. "If he has an EEG, it'll look like a seizure."

"But when he wakes up, he's going to be mad as hell, and he's going to tell them what happened, and we're both going to be in deep shit."

"No, we won't. He won't remember a thing."

"They'll find the burn mark."

"There isn't one. Make the call, okay? I can't do it."

Harry called 911 and told the dispatcher that a guest had had a seizure in his living room during a visit to his house after a party. The dispatcher asked him a number of annoying questions: Was he breathing, was he in any danger of hitting his head on anything, were there any drugs involved. Harry said that, as far as he knew, Jonathan had had a few drinks at the party, but he didn't think he'd ingested anything more sinister, though of course he couldn't be sure. He wasn't particularly interested in preventing Jonathan Ziegart from having to defend himself against drug charges. The dispatcher wanted Harry to stay on the line until the ambulance arrived, but Harry cut her off and hung up the phone. He went into the kitchen, where Maggie was opening and closing cabinet doors. "I can't find the coffee," she said, her voice hitching. Her hands were shaking, and tears were running down her face. Harry put his arms around her, making sure that there was nothing in her hands. Her whole body was trembling, so he pressed her to him more tightly, trying to warm her up.

"You're in shock," he said.

"I know," she said.

"Where's the stun gun?"

"I put it in that drawer," she said, pointing to one by the refrigerator that contained screwdrivers and spatulas. "No one should know about it."

"Where did you get it?"

"Someone gave it to me. To Josie and me. Protection. You know."

"Who?" he said. He tried to imagine Emily Timms giving them such a thing, and couldn't.

"It doesn't matter."

"And you carry it with you? Were you planning on using it on me?"

"No!" Her face scrunched up as though something hurt her. "No, I put it in the car sometimes. When I'm out at night by myself." She put her head on his shoulder, leaning her weight into him as though her legs weren't working too well. "Josie worries about me."

Harry was about to say, but that doesn't explain most of this at all, when the sound of sirens derailed his thoughts. He sat her down on a kitchen chair. "When you can stand up," he said, "the coffee's in the freezer."

Two policemen arrived a few minutes before the paramedics. The cops were bored, and the paramedics were satisfied that Jonathan Ziegart had had a seizure. While uniformed men worked on Ziegart, Harry called Serge, relieved that he was still awake. To his surprise, the party still seemed to be going on. He gave Serge a cleaned-up version of events and asked if someone there would go to the hospital to handle whatever paperwork was needed. Serge was understandably surprised by the whole affair, but after a quick conference away from the phone, he told Harry that Frank Milford was still there and had volunteered to go. Harry thanked him, told the police about Milford and that he himself barely knew Ziegart.

Maggie stood off to the side, saying nothing, staying out of the way. She wasn't crying any longer, but she had her arms tightly crossed, staring with enormous, tired eyes as the gurney was wheeled out the front door. The youngest of the officers asked Harry if "his girlfriend" was going to be okay. "She looks pretty pale. You want one of the EMTs to take a look at her?"

"No," said Harry. "She's shook up, but she'll be all right."

The policeman looked at Maggie longer than Harry was comfortable with, then said, "You're a lucky guy. You keep her warm tonight."

Harry stood on his front porch for a moment as the emergency vehicles pulled away. Serge was next to him; Harry thanked him, told him he'd call tomorrow, and got his friend to go home. He walked back into his quiet house. Maggie sat at the kitchen table, her head on her arms. For the first time since Jonathan Ziegart had been thrown across his living room by a bolt of lightning, Harry could feel the alcohol in his system. His eyes would open only halfway, and he wasn't sure how well he could talk. But he sat down across the table from Maggie while water dripped and gurgled in the coffee machine. "What the hell happened here?"

Her head rose slowly. "I don't know."

"Was he going to attack you?"

"Yes."

"And you happened to have brought the stun gun thingy into the house?"

"Yes."

"Why?"

Maggie wasn't looking at him now; instead, she watched the coffee plop in dark blobs into the glass carafe. "I could see it in his aura," she said.

"He made a pass at you? Back at the party?"

"Sort of." She shook her head. "I know you don't believe me. I don't want any coffee. I'm going to go." She stood up, bracing herself against the table as though her legs still weren't working right. "Should I take it with me?"

"I guess. I don't know. If there are any questions later, maybe it shouldn't be here. Have you zapped anyone else with that thing?"

"Josie has."

"Oh God." He stood up, not any surer of his footing than she seemed to be.

"I'm sorry for all this," Maggie said.

"It wasn't your fault. Was it?" He reached for her, but she pulled away.

"You shouldn't come walking with me anymore," she said. "If I was your wife, I wouldn't like it."

"Don't go."

She found the flashlight-shaped stun gun in the drawer. "I'm sorry I can't be Emily Timms for you, Harry." Then she added, "You should think about going to AA. Good night." She was quicker on her feet than he was and was out the door before he could stop her.

Josie could tell by the sound of the car in the driveway that it hadn't gone well. Part of her had known from the beginning it wouldn't, had known that all those rich college folks weren't likely to be kind. Josie was ashamed at how much of her had been glad about this, but there wasn't much she could do about it, and now that the shit had hit the fan, now that poor Maggie was crushed and crumpled by the weight of all that snobbery and blindness, Josie could at last feel the pain of her sympathy. Maggie came in the door, shrouded in black mist dotted with specks of brown, stinking of misery. As Josie put her arms around her, she remembered the little blond girl coming home from school, eleven years old, having been beaten up by a big farm girl named Tyrena because Maggie had made a drawing of the layers of the skin in health class that was too nice. It was so strange, how the poor girl was spat upon by the low and the high. Maggie had cried then as she was crying now. "Everything is ruined, I am a retard, I can't do anything right," while Josie once more shushed her and called her "my baby" and told her how beautiful she was.

35

PAGE OF
CUPS

REVERSED

*Seduction, but the truth
is soon revealed.*

His son was so skinny, he thought. He
looked like he hadn't slept or eaten for a
week. "What the hell's wrong?"

Dusty shrugged and said, "You know.
Nothing. Same old same old."

"You look like shit."

"Thanks, Dad. Good to know I can always count on you for a boost to my self-
esteem."

Harry had had only two hours of
ugly sleep peppered with quasi dreams
of Maggie drowning in a sinkhole and

Jonathan Ziegart frying in the electric chair. He'd gotten up at six
and drunk a pot of coffee, packed his bag, and driven to Orlando.
He'd thought about calling Maggie on the road but realized it was
Saturday, which meant that she was already at work. Instead he'd
called Ann at about eight while at a rest stop, hoping that she was
up. His cell phone worked only intermittently, but well enough to
warn her of his imminent appearance. He hadn't been able to gauge
her reaction through the static. He had cursed the pimply clerk at
the cell phone store out loud.

Now Harry pestered Dusty until the fourteen-year-old put up his hands in a gesture of silent denial, after which he put on headphones attached to a white wire that disappeared into a jeans pocket and walked away. A moment later, Harry could hear the door to a bedroom close. He went to the kitchen to find Ann.

"What's going on?" he said. "Have you taken him to a doctor? Is he sick? He looks like a junkie." Harry began to pace. "You didn't tell me that he's falling apart."

Ann stood by a metallic refrigerator, her arms folded across her chest. There were no magnets on the refrigerator, and so there were no photos, notes, lists, or examples of Dusty's artwork. "Calm down," she said. "He's just moody. Teenagers are like that."

Harry said, "It's only been a month since I've seen him. I know he hasn't been all that happy here with you." At her look, he added, "I'm not criticizing, I'm just saying, he doesn't like it here. It's not your fault." He thought, But maybe it is. I always try to be nice to her, he added to himself. Why is that? She's seldom that nice to me. He tried to focus on the issue at hand. "He looks like he's lost weight, like he's not sleeping. Do you know his friends? Have you talked to any of their parents?"

"What am I supposed to say to them? 'I'm sorry, but is your son doing drugs, and giving them to mine?' And anyway, the problem isn't that he runs with a bad crowd. It's that he doesn't run with anyone at all. He's too much of a loner." She pointed at his chest. "He takes after you, obviously."

When he called Maggie, Josie told him that she was out. Her tone was cold; he remembered that he'd wanted to ask her more about Emily Timms, but she hung up on him when he asked when Maggie might return. Then he called Serge, who told him that Jonathan Ziegart was "resting comfortably" in the hospital but was being kept a day or two for observation. "Frank Milford says he seems fine, just confused." Serge wanted to talk longer, but Harry cut him off, although less rudely than Josie had him.

The three of them had dinner together, Chinese takeout that was wasted on Harry. He picked at it and watched Dusty do the same. Ann talked all through the meal. Later, Harry couldn't remember anything she'd said.

That night, Ann seduced Harry, and he let her. He knew that later it would haunt him with shame, that he hadn't put her off, hadn't been honest enough to tell her he wasn't going to live with her again, that he was going to leave as soon as he could get Dusty packed to come with him. But she was so beautiful, so good at seduction, and he'd been abstinent a long time. The sex was shockingly good, but his shame started the moment they were done. He lay next to her, sweaty and tired and suddenly hungry. He thought, When is the appropriate time to tell your ex-wife that you just fucked her because you've been so horny for so long and had no one to service you, and thanks a lot and good-bye, you've got a thing for a psychotic cook with no social skills? They lay there for a half hour, Harry thinking that Ann had fallen asleep. Presently, however, she moved, leaned over and pressed her breasts to him. She whispered, "You look good, you know. You've lost weight. You're almost hot now."

The oddly repellent compliment freed him in a way that he thought nothing else would have. "Ann, I'm sorry," he said softly. "But it's not going to be the way you said."

Ann startled him by laughing. "It's not going to be anything. Now that you're here, I can see that. You piss me off. But you haven't been hot in a long time. I wanted to find out if it was any better. It is, but not so good that I want everything that comes with it."

And that was when Harry finally heard the little voice that had been trying to get him to listen for weeks. She's always been like this, it said. She just wanted you to want her back. Ironic, isn't it, that you were never in any danger. It was a relief, but it nevertheless made him feel like shit. He left her alone in her bed and took a shower. While the water ran over his newly acceptable body, he remembered the last night they'd lived together. Lawrence had been in his grave for three weeks. Ann had said, "Maybe you'd be enough for someone, but you're not enough for me." She'd added, "You need someone unsophisticated, uncomplicated. I think you could handle that." He hadn't written a word since. He lay in the guest room for the rest of the night, eyes open, staring at the ceiling.

As soon as it was light, Harry used Ann's desktop computer to print out a map of the location of Todd Greenleaf's house. He wrote a note and put it on the kitchen counter before he left.

He wasn't sure why he hadn't called first. The traffic was already thick, even this early on a Sunday. Thousands upon thousands of people made the journey each year to the hot, tax-free South, either to live in condos by oily canals or to visit the man-made attractions, Disney World and all the gaudy fun it had spawned around it. Once the land had seemed endless with orange groves and marshes; now it was jam-packed with people and buildings and roads and cars in astronomical numbers. Harry felt a profound relief that at last the question of whether or not he should move here for Dusty's sake was answered.

He ate breakfast at a café that had outdoor seating. His table was on a deck that overlooked a large holding pond. He watched an egret spear a small fish in the tall grass at the opposite edge of the water. He suddenly missed Maggie so terribly his chest hurt. He could smell moisture tinged with diesel fuel, and wondered if the tainted air would make her sick.

. . .

Todd Greenleaf lived in a well-maintained trailer park by a canal. The "modular homes" were set on cinder blocks and were neatly aligned at forty-five-degree angles from the road that afforded everyone a view of the water. A small concrete walk led to each front door. The muddy canal made the top of a T at the end of the little road. It smelled of algae and brackish water; Harry wondered fleetingly how often neighborhood pets were eaten by alligators.

He left his car on the edge of the road in the narrow space between the road and the storm ditch. Number 615 was only a few feet away, a yellow single-wide with plastic geraniums in a long planter that hung neatly under the bay window on the short side. An aluminum porch with a moss-colored awning was tacked to the side with the door. The lanai, Harry thought. A man was sitting in a green lawn chair on the porch, a can of something in his hand. Harry looked at his watch. It was 9:14 A.M.

He walked to the porch, his hand raised in greeting. Greenleaf was around seventy and was wearing white shorts over skinny white legs and running shoes on oversize feet. His belly was so distended he looked pregnant. He had on a Florida Marlins cap, and the bristles on his loose cheeks were so white Harry couldn't tell that Greenleaf hadn't shaved in a while until he was on the porch itself.

"Mr. Greenleaf?" He spoke loudly, remembering that the man was hard of hearing.

"Yeah," Greenleaf yelled in a harsh, familiar voice.

Harry introduced himself and extended his hand. The old man lifted the can and said, "Wanna beer?"

"I better not, thanks."

They wasted some time in chitchat about living in Florida. Greenleaf said, "You moved down here to get away from income tax, too, eh?" He shook his head. "In Pennsylvania"—he pronounced it "Pennsivania"—"the taxes are so high all you got left are the people who are too poor to move. Main thing I miss are the sports teams. The Stillers and the Iggles."

Harry bore it as best he could, then directed the conversation where he wanted it to go. He went over the same ground he'd covered many times now: Had Greenleaf heard any allegations of foul play in the death of Charles Ziegart or had he remembered anything more about Emily Ziegart or her suicide.

"No foul play," Greenleaf said. "Why would anyone want him dead? No motive at all. Her least of all. He was her meal ticket."

"If he stole her work, she might have been mad about that." Harry didn't like making the suggestion himself, but he couldn't ignore the possibility.

"Nah. She was a broad, right? He made her rich, got her a place at the university, got his big name attached to hers. What's wrong with that?"

"But he didn't 'get her a place' there," Harry said. "She got accepted at Cantwell as a student before he met her."

"Whatever," Greenleaf said. "You know what I'm sayin'. You wouldn't want to kill the fatted calf."

The goose that lays the golden egg, Harry thought, but he didn't bother correcting the man's cliché out loud. "What do you know about Doug McNeill? Ziegart's student who died not long before he did?"

"Oh yeah. Fat guy who choked to death. That's what I know." Greenleaf took a gulp of beer.

Watching his Ping-Pong-ball Adam's apple bounce up and down made Harry a little queasy. Thank God I don't actually want a beer, he thought. "What about the scholarship?"

"What scholarship?"

"The one in Doug's name. At Cantwell. It's funded by one of Ziegart's patents."

Greenleaf scratched his shoulder and stared at the canal. He had little, watery eyes with tiny brown crusts at their edges. "Oh yeah," he said. "I'm remembering this." He absently massaged his left arm with his right hand. Uh-oh, Harry thought. Angina. I hope he's got a good cardiologist, but I bet there are thousands of them down here, making a killing, no pun intended. Greenleaf went on. "I interviewed the widow, a year or two after Charlie died." Harry's pulse quickened. "They were naming something after him at the school and there was a big to-do about it. Features weren't normally my thing, but I was helping Bella out. Our features gal. The subject of the scholarship came up, I think because Bella had written it down that she wanted me to ask about it. The wife says that Ziegart himself started it before his death, and what a great man he was, blah, blah, blah."

"So you actually interviewed Emily Ziegart? Why didn't you tell me this before? I never saw that piece in any of the archived material online."

"Not Emily. The real wife. What's her name. Pamela. I didn't tell you because I forgot. The piece never made it to press anyway. I told you, 9/11 took all the space in the paper for a long while right around then. Lots of other stuff never got ink."

"Did Pamela tell you why Charlie started the scholarship?"

"Not really. He was a great humanitarian and so on, honoring a dead student, blah, blah, blah."

"You never wondered if there was more to it than that?"

"Of course not. Why? Do you think something was up there? You think Charlie was having some gay-type affair with poor old Dougie? The Brainiac and the Blimp?" Greenleaf laughed, phlegm rattling like a pair of maracas in his chest. He coughed a few times, making Harry fear he would project mucus onto his shoes, but mercifully it stayed put. Greenleaf wiped his eyes. "I'da loved to be able to print something like that. Woulda made my career."

"So you never met Emily?"

"Nah. Went to the hospital after the accident. The first wife was there, along with the pip-squeak son. She wouldn't let me see the second wife. Said press were 'banned' from speaking to her."

"I doubt she had any legal standing."

"Didn't matter. The docs weren't enthusiastic about having strangers in her room either. Besides, Pamela had a lot to say and stood in front of all the cameras. Her and that son. It was a little creepy, if I remember right, how much he seemed to enjoy all the attention. I saw him pose for a picture once, the saddest teenage boy-face you've ever seen, and as soon as the flash faded, he was all grins. Maybe shock or something. Grief does all kinds of weird shit to people, especially kids."

"Yes, it does," Harry said. "You still have any of your notes?"

"Nah. All in storage. Probably couldn't find 'em anyway." For the first time, he looked Harry in the eye. "What exactly is this book of yours about anyway?"

"I have no idea," Harry said.

After leaving the trailer park, he stopped at a chain bookstore and bought a biography of Nikola Tesla. When he got back to Ann's house, Dusty was still in bed, although Ann had left, apparently for church. Harry went online again, made rental car reservations, and bought round-trip airplane tickets for two to Harrisburg. Then he made some more coffee.

When Dusty woke up, he told him to eat breakfast and pack. As his son grumbled off to his room, he checked the time. When he saw that it was late enough for certain people to be home from church, he called a number in Downesport, Pennsylvania, that he hadn't dialed since the night before Lawrence's funeral.

May Wiley answered the phone after two rings. It took several exchanges before she understood who Harry was. She sounded moderately pleased to hear from him. When he told her that he was planning to be in Pennsylvania for the next few days, she didn't immediately ask him to visit. "I'm bringing Dusty with me," he said, and as he'd expected, that secured the invitation.

"How old is he now?" she asked.

"Fourteen. He'll be fifteen in August." He didn't want to tell her why Dusty had so much time free before the school year was over but was a little disappointed that this didn't rouse her curiosity at all.

"You should both come by one morning. Thursdays are best. Before lunch."

Harry had expected an invitation to spend the night, or at least to have a meal. He thought, I'd forgotten how little they liked me.

"Make sure you call first," she said.

Ann said, "When will you be back?"

"I don't know, exactly."

"We haven't talked about what to do about our son."

"There are only a few weeks of school left after his suspension's up. We'll be back by then. He'll finish out the year here, then he'll come back with me for next year."

"Country schools? Come on, Harry."

"I have it on good authority that they're not so bad." He wasn't surprised she didn't fight harder to keep Dusty with her.

"Are you seeing that waitress?" Harry poured himself another cup of coffee to buy himself a moment. She continued, "At least you didn't say it's none of my business. I guess it isn't, but Harry, I hate to see you settle for someone just because they're inferior to you. Even though I know it must be a boost to your ego."

Harry said, "You've changed your tune," but she didn't seem to understand him, and he didn't say anything else about it.

Dusty was sullen about the trip, but Harry was surprised that he didn't get more resistance from him. Ann drove them to the airport. She gave Dusty a kiss on the cheek and ran out the automatic doors without a backward wave.

36

PAGE OF
CUPS

A young man of principle;
kind, an artist or a poet

After the seat belt sign went off, Dusty replaced his earbuds and closed his eyes. Harry found that the purple-checked pattern of the upholstery on the seats in front of them was oddly hypnotic when stared at for minutes on end; it made him think of Miss Tokay. He had to nudge his son several times before the earbuds came out again.

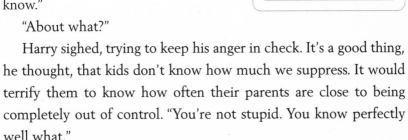

"What?"

"We've got to talk sometime, you know."

"About what?"

Harry sighed, trying to keep his anger in check. It's a good thing, he thought, that kids don't know how much we suppress. It would terrify them to know how often their parents are close to being completely out of control. "You're not stupid. You know perfectly well what."

Dusty went for the earbuds again, and Harry grabbed them. His son's hands were too big for his skinny arms. He's going to be gigantic, Harry thought. I'd better get my bluff in now. "No more iPod till we both agree we're finished. For the moment. Your mother bought you another one?"

"Grandma did."

"I wouldn't have. How many is it that you've lost now?"

Dusty shrugged.

"So what the hell is up with you? You spray-painted 'rich bastards' on the wall of the gym."

"It was 'rich bloated bastards.' "

My literate son, thought Harry. "I'm willing to concede that you go to school with a bunch of them, but you know what? I'm not home-schooling you. Neither is your mother." At that, Harry couldn't prevent the laugh provoked by the image of Ann sitting in front of Dusty in front of a chalkboard, pointer in hand. Dusty suddenly laughed, too, and for several minutes they both laughed harder and harder till the tears were rolling from their eyes. It took almost a minute for each of them to sober up.

"Good one." Dusty leaned back in the seat and closed his eyes again.

"Not sleeping, huh?"

"Not too well. It's okay, though."

"Teenagers never get enough sleep. I didn't. Unfortunately, I don't now either." He looked at the earbuds in his hands. "So what happened?"

"Nothing happened."

"Was it that girl again?"

His son pursed his lips, his eyes still closed, and sighed. "No."

Inspiration came. "Does it have something to do with all the sh— stuff you've been losing? Is someone ripping you off?"

Dusty opened his eyes, turned, and regarded him the way one would a hopelessly incontinent puppy. "You don't say 'ripping you off' anymore, Dad."

Two can play the sarcasm game, he thought. "Yes, that's the important issue right now. Answer the question."

"No one stole anything." Harry waited, pretending to be Maggie, figuring if he sat and stared at his son long enough, he'd cave and spill everything. Dusty carefully looked out the window at blinding light reflected off cottony clouds. "I gave them away."

Harry forbade himself from saying anything, although he wanted to yell questions. He "did a Maggie" as he imagined Dusty would call it and continued to look silently at his son.

"I met this guy. A kid. A little older than me. He was homeless. He smelled pretty bad. He borrowed my iPod."

Harry dug a fingernail into his palm to keep himself from grabbing his son by the lapels and ripping the whole story from him at once. "Oh?" he said casually. "Where did you meet this kid?"

"At the bus station. When I came back from seeing you at Christmas. Mom was a few minutes late getting me."

"She was?" Harry swore in his mind, loudly.

"I went back a week or so later. After school. I saw him again. He told me he'd sold it. He got forty dollars for it, and to him that's a whole lot of money. So I said okay, and I gave him my cell phone."

"What's he doing at the bus station? Panhandling?"

"Yeah, I guess that's what you call it. He has a cup and sh— stuff."

Harry waited, every muscle in his body hard as stone.

"I went back every now and then. It's kind of a long bike ride, but not that long. I kind of, you know, worried about him. There was an old guy who hung around some, who seemed to kind of look after him. Not his dad or anything. I asked." Dusty seemed to think that this made the relationship more acceptable. It filled Harry with horror. "I talked to him a lot. I told him about Michelle calling me gay and all. I knew it was weird that I was friends with this guy. I thought about what the shrink would have asked me."

Harry waited.

"And I thought it was pretty obvious. If this kid had been in my school, and cleaned up and all that, we might have been buddies. Or, like, if you guys were gone, it could be me. But I knew that Mom would absolutely freak if she knew I was friends with a homeless kid. Even one that was pretty cool, an okay guy, really. He's not mean or a criminal or on drugs or anything, and we like all the same stuff, the same music, everything. That's how we got onto the iPod in the first place. He liked everything I had on it." Dusty looked sad, like an old man remembering his lost children, and Harry wanted to put his hands on his son so bad it hurt, to hold his hand or put him in his lap the way he'd done when the boy had been five. And then for no reason Harry remembered how much Dusty had loved his uncle Lawrence, and he felt like crying. But all he said was "What's this kid's name?"

"Jake." Dusty swallowed. "I gave him another iPod and my Game Boy. I kept hoping he'd keep them since I knew he liked music so much. But he kept selling them. He needed the money." Or his pimp did, Harry thought. Dusty went on. "I gave him my second cell phone, too." He shrugged. "I didn't have anybody to call anyway."

Harry resisted the urge to say, You could have called me. Maggie's warning still scratched at his brain; it's not his job to make you feel needed. He said, "When did you last see him?"

"About a month ago. Then I went to the bus station last Saturday. He was gone. The old guy was there. His name's Quick. That's it, just Quick. Anyway, Quick said that Jake had gone home, but the way he said it was funny and Jake had said he didn't really have a home to go to. But Quick wasn't going to tell me anything. I asked the security guard there if he knew where Jake was, but he just looked at me like I was crazy, so I had to leave. I went back two more times. Even Quick was gone by then."

Harry praised the stars that Quick hadn't decided to grab Dusty and do to him whatever he'd done to Jake. But those stars hadn't done much for the homeless boy. Dusty said, "Then I was at school, and it all seemed so weird, you know, the girls and their shoes and their hairdos and the guys with their muscles and their cars. Every time I saw someone with a Game Boy 2 or a PSP, I'd start to get all angry." He shrugged again, his favorite gesture, at times his only one. "So I got a can of paint from Mom's garage and went all mook on the place." His face was red now, his skin uneven with the first sproutings of hair on his upper lip, a few curling under his chin. An ungainly and beautiful boy, thought Harry. He thought about what he could possibly do for the lost Jake. Nothing. It was a moment before he spoke.

"The trick," he said, "is not to get caught."

37

FIVE OF WANDS

Hard times ahead

"We should go stay with Miss Tokay," Maggie said.

"But that place is full of termites."

"It's a real house. Termites or no, she's got better locks. We're not safe here. It's just a matter of time before something bad happens."

"Like what? We're not breaking any laws, and this is America. People aren't just going to come into our house and kill us or something. We don't have enough to rob, at least not that anyone knows about. And this *is* a real house."

"I mean it, Josie. We need to stay over there. Miss Baby and the girls, too. I don't know if they're in any danger, but we are. I talked to Miss Tokay this morning. It's all right with her. I think she'd like the company, actually. Please, Josie. You might want to cancel all your appointments. For the next few days, at least."

"I told you that that college man wasn't going to work out." The heat and the lack of alcohol in the house were making her cranky.

Maggie sat down on the couch next to her. Josie expected to be cajoled or given some reasoned argument to convince her. Instead, Maggie looked as hard as metal, blue eyes bright and flashing. "Staying in Miss Tokay's fortress of a house is the only thing my retarded brain can come up with to keep both our asses intact. So please quit arguing with me and just do it." Josie stared at her, fear in her belly now as Maggie added, "I love you, but you can be stubborn as hell when you don't drink."

When Jonathan Ziegart got out of the hospital, he was still very confused. He didn't know what the woman had done to him. She'd done something; no one could find the slightest reason for the seizure, and he could remember almost nothing after the Olnikoffs' party. The doctor had assured him that he hadn't been drugged. Maybe, they said, some obscure allergic reaction to alcohol. He'd left them shaking their heads and no doubt thinking about ways to write him up to further their careers. He knew all about that and was having none of it; he refused to sign any release forms. After two days, they'd wanted him to stay, but he left "against medical advice." He knew there wasn't anything wrong with him. But he decided that his father's handkerchief was never, ever leaving his pocket again.

Harry got a rental car at the Harrisburg airport, and within an hour of landing he and Dusty were on their way to a cabin that Harry had rented in the Tuscarora Mountains. They drove through deep hills and green fields, barns and cows punctuating the landscape. "God, it's pretty here," said Harry. Dusty didn't answer. Near the state park where the cabin was, they found a small grocery store and a tackle shop, and bought supplies: food, charcoal, rods and reels, a large plastic bucket and some bait. At both stops, Harry had to coerce Dusty into coming into the store with him, making him leave the iPod in the car each time. Harry rang up each purchase on his credit card, wondering idly how long it was going to take to pay off the bill. A lot of it's deductible, he thought. He imagined Maggie doing his taxes.

Josie suggested that Maggie leave the trailer when Roy came over. Maggie said, "Is he going to be driving that big truck of his?"

"That's all he's got, so I'd guess so."

"Would he let me borrow it for the day, do you think?"

"If I ask him right, he'll let you have it for keeps. What do you want with it?"

"I want to move some stuff from the temple. I'd need it for most of the day. He could use my car if he needs a ride while I'm gone."

"You know how you could sweeten the deal."

Maggie sighed. "I've got a lot to do. But okay, okay."

Jonathan Ziegart felt real affection for the scrawny, sweaty man in front of him, although he didn't know why. He was honest enough with himself to realize that it probably was because Darcy obviously thought so much of Jonathan, was so completely impressed by his stature and intelligence and air of authority.

"So, these folks are really that bad, eh?" Darcy said, perspiration decorating his upper lip.

"I'm afraid so, Mr. Murphy. I can't say more at the moment. I know you understand why." He knew Darcy didn't, but he also knew that the man wasn't likely to question him. He hadn't let him look long at the paper FBI identification card that Jonathan had retained from his one-semester internship. They were at a chain restaurant off an interstate exit about twenty miles from downtown Stoweville. Darcy's supervisor was ignorant of the meeting, which suited both men just fine. "All we need you to do is a stakeout. We just want to know the comings and goings in that house. Your van is known in the neighborhood. That's to our advantage; no one will question why you're there."

"The fortune teller will. She's quite the bitch."

Jonathan couldn't figure out why he seemed so afraid of a middle-aged hippie who lived in a trailer. "Has something happened that you're not telling me? We need to know everything, Mr. Murphy."

Darcy twitched as though something had stung him but said only "No. No. Not that I know of."

This was such a peculiar response that Jonathan was going to pursue it, but the waitress picked that moment to ask them if they wanted anything else. Jonathan let Darcy answer, which he did only after a moment's questioning stare at the younger man. "No, I guess not, honey, I guess not," he said finally, and the young woman walked away with a disgusted look on her face. Jonathan resolved to leave a two-dollar tip, not small enough to earn her anger, not large enough to be memorable.

"I don't like that place," Darcy said. "I don't want to spend any more time there than I have to."

"Why not? It's an unusual assignment for a civilian. But it's not a difficult one, nor is it dangerous."

"I know," said Darcy, "I know. It's fine. I'll do it. It's fine."

Not only was Roy persuaded to let Maggie borrow his truck but he even helped her move some of the heavier items from the temple while Josie looked on, the sun shining on her hennaed hair. Roy said, "Where you goin' with this stuff?"

"Better you don't know."

"Josie said you'd work on the tranny for me."

"Sure, Roy. It's the least I can do. I'll be back with it tonight by dinnertime."

38

SIX OF CUPS

REVERSED

*Stuck in an
unfortunate past*

Darcy Murphy told his supervisor in person on Monday morning that he needed more time off; he looked unwell enough that the Little Shit didn't require a lot of convincing. Darcy suspected that his supervisor was relieved he wasn't going to be coming into the office again for a while.

On Tuesday, he sat in the van, which wasn't supposed to be used for personal business, but this didn't count as personal business; he figured when everything was all over, the government would reimburse his employers for whatever wear and tear the van suffered. He worried that it would overheat because he needed to run the engine to keep the air-conditioning going; when he turned the motor off, the heat became intolerable within minutes. "I hate the fucking summer," he said aloud. There was little traffic on the road, and what there was rarely stopped, just big rigs that sailed past twenty or thirty miles an hour over the speed limit, causing the van to rock in their wake. He had pulled onto the berm a hundred feet or so down the highway from the double-wide and had sat for two hours, alternately turning the engine off and baking, then turning the engine on and watching the temperature gauge climb slowly into the red. The tall black woman went in and out of the salon several times, once with two little girls in her wake. He must have nodded off, because a rapping on the window almost sent him bursting through the roof like a bullet. Her name, he remembered from his paperwork, was Thorpe. She made a rolling motion with her hand, and he lowered the window.

"What the hell you doin' here?"

"Takin' a nap," he said, having had the answer ready just in case this very thing happened. He noticed that the heat gauge was reading alarmingly hot, so he turned off the key.

The big woman said, "This is a pretty funny place for it."

"You don't tell my supervisor, I don't tell him you're stealing nothin'."

"I ain't stealin' a damn thing, as well you know, or you ought to by now. Damn electric company. I got a mind to lodge a complaint. It's harassment."

"I ain't harassing nobody, woman. Leave me be."

She waved a dismissive hand at him. "Pooh on you," she said. "Wastin' gas, that's what you're doin'. Should be ashamed of yourself."

"I can live with myself just fine, thank you very much. You watch out for your own conscience."

She walked away with another wave, her hand flapping down as if to say, "you're nothing, you're too low for me," and went back into the salon. Darcy thought about what to do now. He could stay for a while, but he hadn't hidden himself well enough, that was for sure.

"You're not calling that man, are you?" Josie said. Maggie had asked to borrow Roy's truck one more time and was taking a break before she went back on the road. She'd been looking at the phone with a strange, sad expression, and Josie could read her mind as sure as if her thoughts were printed on a piece of paper right in front of her. Maggie wanted to call the college boy, no longer bearded, no longer as chubby as he'd been when Josie had first seen him, which was some kind of a miracle, but Josie also knew that things were bad between them. Maggie had never told her exactly what had gone wrong, other than the incident with the stun gun. But she could guess some of the rest. And why would someone like Harry ulti-mately want Maggie, when college men like him could get all the sex they wanted anytime, all those coeds hanging around them like they were gods? There was nothing that a man liked more, Josie thought, than to be thought divine. She remembered Duncan again, how he'd treated her like she was the one who walked on water. She wished she didn't miss him so much, wished she could recall more of the bad times or the static he'd given her when she'd drunk too much. Of course, she hadn't been in the habit of drinking quite so much when he was alive, but still, she'd put it away a few times when he hadn't liked her to.

By the time Maggie answered her question, Josie had already for-gotten it, so she couldn't figure out what she meant at first when she said, "No, I was thinking about it, but I won't. There's no point." Oh, thought Josie, remembering now, oh, Harry. She's not going to call him. Good. Then she made a bargain with herself that as soon as Maggie left again, she'd go to the package store and get a pint, or maybe a fifth, of vodka or rum. Something you could put into some-thing cold.

The tiny cabin faced a brown lake flanked on all sides by trees in full leaf. Harry had grown used to long vistas of southern pines; he'd almost forgotten the old deciduous forests of his youth. The air smelled different, not cleaner, certainly, but cooler; he imagined that if he could put the air on a slide and look at it under a microscope he'd see a few microbes dancing and darting. The air of Gunhill Park, on the other hand, would be crammed with all manner of minuscule bugs buzzing through the damp, dense as an electron cloud.

The next two mornings they swam at a man-made beach of gray sand a half mile from the cabin, then spent the afternoons fishing and hiking through the wooded hills. They didn't talk much at first, but at least the iPod stayed in the car. The first afternoon, they caught two largemouth bass and three crappies. They reminded each other how to clean, fillet, and lightly batter them, which resulted in a sparse but satisfying dinner in the dark on the buggy porch.

While fishing the second afternoon, Harry broke the silence by asking Dusty how his grandfather was doing.

"He's okay now. They said it wasn't a bad heart attack. Grandma says in a way it was a good thing. It'll force him to eat better and exercise more. You've been working out or something. The last time we hiked anywhere, I thought I was going to have to carry you." Harry grunted at this. Dusty put his rod and reel down on a rock and said, "When are we going to see your parents?"

"Why haven't I ever met them before?" Dusty asked.

The car curved and swooped among the hills that complicated the drive along the big river, the Susquehanna, once beautiful, now ashen and filled with poison. Harry mentally corrected himself; the steel mills are mostly dead and the water's supposed to be cleaner. I still wouldn't eat any fish out of it, though. After a few minutes he said, "It's kind of complicated. You know that my biological parents are dead."

"Yeah. The camping accident."

Harry debated for a moment whether or not to tell Dusty the

whole truth. Not yet, he thought. Too many adult-size burdens already. He said, "Bernie and May were my foster parents. You know what that means?"

"They adopted you."

"No, Uncle Lawrence and I were never actually adopted. We just lived with the Wileys and they took care of us. The state paid them to do it."

"They did it for the money?"

"Partly. They also thought it was a good thing to do, to take care of kids who didn't have anywhere else to live or parents that were able to do a good job." Harry stopped, then added, "You can decide for yourself what you think of them."

Bernie Wiley was working on a car in his driveway, an old gold Buick that had so many patches of rust creeping from its underbelly that it looked two-toned. The hood was up, as were Bernie's sleeves as he twisted a ratchet around and around, *snick, snick, snick,* as though the engine needed winding up. He looked up as Harry's rental car pulled in behind the Buick, then stood up straight, the socket wrench in his hand like a weapon. Harry felt his stomach tighten at the thought of seeing the Wileys face-to-face again after so many long, complicated years.

Dusty had the sense to leave the iPod on the seat; Harry was embarrassed at how glad he was that Bernie and May wouldn't have his son's bad manners to criticize, at least in that respect. He said, "Hi, Bernie. How is everything?"

Bernie nodded, then said, "Not so bad. Can't complain." That'll be the day, Harry thought. "She's waiting for you inside."

The house was bigger than he remembered, which was the opposite of what he'd expected. He thought, You always hear that, as you grow up, things shrink. But he'd always seen the little brick salt-box house as a circumscribed place, the walls so close, the rooms so cramped and dark. When he'd read the first Harry Potter book to Dusty, the boy magician's closet under the stairs had reminded him of the little bedroom he'd shared with Lawrence: the narrow, hard cots; the tiny, high window; the bare, cracked walls; the stacked cardboard boxes whose contents he never saw but whose labels he read every night before he went to sleep: "B's sum clothes," "Mom's cookbooks," "Photos." He had no idea if the labels meant anything or if the boxes had changed contents over the years without any attention paid to the words written on them. They were taped shut, and his curiosity about them never rose to the point where he'd cut them open and risk May's anger at his intrusion. The only box that held any real interest for him was the one labeled "Photos"; he wondered whose pictures were in there, if the label was true. Bernie as a child? May? Pictures of other children they'd fostered? Other blood relatives? Harry had asked once, and May had said only "I don't remember, Harry. Tend to today, not yesterday." Harry never knew exactly what that meant. He always felt he was tending to yesterday, today, and tomorrow, although while living with his foster parents, he never felt like he was getting anywhere no matter how much tending he did.

Now he and his son entered the house, which still smelled of cabbage and air freshener. "May?" he called from the front hallway, not seeing her in the living room. He knew she was probably in the kitchen but was reluctant to walk any farther in without an invitation.

"Is that Harry?" he heard an old woman's voice call from the rear of the house.

He put his hand on his son's shoulder, guiding him beyond the living room into the little white kitchen, where a short, elderly woman was chopping potatoes. "Harry?" she repeated as he came in, Dusty at his side. Harry went to give her a kiss. She jerked back at first, just a tiny movement, then let him finish the gesture, his lips touching her cool, dry cheek for an instant before she pulled away for a second time. Had he expected a hug? He couldn't remember what his expectations had been. He said, "You're looking great, May," which wasn't particularly true; she looked shorter and thicker than he remembered, her hair whiter, which wasn't surprising. But her cheeks were more sunken than they'd been before, at odds with her stoutness, and her skin was sallow, an unhealthy white-yellow under a layer of powder that didn't bode well for her health. "How are you doing?" he said, hoping that if she had a serious health issue, she'd tell him. Although, he thought, why should she? What would I do if I knew something like that? What would she think I could do, or would do? Then the real sadness hit him. Nothing, he thought. I'd do nothing. They'd expect nothing of me, and that's what they'd get.

"So this is Dustin," May said, chopping again.

"Yes," Harry said, holding his hand out toward his son as though he were offering him up.

"Hi," Dusty said, his voice as blank as his face.

"I haven't seen your father in, how many years has it been, Harry?"

"Twenty, give or take."

"You're not married to the boy's mother anymore."

"No."

"Well, it's just as well we weren't at the wedding. It wasn't a proper one anyway. Not in a church." Her eyes focused on Harry, the chopping ceasing for an instant. "She was pregnant, too."

Thank you for that, Harry thought sarcastically as he saw Dusty's eyes widen a bit. He hadn't known, Harry thought. He'd never done the math.

Harry said, "I thought you folks were all about forgiveness. Those without sin cast the first stone and all that." Oh God, he thought, this was a terrible mistake.

"You always were one to misinterpret scripture, Harry." She looked at Dusty. "Your uncle was the one we had hopes for. I'm sorry to say that Harry turned out as we feared."

"What fears are you talking about?" Harry said, forcing her attention back to him. "I'm not a criminal, May."

"Not in the eyes of the law, maybe. But you are walking a dangerous road, Harry, always have been. Nothing's changed. I knew you weren't going to stay married. Who's raising your boy?" She turned back to Dusty. "You go to church?"

Dusty looked startled again. "Sometimes."

"What does that mean? You find yourself a good church, boy, get yourself in right with Jesus."

"I'm not a big sinner, ma'am," Dusty said.

"We're all sinners, boy. You remember that, you'll be doing better." To Harry, she said, "I was real sorry to hear about Lawrence." Chop, chop. "The wages of sin, not even his."

Harry wanted to say, It wasn't my fault. But of course it was, in a way. Maybe I wanted him dead, Harry thought, but I would have stopped a bullet for him anyway.

Dusty said, "You think it's my dad's fault that Uncle Lawrence died?"

The knife stopped, completing the indoor silence. Outside, Bernie ratcheted something else in the big engine, *snick, snick, snick.*

"It was that story he wrote," May said. "Got people all riled up. The judge was a good man."

Harry was about to correct her when Dusty said, "He was a crook. And my dad got him locked up, which he deserved. His son was a psychopath, and murdered my uncle while trying to murder my dad. Are you saying"—Dusty moved a step closer to the old woman with the knife—"that he should have shot my dad instead?"

May held the knife in front of her like a shield, staring at the heated boy in front of her. "No, of course not. But you reap what you sow." As she looked at Dusty's face, something like fear or distaste colored her yellow cheeks.

"What do *you* sow?" Dusty said, now as angry as Harry had ever seen him, and he couldn't figure out his own reaction, something big and swelling and hard. Love, fear, something else. Pride, or elation. That's not good, he thought. I should be horrified. He realized that Dusty might blow altogether any minute, might say something that would make him feel bad later, might cause May to call Bernie in, the whole thing might become physical. Before May could answer Dusty's question, Harry said, "We'd better go. Come on, Dusty. Take care of yourself, May. I'm grateful for the bed, and the food. You gave me Tylenol once when I had a fever. Thanks for that, too." He took Dusty's arm, pulled gently, saying, "We've got to go."

To his relief, Dusty didn't resist the tug on his arm and walked with Harry out the front door and down the porch steps. As they passed him, Bernie said, "Did May set you straight, Harry?"

"Oh, yeah," Harry said. "Straight and narrow."

39

FIVE OF
CUPS

REVERSED

*The one you love
returns to you*

They were both quiet as they drove back
to the cabin in the woods. As the hills
flew by, Harry compared the peaks and
folds of the land with the flatness of
Florida, mostly because he didn't know
what to say. Should he upbraid his son
for speaking so to an old woman, or
should he thank him for coming to his
old man's defense? Neither seemed to
reflect the way he felt; mostly, he admired the way his son had exploded
outward with his feelings, had been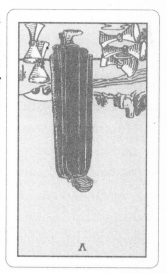
plainspoken without being rude. Although he supposed May Wiley
had thought him rude. Harry wondered if Ann would have thought
so. Maggie, he supposed, would have just nodded in agreement.
Dusty spoke, startling him.

"Was she always like that?"

"May?" Harry said. "Yeah, pretty much."

"Why doesn't she like you?"

Harry tried to think of a way to frame his answer that wasn't just a string of expletives about the Wileys, that wasn't simply judgmental.

"They're mean, in the literary sense. Stingy with their affections. With their money. With their entire selves, really."

"No wonder you don't deal with them. They suck."

Harry felt compelled to defend them, though he wasn't sure why. "I think they're scared," he said, realizing that it was something he believed to be true. "I didn't use to understand that, but they keep their world as contained as possible so that it's not too scary. I always wanted to know everything, always wanted to know the why of everything, too. That irritated the shit out of them."

"She liked Uncle Lawrence."

Harry thought before he spoke. "Lawrence was a pleaser. He told them everything they wanted to hear. He was pretty wild when he was a teenager, you know, but they never knew it. He got caught with a joint once, behind the high school. May and Bernie swore that I must have given it to him, but I didn't. He'd given me one, though, the month before. I coughed for two days and it made me so paranoid that I couldn't look anyone in the eye for about the same length of time. I never saw the fun in it." He looked sideways at Dusty. That last bit is a lie, the judge said. Just make sure that when you're lying to him, you know you're doing it.

Dusty looked away from his father, watched the gleaming trees speed by. Harry asked, "Have you ever tried it?"

Dusty shook his head, and Harry thought it was probably the truth. He was getting his father mojo back; he was beginning to be able to read his son's face and body language again. "That's good. You'll probably do all sorts of terrible and stupid things once you're in college; most kids do, but in high school you're just not equipped. I know that's a cliché, but it's true. All teenagers get stupid. No offense. It comes with the crazy hormones and the growth spurts.

You're not immune, you know. You'll be stupid sometimes, too. The important thing is—"

Dusty said, "To not get caught."

Dusty's face broke into a small but welcome smile when Harry laughed. "Well, yes, but it's more important that you know what you're putting in your body, which means you have to pick your friends pretty carefully, because an awful lot of people will think it's funny to watch you eat poison and then squirm or hallucinate headless clowns or die or something."

"They tell us all that stuff in school, Dad. I know not to get addicted to anything."

"You better not or I'll kick your ass."

Dusty shifted in his seat, looking out the window. After a few minutes he said, "Soon I'll be big enough to kick yours."

"What the hell does that mean?"

Dusty looked back at him, his face hard. After a long time, he said, "When's the last time you got drunk, Dad?"

Darcy Murphy pulled the van into a vacant lot a half mile down the highway. He hated getting out of the cool interior, into the weight of the air, the heat making him dizzy. He murmured a few choice obscenities, made sure his cell phone was in his pocket, and locked the van door. He trudged along the edge of the asphalt, not easy in heavy work boots on the tilt of the sandy grass, sloping on his left down to the drainage ditch. There was no chance of rain today, no help from the clouds. The sun lay on his shoulders like a woolen shawl. He thought of his grandmother. She would have said it was a beautiful day, loving every degree above ninety. The sweat ran down him thick, like oil, into all the crevices of his body, making everything burn and itch.

A couple of big rigs passed him, along with a low-ride Camaro, but the good ole boy inside didn't give Darcy a glance, not a look, not a holler. That was good, Darcy thought, although it was no comfort when he considered that he might well pass out if he didn't hit shade soon.

He got to a pair of palmettos that grew at an angle across the road from the Babyface Salon. One trunk lay on the ground almost perpendicular to the other, and their pointed leaves spread wide apart, making the shade intermittent but better than nothing. He hadn't thought to bring a bottle of water or even beer, which was stupid. Although it would already be hot enough to steep a tea bag in by this time, he thought, but he knew if he kept the image of a glass of iced tea in his head long enough, he'd be insane by nightfall.

He hunkered down in the crotch of the palmettos, binoculars around his neck. He scooted his rear end around several times until he found a spot where he could sit upright in reasonable comfort without putting too much weight on the wrong part of his body. He couldn't lean back, the bark being rough and sharp; he remembered an old high school classmate describing punji sticks to him, a favorite wounding device of the Vietcong. Bamboo rods sharpened to fine points and then laid in a grid in a camouflaged hole in the ground; unlucky soldiers would fall in and be skewered in forty places. Darcy imagined some passerby finding him in a day or two, stuck to the tree and barbecued by the heat. Then he thought of iced tea again, and almost got up to leave.

But then he saw the giant Thorpe woman leaving the salon once more, the two dark little girls trailing after her. She locked the door of the salon, then turned and walked not to the shotgun shack where he knew she lived but to the double-wide beyond it. She and the children knocked on the door of the trailer and were let in. Darcy wasn't sure this was worth much, figuring they might just be visiting since there seemed to be such chumminess in this neck of the woods, but then the front door of the Dupree house opened again, this time disgorging the entire Thorpe party, as well as the two women who lived there. The fortune teller and her blond niece left the double-wide with two small suitcases and walked toward the big house behind the purple shrine. The Thorpes followed them, empty-handed. They disappeared through the pine trees, although it seemed likely that they were headed for the Purple Lady's house. He was pretty sure they hadn't spotted him. He got the cell phone from his pocket and pushed the call button, having the number already programmed in. He loved his country, but after he reported in, he was going home for a shower and a cold, cold beer.

From a pay phone in the parking lot of the park office, Harry called to confirm the appointment he'd made the following day with Louise Glade at Cantwell University. They had the rest of the day free, their last in the cabin, so they made one more fishing expedition on the big lake. A cooler lay next to Harry, placed on a large and level rock. When Dusty was little, they had fished all the time at different places in northern Virginia and southern Maryland, the same cooler between them. At that time, Harry would occasionally risk putting one beer in and had never thought much about it. Now he knew one beer was potentially disastrous; the cooler contained only soda and Gatorade.

"You should know that your mom and I are not getting back together," Harry said.

"I figured."

"You okay with that?"

"Does it matter? I mean, whether or not I'm okay with it won't change anything, will it?"

"I guess not. I just wanted to know. Your mom said something about you wanting us to be a regular family again. I thought you had a right to know that it wasn't going to be like that."

"It was never like that, Dad." This was a mutter, and Harry wasn't sure he heard it right.

"What?"

"I never thought we were gonna be all happy-happy anyway. You know Mom's got a boyfriend, right?"

Harry hadn't known but wasn't as surprised as he should have been. "Oh. Well, I guess it's good that it's all right with you."

"I didn't say it was all right with me. It's just the way it is."

Harry thought for a moment, then said, "You miss your uncle."

Dusty seemed taken aback. "Well, yeah, I guess."

"I miss him, too. But it's not as bad as it used to be. You just have to wait awhile and let time do its thing. Most things don't hurt as bad after a while as they do at first."

"Did time make you hate Mom less?"

"I don't hate your mom."

"I do."

Harry was surprised by Dusty's frankness. "Why?" he said before considering whether or not he wanted to hear the answer.

"Come on, Dad. Did you really not know? Uncle Lawrence was always at our house, mostly when you weren't there." Dusty was facing the water, his jawbone poking through his thin cheek as he ground his teeth between sentences. "When you were traveling. Didn't you know? How could you not know?"

Harry realized he was holding his breath, his hands gripping his pole. He didn't say anything for a few minutes while looking for a place to put it down. He found a pair of rocks where he lodged the handle of the rod just above the reel, knowing that if a fish took the bait now, he might lose the whole thing. He turned to look at his son, who had a scared, mulish look that Harry hated.

"Talk," Harry said.

Dusty stared at a squirrel in a tree across the lake that seemed interested in the two of them. "I walked in on them once." His face was so white it looked like cream. Harry could see the pulse beating in his slight neck, a blue throbbing under delicate skin. "I thought either you knew and you were, you know, like, a wimp, or you didn't, and you were stupid." Dusty started crying, and Harry's arms went around him.

"I was both," Harry said into his son's thick hair.

40

SIX OF
SWORDS

Going somewhere.
Things will improve.
A little

The next morning it rained; Harry thought that they had timed their fishing well. They left the cabin and drove east, stopping early at a family-style restaurant on the highway. Over breakfast, Harry told Dusty as much as he knew about Charles Ziegart and Emily Timms. "I've been reading a biography of Nikola Tesla, Emily's hero."

"Another science chick?" At least his son seemed to be getting the idea that it was good to occasionally swallow before speaking.

"He was a science dude." Dusty smirked. Harry went on, "He was Serbian but became an American citizen. He was a contemporary of Thomas Edison's. They hated each other, Tesla at least with some reason. Edison essentially stole the whole idea of alternating current from him."

"I've heard of it, but I don't know exactly what it means."

"Alternating current is what powers virtually every electrical outlet in the world. It's efficient and incredibly safe. Edison's original system used direct current, which is neither. Tesla was working for Westinghouse when he designed an AC system, so Westinghouse, and later Edison, got all the profits."

"That sucks."

"You bet. Tesla invented radio, too."

"I thought it was that Italian dude."

"Marconi. He took credit for it and got rich, but even the federal courts ruled that the original concepts belonged to Tesla. He invented lots of other things. X-ray machines, remote-control ships, even some of the technology used in cell phones. And this was all in the early twentieth century, when a lot of this kind of stuff was only taken seriously in science fiction. He offered his services to the American government over and over, but they ignored him while he was alive. He was too far ahead of his time in all kinds of ways, so a lot of people thought he was crazy."

"Like da Vinci. Inventing submarines before there were engines that could power them."

"Exactly. After he died, the FBI took away most of his notes and they disappeared."

"Whoa. Like *The X-Files*."

"But real. He'd figured out a way to generate a huge amount of electricity for almost no cost, no fossil fuels needed. Sometimes he gave demonstrations for big audiences, where he'd do things like turn on lamps by plugging them into the ground and make bolts of lightning in the sky over his lab."

"How?"

"No one knows. The biography I read said that he could take just a small bit of power and somehow send it into the ground; the beam would go back and forth through the earth, stopped by the crust, back and forth, over and over, building and building with each pass. The beam travels at the speed of light, so the whole process only takes a fraction of a second. When you tap it, the result is a huge amount of power, amplified thousands of times over the original source. One of his big dreams was to build an enormous tower and broadcast electricity so everyone could pick it up on a receiver and use it for free, like radio."

"It could, like, stop global warming."

"It could help, anyway. The problem was, who'd pay for the tower? People don't like giving stuff away for free, especially when it's stuff they're already selling. He actually started building it, but the money ran out, so it was never finished. Eventually the tower was torn down for scrap metal."

Dusty said, "I can see why he'd be a hero to a science nerd like Emily Timms."

"Damn right. All she wanted to do was save the world." He said before he remembered who he was talking to, "I'm wondering if someone killed her for it."

The waitress was bored, which suited Jonathan just fine. He said, "You understand the instructions I've given you?"

Darcy nodded, three quick jerks.

"You have any questions?"

"There'll be backup, you said?"

"Plenty. Don't worry, Mr. Murphy. We wouldn't leave you on your own. There is some risk, I won't lie to you about that. But because you're a familiar face in the neighborhood, you won't be arousing any premature suspicion. It's really fortunate that we could find someone of your caliber so perfectly situated for our needs." Jonathan hadn't taken a drink of his coffee. He had on glasses that he didn't need, and a baseball cap that he'd bought that morning at a truck stop even farther out of town than this hellhole. He intended to leave the Tampa Bay Bucs T-shirt in a Dumpster along with the hat and glasses. It was unlikely that anyone would remember the two of them, but even if they did, it was far less likely that anyone would remember his face. He'd probably throw the cell phones into Lake Austell, heavy metals be damned. "All we need you to do is draw the old lady out of her house. We really want the fortune teller's niece, but the older woman will do if she's all we can get."

"What do you want me to do with my gun?"

"Nothing. The only reason I suggest it is that you might need to show it to the old lady, but only if she gives you any serious trouble. I wouldn't even load it, if I were you. We don't want you shooting anyone." He watched while Darcy took a sip of coffee with a very slightly trembling hand. "Mr. Murphy," he said, giving Darcy a sweet, confident smile. "I've got your back."

Louise Glade ate her steak as though she was on death row. "I love this place. I only come here once a year with my husband on our anniversary."

"If I pay, it's deductible," said Harry, relieved that he only had a salad. Dusty had gotten a hamburger and French fries. The three of them were sitting in a chain steak house on the outskirts of Lucasta, Pennsylvania. The decor tended to faux-medieval: resin casts of suits of armor, halberds crossed on the fake wood walls, coats of arms and tapestries hung at regular intervals. It was dark, and the light had a reddish-yellowish tint, brought on by the orange globes in the hanging wooden light fixtures; they were covered with metallic studs and made Harry think of saddles.

"I hope you do right by Emily," said Louise around the plank of beef that she'd just put in her mouth. Harry had been hoping to speak to Gillian DeGraff, to Pamela Ziegart, to anyone in the Ziegart School. The only person he'd found in was Louise, who'd looked around as though she was being hunted and scooted Harry and Dusty out of the office. The term had ended and she said most everyone was out of town or recreating in some way. He hadn't called to make appointments with anyone else at the university because he was fairly certain that no one would see him if he warned them of his trip. Even if he talked to no one at Cantwell besides Louise, he still wanted to take a look at the campus, at where the Ziegarts had lived, where the accident had happened. Louise had hinted that she was hungry and that her husband would be working the night shift. When Harry had offered to buy her an early dinner, she had been so happy that she was almost pretty.

"I'll do my best to be fair to Emily," said Harry. "To be honest, I'm not even sure I'm going to write anything about her. I do find it interesting how many people around here seem angry at her. I understand that she didn't break up Ziegart's first marriage. But I guess if she threw herself at him, that could have put a lot of people off."

Louise swallowed a large bite of meat, then wiped her mouth. "Oh no. Oh my God, no. She wouldn't have gone near him in that way. Charlie went after *her*. He swept her away the moment she walked through the door into the office. You can't imagine the force of his charm when he had it on full blast. She was fresh from the farmhouse by the look of her, and she didn't have a chance."

"Why?" Harry asked, although he was pretty sure he knew.

Louise looked at him with pity. "So he could take her work, of course."

Dusty spoke for the first time, having overcome his fascination with the extravagant way that Louise attacked her dinner. "It's so bogus that he could do that."

Harry had already explained to his son the position that most graduate students were in regarding their research, so he ignored the remark. "Did she have any friends here? Besides you? Any other students?"

Louise nodded. Harry blessed the fact that her mouth was closed so nothing tumbled out with the motion. She chewed for a bit, swallowed, and said, "Fay Levy. Sorry I didn't think of her before, but she wasn't a graduate student. She was a physics major while Emily was here."

"An undergraduate?"

"Uh-huh. There weren't a lot of girls around, and I think that alone gave them something in common. Fay worshiped Emily. Her role model, and so on."

Harry said, "I'm guessing that didn't work out all that well."

"You said it," Louise said around an enormous wad of meat. Harry had a hard time looking at her; she'd apparently never been taught to close her mouth when it was full of food, even if the food tended to fall out. "Fay managed to graduate just after Charlie died. I haven't seen her since."

"Do you know where she is now?"

Louise shrugged, dislodging a fragment of French fry from the side of her mouth. "I know she didn't go to graduate school anywhere. No one in the department was asked for a recommendation letter. I would've been the one to type it."

"Anyone I could ask who might know where she is?"

Louise shook her head again, then said, "No one's around, so we could go back to the office and you could hang over my shoulder while I do an online search. Even if we just find out where she's working, I have phone books in my desk for most of the towns around here. You could look in them, see if her name's there. I've never had a reason to look before. But if she got married and changed her name or if she moved out of the area, it won't do you any good. Although," she added, swallowing her last enormous bite, "I doubt she's married. If you know what I mean."

"It's worth a shot," Harry said, thankful that she was finished with her meal. "I appreciate it."

"It's okay," said Louise. "What's for dessert?"

. . .

The department offices were as quiet as a desert. There was no Fay Levy in the local phone directory, but Louise had luck on the Internet. She was listed on the faculty of a private girl's high school in Godfrey Lake, a town about fifty miles from Lucasta. Louise found a listing for "F. Levy" in the white pages online. She even allowed Harry to make the call from the office phone since he couldn't get his cell phone to work. He left a message on an answering machine, including the number of the hotel where he and Dusty were staying. He thanked Louise and promised her that, if they returned, she'd be treated to another steak dinner.

"I need to check in with Mom, and see how Grandpa's doing. Can I try your cell phone again, Dad?"

"Your mom didn't buy you another one, eh?"

"No. She said you didn't think it was a good idea."

"See if you can get it to work. I haven't had any luck."

Dusty took Harry's cell phone and power cord. Seeing the phone's blank display, he plugged it into the outlet in the car under the CD player. He stared at the display for another few minutes, then said, "It's not charging."

"Shit," said Harry. "I mean, crud. I got a new battery from the guy at the phone place. Or rather, a recycled one. It worked for a few days."

"It's not working now."

"You can call her on the phone in our room. It'll cost a million dollars, but I don't know what else to do. I can't even check my voice mail. We should go back to the hotel anyway. Maybe we can find a good movie on pay-per-view or something. I want to stay by the phone in case Fay Levy calls. I can't do much else after that meal anyway. I feel like Caligula when he couldn't take time out for a trip to the vomitorium."

"Gross."

"That's my special charm, son. I hope you inherited it. It drives the ladies wild." A moment later Harry said, "Speaking of which, I'm about to start seeing someone. Well, I guess I've already been seeing her. But not really."

Dusty rolled his eyes. "God, I don't have a chance at being anything but a geek, do I? Mom keeps saying I got all your genes. You're not making me feel too optimistic about my future."

"We're not geeks, we're intellectuals." At Dusty's look, Harry added, "I know; in high school they're the same thing. Anyway, this woman and I have been friends for a while. I've been hesitating for a lot of reasons, but they're all pretty bogus."

"The Waitress?"

"She's a cook."

"Does she like you?"

"I think so." He thought about Maggie's face when he'd asked her to go to Serge's party. There was only one likely reason that she'd said yes, yet he'd more or less stomped on her emotions once she'd arrived at his house. The realization made him feel sick. "I've hurt her feelings pretty badly, so this may not be a simple matter of just asking her out."

"Are you supposed to give her jewelry or something? That's what Mom always says you're supposed to do when you want a girl to like you."

"I don't think buying Maggie jewelry will impress her at all. Maybe if I can keep her out of jail for zapping people with a stun gun, she'll decide I'm okay."

"She zaps people? Cool."

Dusty phoned his mother from their room. Harry was glad the call was short because he knew it would cost the moon, but it was depressing how little his son and his ex-wife had to say to each other. Then Harry made another expensive call to his own machine. There was only one message, Julie Canfield reiterating her offer to help him with his research over the summer. He shook off his dismay at this and called Maggie's house. The phone rang and rang, but no one answered. Oh, well, he thought. At least I don't have to say "I want to be your boyfriend" on an answering machine.

They were in the home stretch of a movie that Dusty had chosen, something involving exploding cars and men kicking and punching and shooting at one another; Harry was gleefully annoying Dusty by making more comparisons with Caligula when the phone rang. He picked it up after telling Dusty to turn the TV down. It was Fay Levy.

41

THE EMPRESS

REVERSED

She loses everything.
She is barren and bereft

Maggie said, "I only need to make one more trip. Everything I want to take will fit in my car. Miss Tokay's taking a nap. Will you check on her in an hour or so? She's talking about ascending again."

Josie sat on the couch in Miss Tokay's once-grand living room, a dozen cards splayed on the dainty table in front of her. "She always does that."

"I know, but she said she saw her lawyer recently and tidied up her affairs. Now she seems more tuckered out than usual."

"When will you be back?" Josie asked, not liking how much her voice was shaking.

"By tonight. You'll be all right?"

"I'll be fine. But the cards are ominous. You were right to bring us here, I guess. But then again, trouble follows me around for sure. I don't know if it matters where I go." She looked up. "You're not going to see him, are you?"

Maggie sighed, an explosive breath out, then spoke with more fire than Josie had seen in her for a long while. "He's not even in town. He's gone back to his wife. That should make you happy."

"Maggie, I only want *you* to be happy. I knew he wasn't going to stick, is all."

"I guess you were right." Maggie's voice was harsh. Josie didn't like when her niece got all feisty and mad. It wasn't her normal way, and Josie feared her sometimes, although she would never have admitted it to a soul, not even Baby. She hated the tiny whispers of doubt about her niece's sanity, but they were there nonetheless, little ghosts of worry that danced in the back of her mind, darting into the front from time to time. Maggie said in a weird, tight voice, "You can stop it now. I don't have any expectations left. The hope's all gone. I haven't quite gotten rid of the wanting part, but I'm pretty sure that'll be killed too if we chisel at it long enough."

"What do you mean? I don't want you to give up all hope. And hope of what, anyway?" Josie hated how weak and silly her voice sounded, as if she was talking with a head full of water.

Maggie leaned closer. "That someday I'll do some of the things that burn in my heart, that I'll ever be able to speak openly about important things. That I won't be all alone, forever and ever. You've got what you wanted. I know it doesn't make you happy, but maybe it'll make you satisfied."

Josie raised her own voice. "I'm sorry I'm not lighthearted enough for you. I apologize for having lost everyone I've ever really loved. A husband, a child, a sister. My whole family." She paused, breathing hard.

Maggie's lips compressed. "I've lost everybody, too. Except for you." She reached for the deck as though she was going to take a card, then pulled her hand back. She said, "At least you had your own family for a while." Without saying anything else, she turned and left the room. Josie heard the Toyota pull away a few minutes later, beating down panic at the notion that Maggie was never coming back. She turned over the top card on the deck, the one Maggie would have drawn. It was the the Chariot, reversed. "An unethical victory," she muttered, the hated quaver still in her voice. She looked at the cards for a few more minutes before she went to find a glass.

Harry had made the appointment with Fay Levy for one o'clock. After eating breakfast, they went to one he'd made earlier at the state police barracks in Bellstade, about halfway between Lucasta and Godfrey Lake.

Commander Matthew Sutton was an inch or so shorter than Harry, covered in freckles and red fur. His hair was short and curly; Harry suspected that the man had had to fight the tendency for everyone he knew to call him Rusty. His eyes were so light that they almost disappeared into the wrinkles around his eyes, although otherwise he didn't look much over thirty. His muscles made his uniform bulge around his arms; Harry flexed his own leaner biceps automatically, then stopped himself, embarrassed.

Commander Sutton was more welcoming than Harry had expected; this was explained by the man himself when he gestured them to two chairs in his tiny industrial office. "Not much to do right about now except to pull speeders heading to Philly on the turnpike. Occasionally one of them sails through a guardrail. A few years ago we had a big drug bust that made the national news. Sometimes people rent old farms, build small grass landing strips and drug labs, and start doing business; they can fly product in and out without much scrutiny. The last one we broke up yielded six arrests and so much meth you could keep a stadium-full of people high for a year. That was the highlight of my career so far." He eyed Dusty. "This is your son, you said?"

"Yes. He's acting as my research assistant."

"Now, that's real nice. You gonna be a reporter someday?"

"Maybe," Dusty said. Harry was relieved that his son's tone was neutral, even polite.

Sutton handed them two manila folders, one fat, one thin. He said they could look at them while he got coffee and disappeared out the door. Harry thumbed through the fat one first, Dusty looking over his shoulder. Harry could feel his son's warm, damp breath on his ear as he quickly shoved the photos of the accident scene under the written report. "Oh my God," he said after a minute.

"What?" asked Dusty.

"Look at that." He pointed to a line in the report. "No one ever said anything."

Sutton came back a few minutes later. He'd brought two paper cups of coffee with him and a can of Coke. Harry took the coffee with thanks, nudging Dusty to do the same for the soda. Then Dusty pulled out his notebook and pencil, and "assumed the position" as he called it, ready to write down everything anyone said.

Sutton said, "When Ziegart died, it was the first time in local memory that we made the national news. The meth lab was time number two."

Harry nodded. "It seems everybody ran Todd Greenleaf's story, picked up from the wire. I spoke to him, but I thought I should talk to you directly. I appreciate your help."

"Glad to do it. How is Todd?"

"Seems to be enjoying himself."

"He always did. Lousy writer, but not a bad guy. At least he did his best to get his facts right before he printed them."

Harry gestured to the folder and said, "I didn't realize how severely Emily Ziegart was hurt in the accident."

Sutton nodded as he leaned back in the big swivel chair. "Poor thing was a mess. All her injuries were internal, so she didn't look that bad. But when we found 'em, they'd both been thrown from the car, and she was the only one conscious. She was giving him mouth-to-mouth and CPR like crazy, and she was crying and all bloody, screaming at the EMTs that they had to save him."

"So you don't think she did anything to try to precipitate the accident?"

"Of course not. If I'd thought that for a second, I'd have followed it up. But there was no doubt what happened."

"Someone suggested that she put the yellow jacket in the car."

"Who? Only if she'd been suicidal. She was devastated afterwards, that was obvious. She kept going back and forth, trying to resuscitate Ziegart, then running back to the car; she tore it apart inside, looking for his EpiPen. He'd dropped it at the party they'd just left. Terrible luck for both of them. The accident ruined her life. I can't imagine why anyone would suggest otherwise."

"I didn't think the claim had any merit, but I had to ask."

"Was it the ex-wife?"

"Why do you say that?"

Sutton paused, looking at Harry over the rim of his cup. "She was all over the place when Ziegart was dying in the hospital, giving orders, acting all broken up, but in this nasty, bossy way. I actually had to put one of my men outside Emily's room to keep her out. The old witch kept trying to go in and harass her, even after the poor girl had found out she'd been all tore up inside."

"I appreciate that you also pulled the file on Doug McNeill."

"Now that one I don't remember so well. I didn't handle it personally. According to the report, it was a straightforward case of choking. He was known to eat too fast, and he lived alone, so when it happened, that was all she wrote."

Harry paged through the manila folder. "He was found by Jonathan Ziegart?"

"Yeah. It's a small town, a small campus. The faculty families mix with the students socially. Jonathan Ziegart dropped by McNeill's all the time. He was just a kid, if I remember right."

"So it says here. Seventeen years old." Harry looked back up at the commander. "I've met him."

"Oh? I saw him at the hospital when his dad was dying, and later at the inquest, but I never spoke to him personally."

Harry said, "No way McNeill's death could have been murder?"

"No way. It's pretty hard to make someone choke to death and leave no trace of it."

"You must know that Emily killed herself not long after she left here, which wasn't long after Ziegart's death." Sutton nodded. Harry went on, "Do you know any details? Where, how, or when, things like that?"

"No, I never got anything official, but there's no reason I should have. By the time she left, the file was closed on Charles Ziegart." Sutton drained the last of his coffee. "You don't remember everybody you come across in this line of work, but I remember her. She was real nice to me when I interviewed her, which they aren't always. Sometimes they blame us or the EMTs for whatever happened, especially when it's really bad. She kept thanking me for trying to help. I was in the room when they told her that she'd lost the baby, and she started crying, and it was just about the saddest thing I'd ever seen. She just kind of crumpled, got all lost-looking. I heard from the doctor later that she couldn't ever have no more, her insides were so messed up."

Darcy Murphy felt his fear like acid eating away at his stomach. He couldn't eat lunch, terror having filled his belly, so he'd broken his promise to his wife and to God and to his dead mother and had what his old drinking buddies called a "liquid lunch." Three shots of bourbon. And some nuts. That was protein at least. He kept telling himself that this was his moment, his offering to his country, to the world. Now he knew how all the great heroes felt. John Wayne, Neil Armstrong, Babe Ruth, this was how they felt before the big scene, the long step, the championship game. Like mice were gnawing at your insides, running around and chattering inside you, making your hands shake and your jaw tremble and your vision waver. When it came to the sticking point, he hoped his courage would screw up nice and proper, and that he'd be able to do his job and make his dead mother proud.

The gun felt cold and heavy in his pocket; he'd loaded it against the agent's advice because he didn't trust anybody, not even the Federal Bureau of Investigation, to keep him safe from the fortune teller. He tried to think of the gun as a shield against danger, but he kept pulling it out and checking the safety; his imagination kept painting pictures of the gun going off in his pants and shooting off his foot or worse. The last thing he wanted was to go out like an asshole, his dong blown off in a fumbling bloody blur. The thought of being a dead joke, a serious contender in the Darwin Awards, made his skin quiver with horror.

It was only ten-thirty when they left the state police barracks, so there was plenty of time to have an early lunch and to make the long drive to Godfrey Lake. They traveled on a winding, two-lane highway through more farm country. They passed a yellow traffic sign depicting a horse and buggy, and Dusty said, "What does that mean? There's a time portal somewhere around here?"

Harry said, "Sort of. Although I think the Amish are masters of the Internet and real estate these days, so it's more like a wormhole to an alternate universe than a trip back in time."

After a minute, Dusty said, "No one ever said she was pregnant?"

"No. Not a soul."

"Do you think it's important?"

"It might help explain her suicide, I suppose, along with the general horror of her whole Cantwell experience. But I don't know."

"You think someone offed her?"

Harry glanced at his son, not willing to take his eyes from the steep curves of the road for long. "You know, this isn't a joke."

Dusty looked sheepish. "Sorry."

"But you're right. I think it's very possible that someone offed her."

He could see the shrine now, down the road, a ghastly thing in concrete and purple paint. It seemed uglier today, an overcast sky making it look like an insane carnival tomb. He'd always felt the wrongness of it, its unnatural colors giving him a bellyache, but now the wrongness was tinged with violence and a hatred for order. He felt it laughing at him like a big, purple clown.

He drove past it, sweat making his back stick to the vinyl seat, and pulled into the empty lot in front of the Babyface Salon. He parked the van and slowly got out, feeling the thump, thump of the gun against his thigh. He took a moment to look up at the blue-gray sky, the heat lying on him like a blanket, thinking, It's gonna rain soon. Will that be good or bad? Then he looked around at the pine trees on either side of the road, at the shotgun shack to the left of the salon, at the double-wide beyond it, then to the other side of the road, where there was a small clapboard house set far back, a lame truck rusting on cinder blocks in the shady front yard. No birds sang, no wind blew. Darcy wondered where all the surveillance was. He looked at his watch. It was four minutes before three. Showtime.

42

KNIGHT OF SWORDS

REVERSED

Lies, bigger lies, and secrets.
Don't turn your back on him

Fay Levy's small brick house was only three feet away on either side from homes that were almost identical to hers. She was short and solid with long dark ringlets and big brown eyes, and she wore jeans and a bright red sweatshirt. She opened the door with a terse smile and only the briefest series of questions as to Harry's bona fides. He almost wished she'd been more reluctant to talk to him; single women should be more careful, he thought. How was she to

know that he wasn't someone untrustworthy, in spite of having his fourteen-year-old with him? He thought about Quick and the lost Jake, and wanted to pull his son to his side and hold him there while lecturing the woman, who had to be almost thirty, about Bad Men and Ulterior Motives, auras be damned. The hallway was dark, with stairs facing the front door leading up into even deeper darkness. The room they followed her into, however, was light and comfortable and pretty, with fat, flowery furniture and a big uncurtained window to the porch. The room was small, with a wall that was almost all fireplace, flanked by tall, crammed bookcases. Here a fireplace makes sense, Harry thought. She offered them hot tea, saying that it was all she had. They both declined. The first thing she said after they'd all sat down was "Why did it take you so long?"

"I beg your pardon?"

"When Charlie died, everyone in the world was wringing their hands and moaning about the Great Loss to Science. Emily kills herself, and it never even made the *Lucasta Mirror.*"

"Why was that?"

"Oh, come on!" Her long feather earrings swayed with her anger, catching in her black curls. "Everyone at Cantwell knew that Charlie was sucking all her work up like a big fat leech and taking all the bows and awards." She shook her head. "After Emily's death, there was nothing about it anywhere. I looked." She stared at a loaded bookshelf beside the fireplace. "If she'd been a man, everyone would have been beating their breasts about what a loss to science *her* death was. Not to mention a terrible injustice. But Cantwell is such a fucking old boys' club." She glanced at Dusty and apologized for her language. "I thought you folks' job was to investigate stuff. No one investigated anything. Lazy sons of bitches. Sorry."

Dusty was furiously scribbling, and Harry feared that he was writing down every obscenity. "You were close to her," Harry said.

"We were best friends. When I came to Cantwell, I expected long nights drinking coffee and beer and smoking endless cigarettes, working out the Theory of Everything with young, excited colleagues." She snorted. "Instead, it was one big frat party. I was the only undergraduate woman in the whole fucking program." Another look at Dusty. "Sorry. But every time I came into a room, all conversation stopped. They made jokes about women's . . . anatomy, and made fun of my hair. They wanted me gone. They wanted Emily gone, too, but she was married to Charlie, so there wasn't much they could do to her. He protected her, in his way." She looked at Harry with shining eyes; he realized she was on the edge of tears. "She wound up protecting me. Because of that, those assholes started rumors that we were a dyke couple. I happen to be a lesbian, which didn't help anything. But no, in case you're about to ask, Emily wasn't my lover. She was completely infatuated with Charlie, for all the good it did her."

Harry glanced at Dusty, head down and writing madly in the composition book. "If Emily was so smart, why did everyone want her out so badly, other than Charlie?"

She looked at him with disgust. "They were jealous, obviously. Don't tell me you've never run into anything like it. If the girl is pretty, she must be stupid. If she's not, then she must be stupid as well as ugly. If she's smart, oh my God, you'd better stomp on her in case she gets any ideas about being as good as anybody else."

Harry thought about Ronnie Ho and Julie Canfield. "So it's a good strategy to hook up with a professor."

Fay got so angry at this Harry could almost see the colors emanating from her, reds and greens and blacks. "That isn't what happened. And it isn't such a good *strategy* anyway if the guy rips you off." Harry almost shot a look of triumph at Dusty but managed to keep his eyes on Fay. "Emily just wanted to do her work and be left alone. She wanted friends, too, but she saw right away that that wasn't going to happen. Charlie promised her eternal love and world peace, and she bought it, at least at first. By the time she knew what she was really in for, she was married to the asshole. And she figured at least she could try to save the world, even if her name was never associated with it."

A gray tabby cat the size of a wolverine wandered into the room and made his way to Fay's chair. She reached down and picked him up; Harry was impressed by her strength, since the cat looked like he weighed twenty pounds or so. "His name's Nick." She stroked him as she said, "That reminds me. You wanted to see her last letter to me." She stood up and deposited Nick on Harry's lap. It felt as though he'd had a piece of furniture thrust onto him. He petted the cat, who seemed reasonably pleased and started kneading Harry's thighs. Dusty appeared to enjoy his father's winces and muted gasps of pain as the cat pierced the fabric of his pants with fine claws. Fay returned in a moment.

"Is Nick named after Nikola Tesla?" Harry asked, half joking.

Fay's eyes grew big with surprise. "How did you guess that?" He shrugged. She said, "You know more about her than I gave you credit for. That's good. I feel better about letting you read this." She handed Harry a handwritten letter on thick parchment stationery. Harry took it and shimmied his thighs enough to get Nick to jump off him. "I've never shown this to anyone," Fay said. "I'm not sure I should show it to you. But I guess it can't hurt Emily now."

There was a monogram on the top, brown in intertwined Gothic letters, CEZ. Charles Edgar Ziegart. The curvy blue handwriting looked as though it had been made with a fountain pen, the shape of the letters feminine and young. He looked at the date; it was six years ago.

> *Dear Fay,*
>
> *Whatever you hear, I want you to know that there was nothing you could have done to change anything. This is the best end to a bad situation. Don't defend me to anyone. It won't help me and it will hurt you.*
>
> *I have too many regrets to count, but one of my greatest ones is that I failed my responsibility to you. I'm sorry most of all about the wheat fields. When you pass them, remember that you are unique in all the world, because I made you my friend.*
>
> *Em*

He gave the letter to Dusty, who read it, his mouth open. Harry restrained an urge to tell his son to close his mouth. Instead he asked

Fay, perched once more in the big chair, the cat returned to her lap, "What did she mean about the wheat fields?"

"It's a reference to *The Little Prince*. It's my favorite book. I used to joke with her about the fox." Her eyes were dim and sad, her hand slow as she treated the cat to gentle wipes down his spine.

Harry said, "I read it a long time ago." To Dusty, he thought. "You'll have to excuse my memory. What about the fox?"

Dusty looked up. "You especially liked that part. Where the prince tames the fox, and he says that wheat fields will always remind him of the prince's hair?"

Harry was surprised that his son not only retained such a sentimental memory but could remark upon it so unself-consciously. He remembered now that he'd almost been brought to tears by it, something about a lonely fox and a lonely little boy, and at the time, he'd been thinking of his brother, Lawrence. Now he realized he'd also been thinking about himself.

Fay Levy got up again, sending the cat to the floor with a loud thump, and went to one of the overstuffed bookcases. She pulled a small hardcover from the top shelf. Harry recognized the book at once. It was missing the dust jacket and was worn around the edges. A silk bookmark with a flower pattern had been placed between two middle pages. Fay handed it to him.

Harry opened to where the bookmark held its place, a passage in which a fox was speaking to the wandering boy.

The wheat fields have nothing to say to me. And that is sad. But you have hair that is the color of gold. Think how wonderful that will be when you have tamed me! The grain, which is also golden, will bring me back the thought of you.

Harry smiled at the memory of reading to Dusty, his head weighty on Harry's chest as he sat in a big chair and hurt his throat making a different voice for every character, to his little son's delight. Harry replaced the bookmark and closed the slim book. "How well did you know Doug McNeill?" he said.

Fay grew quiet at that, her eyes squinting as she sat down again. "The three of us were pretty close. Doug was her only other friend besides me. The Three Freaks, I believe we were called. Poor Doug. We both were always trying to get him to exercise with us, but he thought walking the half block to campus was like running a marathon."

"Did Doug work with Emily on the Ziegart effect?" Fay shook her head. "Then how come he was on the original paper?"

Fay looked at him, considering her answer. Then she said, "He and I were the only people who seemed to think there was anything wrong with how Charlie was using Emily. I was only an undergraduate dyke; no one was going to listen to anything I said. And Doug was dismissed as a fat underachiever. That was kind of true, unfortunately. But Doug talked to Charlie one night when they were alone in Charlie's lab. He said he was going to call someone he knew who worked at *Scientific American* and tell them all about how Emily was responsible for the Ziegart effect, not to mention most of Charlie's other 'achievements' after they got married. She let him have all of them."

"Such as?"

"For one thing, using chlorophyll as a medium for the storage and transmission of solar energy. There were lots of others."

Bingo, Harry thought. The green solar panels. "Why did she let him do this to her? Didn't she ever get angry about him taking all the credit for her ideas?"

"She loved him. And she didn't care about fame and all that. She just wanted the work to get out there, you know? If Charlie hadn't died when he did, she would have had her Ph.D. in another few months. She thought she'd just keep working at Cantwell afterwards as junior faculty, which would have suited her fine."

And given her no motive for his murder at all, he thought, at least not then. "What exactly did Doug want Charlie to do?"

"Put Emily on as first author on the Ziegart effect paper. And put Doug on as third author. We all knew that the Ziegart effect was going to be a big deal."

"Doug blackmailed Charlie."

"I guess. I thought it was terrible of him, but I couldn't totally blame him either. It was a once in a lifetime chance; he took it. Emily was furious."

"And then he choked to death."

"That was a few months later." There was something different in her manner now. Harry waited. After a moment, she said, "Doug's death gave us both nightmares. But it spooked her even more than it did me. She was pretty superstitious, so I thought that she'd decided the project was unlucky or something."

"Charlie's son found the body."

"Yes." There was a trace of distress in her face now, and Harry wanted to push on it and squeeze something out of her, something that he was sure was there. He said nothing and waited again, the only sound in the room the soft rasping of Dusty's pencil against paper. Fay shifted in her chair as though she had an itch in her shoulder, a quick, jerking movement, and then she said, "Jonathan had a thing for Emily. He made a pass at her once." The room stayed silent while Harry mentally pushed some more, keeping his face and body impassive. He wasn't as surprised as he should have been, he thought. Fay took a breath and continued, "As far as I know, she never told Charlie. I think she was so shocked when it happened that she had no idea what to do. The weird thing is, Jonathan adored his dad. I guess a shrink would say he was trying to merge with him or something. And to merge with his wife," she added, making the last a failed joke.

"And he found Doug's body?" Harry repeated, his voice calm and low.

"Yes. Yes." She looked away at the bookcases. "He didn't deliberately kill Doug, or anything like that. But if you happen to be in the room with someone when he starts choking, and you just stand there, doing nothing"—she paused, still staring at the bookcases—"are you breaking any laws?" The room was very quiet now. Harry could hear the *thuck thuck* of a small clock on her mantel.

"Depends," Harry said quietly, thinking, No wonder he gave me the creeps. Then he said, "But why would he do that?"

She shifted in her chair again as though she couldn't find a comfortable position. Then she finally faced him. "He knew Doug was making things hard for his father. He might have thought he was helping."

Harry wondered suddenly where Jonathan Ziegart was right now. Fay's eyes grew panicky and wide. "Wait, I don't know that. I don't know anything. Emily and I never talked about it. You can't print that. I'll get sued for slander or something." She repeated, "I don't know anything."

Another idea snapped into place in Harry's mind. "Did you know she was pregnant when she and Charlie were in the accident?"

Fay's hand went to her mouth in horror; Harry believed her when she said she hadn't. She started to cry, and Dusty looked appalled. Harry had a bad feeling that Jonathan was still in Stoweville, and might think that Maggie had made things hard for him.

The walk to the front door of the Purple Lady's house took longer than four minutes, and Darcy had a panicked moment when he thought maybe he'd blown the whole operation, being late. But he thought, They can see me, they can hear me. They know where I am. Close enough.

The front door was the same blasphemous color as the shrine, although a little brighter, with newer paint. Darcy felt the hard weight of the gun against his thigh again as he climbed the front steps. Safety's on, he told himself. You won't shoot nothing off yourself. No accidents. He raised the knocker, dropped it. It didn't sound very loud, and he was about to do it again when the door opened, causing his stomach to do a flippy-flopping kind of thing that made his hands shiver. He put them in his pockets so that whoever answered the door wouldn't see them shake; his right hand felt the gun and he gripped it, only for something for it to do.

Harry assured Fay that he wasn't going to print anything she'd said about Jonathan Ziegart, then explained that his cell phone didn't work. She reluctantly let him use her phone to call Florida. No one answered at Maggie's home. He called Serge, but only got his voice mail. He didn't bother leaving a message. When he returned to the living room, Dusty was reading *The Little Prince*. He put it down when he saw Harry. "Fay's gone to the bathroom," he said. "She said she'd be back in a minute. Are we going to leave?"

"Yeah," Harry said. "Unless I can think of any more questions to ask her."

"I thought you'd be all prepared, you know, have 'em all written down."

"I'm prepared. But you never know when you'll get an answer that takes you somewhere you didn't know you were going to go." Harry picked up the book and let it fall open to the weight of the lacy bookmark.

He was only a fox like a hundred thousand other foxes. But I have made him my friend, and now he is unique in all the world.

He glanced down the rest of the page, then turned to the next and froze after he'd read just a few lines farther. A fragment of memory, a little nagging something had been floating around his brain for the last half hour or so, and now here it was, the answer to a question, the thing that had been gently poking at him. Oh God, Harry thought. I've been such an idiot.

43

NINE OF
SWORDS

Very bad things.
Injury,
terrible bereavement

When Josie saw Darcy Murphy standing in the doorway, she thought she might faint for the first time in her life. She hadn't fainted when they'd told her that Dee was dead, she hadn't fainted when she held Dunc's hand as the life passed from him and his skin got cold and quiet. But now, of all times, she was facing a man whom she hadn't really wronged, yet she felt her breath leave her lungs as though sucked out by a vacuum and her eyes saw everything get wavy and too bright and her head felt as though it was stuffed with helium and might float off her shoulders altogether. She'd had three rum and Cokes on the sly, and figured that that was probably the cause of it, this terrible unsteadiness. She wasn't drunk, but she wasn't fully there, and right now she had a sense as clear as clean water that she needed to be. Then she thought, I should have the goddamned flashlight, even as Darcy's eyes traveled to her hands, no doubt unconsciously expecting to be zapped. But she was fairly certain she would never be able to push that button again, or even touch the goddamned gizmo.

"What in the name of all that shines do you want?" she said.

"Just to talk," he croaked, his voice odd and stiff, like he'd turned into a raggedy robot.

"About what?" she said, and she knew she was showing fear. They're going to put me away for using that damn weapon, she thought, and then she imagined the hard clang of a cell door, the unbearable stink, the cold metal all around, the colder faces, enough pain in the air to make any psychic go mad in a day, and she realized for the first time just what made Maggie so afraid. Maggie, who was away doing what she always did when she wasn't working at one thing or another, or walking with nosy college boys; she was at the public library. She was too much in her own head, that was what she was, although at least she had the girls with her, so they were safe. But Baby was gone, too, off shopping for supplies as if they were laying in for a siege, and here he was, the enemy himself coming right to their door and Josie too drunk to know better than to open up and let the bad colors inside. If Maggie were here, she'd know what to do with this worthless piece of garbage oozing all the colors of death and fear and hatred.

"You look good," Darcy said for no apparent reason, and that's when they heard the unmistakable sound of a shotgun being cocked.

She looked behind her and saw Miss Tokay in the hallway, standing in front of the grandfather clock, holding the biggest gun Josie had ever seen in her life; it looked like one of those bazooka things you saw in old war movies. Miss Tokay was aiming right at Darcy Murphy's chest, and the old lady said in a tone that sounded kind, "You get out of here, boy."

Then Josie heard something else, the sound of cars pulling up the dirt driveway, although she couldn't see them yet because she couldn't see much of anything other than the giant gun. Miss Tokay said, "Pull your hands out your pockets, boy," and Josie turned back to him, hoping he would obey the old woman, who Josie could see now had entered some mad place. Darcy did as Miss Tokay asked, a wide-open, stupid expression on his face, one of those grins that means you're shit-scared, and as his hands came out of his pants a pistol, a big one, was in his right hand, his tight fingers wound around the grip as though rigor had set in, the knuckles blue-white, the thin bones prominent. Josie could hear cars crunching up the driveway louder now, although she couldn't see, couldn't look away from Darcy Murphy's hands, and then she saw him raise the pistol, the fear-grin still eating up the lower half of his face. "It's all over now, ma'am, you got to let go of that shotgun." Who the hell does he think he is? she thought. John Fucking Wayne?

Miss Tokay walked forward, the big shotgun not wavering a bit. Josie thought, If I had a level, I bet the bubble would stay right in the center, and oh God I wish I was sober, maybe then I'd know what to do. She almost called Maggie's name out loud but remembered that Maggie wasn't there, and maybe that was a good thing, but she and Miss Tokay were there, sure enough, so it maybe wasn't so good at all, people were going to get hurt. Or going to jail.

Miss Tokay kept moving, the big gun like a prow on a comical little ship with a good wind in its sails, pushing Darcy back from the door. "You tell my nephew-in-law that he can't have none of it," she said, calmly and sweetly. "You tell him that, after you put that silly gun down."

Darcy held his gun out still, and Josie thought this had to be the worst thing, the most dangerous situation she'd ever been in. I should've let him rape me, she thought. Maybe then we'd all be safe. I would've survived, and someone isn't gonna survive this. She knew this as deep as anything, that someone was going to die here today. It might be me, she thought. It might be. Oh, Maggie, oh, Maggie.

Darcy raised his gun just a little higher, as though righting his aim a bit, then said in a louder voice, no croaking now, "Put the shotgun down, ma'am, the game's over. You're caught, you know. The authorities know."

"They don't know nothing, sweetheart," said Miss Tokay. Then Josie heard an explosion like a bomb going off in her head, felt heat and wind, and Darcy Murphy grew smaller and smaller, as if he was being sucked down a tube and then disappeared. Josie realized that he'd been hit by the blast, been knocked clean off the porch. She stood for a moment, paralyzed by horror and indecision. She turned to Miss Tokay, who was sitting in a chair in the hallway, having been knocked backward by the recoil of the big gun. Josie went to her first, and pulled the heavy shotgun from the old woman's thin hands. She said, "Miss Tokay, Miss Tokay," and Josie realized that she was crying, and she lifted the gun, feeling the horrible, warm weight of it. She should have put it down, but she couldn't, she was so afraid that the old woman might pick it up and shoot again. The gun fell a little as Josie moved back toward the outside, frightened out of her mind, dragging the big gun with her out the front door, out to where Darcy was lying in a strange, bony pile half on and half off the porch. She pulled herself closer to him, seeing the blood-and-bone mess of him, his chest a grisly mix in the middle of his body. She reached the edge of the porch and looked down on him, strangely unafraid of the gore painting him, and saw his gun pointing up to the sky, his arm propped against the planks of the porch.

She thought, I have to put the shotgun down, and only then did it occur to her that she might be blamed for having shot him, that now her fingerprints were all over the big gun and Miss Tokay wasn't in her right mind and might not tell them what really happened, might not even remember, and Darcy Murphy was certainly dead. She lifted the big gun again, not wanting to drop it on the porch and have it shoot, not knowing where to put it away, out of reach of anyone else crazy enough to use it, and then she saw the spinning lights, beautiful, like Christmas, on the roofs of several blue and white cars parked in a zigzag line in Miss Tokay's grassy driveway; she had the impression of the face of a terrified white boy wearing a grown-up deputy's hat; the boy was hunched behind an open car door, staring at her through the window. She thought, Have they come for me or for the Purple Lady? And then she heard a crack, a ping, felt something very hot in her shoulder, and looked up to see the trees and the sky, felt the rain hit her like bullets. They think it was me, she thought as she fell, the enormous shotgun clattering on the wooden floor next to her, and she was surprised by how much her back hurt, by how hard and cool the wood felt on her bare arms as her body went down. I'll find out now where you go, I'm gonna know for sure. Duncan, she thought, and would have sworn, had anyone asked her, that she heard an answering "Josie Posey Puddin' and Pie."

44

FIVE OF
SWORDS

Wanting the wrong thing,
and getting what you want

Harry used a pay phone in a small grocery store a few blocks from Fay Levy's
house to call Maggie. No answer. Then
he called his own house to check his
answering machine again. There were
no new messages, and he realized with
a mental obscenity that everyone would
assume he could get to his cell phone
voice mail. Goddamn the motherfucking
information age, he thought.

He got Serge's machine again and left
a message, saying that he was coming
back to town soon and that he was worried about Maggie's safety.
He added that Serge shouldn't trust Jonathan Ziegart. He had
planned to stop in Virginia to visit Grenier University before flying
back to Orlando. Now, however, he felt certain that getting back to
Stoweville as soon as possible was imperative, although he didn't
know what he intended to do when he got home. He called the airline; after wading through an intricate series of phone menus, he finally spoke to a real person who told him that the soonest they
could leave Harrisburg was the next afternoon. The charge for

changing their itinerary was jaw-dropping. Harry didn't change anything, not trusting his instincts. Staring at the phone after hanging
up, he trusted them again and swore aloud.

Dusty and Harry ate dinner in a restaurant on the outskirts of
Lucasta, then went back to the hotel. Harry called Maggie and Serge
again with no more success than he'd had before. He left the number of the hotel on Serge's machine. Dusty watched another bad
movie while Harry read his book on Tesla.

They had breakfast the next morning, then came back to the
room to pack. Dusty called Ann to check in again; after a short in-
terchange with her, he handed the phone to Harry. "She wants to
talk to you."

Harry wasn't eager to speak to his ex-wife, but he took the
phone and said, "What's up? Is your father okay?"

"Serge has been trying your cell phone for the last twenty-four
hours."

"It's dead." Harry had a bad feeling in his stomach. "What's happened?"

"I don't know exactly, but he said it was urgent that he speak to
you." Harry said he'd call the Olnikoffs immediately, furious that
Serge hadn't called the hotel. He hung up, feeling like wringing his
hands, something he'd never actually seen anyone do. He tried
Serge's again; no answer, but this time Harry's message was more to
the point. "What the hell's happening there? I talked to Ann. Call
me. At the hotel, not on my goddamned cell." He dialed the airline
again, willing this time to eat any extra charges for changing flights
from Tacamaw, Virginia, to Orlando. All the Orlando flights that afternoon were full, the agent said. Now the soonest they could leave
was first thing the following morning. Harry was alternately hostile
and apologetic to the ticket agent while he made the reservations, so
frustrated at the capriciousness of other travelers that he wanted to
throw the phone across the room. After he'd finished with the air-

line, he wanted to take Dusty for a long walk, but instead he let his son listen undisturbed to his iPod while he paced around the room, waiting for Serge's call.

The hotel didn't have a restaurant, so they had to leave the room for lunch. There was an omelet house a mile away, and they had a brief debate about whether or not to leave Dusty in the room, but he couldn't tell Harry what he wanted to eat without seeing a menu. So they drove to the restaurant and ordered their food to go. Dusty was now infected with his father's urgency; he didn't want to miss a call from Serge any more than Harry did. They got back to the room within an hour of leaving it; there was still no message from Serge. Harry called the Olnikoffs' again. This time, he got Amelia.

"Serge is at the courthouse with Tony Frantz, filing papers to keep that crazy old lady out of jail."

"Which crazy lady? You mean the fortune teller? What the hell's she done now?"

"Oh my God, Harry, you haven't talked to anyone here? You don't know what's happened?"

"I know nothing other than I leave town for a week and everything seems to have fallen to pieces. What the hell's going on? I left our number on your machine. Why didn't he call me on it?"

"He tried. He kept getting a gas station."

She repeated the number he'd left; the last two digits were reversed. He let loose a colorful string of expletives in his mind, almost feeling the seams of his body rip apart with the effort of keeping them to himself.

Amelia was saying, "Oh God, I didn't want to be the one to tell you all this." Harry thought, Something's happened to Maggie, but Amelia said, "The fortune teller's dead, Harry. She was shot by the police."

"What? Josie Dupree? You mean her, right?" He had a sudden

horrible worry that Maggie might be labeled a fortune teller, too, by people who didn't know her.

"Yes. Josephine Dupree." Harry's relief made him feel sick with guilt. "It's a huge mess. Serge says it's all a terrible cock-up by the sheriff's department, but we don't really know for sure."

"How's Maggie? Has anyone talked to her or seen her? Is she all right?"

"She's okay. She called Serge last night. She was very upset, obviously. She begged him for help because the old lady they were staying with had been arrested. They think she shot someone, a meter reader or something. None of it makes sense yet."

Why the hell were they staying with Miss Tokay? Harry thought. Why in hell did she shoot anybody? And who knew she had a gun? He said, "Did Serge get Miss Tokay out?"

"Eventually. Actually, Tony did. You know he's the best criminal defense attorney around here. He's semiretired and mostly teaches at the law school now, but Serge strong-armed him. You know how he can be when he's wound up. He knows that Maggie is important to you, so he really threw his weight around."

"Is Frantz doing this pro bono or is someone going to have to come up with a billion dollars later?"

"I don't know. We'll work something out, I guess. The important thing is that Miss Toky is out of jail on bond, and is home now. I gather that Maggie is staying with her."

Harry didn't correct Amelia's pronunciation of the old woman's name; he knew that it was misplaced gratitude but at the moment didn't know how to express it any other way.

"When are you coming home, Harry?" she said.

"Tomorrow," he said. "Goddamnit to hell, it's the soonest I can make it."

. . .

The sheriff's department no longer looked like the calm, well-run establishment it had when Jonathan Ziegart had been given the tour by Lieutenant Deputy Faber. The place was both noisier and quieter, in that there was much silent walking around by various employees, all at work even on a Saturday, muted phone conversations at desks as deputies talked intently to members of the public, the press, and Jonathan imagined, employees of the Florida attorney general's office. He'd read the local paper; the sheriff's department hadn't come off well in the "shrine shoot-out" as a headline dubbed it. Jonathan greeted Serena the receptionist with a sympathetic smile. He took her hand and said, "Hard morning?"

She didn't smile back, but she seemed to relax in the way that people did when they were happy to see someone under miserable circumstances. "Things are bad. The sheriff's not here. Do you have a meeting with someone?"

"I've offered my services to Lieutenant Deputy Faber. I imagine he could use any extra hands he can get investigating this thing."

Serena shook her head. "Wally can't investigate himself, Jon. That's up to the Law Enforcement Review Board."

"Faber's being investigated?"

Her voice dropped. "It's automatic when any officer uses deadly force, and now it's not clear whether or not it was called for. It looks like he bypassed all the appropriate protocols when he took a bunch of guys out there in the first place. But I think it'll all come out all right. These things usually do."

Jonathan had to exert some effort to keep from asking Serena about the tip Faber had gotten while the sheriff gave a speech on compassion and tolerance to the Elks club. There hadn't been anything specific about it in the newspaper. He said, "I understand he had some sort of information about the old lady. You know, operating one of those doomsday cults on her property."

Serena fluttered her tongue between her front teeth, making a tsking sound. "The sheriff's grandmother went to school with Edith Tokay. He went to her house for barbecues when he was a teenager. She's crazy all right, but about as dangerous as a dead cat."

Jonathan thought, They're more dangerous than you might think. Dead claws are still sharp. He soothed and flattered until she allowed him to pass into the large open office area behind her. The sheriff was nowhere to be found; Jonathan assumed he was being yelled at in the office of the mayor or the district attorney. Jonathan spotted Wally Faber at the coffeemaker; he was holding a cup and looking earnestly at a tall man in a navy blue suit with thinning hair and a long nose. The man in the suit was talking not to Faber but at him, pushing his index finger dangerously close to the younger man's chest. Jonathan recognized the suit at once: the uniform of the FBI. He heard Faber say, "Look, Agent Soames, everyone knows the old lady's batshit." The voices of the two men were low but still loud enough to be audible to anyone interested in their conversation. Jonathan imagined he wasn't the only one in the room listening with straining ears.

"So now you're a psychologist as well as an antiterrorism expert." The man named Soames was drawn and angry, and he saw Jonathan and said, "Who the hell's this? Somebody's nephew, playing cop? Jesus Christ, are you people for real?"

"I'm Jonathan Ziegart," Jonathan said, extending his hand.

The FBI agent didn't take it. "Bully for you. Go back to your dorm room."

Faber said that Jonathan was a forensic anthropologist who had offered his services to the Stowe County Sheriff's Department on an earlier occasion. Soames didn't appear impressed at all; he said simply, "Don't talk to him about anything, Faber." Agent Soames disappeared into the sheriff's office, which he appeared to have commandeered.

Jonathan said, "Can I help?"

Faber considered this. "No, Jon, but thanks. There's nothing exotic to examine. Fingerprints. Crime scene photos. You know, the normal stuff." Faber shook his head. One eye was twitching with such regularity that Jonathan found himself timing it. He knew that, if he waited, Faber would talk more than was wise; sure enough, after six twitches, he said, "The inspector for North Florida Light, the one that was killed, he had a grudge against the old lady and her neighbors because they used solar panels. Makes you think, eh?"

Jonathan wasn't sure what it was supposed to make you think of, but he agreed, keeping his voice pleasant. "What happened, Wally?"

"A tip. A series of 'em, actually. One said that the Purple Lady's cult had started up again. The sheriff didn't take it serious, but I wondered. Lots of militias in the central part of the state. You always have to keep watch, especially these days." Jonathan agreed again, happy that Faber had apparently decided to ignore Agent Soames's orders. "We got a second one when Sheriff Kimble was away. The caller had his voice disguised with one of those computer thingamajigs. The call was recorded, but the lab guys say there's not much likelihood of ever IDing it. The phone was a prepaid cell. We don't even know if it was a he or a she, but the caller said that somebody was building a dirty bomb in the old lady's garage. Murphy, the inspector, was maybe in on it with her. Maybe even the instigator."

"You thought it was a credible threat?"

"Nothing else was going on, and I figured it was worth a look-see, you know? I took some guys, and then there was a shot and some guns drawn, and the next thing you know, it's all a big fucking mess." Faber wiped his hand over his face. "I may need to go job huntin', Jon." Jonathan saw with interest that the lieutenant deputy was close to tears; his hands were shaking, and there were dollops of sweat the size of peppercorns speckling his forehead. It was unpleasant to look at, although he found it fascinating when two drops starting traveling down toward the deputy's left eyebrow. He said, "I'll make a call to the Lucasta Police Department. They might need somebody."

It was meant as a joke, but Faber didn't smile. It looked as though he was trying to, but instead his upper lip lifted in a sort of grimace, exposing his front teeth, one of which was outlined in gold. Jonathan found that fascinating as well. He said, "So, no trace of dirty bombs anywhere, I guess?"

"No. Miss Tokay lets a friend of hers do fix-it jobs in her garage. A junk dealer who repairs people's toasters. There were a few engine parts lying around, but nothing that amounts to anything. Soames is looking into his background, but he's local, been here forever, no complaints, no sheet. Nobody knows why the inspector for the electric company showed up on her porch. He may have meant the old lady harm, but maybe not. We don't know why he had a gun on him either. The old lady says he was there to scare her off her land. Maybe he was. Soames is looking at her nephew, thinking maybe Murphy was working for him. He's known to be eager to get his hands on the place."

"So she wasn't the one killed? I read in the paper that a woman was shot. A fortune teller or something? I assumed that she was the crazy shrine lady."

"Oh no. It was another neighbor. We're not even sure which crazy woman shot Murphy. On the videotapes, you can't see what was going on in the house when he pulled his gun." He stopped and took a shaky breath, then turned to the coffeemaker. "He left a wife. No kids, thank God. The fortune teller just left a niece."

"She wasn't there?" Faber looked surprised at the question, and Jonathan took a breath and told himself to calm down. He felt in his pocket for his handkerchief, but he didn't pull it out.

"She was at the library with two little girls. Other neighbor kids.

She's all grown up. She'll be all right." Faber tried to pour coffee into a cup, but he couldn't still the trembling of his hand enough for any kind of accuracy, so he put the carafe back on the burner. He put the clean mug back with its fellows on the paper place mat that sat next to the coffeemaker. There was also a jar of nondairy creamer, a cup of plastic stirrers, and a box of sugar packets along with the mugs. Jonathan didn't like powdered whitener, so he didn't pour himself any coffee.

45

THE MAGICIAN

*She holds the four symbols of
creation: a wand (fire),
a cup (water), a sword (air),
and a pentacle (earth).*

THE MAGICIAN.

Harry got into the outskirts of Stoweville by noon. Dusty was mad at being left at his grandparents' house in Orlando, but Harry had said, "You go back to school in three days. You'll be finished in two weeks. I'll come down the day you're done and we'll pack you up and bring you home with me. I'll call you every day and let you know what's going on. But right now I need you to help your grandmother take care of your grandfather, and to be as nice as you can to your mother." He'd added with emphasis, "And stay away from the bus station."

He still hadn't spoken to Maggie. He'd tried Miss Tokay's house when he got to Orlando, but the phone was "temporarily out of service." There was no answer at the double-wide. Serge hadn't spoken to Maggie since the previous evening; he didn't know where she was either.

Harry went to Crane's first. She wasn't there, but Shawntelle was, and she didn't look amused anymore. He was greeted with warmth by Dottie and Fat Calvin. The latter looked shrunken and bereft. Neither knew anything useful, although Dottie wanted to engage him in long, pointless, if well-meaning speculation. He left with promises to let them know if there was anything they could do to help.

He drove by the trailer and saw only Josie's car, so he didn't stop. He backtracked to the shrine, noticing now how it was pitted and blackened; he stopped at the edge of the driveway and rolled down his window to get a better look. Someone had shot it enough times to make it looked frayed around the edges, burned and wounded. There was a lot of trash: empty paper cups and the wrappers of burgers and candy bars. The detritus of reporters and rubberneckers.

He continued down the drive, stopping the car and getting out to move the chain from across Miss Tokay's driveway, then pulled his car up to the house. There was crime scene tape all around the front porch and a horrible stain on the edge of the wood flooring. There was no other vehicle in front of the house and no answer to his knock when he hammered on the solid purple door. Behind the house he could see the Purple Lady's temple, the second one, which had once been a garage and was now just for storage. There was no car in front, where the big doors had long ago been boarded up with plywood. He thought he could hear music, far off in the trees, like nothing he'd ever heard before. Alien music, but so faint it rose away from him in the heat and then was gone. He listened to the silence for another minute before he got back into his car, welcoming the air-conditioning; then he drove to the cemetery.

He didn't see the Celica in the parking lot, but he knew there were other places she could have left it; he didn't know whether or not she was avoiding him. He wove his way between headstones by the stream toward the break in the trees where she always entered the hiking trail. His eye caught one of the graves: Duncan Dupree, her uncle. Next to it was a perfect rectangle cut deep into the earth, and he knew that it was for Josie. For the first time he could conjure up something like affection for her, useless and too late. Then in his peripheral vision, a name grabbed him that had a resonance it hadn't before, which was the only reason he could give himself for why he'd never noticed it. It was the grave of Marlene, Maggie's mother.

He walked the entire park before returning to the double-wide. Under other circumstances, he would have felt great about how effortless the entire thing had been. He was in the best shape of his life. After parking in the gravel and oyster-shell driveway, he walked back by the trailer, past the thriving little vegetable garden, understanding for the first time why they had no flowers, and down the worn trail in the grass and pine needles to the shotgun shack where the Thorpes lived. Miss Baby's Buick was parked in front. When he knocked on the door, she opened it and burst into tears at the sight of him. He had to beg her a little, tears in his own eyes that convinced her to help him.

She had a ring of keys like a jailer and walked in front of him toward Miss Tokay's house, cutting across the field behind the double-wide and then into some pines. There was just a hint of a path here, a narrow, matted bit of pine straw through the shadows, wide enough for only one. It broke through the trees into a small yard by the new temple, the old garage. They were approaching it from the rear this time, and he saw Maggie's car parked six feet from its sturdy door, out of sight of the main house. It had been there all the time. His heart sped up.

The door was badly in need of paint, but the wood was thick and the lock was bright gold, new and intimidating. Now Harry could hear that music again, large, melancholy chords coming from inside the building, but they sounded far off at the same time, faint, as though they were emanating from another sinkhole deep underneath it. There was crime scene tape here as well, but it was torn, bright yellow shreds lying in the grass under the few boarded-up windows. It looked gay and dissipated at the same time, like the mess after a drunken party.

Miss Baby gave a loud knock on the door. When no one opened it, she lifted the keys, found a large one the same gold as the lock, and used it. Harry followed her in.

The place seemed enormous, the bare rafters an extra story above them. From them were suspended large, oval bulbs that gave off a warm yellow light. There were plants on a table along one window, ivy and asparagus fern and rosemary, giving the place its only green. Along the three windowless walls were shelves of wood, of metal, even several of the same resin that made up Josie's old porch set. On a number of them there were neat rows of magazines: *Scientific American, Science, Nature, American Engineering*, the *Northeastern Journal of Physics and Engineering*. Several other shelves were covered with parts of engines, of motors, cylinders, gears, pulleys, wires, although many shelves were bare. It was cool, and he followed the movement of the air to a large metal box coated in droplets of condensation that looked like an overgrown space heater by the door; cold air poured from it, blown by a fan inside that looked like it dated from World War II. The music was loud enough that Harry realized the place must be soundproofed or it would have throbbed all the way to the highway. It was something Harry had never heard before, many women's voices singing in angry harmony in a language he didn't recognize; the women sang urgently at him from a small speaker suspended from the rafter nearest the door. Nothing seemed real.

Maggie sat on a bench in front of a large wooden table in the center of the room, which was strewn with wires and circuit boards. Her head was down, her face resting on her bent left arm. Her right hand lay splayed out as though her arm had dropped as she was signaling hello to someone. Next to her hand was a soldering iron in a metal cradle; the first thing Harry did was put his hand close to the bit to see if it was hot. It wasn't, but he moved it farther from her still hand anyway, then, breathing hard, he put two fingers on her neck to see if she had a pulse. She jumped, a soft gasp escaping her as though she'd been pricked; her head jerked up, and she turned her face to him, eyes wide and glassy. She had been crying, but she wasn't now. She looked indescribably tired. She stood up slowly, put her arms around his shoulders and said his name into his neck. Then she fell asleep.

He managed to get her disentangled, leaving her semiconscious and in the care of a confused Miss Baby while he brought his car to the temple door. He got her into his car without mishap, her head lolling as she kept falling asleep against him while he told Miss Baby that they were going to his house, and not to worry, and thank you. At his house, he half walked, half carried Maggie up the porch steps, held her up with one hand as he worked his keys, careful to throw the bolt behind them, then held her up again as he walked her to his bedroom. She flopped down on the bed, almost asleep again. Harry got her shoes off, then his own, and lay down next to her, putting his arms around her waist, laying his head on her shoulder, not fully so that the weight would be a problem, but with his face in her neck. Her T-shirt was fragrant with lemon and something piney. Rosemary, he thought. He said, not sure if she was awake enough to hear him, "Were you lying when you said your middle name wasn't Emily?"

She took in a deep, sleepy breath, then said, her voice soft and slightly hoarse, "No." A pause. "My middle name is Magdalene. My first name is Emily. My dad picked it, but my mom always liked Maggie better."

"Your mother. Marlene Timms."

"Mmm." Her eyes were closed.

Harry said, "Huh," in response, then fell hard into sleep.

46

THE MOON

REVERSED

Lies uncovered.
Love, hard-bought

The phone woke Harry once when the sun was slanting through the west-facing window so brightly that it made his sleep-filled eyes hurt. He unplugged the one by his bed, having a groggy notion that he'd listen to his machine sometime later. He thought briefly about Serge but was too close to sleep to care. Maggie was unconscious on the bed next to him, her mouth slightly open, her hair in a tangled halo around her head. Harry lay down next to her again, pulled her close, and fell back into a beautiful sleep.

When he next opened his eyes, there was still some light from a dying sun, turning the bedroom orange. They faced each other across the divide between their pillows; there was just enough light to see that Maggie's eyes were open.

"Hi," he said, his voice a sleepy rumble. "You're the Magician." He yawned. "In the Tarot reading you gave me." She didn't answer. He wriggled to get closer to her on the bed, working an arm under her shoulders, pulling her to him till her head was resting on his chest. She moved her thigh, resting it on top of his, and draped her arm over his stomach. He could feel himself becoming aroused even as he knew he was too sleepy to do much about it. Her hair glowed in the half-light: the color of the wheat fields, he thought.

"Did I hurt you?" he murmured.

Her voice was soft, an exhale. "You know you did."

"I'm sorry."

"Apologies are cheap." Slow breath in. "You slept with her, didn't you?"

Oh God. "I know I've been an asshole."

"Yes, you have." Her voice was sweet and warm. He wondered if she was talking in her sleep. "Just admitting it doesn't make it okay, you know."

"Are you going to forgive me?"

An intake of breath so that her head moved slightly closer to his. As she exhaled, she said, "I don't know."

When he woke again, the window was filled with nothing but black sky. He looked at the clock; it was almost one a.m. Maggie wasn't in the bed; he heard the toilet flush, then saw her emerge from the bathroom, her eyes tense.

"What's wrong?" Harry said. His voice didn't work all at once; he had to clear his throat a couple of times before it came out right.

"I don't have any of my stuff." She looked away from him, back at the sink through the open bathroom door. "I don't have my tooth-brush. I need to brush my teeth." She looked as though she were about to cry. He got up and showed her the drawer under the sink that held spare toothbrushes, razor blades, and bars of soap.

"Here," he said, handing her a packaged toothbrush. She took it and looked at him with big, shattered eyes.

"But you won't be able to use it again," she said.

"I know," said Harry, glad he didn't feel the urge to laugh. "That's okay. It's yours." He nodded toward the sink. "You can even use my toothpaste."

He joined her, and they brushed their teeth side by side, taking turns spitting into the sink. Maggie rinsed off the toothbrush, and holding it in her hand like a magic wand, she said, "I'll take it with me, if that's all right. That way it won't go to waste."

Harry said, "You could leave it. You know, for when you're here."

She didn't answer, just stood there motionless, staring at him. Then he guided her out of the bathroom so he could have it to himself for a few minutes, closing the door behind him. When he came out again, she was gone. He muttered a swearword and ran into the living room.

She was opening the front door. She turned when he said, "Where are you going?"

"Home," she said.

"How were you planning to get there?"

"It's a cool night. I'll walk." Her voice and face were completely devoid of expression, and Harry thought, We're back to the beginning. He said, "It's at least eight miles."

"I've walked that far before." She felt in her pockets but didn't seem to find what she was looking for. Harry thought that maybe this time he wasn't taming her as much as trapping her; he hadn't meant to, but he'd left her no way to get home, no way even to get into her own house. She had no keys, no money, no car, no extra clothes.

"I'll drive you if you really want to go. But I'd rather you didn't. Come on, Maggie."

"I'll call Miss Baby, if I can use your phone."

"You can use anything, but it's one in the morning."

"Oh," she said.

In the half-light shed by the floor lamp, Harry felt as if he was seeing her clearly for the first time. What do I do? he thought. What do I say? "I know you thought it was a class thing. It wasn't. You were just so fucking young, or I thought you were."

"Oh?" she said again, tilting her head to one side. "I'm thirty-two. Is that old enough for you?" Her voice was light, but her eyes were cold. "You know why I didn't want to go to that stupid party? You thought it was because I was afraid of all those important people. It was really because most of them make me sick." Her voice got louder as she spoke, bit by bit, as though someone was slowly turning an invisible volume knob. "All those self-important colors, all that ignorant moneygrubbing, it's all about power and getting over on people and eating as much of the planet as they can while little kids go blind in sweatshops making their expensive clothes and all the cheap toys for their trophy kids. They get their big houses and their huge cars and they work eighty hours a week to pay for all that petroleum they burn, and then they'll die in their expensive hospitals. Their kids will hate them, but at least they'll be rich." Her chest was heaving with anger now, eyes flashing and fists clenched. "You can go crawl into a bottle with them and drown."

He forced himself to keep his voice soft. "They're not all that bad. Everyone's just trying to live their lives, Maggie."

She picked up a magazine that was lying on the end table closest to her and threw it at him. It fluttered loudly and hit him in the face. He caught it by a page, and it tore as he caught the rest in his other hand. By this time she'd moved to his big oak desk; first she grabbed the biography of Tesla that was by his laptop. She threw it at him; it hit him in the shoulder. To his horror, her hand moved to an empty ginger ale bottle; she picked it up by the neck and hurled it at him. He ducked in time for it to sail past him and smash into a bookcase. He went toward her with the intention of holding her hands; as he did, he said, "It's about time you got mad." That's when she slapped him.

It was loud, like a gunshot. Harry said "Ow!" and put his hand to his cheek at the same time Maggie put hers to her mouth and started to cry, saying, "Oh God, I'm sorry." Harry moved toward her again, trying to put his arms around her, his face stinging but not really hurt. She pushed him away with some force, then turned and yanked the front door open. Harry moved fast, thrusting the door shut with a hand over her shoulder. She rested her head against the door, crying harder. He stood a few inches from her, her hair brushing his chin. He touched her, and she started, almost clipping his jaw with the top of her head. He moved back a few inches, giving her just enough room to turn to face him. He said in a low, hoarse voice, "I tried to call you every single goddamned day I was gone, and I could never get you, which is the same thing that's happened to me almost every other time I've tried to call you. I'd get Josie telling me in so many words to back off, or I'd get no answer at all. I mean, Jesus Christ, how much does an answering machine cost? If you go back to living in that goddamned trailer, I'll buy you a goddamned answering machine so I don't have to listen to that goddamned end-less ringing anymore. If my goddamned cell phone hadn't crapped out on me, I would have been calling you six or seven times a day till I actually got you on the phone, and the moment I heard what had happened from Serge, I got on the next plane I possi-bly could, dumped my son, and came back." He was breathing hard, his forehead now pressed against the side of her head, and he could feel her body heat, could smell her perspiration and the peppermint of the toothpaste she'd just borrowed from him. "I love you."

She put her hands on his chest and shoved him away. "You only say that when you're drunk."

"I'm not even slightly drunk. Can't you see my aura or what-ever?" he said. "Can't you tell?"

"You can't read them once you're too involved with someone." She was still breathing hard, her eyes sleepy and swollen. "When your emotions are all jangled like that, you can't tell what's yours and what's theirs."

"What do you see now?"

"Anger."

He felt a frustration so great he was surprised he could get any words out. "You know we're going to be here in the end anyway."

"Where?"

"Together." He stepped forward again and dropped to his knees, putting his arms around her hips, pushing his face into her belly. His grip was tight because he expected her to push him away again, but she didn't. The button on the fly of her jeans bit into his stinging cheek, and he felt her fingers in his hair. They tightened to where it was just painful as she said, "You put me between you and your son. That's a terrible place to be." She pulled a little harder. "And then you slept with her. I'm not sure I'll forgive you for either thing."

Harry looked up and saw she was crying again, and he remembered how she used to be, all silent and blank, and remembered how much she boiled under all that careful blankness. He said, "He loved you, too." He thought, Do you realize how much of a sacrifice this is? Do you understand what I'm doing for you?

"What?"

"I know he loved you. Because he couldn't have known you well and not loved you."

"You don't have to do that. Don't say that."

He said into her stomach, "We're not all like that, like you said. Not everyone. Forgive me. Forgive me. Forgive me." She tightened her grip till it was genuinely painful and finally pulled him up by the hair, saying, "Stop. I do. Stop."

47

FOUR OF SWORDS

Time to rest
after a great struggle

He said, "It's customary that you say it back when someone tells you that they love you. Especially when they say it over and over again. If you don't, the lack is significant, if you know what I mean."

Her head was on his chest, and she moved it quickly to look into his face. "Every time I say it to anyone, they're dead or dying within twenty-four hours. I'm a little superstitious."

"Oh," he said. "Who?"

"My mother. Charlie. Josie. It was like I put a bull's-eye on each of them. I don't want to put a bull's-eye on you."

He was ashamed at how much better her stricken look made him feel. He said, "A little while ago you wouldn't have minded. What if I ask you a yes or no question?"

"What?"

"Do you love me?"

"Yes," she said. She gave him her first smile; his relief was enormous. "Of course I do." After few minutes of silence, she asked, "Did you have a good time? On your fishing trip?"

Harry burst out laughing. "Yeah," he said. "Actually, it was a really . . . what's the word I want? Potent. It was a potent trip." He kissed her.

"It was true what I said. I was always going to try to convince you to be with me. Even before I knew about Lucasta and Cantwell and all that. You should know that."

He could feel her shrug sleepily against him under the covers. "Josie would probably say that that was important. But now it doesn't matter to me at all." Harry could feel himself drifting off to more blissful sleep when her voice brought him back. "You'll have to go to meetings, Harry. I did it enough with Josie. I'm not going to do it with you. I'm not carrying you drunk to bed. Not ever again."

Harry felt suddenly cold, and sad. So humiliated. "God, I'm sorry."

"Don't apologize. Admit it, and move on." She lifted her head, and her eyes were huge and dark. "I'll stick with you through anything and everything, illness and the end of the bloody world, if you do your part." Then she climbed on top of him and kissed him, and he didn't feel humiliated anymore.

It was three a.m. by the time they found themselves in the kitchen. Harry insisted that he make the omelets this time, which didn't turn out as well as they would have had Maggie made them, but they were good enough. She was wearing one of his bathrobes, having a horror of getting back into her soiled clothes after a shower. Harry tossed them into the washing machine with a small load of his own laundry. He made a production of it, saying that if she came to live with him, these were the kinds of superior amenities she could expect, a washer and dryer on the premises, and was delighted with himself that he made her laugh. He said, "What was that music you had playing in the temple?"

"A Bulgarian women's choir."

"I've never heard anything like it. It was amazing."

"No matter what they sing about, herding sheep or washing clothes or feeding horses or whatever, it always sounds holy." She took a bite, swallowed, then said, "I decided not to learn the language because I thought it sounded more beautiful if you didn't know what they were saying."

The guilelessness with which she said this filled Harry with a burst of desire so strong that he leaned across the table and kissed her hard on the mouth. He thought, It never occurs to her that other adults do not usually have to resist learning a foreign language. "Those tests that your dad made you have." She was still looking surprised from his sudden kiss. "Was one of them an IQ test?"

Her face became still. "Yes," she said after a moment.

"So what was it?" She closed her mouth and shook her head as though that answered the question. "Is that when he left? After that?"

She nodded. He asked, "How old were you?"

"Fourteen." Then she added, "He said that I didn't need him." She pushed her plate away, half the omelet uneaten. "I told him I did, but he didn't believe me." Her elbow rested on the table, and she dropped her chin into her cupped palm. "Mamma was sick of him by then. She told him he was right. I never saw him again. He died a few years later."

Harry finished his omelet in silence, thinking about James Roth and how to make your children crazy. Maggie said, "How did you figure it out? No one in Lucasta knows about me, do they? Now, I mean?"

"You mean, does anyone there know you're alive? Not unless Jonathan Ziegart has told them. I didn't, if you're wondering."

"So how did you figure it out?" she repeated.

"The Little Prince."

"Oh God. You saw Fay Levy."

"Yes. She showed Dusty and me her copy of the book. I'd read it, but it's been a while. I came across the line you quoted, the fox saying, 'You become responsible, forever, for what you have tamed.' " His plate was empty. "Who was taming who?"

She smiled. "I don't know. You can decide."

He reached across the table and took her hand. "You've got to tell me everything, you know."

She gave his hand a squeeze and took a deep breath. "Growing up, I was always Maggie. When I went to college, I decided to use my first name. I thought it made me sound classier."

Harry got up and put the kettle on. He asked, "Dee wrote that letter about your suicide?"

"She sent it when she was in Denver with her boyfriend. I wrote it."

"Everyone thought she was your sister."

"The letter was vague. I guess everyone assumed stuff."

"You were afraid of Jonathan?"

She nodded. "I didn't hide myself so well that a real detective couldn't find me. But just so they couldn't open a phone book and see my name. That was enough."

"Till I came to town and blew your cover."

"I tried not to lie to you, Harry. I mostly didn't."

"You got Miss Tokay and Miss Baby in on it. They spun a good story."

"They mostly kept to the truth."

"Miss Tokay said you were dead."

"No. She said I'd ascended. I'm sure she could defend that to you somehow."

"You sound like an attorney." He let her smile linger for a while before asking, "You made the stun gun that looks like a flashlight?"

She made a motion with her hand as though waving away his

words. "They're pretty simple. I got the empty casings from a friend of Josie's. He has a junkyard."

"Why?"

"You never know. I had a feeling that one day I might have to use it."

"And you stayed at my house the night of the party to protect me from Jonathan?"

The smile went away. "He'll keep trying to hurt you. Especially if he thinks you're dear to me."

Harry liked the old-fashioned phrase. He said, "And if he thinks you're dear to me?"

Her face screwed up as though something suddenly hurt. "Especially if he thinks that."

"Because he loves you."

"Yes. And because he hates me."

"Like with Charlie." Maggie nodded again, and Harry said before thinking, "And the baby."

He could have punched himself, but Maggie's only response was to shake her head and say, "Oh no. That was all hate."

They talked for a long time. After a while, Harry went to his desk and found the picture he'd printed from Louise Glade's e-mail. He could see Maggie in Emily's face now, amazed at how he'd missed it before. Her hair was lighter now from the sun, and shorter with curls that hadn't been there when it was long. So many years earlier, her face had been round, childish, undefined. It was amazing how much the same she looked now, and how different. Still young, but not remotely childish anymore.

He handed her the flimsy photograph, printed on plain paper. She looked at it for a minute, then said, "That was the day Charlie died. After that, I really did become someone else."

"If I'd been able to see your eyes," Harry said, "I'd have known right away it was you."

Maggie helped him clean up the shattered ginger ale bottle; then she washed the dishes while Harry listened to the messages on his machine. Serge had called three times: "I know you're there, Harry. You're pissing me off. Oh, hell, I guess you're sleeping. Call me when you wake up." It was four a.m. They went back to bed.

Four hours later Harry woke again, so disoriented that at first he didn't know where he was. Maggie was asleep next to him, and it took several minutes before he could convince himself that everything that had happened to him in the last two days was real. The most astonishing thing about the whole business was how well he'd slept.

He called Serge while the coffee dripped and Maggie took a second shower. Serge told him some things he already knew and many things he didn't. "The sheriff's department got an anonymous tip that they were a bunch of terrorists; for some reason, that idiot Faber believed it. The call was very specific, implicating a hapless line inspector for the electric company. They fucked up badly, and now the poor fellow is dead, along with the fortune teller. Then some asshole took advantage of the whole thing and waited till the cops had gone and used the shrine for target practice. The sheriff's got people talking to Hugh Covington about that; he's the developer nephew. Anyway, they plan to release Mrs. Dupree's body tomorrow. I don't know when the funeral will be scheduled. Have you talked to Maggie yet?"

"Yes."

There was a pause. Then Serge said, "Is she with you?"

"Yes."

"Oh." Another silence. "I guess Amelia was right. I now owe her a night out."

After the Olnikoffs arrived, Serge said to Maggie, "I feel like I should make a joke about fireworks, but I won't."

She said, "Barium makes green." Everyone looked confused, so she added, "No one knew at your party." There was more silence. Then she shrugged and said, "It's not the explosion that makes the light. It's when the stuff in the fireworks starts cooling down as it falls. That's when you see the colors."

48

FIVE OF
PENTACLES

REVERSED

Coming in out of the cold.
The tale of a monster

Serge and Amelia insisted that the four of them go out for breakfast. Harry explained about Maggie's sensitivity to fluorescent lights; Amelia suggested a coffeehouse with outdoor seating far enough from campus that they wouldn't bump into anyone they knew, especially during the university's summer session. The weather was fine. "There's an awning," she said. "So we won't get burned."

"Thank you for all your help," Maggie said to Serge, who shrugged it away.

"I'm sorry I couldn't do more personally. I do environmental law. I've been told by a lot of my colleagues that that makes me useless when it comes to people." Maggie gave Harry an apologetic look; he smiled back at her, trying not to look smug, and made a mental note to tell Serge that he had gone from okay guy to comrade in an instant. Over cappuccinos and blueberry scones, he told the Olnikoffs about his trip to Lucasta, checking with Maggie at intervals to see if she wanted to make corrections or add anything to the story as he knew it.

"*You're* Emily Ziegart?" Serge said.

"Close your mouth, Sergei," Harry said.

Serge ignored him, gaping at Maggie. "Why did you leave Cantwell? Charles Ziegart's death was a tragedy, obviously, but why would you give up everything after that? Surely he wanted you to have his name, his property, your position there, everything you'd worked for?"

Maggie looked at Harry, who nodded. Then she answered him, "Because his son would have killed me if I stayed."

The silence that greeted this was profound.

"Jonathan Ziegart," Amelia said. "He pretended he didn't know you because . . ." Her question trailed off.

"Because he intended to kill me," Maggie said.

"Why?" Serge said, letting his cappuccino cool and leaving his scone untouched. "Why does he hate you so much?"

Maggie didn't answer, plainly reluctant. Harry stepped in. "Partly because she rebuffed him."

"Ew," Amelia said. "When he was your stepson?"

"And because she got pregnant," Harry added. "He didn't want a sibling."

"Oh my God," Amelia said.

"So you came back here and changed your name?" Serge asked.

"Just my last name. My father's name was Roth. I've always been Maggie here, so that wasn't anything. I didn't think Jon was going to look that hard for me if I went away like they wanted me to. He didn't have my address down here."

"But she died, too, just in case," Harry said.

Serge stirred some sugar into his coffee. "He's that dangerous?"

"He killed his father," Harry said. "He tried to kill Maggie, too."

"How could someone get away with something like that in this day and age of forensic everything, when you can be convicted because of your goddamned *spit*?" Amelia was unusually worked up. Harry liked it.

Maggie regarded her, and Harry could tell she was surprised at Amelia's heat. "He doesn't really commit crimes," she said. "Or if he does, they're little ones that are easy to get away with. Like just letting Doug die. I think that was the first time he did anything really awful."

"Why?" Serge asked again. "Why did he let that poor boy choke to death?"

"Doug was giving Charlie a hard time. Afterwards, Jon told Charlie all about what happened. He expected his dad to be proud of him for fixing things."

"And I guess he wasn't," Serge said.

"He was horrified." Maggie's chair was close to Harry's, and she leaned very slightly against him. "That really hurt Jon's feelings." Her face was no longer calm; she looked pale and ill.

Harry couldn't help imagining what it had been like, witnessing Doug McNeill choking to death, and what it would take to stand and watch, doing nothing. Waiting. God, he thought, Jesus Christ.

Maggie said, "Even Jon was surprised it didn't bother him. Watching Doug die. I was in the room when he told his father how interesting it was." Her mouth bent down at the edges, like she was going to be sick. "He's a sociopath. That's the first time I realized it. Charlie realized it, too."

Harry said, "Somehow he managed to wrap a couple of yellow jackets in a handkerchief and then put them in his dad's pocket, after tossing his EpiPen. Then he let nature take its course. If something bad happened, great. If not, oh well. No great risk to him."

"He probably didn't plan it," Maggie said. "I imagine he saw the wasps on the melon, and just took advantage of how easy it was to scoop them up."

"Holy shit," Serge said.

"What does any of this have to do with your aunt's death, Maggie?" Amelia asked. "I don't see how Jon could've had a hand in that."

"He set it up somehow. That's what he does. We may never know exactly how he did it."

"The tip to the sheriff's department," Serge said. "Although why he thought they'd buy it, I can't imagine."

"But he was right," Harry said. "He probably succeeded beyond anything he expected."

Amelia continued to look anxiously at Maggie. "He's a free man. The police aren't even investigating him. They have no reason to. So the big question is, What do you think he's going to do next?"

"He'll come after me one way or another. Or you," Maggie added, looking at Harry.

49

FIVE OF
SWORDS
REVERSED

A funeral

The rush of perfect completion was almost orgasmic, the way his plans clicked and circled and purred like a beautiful piece of engineering. It had happened only a few times, this flawless convergence of mechanisms he'd set in motion, a whisper here and a smile there. He thought of the woman on the road, there by chance, alone, unguarded, unwitnessed, and a simple flick of the steering wheel altering worlds. His hands still remembered the cool feel of melon, the angry movement of wasps in the folds of a handkerchief, the stomach-tightening excitement as he slipped the toxic little bundle into his father's jacket pocket, no one seeing, no one looking at him. He'd loved his father but had been strangely elated at his death. He'd never understood why, but the satisfaction had fueled his best dreams for years. Now he'd hit a stride again, now his life was moving. Nothing was as satisfying as this, being the butterfly whose tiny flutterings birthed the hurricane.

God, he was in love with her. He thought that he'd loved her before; he thought that he'd known fulfillment before. But seeing her again, and so blooming, so aglow, as if whatever was in excess had burned away until what was left was only her brilliant core, and when she looked at him now, she saw him truly, in a way no one else ever had.

His father was a shadow now, a ghost that he conjured when he looked in the mirror, the reflections merging beautifully. He wanted Emily in a way he couldn't have imagined at seventeen, wanted her to look at him the way she'd once looked at Charlie. He combed his hair. He put his father's handkerchief in his pocket.

The weather held for the funeral, hot and bright and humid. The service was to be at the graveside; Josie hadn't been inside a church since she'd gotten married to Duncan Dupree thirty-five years before. There was a large white canvas canopy set up in a grassy area by the coffin, suspended above the rectangular hole where Josephine Timms Dupree was to be laid to rest. Underneath the canopy were rows of metal folding chairs. Serge and Amelia joined them, looking somber and well-groomed. Amelia hovered sweetly around Maggie, patting her hair and whispering encouraging words in her ear that Harry couldn't hear. It was almost funny, he thought, how maternal she was being, even though Maggie was her senior by several years. But Amelia was almost a half foot taller; maybe there were times when height stood in for age. Maggie took it with good grace, looking surprised but grateful. Harry wondered if Amelia was trying to replace Josie, if only for the day.

There was only one reporter from the *Stoweville Register,* along with a single photographer, a woman wearing jeans and a T-shirt that proclaimed "Life is Great!" Harry wondered what thought processes, if any, had gone into the choice of the shirt. The reporter made his way to Maggie after talking to a few people on the outside edges of the crowd. Harry watched a young white woman with a baby in her arms point to Maggie after speaking to him.

"Hey, Maggie," the reporter said after making his way across the grass. "What do you have to say to the sheriff's department's allegations that your aunt was a terrorist?"

"No comment," Harry said. Serge moved next to him, his expression as close to menacing as he could get. Maggie looked at Harry, then at the reporter, but said nothing.

"Who are you?" the reporter said to Harry. The camera flashed behind him.

"Her attorney." He thought, I'm not exactly lying. "If you print anything that isn't true, we'll sue your ass from here to Mars." The camera flashed and clicked, but the reporter moved away. Wimp, Harry thought.

Miss Baby appeared from beyond the canopy with Charlotte and Tamara. Both girls wore chiffon dresses, Charlotte's pink, Tamara's yellow; Harry was reminded of Easter eggs. Maggie and Miss Baby hugged each other for a long time, Miss Baby in tears, Maggie dry-eyed. When they broke apart, Tamara and Charlotte flanked Maggie, putting their arms around her waist as she enveloped them, leaning down and kissing each girl in turn on the top of the head. Harry felt in the way until Miss Baby, still crying, threw her arms around his neck, squeezing him so hard it hurt; he hugged her back, feeling mortified, bewildered, and gratified all at the same time. After she let him go, Harry made the introductions. Amelia looked a little chagrined; Harry suspected that she was jealous of Miss Baby's prior claim to Maggie.

Maggie held the hands of the girls as a number of mourners approached them. There was a procession of black people and white people, young and old, male and female. A few faces were familiar to Harry, like Dottie the waitress, but most were strangers to him.

Miss Tokay wasn't anywhere to be seen; Miss Baby said that she was being looked after by her niece and the objectionable developer husband. As the line grew, Serge and Amelia moved away to observe from the margins, as well as to keep an eye on the reporter and his boorish photographer.

Harry wasn't sure where to stand, but Miss Baby took his hand and kept him in the line with her granddaughters and Maggie as they received the good wishes of one person after another. Most of the comments were about Josie: "She knew the treatment would come out all right, she said so, she was right." "She said my mamma wouldn't suffer none, and she didn't, it was peaceful, thank God." "I left the bastard the way she said, and now I'm better off, I sure am." But then a middle-aged woman with hair so thin her pink speckled scalp showed through the strands thanked Maggie for fixing one appliance or the other; an old man with a hump on his back that was painful to look at gripped Maggie's arms while telling her how well his pickup ran after she'd done something to it. Through his tears, Calvin Crane told her how much he'd miss Josie, then added almost casually that two lightbulbs had burned out and asked when she could replace them. Harry thought, thunderstruck, the beautiful light in Crane's, it was from Maggie's hands. It was then that Josie's words about the responsibility of taking care of Maggie came back to him with force; it was much more profound than shielding a shy girl from social slings and arrows. He felt a sudden panic and thought, God, I hope I'm man enough.

His chest gave another unpleasant little thump when he saw three women walking across the cemetery lawn. Two were wearing smart, silky pantsuits: Julie Canfield and Ronnie Ho. Ronnie in particular looked surprised to see him. Judd Lippman wasn't with them; Harry seemed to remember Amelia saying something about Ronnie dumping him in front of a bunch of other students at the Brew House. The third woman had a simian, acne-scarred face and was wearing jeans, a white blouse, and a tweed blazer. Harry suspected that she was Ronnie's roommate, the physics student from a thousand years ago, the one Josie had told about the stolen Ziegart effect. Julie broke away from the trio and came to his side while Ronnie and her roommate approached Maggie, each in turn shaking her hand. Julie said in his ear, "Poor Maggie. Ronnie and Cheryl thought the world of her aunt. I thought I might see you here." She gave him a quick, rueful smile and moved toward her friends. Ronnie's roommate, Cheryl, was telling Maggie how sorry she was while Ronnie nodded in agreement. Harry wondered what her reaction would be if she ever learned that she had just shaken the hand of the true inventor of the Ziegart effect.

It wasn't long before the memory of Lawrence's funeral hit him gently; it had been sparsely attended but just as miserable. He thought about Dusty's wooden face, so much younger then, and Ann's open sobbing. He'd thought at the time that her overwrought displays of emotion didn't allow him room to express anything; now he thought, I can blame her for a lot but not for that. I was so goddamned mad at him, he thought. Maggie nudged the girls in Miss Baby's direction and came beside him. She took his hand. "Funerals suck," he said.

A tall, skinny man of about sixty, skin toughened and coffee-colored from too much sun, stood off to the side of the other mourners, a bewildered look on his face. Harry asked who he was; Maggie murmured, "Roy Crawley. He runs a junkyard. He was in love with Josie." Harry believed her; the man's face was heartbreaking in the understated way of some men's terrible grief. Harry noticed that Calvin Crane was now openly crying while taking obvious pains to stay on the other side of the gathering from Roy Crawley. The latter made his way through the crowd to Maggie. As soon as he was an arm's length away, he said, "I woulda married her, Maggie."

He fell into her arms, silent, but the movement of his broad, bony shoulders giving him away. "I know, Roy, I know," she said, patting his back while he leaned on her. It took Harry a second to take this in, that this man was so lost for Josie Dupree that his self-control would desert him in public. Roy pulled back after a minute or so and said, "You just call me if you need anything, you hear. I got some stuff for you. You come see when you're all settled down."

Maggie said, "Thank you for taking the blame for the workshop."

"Taking credit's more like it. My tranny hums now. You doubled my gas mileage. I got a block, a driveshaft from an old Dakota. A bale of copper wire. You come see me."

Maggie thanked him again as he walked away, back to the farthest reaches of people, beyond the azalea bushes.

"Your supplier."

"Yes." She looked solemnly around at the crowd, not seeming nearly as distressed at dealing with them as she had been the people at Serge's party. Then Harry remembered that Jonathan Ziegart had been there. He said, "No one told the sheriff's people that the workshop was yours?"

"No."

"But if the truth came out, they'd know your connection to Jonathan. Maybe they could find a link between him and what happened to Josie, and to Murphy."

Her eyes were not as tired as they had once been, but the sadness was back. "And they'd be able to prove nothing. And he'd be so mad at me I'd be dead in a week." She sounded so certain that Harry believed her.

The service was short in the sunlight. Miss Baby was the first speaker, using a churchy cadence that Harry found moving and oddly comforting. No one made Maggie get up and talk; no one seemed to expect her to, and Harry found that the most moving thing of all.

The eulogies ended with Josie's plain casket being lowered into the ground. The winch creaked in the silence, and soft sobs broke through the birdsong and the sunlight and the clatter of a pileated woodpecker ripping open a distant, dying tree. Maggie was quiet and dry-eyed as she watched the wooden box descend, but she squeezed Harry's hand as it disappeared. In the near silence, Harry heard the sound of someone else approaching from the parking lot, soft footsteps on grass, and he turned to see Sheriff Melvin Kimble in an impressive dress uniform walking toward the funeral party, followed by a black-suited Jonathan Ziegart.

Calvin Crane had closed his restaurant in honor of Josie's passing, and the mourners were directed to go there after Josie's body had been lowered into the ground. The sheriff and Jonathan had stayed in the background, a few feet beyond the canvas canopy. Now people were standing, murmuring, preparing to walk to cars and ride the short mile to Crane's, or to leave altogether. Maggie lifted herself from her chair as though her weight approached Calvin's, slowly and with attention to her joints. She let go of Harry's hand for the first time in an hour, rubbing her elbows and then her neck as though she was in pain. Amelia moved in on her again, taking her arm. Maggie saw the sheriff and the man behind him before Harry could warn her. She didn't move, just stared at them with her great blue eyes. He took an involuntary look at her hands to make sure there was nothing like a flashlight in them.

Sheriff Kimble approached them first. Harry watched Jonathan move off to mingle; he couldn't imagine what the young man would have to say to any of the strangers in the crowd but saw him walk toward Julie Canfield. Harry wondered what his responsibility was; should he warn her of something? He could imagine pulling her aside and telling her that Jonathan Ziegart was dangerous, but Julie was practically a lawyer and he had few facts. He sighed internally, knowing his job was to stay with Maggie.

The sheriff said to Amelia, "I was wondering if you'd give me a private moment with Miss Roth?" Maggie nodded at Amelia's questioning look. Serge was right behind her and looked for confirmation at Harry, who gave a tiny shrug. He said, "You two go on to Crane's. We'll follow you there in a few minutes."

"You sure?" Serge said.

Harry assured him that he was, and the Olnikoffs moved away into the thinning crowd, casting back anxious glances.

The sheriff had an appropriate expression, sad and ingratiating. "Miss Roth," he said, extending his hand. Maggie looked at it for a moment before extending hers. "I wanted to express my condolences personally. A terrible thing." Maggie said nothing, just stared at him while he went on. "I hope that you know that the Stowe County Sheriff's Department only has the interest of the residents of this county at heart. I hope you understand that, honey," he repeated.

Harry said, "If you're asking whether Ms. Roth is planning on bringing a wrongful death suit against the department, we haven't yet determined if she has grounds. We're looking into it."

The sheriff turned to Harry. "Are you licensed to practice law in this state, Mr. Sterling?"

Harry was about to assure him that he'd passed the Florida bar exam when Maggie said, "I won't be suing you," startling both of them. "I wish you people were better at your jobs than you are, but you got voted in, so it's just as much the fault of the people that voted for you."

The sheriff looked confused, not sure how to reply to such a candid speech, then regrouped and said, "Well, I hope we can change your mind about that someday. Everyone in my office takes their job very seriously, I assure you. I hope there's no hard feelings, and that we can move on."

Maggie stared at him for a moment before saying, "Time moves on no matter what any of us do. My feelings are very hard, but most of them don't have anything to do with you."

Harry said, a thought occurring to him suddenly, "Sheriff, I have a favor to ask."

The sheriff didn't look pleased at having such an immediate opportunity to change anyone's mind about how helpful his office could be to civilians. Harry went on. "A boy disappeared in an Orlando bus station a few weeks ago. A homeless boy. All I have is his first name, Jake. He was last seen in the company of a man named Quick. I'd appreciate it if you'd make a call or two and see if the Orlando police know anything about what happened to him."

Kimble turned back to Maggie and seemed to mull it over as he looked at her, silent in the sunlight, regarding him with no expression at all, but Harry was willing to bet that, to the sheriff, she looked accusing and potentially threatening. Then he looked at Harry again. "I can make a call. I can't promise a thing. You know that."

The reporter was approaching again, and the photographer followed behind, raising her camera as she walked. The sheriff grabbed Maggie's hand again and pumped it with a look of earnest condolence while she looked blankly back. The camera whirred and caught the image. With another brief and slightly sour look at Harry, the sheriff left them to shake the hands of the more prosperous looking people still gathered around the grave. Harry glared at the reporter, who then led the photographer off in the sheriff's wake.

Harry said, "Are you sure you don't want to try to sue? We could talk to some of Serge's friends. You might have a good case."

Maggie said, "In this town, it isn't likely we'd win. Even if we did, we wouldn't get enough money to make it worthwhile."

· · ·

Jonathan Ziegart was waiting for them to approach him. Harry expected Maggie to try to avoid him, but after the sheriff was out of earshot she walked to where Jonathan was talking with an elderly black couple, dressed in church clothes and smiling. Harry followed Maggie and heard the tail end of a conversation in which the older man was explaining to Jonathan how many of Josie's suggested numbers had hit on the lottery. "I made me five hundred dollars once." When the man saw Maggie nearing them, he stopped as though caught in something unsavory. He said, "Now don't give me one of your lectures on how the lottery is 'the poverty tax' again, Maggie. I heard you the first ten times. I'm still ahead, you know. I ain't played it five hundred times."

"No, only about three hundred. So you're ahead, but not by much. And you'll fall behind fast if you don't stop."

"Your aunt always said the same thing, although I always got the feelin' she was just quotin' you." He smiled sweetly and shook her hand as his wife nodded and smiled too. They made their good-days, promising to see all of them at Crane's, and left.

Maggie and Jonathan faced each other, a short strip of healthy grass all that lay between them. Harry stood at Maggie's side. Jonathan's suit looked expensive, and he'd gotten a haircut since they'd last met. My God, thought Harry; he looks like Charlie. Maggie said in a calm, reasonable voice, "You got her killed, you son of a
. bitch."

50

JUSTICE

Something like it,
anyway

Jonathan looked hurt; Harry thought, It looks like he's about to cry. He'd always thought Jonathan's affect was somehow distorted, and now the effect was horrifying, like sticking your hand into a bucket of something squirming and wet.

Jonathan said, "You look beautiful." He moved a step toward her, his hand reaching out. Maggie jumped back as though he had a gun in it. Jonathan stopped and looked hurt again. "I understand what it is to lose someone so important to you. I'd like to help." He was smiling now, but it had an odd, glassy quality; he looked as if he was on an intense and unhealthy stimulant. "But I guess I should remember how shy you are."

Maggie had moved a few inches away from Harry, just enough, he realized, to avoid giving Jonathan Ziegart any more reason to think that Harry was dear to her. Fuck that, he thought, and reached out to take her hand in his. This at least got Jonathan to look at him. The anger in those bright, wet eyes was so hot that Harry almost felt the burn of it. Then Jonathan made to ignore Harry again, turning back to Maggie. He said, "I'm not allergic to anything, Emily. Which is good, because I am considering living here, and the place is full of bees." A puff of dandelion landed on his lapel, and he brushed it away with a thin hand; it was shaking. Then he looked from her to Harry, at their joined hands, and said, "You have a son, don't you, Harry?" It was said conversationally, pleasantly. Jonathan's hands opened and closed as if he was a pianist warming them up before a concert. "I hear he lives with his mother in Orlando. I've always wanted to check out Disneyland."

Harry had once interviewed a prizefighter who'd lost everything because of an addiction to oxycodone. The young man had been almost comically huge, a half a foot taller and a hundred pounds heavier than Harry, who wasn't particularly small. He had seemed to be made entirely of muscle; no visible skin drooped or dangled. He made his living by hurting people, probably killing a few; he had worked for the second busiest drug dealer in the DC area. Harry had been surprised by how much he liked the murderer, how affable and intelligent he was. They'd started talking about how to damage someone so that it didn't show, the attorney in Harry being interested in such things. "Hit 'em in the belly," the boxer had said. "Fewer marks. The face bruises too easy and bleeds too much. You hit 'em in the jaw, you break all the little bones in your hand and it hurts like hell."

Now Harry said, "Disneyland is in California. Here, it's Disney World," and punched Jonathan Ziegart in the stomach.

He was dimly aware of Maggie's hands on him, one around his upper arm and the other pulling on his jacket. There were others around them, too, big hands against Harry's chest, pushing him away from the man at his feet. These impediments irritated him mildly since he'd gotten to hit Jonathan only once. Jonathan had let loose a shocked bark of pain and was half sitting on the ground. For a second Harry was puzzled about how he'd gotten there. Then the judge spoke in his mind: You're going to pay for this. But when he saw the happy look on Maggie's face, he thought, I don't care. Jonathan stood up with the help of Roy Crawley, anger and pain making his face dark and veined. His nose was bleeding, and he pulled a white handkerchief from his pocket and pressed it to his face. Harry wondered if Roy was ever going to know the role of the man he was helping stand up in Josie Dupree's death. By the look of him, Roy was another one who would kill someone given a good enough reason.

The sheriff and the reporters were gone, so the only witnesses to Harry's assault on Jonathan Ziegart were the few people who hadn't yet left for Crane's. Miss Baby was among them, and she hurried over, looking alternately at Jonathan and at Maggie. "He the one, sugar?" Maggie nodded, and Miss Baby turned on Jonathan. "You best leave, boy, before you're pounded to a pile of bone and grease by the assembled party."

Jonathan didn't follow them to Crane's. Calvin served no alcohol, although Harry was surprised to find that he didn't feel the need for a drink anyway. He thought, From now on, I'll need my wits about me.

51

STRENGTH

*The Seeker
gets a backbone*

Harry expected a knock at any moment from the police or the sheriff's department to haul him off for assaulting Jonathan Ziegart. "Maybe we should both get out of town for a few days, before the sheriff tells either of us that we can't," he said to Maggie. "We should go to Pennsylvania. You need to pay a visit to the good people at Cantwell." At her worried face, he said, "My treat. Can Calvin spare you for a few more days?"

"I already told him that I might not be back at all. But I'm not sure what to do. I don't have any money in the bank."

Harry said, "They don't have as much power as you think they do. We'll have to decide what to do about Jonathan later. Let's at least set you free from those pompous assholes at Cantwell, and stop them from shutting you up."

She stared at him for a moment and then said, "You think we could get some money out of them?"

"I'll bet we could," he said. "How much money do you want?"

She thought for a moment. "A lot. Tamara needs braces."

Before they left, Maggie insisted that they visit Miss Tokay. Maggie put her hand on her stomach when they passed the shot-up shrine as though it hurt her in the middle to see it. There were chunks of purple concrete lying around the steps. The heart had been the main target; only a third of it remained intact, a jagged half-moon dotted with black holes the size of coat buttons.

"Was it the nephew-in-law?" Harry said.

"Of course it was," she said, her voice bitter and hard. "He's always hated it. He said it brings down the value of the property."

The niece, Gretchen Covington, was there without her husband. She didn't want to let them in, but Harry gently threatened her with a call to Social Services if she wouldn't let them see the Purple Lady and make sure she was being cared for properly. The niece was easily intimidated; between that and the ruination of the shrine, Harry had an idea of what the husband was probably like. She was a thin, overly tanned woman, well dressed in pale silk slacks and blouse, and she talked incessantly as she led them through the dark hall into the sitting room, where Miss Tokay sat on her Victorian divan in her voluminous purple shawl. Maggie sat next to her, asking how she was, did she want a cup of tea or coffee, had she been eating. Harry was appalled at the poor woman's face, shrunken and wrinkled. He didn't know if what ailed her was mostly dementia, guilt, or sorrow at the destruction outside her front door.

Miss Tokay's expression didn't change at first, although she looked at Maggie through rheumy eyes; Harry wasn't sure she was registering who Maggie was. But when Gretchen left the room to call her husband, the old woman's face shifted into recognition, lighting up. "Maggie," she said, so quietly he almost couldn't hear her, though he was standing only a couple of feet from where they sat. She didn't seem to recall that anyone had died on her porch recently, although she didn't ask after Josie, so Harry had to wonder how much she really had forgotten. She seemed to notice him for the first time after a few minutes and told him to sit as though she had been remiss as a hostess, offering him something to eat or drink. He told her he was fine and sat down on the dainty little chair across the coffee table from her.

"We're going out of town for a few days," Maggie said. "Are they treating you all right? Anything I can do for you before we go?"

"I'll be fine. You're coming back, though, right, honey?" Miss Tokay's voice had a trembling sharpness that Harry had never heard in it before, although he hadn't talked to her much. Maybe she got this odd intensity often. But Maggie looked both worried and sad, and Harry suspected that the old woman's need for her cut her heart.

"Yes, ma'am. I'll always come back. Don't you worry."

Miss Tokay assured them that she wasn't suffering any abuse from her niece or nephew-in-law. "They think I'm loony, of course," she said with an unexpectedly lovely smile. Then she asked Maggie when they planned to return.

"Take this," Maggie said, handing Miss Tokay a small piece of yellow paper with a string of numbers written on it. "Harry has a cell phone, so you can call us anytime."

"It's brand-new," Harry interjected, then felt like an idiot as the two women looked blankly at him.

52

ACE OF
SWORDS

The Seeker gets ready
to kick some butt

"I don't want to do this," she said. They were on a plane to Atlanta, where they would catch another to Harrisburg in a few hours.

"I know," Harry said.

"I'm afraid that Miss Tokay isn't going to be alive when we get back."

"Do you think Jonathan will try to do something to her?"

She shook her head, looking out the window at billowy clouds and a bleached sun. "He's already done something to her. I think he's just going to let the law take its course. Or nature."

"Did you see something in her aura?" Harry said, surprised to hear himself ask the question.

She looked back at him and said, "It was sickly. But also, before we left, she asked me if I wanted her to tell Josie anything for me."

They rented a car in Harrisburg. The closer they got to Lucasta, the more agitated and restless Maggie became. They checked in to the same hotel that Harry and Dusty had stayed in, and then they discussed for the third time when and if they would call Fay Levy. Maggie didn't want to deal with the scene that would inevitably follow, so Harry agreed to at least wait until after they'd had their appointment at Cantwell. They got a take-out dinner at the nearby omelet house and ate in the room. For the first time since they'd been together, neither of them slept well. Maggie tossed so much that Harry pulled her to him and held her and murmured calming things to her until she put her hands on him. Afterward, her puffy blond hair tickled his chin, and he kept jerking and pushing it off his face to try to get her to laugh. It was only slightly successful. He said, "I'll be with you every second. Remember not to touch me, though. It'll be better if we don't come off as a goofy in-love sort of couple. I'm going to act the part of your hard-assed attorney, as well as a crack investigator. It doesn't matter that I'm not licensed here. They'll know as well as we do that we can hire a local in seconds."

She said, "What's the name of Serge's friend up here?"

"Rick Clooney. He's a friend of a friend. I'm only going to call him if we need to. But we have permission to drop his name." He stared at the ceiling, filled with dots on ugly acoustical panels. Why would they drop the ceiling in a nice old building like this? He wondered if these dots were anything like Maggie's. Of course not, he thought, grimacing at the idea of a world that was made up entirely of cheap ceiling tiles and paneling. He said, "You could make better looking ceilings than that, I bet. Acoustically sound, and all that."

"Hmmm," she said, looking up.

He contemplated the offending ceiling, then said before thinking, "Do you miss him?"

She turned over onto her stomach, her fists on his chest making a support for her chin. The room was dark, but he could still see her eyes, gleaming as they caught the light from the open bathroom door. Her breath tickled his chest hair as she said, "I always wondered how those whales and dolphins at SeaWorld feel about their trainers. I imagine it's kind of like I used to feel about Charlie. Grateful and resentful at the same time. They can swim and eat, but not like they want. Not like what's natural for them. I suppose they're happy when they get their buckets of fish. I didn't get enough fish." She kissed his chest, then put her chin back on her fists. "I like your fish better anyway."

"I'm trying to figure out what that's a metaphor for."

She laughed and said, "Forget the fish." She kissed his chest again. "The moment I saw you, I knew that you were going to be important to me somehow."

"I was drunk and puking on your porch."

Her smile was so beautiful, even in the dark, it almost hurt to look at it. "I never said that you were a sweet talker. And I didn't know if I was going to be particularly important to you."

He said, "I hope you know that now," reaching for her again as she finally answered his question. "I don't miss him anymore, Harry." Then she added, "Have you found out about meetings up here?"

"Dusty e-mailed a list he got on the Internet." He studied the dots in the ceiling one more time, then said, "He's going to Alateen. I'm not quite sure how I feel about it."

"He loves you."

"Yes, he does. Do you love me?"

She smiled her beautiful smile. "Yes."

"A lot?"

"More than anything." She kissed his chest. "More than anyone." He relaxed and after a while, slept.

53

TEN OF WANDS

REVERSED

A sweet talker.
A demon

Jonathan Ziegart got a copy of the incident report of the shootings of Josie Dupree and Darcy Murphy from Serena. He had almost asked her out, but not quite, so the young divorcée had hopes of him. He told her that the information in the report would be useful for his dissertation research but promised that he'd change the names and dates and places so that the case itself would never be recognizable to anyone outside Stowe County. She believed him.

He read it with some care in his room, drinking a can of root beer from the minibar and making notes on a yellow legal pad as he sat at the small round table that the hotel provided for just such work. There was a search, he read, of the big garage at the old lady's house. A junk dealer, Roy Crawley, used the space as a workshop. Jonathan thought, junk dealer my ass. It has to be Emily's. The dimwits hadn't found anything in it of interest. He could imagine the old lady conning them, or maybe Emily herself saying, Oh, Mr. Policeman, just some old notebooks, no need for you to bother to get anyone with any education to read it. And they would believe a propertied southern lady like Miss Tokay. God, he thought, the stereotypes were true; the sloppiness and stupidity of the southern swamp police were boundless.

He was so angry that he was scaring himself a little. He breathed in and out, deep cleansing breaths. Think of the positives, he thought. Darcy Murphy was dead, so he couldn't tell anyone they'd ever met. No one else knew; there was no reason for anyone to even ask. His supervisor's statement was in the file, as was the statement of Murphy's wife. Both confirmed that he'd had an unhealthy interest in the fortune teller. He seemed to have it in for her for no other reason than his general distaste for the profession. Jonathan could have told them that Darcy had also had the hots for Josie Dupree, but no one else seemed to have gleaned this fact. Just as well, Jonathan thought. Murphy's wife had also told them her husband had started drinking after having been sober for several months. Jonathan made himself smile, but the anger was still there, unmoved, like a cancer.

I could kill her, he thought. I might kill her. I might not. He sweated and thought. But maybe it would be better to watch her try to save herself against terrible odds. Maybe I could even rescue her. This brought a memory back to him, a violent memory that never failed to give him goose bumps, to make his heart race and shudder. Doug McNeill flailing and huge, a gargantuan choking thing, his airless moans almost musical, his eyes bloodshot in a blue face. When Fate had seen fit to kill an enemy of his father's, it had seemed like marvelous luck. But it had forced Jonathan to discover a dead part of himself as well. Because he'd found Doug McNeill's death dance beautiful, fascinating, awe-inspiring. And it never once occurred to him to try to save the man's life.

Sorry, Emily, he thought; rescuing people is not my forte. Still, he thought, I could allow for it as a possible outcome. My redemption.

It might be a simple matter of putting something in the temple, something more interesting to the sheriff, or likely to catch the eye of Homeland Security. Then a few phone calls, an anonymous party interested in restoring the reputation of Wally Faber and the sheriff's department in general. They'd have to take it seriously. Mention Emily's name, or rather her new name. She was bound to have left fingerprints and DNA evidence all over the place, even if none of the crackers who knew her would fess up that the workshop is hers. He had notes of his father's, some unfinished and impractical designs for weaponry. He remembered his father's hopes that the so-called Star Wars initiatives would be reinstated. The software involved was not Charlie Ziegart's strong suit, but the hardware, ah, his father told him about dreams that he had, literal dreams; he'd awakened one morning and drawn plans in the notebook he kept by his bed of a laser that could fry a scarab beetle on a tent flap while orbiting on a satellite two hundred miles above the ground. The computer simulations had never panned out; all the contracts Charlie won were for power systems, but he had hopes, always hopes. And Jonathan had some of the notes, a few abortive schematics, calculations, and spreadsheets. Not all of them, but a few. Enough. And he was on a roll.

It would be an interesting problem, he thought, how to generate copies without them being linked to any printer he was associated with. Laser printers left encoded signatures on documents. I'll have to go to a chain copy store, he thought. But I've got time. I'll have to see the place for myself first. Get the lay of the land.

I need her notes, he thought. She used to be obsessive about making them. Emily generated even more notebooks than Charlie. I can reorganize them; I'm sure I could come up with something absolutely fantastic for Homeland Security.

He mused for a while, thinking, It'll come out that we're connected. He liked the sound of it, so he said it aloud. "We're connected." How to explain that? Tell the truth, he thought; that's always best. I found out she was alive from Gillian, or suspected that she was, and came down here to see her. She didn't want to have anything to do with me. I had no idea that she was up to something so heinous, that she'd become so twisted. But she was always odd, a loner. He thought it would feel so good to say to a policeman at last, I always thought that she killed my father. But I just couldn't believe it.

Maybe she'd be extradited. Pennsylvania had the death penalty. But then so did Florida. He would be her only visitor on death row. She'd look so beautiful in orange. At least he thought prison uniforms were orange. Easy enough to check.

An inspiration leapt into his mind from its underbelly, the way the best ideas always do, when you're not trying so hard, when you're thinking about something else. He thought, I'll find a copy place in Orlando.

54

SEVEN OF
SWORDS

A nasty bunch,
but not as smart
as they think they are

Gillian DeGraff and Pamela Ziegart had
agreed to meet with Harry and Maggie in
DeGraff's office at eleven o'clock. Maggie couldn't keep still all through breakfast and ate almost nothing. Her nerves
made Harry drink too much coffee, and
the eggs he'd ordered weren't sitting well
in his stomach. Afterward they went for
a walk before their appointment. The
campus was larger than was justified by
the size of the student body. A section to
the east gave way to a vast complex of
formal gardens. Maggie explained that Cantwell had a horticulture
school that maintained them.

"I used to walk here all the time. Sometimes with Fay, but mostly
alone."

"It seems tame compared to Gunhill Park and Miss Tokay's land."

She smiled. "That was one of the good things about my leaving
here in disgrace. A wilder place to walk."

Harry said, "Why Crane's? I mean, why didn't you just go to another school or get a job somewhere in a lab?"

She slowed, gestured to a stone bench by a sea of lamb's ear. "I could use a breather. It's been a long time since I walked where it's hilly." They sat, and she looked up at clouds that formed white fingers in the blue sky. Cornflower blue, Harry thought. She said, "I couldn't get a letter from anyone. Gillian made it clear that they'd trash my name to anyone who inquired about why I was transferring."

"You can sue people for that, you know."

"I couldn't," she said. "You have no idea how frightened I was of Jon."

"But what about after you came home? Couldn't you have worked for an electrician? I know it's not the same, but at least you could have been better paid and gotten to use some of your skills."

She smiled again. "I did. I don't have a license, and I didn't want to have to go to a technical school to learn what I already knew. So I apprenticed." Her smile got wider. "Twice."

She stopped talking, her smile fading. Harry said, "It didn't work out?"

"No." She leaned down and touched one of the soft gray leaves. "I kept questioning them. About every procedure, every material. I kept trying to improve things. The first man I worked for thought I was too uppity. The second thought I was crazy. They both thought I was hopeless. I couldn't find a third. And I still didn't have a license." She inhaled the warm, sweet air of the garden. "I couldn't shut up. I tried, but I just couldn't."

"So then you just shut up altogether."

She shrugged. "I guess. But once Miss Tokay let me use the new temple, I was okay. Better than that, actually. Free."

They went back to the hotel to clean up and change. Harry said if they smelled bad enough it might give them the upper hand in their negotiations. "They'll give us whatever we want to get us out of the room." Maggie laughed but showered anyway. Harry had gone with her before they'd left Stoweville to buy a brown tweed suit and some leather shoes; he'd brought his own best black pinstripe. He wanted them to look intimidating. As they stood side by side in front of the thin mirror in their room, he thought they'd succeeded, although Maggie looked too pale. "Deep breaths," he said, and she nodded jerkily.

On their way to the appointment, they passed a building shaped like a large brick cube. Attached to it like an unsightly growth was a metallic addition, doubling the size of the building. Maggie stopped to stare at it. There was a sign mounted in the grass beside the concrete walkway leading up to the main door. It was bronze, half the size of a coffin lid, and announced that this was the home of the Charles Ziegart School of Physics and Engineering.

"That's where I used to work."

"I know," he said.

"I forgot that you've been here. They added that thing"—she pointed to the huge architectural tumor—"after I left. I didn't know they'd changed the name of the school."

"Where do you think they got the money?"

"They design a lot of components of weapons systems," she said. "Power supplies. Big government contracts. That's another reason they didn't like me much. I wasn't very cooperative. They said I shouldn't have come here if I didn't 'share the vision' of the school. They were right. It was Charlie's vision, too. He loved being rich. And famous. But I didn't do enough research on the school before I came. I was so flattered and excited. And stupid."

"You weren't stupid, you were young. I bet they didn't tell you they wanted you to work on military contracts when they invited you."

"No," she said. "They didn't. But that was back when they had hopes for me."

. . .

They were ten minutes early. "Is that bad?" Maggie asked.

"No," he said, although he would have preferred to keep them waiting. It was unprofessional, but just ornery enough that it would have been satisfying. But rather than take more time sightseeing around the grounds, they climbed the cement steps into the main administration building. It was grand and Georgian, four stories of freshly repointed brick and large white-trimmed windows. The ceilings were high and old, pressed tin in flowery shapes. The inside of the building smelled of paint and was cool, with the light illuminating tiny specks of dust in beams that stroked the broad marble floor of the hallway. There was an elevator, but Maggie shook her head. "It vibrates," she said. "It makes me hyperventilate." So he held her hand as they climbed the stairs to the fourth floor.

They came to an open reception area with a phone bank and three computer terminals on broad oak-stained desks. There was no one in sight. Behind the secretarial stations was a frosted glass door with "Office of the Dean of Arts and Sciences" painted on it importantly in gilt letters. He led Maggie to it, then let go of her hand. Then he reached into his pocket for his cell phone and turned it off. "Don't want to be rude," he said.

There were two women and one man in a beautiful office that seemed soaked in cherrywood paneling and brass trim. They were seated, but they stood when Harry and Maggie entered the room. The man offered his hand first; Harry shook it firmly. "Wesley De-Graff," the man said, looking calm and confident. He wore a gray suit and red patterned tie and was well-built with a big chin, small nose, and very little hair. "I'm Cantwell's chancellor."

Harry merely nodded as the rest of the introductions were made. Gillian DeGraff didn't look like Harry expected, short and squat and dark when he'd been prepared to see someone tall and willowy and aristocratic. Pamela Ziegart was another matter, a tall, aging woman with a face like a mosquito, all points and squints. She wasn't unattractive, but she looked as if anger sat on her face all year round and as if she disdained most things. He could see a few traces of Jonathan in her, but not many. No one needed to introduce Maggie. Wesley was again the first to address her. "Hello, Emily," he said. "It's good to see you again. A shock, as you might imagine, but a pleasant one." Maggie didn't answer, just stared at him with her wide, bright eyes.

"Yes," said Gillian in a voice that Harry recognized from the phone, all patrician and good vowels. "So nice to hear that you're not dead after all."

"Well," Wesley began after they'd all sat down, "as I said, I'm delighted that Emily is no longer lost to the world of the living, but I'm not sure what we can do for you. I assume that this isn't a social visit?"

Harry said, "As I'm sure you all know, for the last five years or so of his life, Charles Ziegart systematically used all of his wife Emily's work, presenting it as his own."

This had the effect that Harry intended. The three of them had almost exactly the same expression, which would have been comical if Harry hadn't already felt needles of anger sticking him. Gillian was the first to speak. "That's simply not true. Besides, she was his student. She worked for him."

Harry nodded. "So I've been told. Legally, you're all safe. But from a public relations standpoint, you've got a problem."

This time it was Wesley who spoke. "If it's your intention to slander Charlie or the university, you're the one who's going to have legal problems, Mr. Sterling." He no longer looked friendly.

"I'm only interested in printing the truth." Harry leaned back in his chair, regarding the three of them, wondering how long it would take for Pamela Ziegart, sitting quiet and imploded in the farthest chair, to say something.

"Get out," said Gillian. Her voice was flat with anger.

"In a minute," Harry said. "I assume you also know that Jonathan Ziegart killed his father."

That did it. Pamela stood up. "How dare you! You have some nerve, coming here and tossing horrible accusations around." Wesley and Gillian had recovered more quickly and were making delicate efforts to shush Pamela, but it wasn't working. She squinted at Maggie. "You hated us, you wanted everything we'd worked for. You couldn't stand it, that he still had a family. Greedy little bitch."

Maggie spoke for the first time. "I didn't take him from you, Pamela. I didn't take anything from you. You know that perfectly well."

Pamela seemed to get bigger as her rage seemed to inflate. "Your goddamned *application* stole him from me."

Maggie's mouth opened, and Harry could see that this was a blow she hadn't expected. He said to Pamela, "You'd better sit down and shut up before you say anything else equally asinine."

Gillian said, "Pamela, calm down. I'm calling security and having the two of them forcibly removed from the premises."

Pamela sat down; then, looking at Harry, said, "Everyone knows that she was responsible for Charlie's death."

Harry said, "That's bullshit. You and everyone else know it's bullshit, including the police. I've talked to Commander Sutton of the state police."

There was a silence in which Harry could hear Pamela's heavy breathing through her thin nose. Gillian's hand was on her desk phone, but she didn't pick it up. She said, "You never answered Wesley's question. If you came all the way from whatever swamp you inhabit to insult us with slurs on Charles Ziegart and his son, there's no point in talking any longer. We have much better things to do with our time, even if you don't."

Harry said, "We've been in touch with an attorney in town, Rick Clooney."

Wesley made a nervous motion with his hands. "He's a criminal lawyer. I can't imagine why you've talked to him. If there has been any wrongdoing, it isn't by anyone at Cantwell." He looked at Maggie, his face no longer friendly. "Your allegations against Jon are patently false, so you can't possibly have any evidence, unless you've manufactured some. I agree with Pamela that this is highly distasteful, and legally actionable if you make these claims publicly. I can't believe that you would try to smear the name of anyone in the Ziegart family, Emily."

Harry said, "Because she benefited so much from her association with them?"

This had the effect he wanted, getting Wesley's attention back to him. "Well, yes. Without Charlie, where would she be, after all?"

"Probably on the faculty of MIT."

This was answered by a general humming of disagreement. "I hardly think that's likely," Wesley said.

"He killed my mother, too," Maggie said with no affect.

There was another thick silence, the DeGraffs and Pamela Ziegart staring at Maggie with collective horror. Harry was glad they weren't looking at him; he was shocked as well, never having considered this possibility. He thought, I bet that's true. Oh my God. We'll probably never be able to prove that either. Bluff, he thought, bluff like you've never bluffed before. He spoke before they could spew out more heated denials. "We are well aware of the limitations of the justice system. We know these allegations are true, but we don't have the kind of evidence that would meet the standard of proof in criminal court. We're being frank with you about this."

"Are you blackmailing us?" said Wesley. "Is that what this is about?"

"Emily relinquished all claim to monies generated by her work and her share of Charles Ziegart's estate because of coercion and threats by Pamela and Jonathan."

"What coercion?" said Gillian. "The only thing she was threatened with was exposure."

"Jonathan said he would kill Fay," said Maggie. "If I didn't leave."

Gillian said, "Who's Fay?" at the same time that Wesley spat out, "This is ludicrous!" He faced Harry. "I can't believe someone of your professional stature would be a party to this. It's all fantasy, and a crass, and probably criminal, attempt to blackmail the university."

Harry said, "It's not blackmail if the money was rightfully hers in the first place."

Pamela made a noise of disgust, a sort of spitting sound. Harry expected her to say something, but she only stared at Maggie with that mosquito glare of hers, hatred making her eyes glassy.

Maggie looked at Wesley. "Pamela's afraid of him, too, you know."

"Of who? Her own son? That's ridiculous. I happen to know how close they are."

Pamela made the spitting sound again but still said nothing.

Maggie said, "You should be careful if he hears about this meeting. He might suspect that we talked about him. He's pretty paranoid. He really wouldn't like it if his mother told the truth about him to anyone." All eyes traveled to Pamela's face, which had undergone a subtle shift. Harry thought, She's afraid but doesn't want to show it.

Gillian said, "Why don't you tell us exactly what you want, and quit wasting our time?"

"You're right," Harry said. "We want money."

Wesley repeated, "That's ridiculous."

Gillian said, "How much?"

Wesley said to his wife, "Don't even dignify this stupid threat by asking that."

Harry said, "Two hundred thousand dollars." There was another collective gasp. "The Ziegart effect patent has brought the university many times that over the years. Emily just wants a small percentage of what she's entitled to." He waited, letting that sink in. Then he said, "Along with the documentation that her Ph.D. is finished, and appropriately favorable letters of recommendation so that she can regain her academic standing and find a job." He looked at Gillian. "We don't want anyone to lie. We just want letters from faculty who know of her work, in the same format they use for any student, honestly evaluating her performance, talents, and potential. They need to refrain from adding prejudicial and unfounded accusations or insinuations as well."

Wesley's face was incredulous and angry, but Gillian said to Maggie, "If we do this, you'll keep these slanders to yourself?"

Maggie said nothing. Harry nodded. "She just wants to be able to work in a lab again, and to be able to file her own patents without fear of retaliation."

Gillian looked at Harry. "You're a reporter. How do we know that you won't put the lies you've told us in print?"

Harry said, "You have my word that I won't publish anything about Jonathan Ziegart's threats and criminal actions, as long as he doesn't try to harm anyone else." Poor Doug McNeill, he thought. No justice for you, or for Josie, or Marlene Timms, or even Darcy Murphy. But without any real evidence, he knew there was nothing they could do anyway. "We could put my assurances in writing if you want." He grinned at her, which she didn't seem to like.

Wesley said, "No. You can print whatever you want. Our lawyers will see to it that you never publish again. Not even a shopping list."

Pamela and Gillian looked at him. Gillian turned to Harry and said, "We need to talk in private for a few minutes. Wait outside."

. . .

There was a bench in the reception area, and the two of them sat down. Harry felt exhilarated, a feeling he'd forgotten, closing in on smug power mongers, getting under their skin, making them itch with guilt and the fear of exposure. He knew it probably didn't speak well of him that he enjoyed it so much. Only people who deserve it, he thought. As long as I'm on the side of the angels.

Maggie stared at the wall across from them. He wondered what the dots of light really looked like, and if that was what she was looking at. She said, "She's probably right, Harry. About Charlie. About why he married me."

"If that was the only reason," he said, "he was an idiot." She kissed him on the cheek and then laid her head on his shoulder as he added, "They're going to give in. I can smell it. How were their auras?"

"Dirty," she said.

A half hour later, they were called back into the room. Nothing was to be put in writing. "If you break our agreement, we'll sue you, Mr. Sterling."

"I know," Harry said. "But Jonathan Ziegart is still a murderer, and if any evidence comes to light about his crimes, old or new, we'll make sure that he gets prosecuted. That's not up for negotiation." He looked at Pamela.

Wesley said, "You understand, no one in this room can control the behavior of another human being. Jonathan is completely blameless. But I don't want you smearing the family or the university if he's caught speeding or something. He's his own man."

Harry thought, his stomach contracting, They all know perfectly well what he's capable of. They believe us. They'll never admit it, but they knew all along. Maybe DeGraff didn't before, but he does now, and so do his wife and the merry widow. Ex-wife, he corrected himself. He clenched his fists, then relaxed them again with great effort. Assholes, he thought, fucking assholes. But all he said was "Why don't you folks try anyway? Give him a talking-to. Maybe you have more influence with him than you think." He looked at Maggie, then back at the trio flanking one another in the stately office. "If he hurts her anymore, you'll have to answer to me."

Maggie spoke to them for the last time. "And if he hurts Harry, I'll destroy all of you."

55

FOUR OF
CUPS

REVERSED

New opportunities

She is so hot, he thought, all sinewy angles and burning color. One thing he had to give Harry Sterling; he had great taste in women. "Mrs. Sterling?" he said to the gorgeous brunette who answered the door.

"Yes?"

"I'm a friend of Harry's. My name's Jonathan Ziegart. When I told him I was going to be in Orlando on business, he asked me to bring your son some books. Is he here?"

"Yes." Ann Sterling looked irritated. "Come on in. I can't believe Harry didn't at least call to tell me you were coming."

She is also dumb, he thought. She left him alone with Dusty for a half hour. He'd managed to charm her out of her fractious mood, and even to cadge a root beer. Then he'd made two references to the fact that Harry had a new girlfriend, a beautiful, petite blonde, and said how happy they looked. That had sent her back into the sullens, but she was too well-bred to kick him out.

The boy was pretty sullen himself, but Jon handed him a boxed set of the *Lord of the Rings* trilogy he'd picked up at the airport bookstore that morning. He never read fiction himself but supposedly all teenage boys loved books about trolls and witches and whatever. "Your dad said that you'd like these."

"I read 'em all two years ago," Dusty said, turning the box over in his hands. "He knows that. This is weird."

Jonathan felt the beginnings of hatred for this dopey-looking boy, his arms far too long for his body, his feet too large for his skinny little legs. He felt certain he could smell him, too, a mixture of churning hormones and sweat. "Well, I guess he forgot. You know, he's old. Getting forgetful. Haha."

Dusty regarded Jonathan through long bangs that threatened to skewer his eyeballs. "What's your last name again?"

Jonathan told him, and the boy's face got a strange look on it, possibly of recognition. Interesting, Jonathan thought. "Has your father mentioned me?"

"Your dad was a big scientist."

"Yes. Your father is thinking of writing a biography of him. That's how we got acquainted."

This got no response but an openmouthed gape. Jonathan decided the interview had become tiresome, so he said good-bye, leaving behind an indifferent mother and a puzzled son. The boy was almost certainly into drugs of some kind. All teenagers took them these days. It had been true of his generation, too, he thought, trying to be fair. He'd always been careful about what he put into his body, but so many of the Cantwell faculty kids, his classmates, treated themselves as lab specimens, trying out every chemical they could find and monitoring its effects with almost clinical interest. He recognized that a lot of this experimentation was fueled by adolescent boredom and depression. He'd read that teenagers were more prone to suicide these days. Dustin, he thought, was a good candidate for that. Nice and surly, divorced parents. Another interesting problem, how to foster that potential.

He wasn't worried that the boy would tell Harry about his visit. The thought of the conversation they would probably have on the phone and the impotence of Harry's worry over it made Jonathan press a little too hard on the accelerator of the rental car. He made himself slow down. He didn't want to get pulled over, and he wasn't in a hurry. There was plenty of time to find a copy center on the other side of town.

56

THREE OF
CUPS

REVERSED

Happy endings turn sour.
Beware of gossip from
an old friend

Harry drove back to the hotel with Maggie silent and still in the seat next to him. He waited for her to speak; when she didn't, he said, "This is all good, you know. You got what you wanted."

She looked at him with big, blue eyes. "I thought it would make me feel better," she said.

"You didn't tell me he killed your mother. Oh God, Maggie, I'm so sorry."

"There was no evidence. Maybe he wasn't responsible for the hit-and-run, but I'm pretty sure he was."

"Why?"

"He knew my mother's address outside Mobile. He was gone from here when she died. He probably just wanted to chat with her, charm her, see what dirt he could find out about me. No one saw anything. She liked to walk on lonely country roads, like me. I'm guessing he just saw another opportunity and took it. Right after that, his mamma bought him a new car. Oh God, Harry, what are we going to do?"

"We're going to have to live our lives as though he wasn't out there. I think it would be a good idea to make your former life or identity public knowledge. Maybe we can get the local press to do a story on it. That way, his relationship with you will be better known. That should buy you some sort of protection, make him have to think twice about rigging something too terrible. But at least you can go back to work now." He thought about Dan Polti's comment about the productive years of the average physicist and felt a pang of sadness for her lost opportunities. She was looking out the window at the passing hills. Then she took in a deep breath and said, "I think you're right. It's time I faced Fay."

Jonathan was back in Stoweville by early evening. The air was moist and cool, and the sun was painting the sky with all sorts of improbable colors. Emily would know everything about that process, he thought, how the light breaks apart as it tears through the sky from the dying sun. So would my father. I'd miss him if I really cared that much about how it all happens.

He stopped his car by the shrine just for a moment because he didn't want to be seen there. Serena had called his cell phone and told him that the nephew-in-law had been formally accused of shooting it up but would probably only pay a fine. He was claiming distress. Distress my ass, thought Jonathan, although you had to have some sympathy for him; all that land, all that money sitting there, useless in the hands of a cult-crazed old biddy. And besides, he thought, considering the broken heart at the top of the now-ruined stairs, somewhere in the man lay a poet.

He made his way down the driveway of the Purple Lady's house, driving easily over the chain lying in the dirt. Her last visitors had left it down; probably the niece and her moneygrubbing husband, he thought. They probably wanted her to be attacked or vandalized or at least harassed. But he had no intention of harassing her at all;

on the contrary, he expected the whole encounter to be pleasant for both of them.

He parked his car at the rear of the house, out of sight of the road, although it was unlikely that anyone could see through all the pines, especially in the dark. But the outside of the house was well enough lit that it was possible someone would spot it if he parked in the front. It was probably unimportant, since he didn't intend the old lady any harm, but you never knew when an opportunity might come along; you never knew when it was better to slide out of a place leaving no mark at all. He patted the handkerchief in his pocket.

They sat in the parking lot of a restaurant on the outskirts of Godfrey Lake. It looked a lot like Crane's, and Harry imagined that the menu was the same sort, laminated and dominated by burgers and familiar sandwiches. Harry had suggested that they go in and eat something before calling Fay, but Maggie had hesitated and finally explained that she could see the fluorescent lighting through the windows.

"Sorry. I forgot." He told her to wait in the car and went inside to get some food to go. Before he left, she thanked him so sweetly and so apologetically that he almost couldn't leave her there, big, tense eyes gazing at him through the open car window, pale hands clutching the edge of the door like Kilroy. He walked back at once, kissed her mouth, then turned to complete his mission. He was starving.

When he returned, the bags he carried already darkening with the grease from two cheeseburgers, she looked even more grave. "I can't bring myself to make the call," she said. "I'm sorry."

Harry took the cell phone, remembering Josie's words again. "It's all right. I will," he said. The phone was still turned off; he pressed the On button. "I missed a call from Dusty. Okay if I call him back first?" She nodded. Dusty answered right away. After hearing his news, all Harry could say was "Jesus Christ, Jesus Christ. Throw it out. He might have dusted it with anthrax or something." Then he made his son bring Ann to the phone. He gave her a simplified account of who and what Jonathan Ziegart was. "Don't let him anywhere near you or Dusty again."

She yelled at him for not giving them some advance warning, which he bore even though he hadn't had any himself. After an awkward pause, she said that they had police protection of a sort anyway. When he pressed her, she reluctantly told him that she'd been seeing an assistant district attorney. "I can make sure he's around the house a lot." Harry didn't bother asking how long she'd been seeing him; he'd known from Dusty that she had a man in her life, and he was sure now it had been going on long before Ann had made that plea to get him back. He felt no twinge of jealousy, which was a relief, but he threatened her with everything he could think of if she let anything happen to their son. "Take him back to your parents'," he said. She hung up on him.

"Oh God," Maggie said.

"Jonathan gave him a copy of *Lord of the Rings*. He was pleasant."

"He wants you to know that he can get to Dusty."

They debated about the value of returning to Stoweville, of flying or driving to Orlando that evening. Harry could tell that Maggie was looking for an excuse to forget the visit to Fay Levy. He thought some more, then said, "I think he'll be okay. I hope so." He rubbed his chin. "I'm not sure what good it will do us to run down there right now. At least Ann and her DA boyfriend know who to look out for."

"But not what," Maggie said.

"No. But neither do we." He felt his stomach rumbling and fished the burger out of the bag. He was surprised he was still hungry. "Dusty's actually kind of psyched to be in on things this much." He took a bite. "I think we should keep to our plans. I don't know what else to do."

They finished their burgers, and then Harry called Fay Levy. He got the answering machine after the second ring. After leaving a cryptic message and his cell number, he turned to Maggie. "We could just go to her house, but I don't know if it's a good idea to ambush her."

"Let's get it over with," she said.

When they pulled up to the little brick house, the windows were dark. There was a lamp on a pole by the front walk that was shaped like an old-fashioned lantern. The light it gave off was dim, and Harry felt like a criminal staking out a future robbery as they sat in the car, watching the moths batter themselves against the metal and glass of the light. Neither one of them had an opinion on how long they should wait for Fay to come home, so they sat in an uneasy silence with the car windows open, the crickets chirping loudly in the dusk. At least Harry thought they were crickets, but when he mentioned this to Maggie, she said, "Tree frogs. This time of night, they're out trying to mate. They make a big racket."

"So I hear," he said. "I'd rather be trying to mate right now myself."

This got a smile from her at least, though not a big one. Then the street rumbled with the sound of an approaching car, headlights brushing them. Harry wondered what their faces looked like, if they were even visible in the brief wash of light. A compact car pulled into the short driveway to the house; its engine went silent and the lights died. He recognized Fay Levy's silhouette as she got out of the car. Harry glanced at Maggie, then opened the driver's side door.

"Fay?" he called softly, trying not to startle her.

The woman turned and gave the impression of recognition, although it was impossible to see her face clearly in the dark. He said,

"It's Harry Sterling. I left you a message, but I assume you haven't gotten it yet. Do you have a few minutes?"

"I didn't expect to see you again," she said, opening her car's rear hatch and bending in, then standing up with canvas grocery bags dangling heavily from her hands. "You could help me get these into the house."

"I'd be glad to. But I've got someone in the car who wants to see you." He imagined peanut butter jars and cartons of milk crashing to the ground the moment Fay set eyes on Maggie. "I think it would be a good idea if you put the bags down first." Fay obeyed him, resting the bags on the concrete of the driveway, where they settled and rustled when she removed her hands from the handles. "Isn't that your son with you?"

"No," he said as the passenger door opened and Maggie got out.

Harry was glad he'd made her put the groceries down, for she surely would have dropped them; she seemed to lose control of her knees for a moment, falling into the car, her hands splayed out on the hood. "Emily?" she said.

Maggie nodded and walked slowly toward the car; Harry imagined it was the way you walked toward a UFO when you were being abducted, with slow steps to somewhere you didn't really want to go, but all volition had been zapped from you.

"You're alive," Fay said in a funny voice, trembly and high. Maggie's mouth opened, but Fay spoke again before she could. "You lied to me. You lied to me about being dead, for God's sake." She stood up straighter. "I can't believe you did such a terrible thing."

"I'm sorry," Maggie said. "I'm so sorry, Fay. Can . . . can we talk? I'd like to try to explain what's been going on."

"For six years, I've thought you killed yourself. How could you possibly have done that to me?"

"In a way, I *was* dead. As good as, anyway."

"Don't play word games with me." Fay turned to Harry, the twilight making her face into a muddy mask, her features appearing to twist and shift as bits of light swam in and out of the topography of her face. "And you knew all along, you son of a bitch. Were you laughing at me? You and your son?" She came around the car toward Maggie, pushing against the hood with her hands as if her legs weren't working right.

Maggie said, "He just found out. Believe it or not, I was trying to do you a favor."

"A fucking *favor?*" Fay's voice was stronger now, and considerably louder. She pushed off from the car, moving toward Maggie with renewed strength in her legs. "Am I supposed to thank you? I cried for a solid year. A whole goddamned year. I gave up graduate school, I gave up everything because I thought you had died, I thought that they'd beaten you, and if you could be beaten, what chance did someone like me have? But they didn't beat you, you snuck off like a goddamned snake into a bunch of rocks or something."

"Fay."

"Don't you 'Fay' me, like all you have to do is say my name and it'll be just fine, all forgiven, no harm done." With that, Fay moved toward Maggie with one arm raised and hit her in the face with a closed fist. Maggie staggered back a pace as Harry lunged forward in horror; he'd expected crying and hugs, or maybe a few recriminations and then tearful forgiveness. He'd never expected Fay Levy to want to beat Maggie senseless.

He reached Fay before she had a chance to strike Maggie again, catching her wrist and holding it in the air as though he were proclaiming her the winner. Maggie was still standing, one hand to her eye, but she made no sound, no defensive movement. Fay ripped her arm from Harry's grip, then stepped back, making a sound like a growl. Harry said, "No one's laughing. It was life or death, and I think you should listen to what she has to say."

Fay turned to him, so angry that Harry could hear her breath fighting its way in and out. "Life or death my ass. I think you should both leave right now. If you come back, I'm calling the police."

On the way back to the hotel, Harry stopped at a small grocery store. He left Maggie in the car since the lights inside it were even more gaseous and bright than the ones in the restaurant. He came back in a few minutes with a bag of frozen peas. "Put this on your eye," he said. She obeyed without a word. Then he said, "It's not your fault, you know. She seems a little crazy."

"Most people thought she was a lot less crazy than me." She shifted the bag of peas and leaned her head against the window. "When Dee sent the letter to the department about my supposed suicide, all I thought about was Fay. I felt so guilty about abandoning her, but at least I figured she'd be safe. Maybe I was a coward. I guess I was."

"You've never seemed cowardly to me. All we know for sure is that Jonathan Ziegart didn't come after her. It's possible that you saved her life. Besides, you learn to live with guilt," he said. "She may calm down later. Or not. We can't do anything about it, one way or the other."

She said, "Let's go home. I never want to see this place again."

57

THE
HANGED MAN

REVERSED

Denial of spiritual truth.
Hard work with no payoff

"Ma'am?" he said. "Miss Tokay?"

"Yes?" she said. Her voice was faint and croaking, barely audible, as if her lungs were too old to work right, not enough muscle power to get the air all the way down to where it could do its work properly.

"My name's Jon. I'm an old friend of Maggie's. I don't know if she's mentioned me?" It was a critical question, he knew, but he had a sense that she'd kept her former life quiet; it was unlikely the old lady knew much about it.

Miss Tokay regarded him for a moment, blinking her damp gray eyes. "My memory is so unreliable." She said it apologetically, and he was starting to get the flavor of her accent. Nice and slow. "You're a friend of Maggie's?"

"Yes," he said. "An old friend from when she was at school. I don't know if you knew her then."

"Not so well as now, of course, but that was a while ago. It's nice to see old friends; I don't have so many left nowadays. Not from school. Not from all that time ago."

"Yes, ma'am. May I come in?" He smiled again and pulled out his identification from his long-ago internship. "May I talk to you? This isn't official, mind you. It's just that I know that my bosses at the bureau are trying to decide whether or not to see Maggie as a 'person of interest.' I was hoping to talk to you because all this unpleasantness happened on your property, and Maggie's a friend of yours. I thought maybe the two of us could put our heads together, see if we can piece together what really happened. Maybe with your help, I can put their suspicions to rest."

"What suspicions?" Miss Tokay's voice rose a little, the tremor strengthening. "Of Maggie? They can't possibly think she had anything to do with . . . what happened?"

"Well, ma'am, the sad truth is they're looking to lay blame. It's all politics and paperwork, to be honest. You and I know that Maggie is the nicest girl under the sun and would never harm anybody. But that's the way the wind is blowing in the bureau; I'm being candid with you here. I want to try to set things right. I was hoping you'd help me."

"If you're a friend of Maggie's," the old lady said, "you're welcome to come in."

She led the way through a warmly lit hallway into a pretty room illuminated by what appeared to be genuine Tiffany lamps. It was cool in the room; he could hear the welcome hum of air-conditioning. He paused in his progression across the parlor, as he named the room in his mind, to examine the shade of a floor lamp with a pattern of hummingbirds pieced together with bits of emerald and ruby glass. "Ma'am, I think I see a chip here. Was there gunfire in this room?"

"Of course not," said Miss Tokay. She had been in the process of sitting down on her sofa, rewrapping her enormous purple shawl around her shoulders before bending her knees. This stopped her. "What chip? That lamp has been on that spot for close to eighty years, and it's never been damaged."

It also looked as though it hadn't been cleaned in at least thirty, he thought; the dust was as thick as his finger. "Come see for yourself, Miss Tokay." She made her way back across the room, fingers tight on the hem of the shawl. Her steps were slow, each foot lifting only a fraction of an inch above the floor so that her shoes made a swishing sound on the wood; to Jonathan it sounded as though someone was using a broom, *sweep, sweep.* She came near the lamp, and he pointed to a spot near the crown where the dust had been smeared by his index finger.

"See, just here?" he said. "It looks like it was slightly tipped by a bullet. Just glanced off it. Of course, if it had been a more direct hit, it would have been blown to bits. It's just a nick. Are you sure there wasn't any event involving a gunshot in this room?" As she shook her head in confusion, he looked around the room as though searching for other evidence. "Maybe a stray," he said. "You'd be surprised how far they can travel. I know that not all the slugs were found by the crime scene folks." This was untrue, but Jonathan doubted Miss Tokay had read the incident report. "Did they look through this room much?"

"They searched it, looking for God knows what," she said. "There was no call to look at the furniture the way you're doing. No one was in here when the . . . when it happened."

"Just as I thought," he said. "If a bullet came through the door and glanced off the lamp, no one would have known about it." He nodded confidently and pulled a magnifying glass from his pocket. He turned to the lamp shade, peering at the imagined nick. "I can see it here. Yes, it's definitely something." He pocketed the magnifying glass. "I hate to say this, ma'am, but I'm going to have to take this to the lab to be processed. It'll be returned to you."

"How long will it take?"

"No more than a couple of weeks," he said. If anyone asks me, he thought, I can say the nephew must have stolen it; I bet he'd love to get his hands on this. "That's enough about guns for now. Please sit down." He touched her under her elbow, which caused her to start. He wondered when a man had last touched her who wasn't a doctor. But she seemed to relax at once and allowed him to guide her to the ornate sofa. He kept his hand on her arm all through her bottom's rickety progress onto the seat. When she was finally ensconced, her shawl carefully repositioned around her, he asked if he could sit as well; at her nod, he took the chair across from her. He said, "Maggie told me that the workshop is actually hers. I'm willing to keep that information to myself, but there have been some suspicions about Crawley's story. I know the previous investigators looked through the papers in your garage. I was wondering if you'd mind if I took a look as well."

Miss Tokay took a moment to think about this. "Papers?" she said.

"Yes. Notes regarding her work there. I assume that's where she keeps them."

"Oh," she said, her head bobbing in comprehension. "Her notebooks."

"Yes, ma'am." Eureka, he thought.

"They're all in the temple, as far as I know."

"The temple?"

"Yes, that's where she's always worked. In the temple. Of course I don't use it as such anymore. Such a shame. The Sky People are going to see that I ascend quite soon, myself. Life is change, I know that, but sometimes it still makes me sad, seeing the temple transformed from a place of worship and wisdom and joy to a place of belts and pulleys and motors. But that's wisdom of a kind, too, I know. Joy, too, at least to Maggie. At least sometimes." She stopped.

She'd been looking in his direction, but her attention had been on her own thoughts. Now she focused on him and gave a small smile. "Do you understand anything that I'm talking about, honey?"

Jonathan gave a small laugh. "Not really, ma'am. But I'd love it if you explained it to me." Her smile spread across her face and he thought that, when she was young, she must have been a looker; even through the wrinkles and the death that were all over her face, the smile was beautiful. Not as beautiful as Emily's, to be sure, but sweet enough to make you speculate on her past. That's how she got followers, he thought; she beguiled them with her beauty.

"I'm speaking of spiritual matters," she said. "I don't know if you hold with such things."

"I have a degree in religious studies, ma'am. It sounds like you're in the tradition of Madame Blavatsky and the Society of the Golden Dawn."

"Oh, yes. I didn't expect such sophistication in metaphysical matters from a Yankee boy such as yourself, if you'll forgive my being so blunt." She smiled again. "Your mother must be very proud, such a fine-spoken fellow as you are." That's when Jonathan decided for sure he wouldn't kill her.

They talked for an hour or so, after she'd apologized for not having any refreshments to offer him. "My niece and her husband consumed everything that was worth eating," she said. He assured her that he didn't require anything. As she told him more about the Sky People and the Ascended Masters, he nodded intelligently from time to time, letting her do most of the talking; this seemed to please her. "You know, everything in the universe has consciousness. Not just the things we normally think of as living. Even the rocks and mountains and water are alive. It's just that the life processes of some things move at such a slow pace, we don't recognize it." She gave him another one of her smiles, and he could see her girl-face again in the shadow of the one she looked through now. "I've enjoyed this. Thank you for tolerating me."

He assured her that he'd enjoyed their conversation as well, which was only partly false. He'd been interested in spite of himself because he loved the minds of others, especially when those minds wandered all over sanity like lost boats on the sea. "But I do need to be going, ma'am. I hope we can talk more soon. But for now, if you'll allow me to take a look at her papers, that would be great." He stood up. "I'll take the lamp now and put it in my car."

"Why don't you get it as you leave?" she said, opening a wooden box on the small table in front of her. "I'll gather some literature to give you." The box tinkled a tune when the lid was lifted. " 'The Dying Swan' from *Swan Lake*," she added. "Tchaikovsky."

"Ah, yes," said Jonathan. "It's beautiful." Valuable, too, by the look of it.

"It's Russian." She pulled a bright gold key from inside the box and held it out. He leaned over and took it. "It opens everything," she said. She asked for his help in standing; he came next to her and pulled her up by her child-size arm. It gave him the creeps how light she was, how thin and hollow her little bones felt. She followed him out to the hallway. He was about to walk out the big front door when she opened a compartment in the big grandfather clock that faced it. She pulled a large flashlight from inside the clock. "Take this," she added. "It's mighty dark out there. There are lights by the temple, but I don't want you falling into the big sink out there. It can come up on you kind of quick. Make sure you use this when you're unsure of your footing."

"Thank you, ma'am," Jonathan said, giving her a smile almost as beautiful as hers.

58

THE EMPEROR

REVERSED

Control slips away.
The Seeker may be seriously
injured in the fracas

The night was crystal clear, remarkably
so for this time of year. Jonathan wondered if they got many hurricanes in this
part of Florida. He was starting to miss
the hills of Pennsylvania, where you
could see for miles from even casual van-
tage points. Here, you couldn't see more
than a few feet in any direction because
of the trees. And the night was *so* dark,
heavy and damp and black. The proxim-
ity of the town didn't help; Stoweville
was so small that its lights didn't pene-
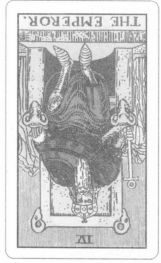
trate even the lowest part of the sky. He thought, Maybe I need to
rethink living here. It's awfully hot.

The tapestry made by the sharp white stars was so bright that his
eyes ached whenever he looked up, his pupils dilated with the effort
to see through the trees. But there was no moon, and the stars
weren't much help in the woods. He let his eyes adjust, took his
time. There was no need to hurry, no need to let haste cause blun-
ders, and it was too muggy to move fast anyway. He walked slowly
along the path the old lady had told him to follow, then saw the cir-

cle of lights girding the sinkhole. He remembered Wally Faber saying that sinkholes were favorite places to dispose of old appliances, and worse. In daylight, he would have taken a good long look, but in the dark, the sinkhole beyond the lights had all the charm of a black hole, the kind his father used to talk about, that could suck in an unwary astronaut or planet or star, elongating it like a grisly galaxy-size rubber band before tearing it apart. His father had always spoken with ill-concealed jealousy of Stephen Hawking, the physicist best known for his theoretical work on black holes and for his imprisonment in a body long afflicted with Lou Gehrig's disease. "Steve's got a brilliant mind all right. Maybe more so than Einstein or Feynman. But he's completely impractical." One time Jonathan had been at dinner at his father's house, and Charlie had said, "You can't fuel a nuclear generator with black holes." Emily had responded in that smarty-pants way she had, "Not yet." His father had gotten furious and stomped off to his study; he hadn't emerged for several hours. Jonathan was pretty sure his father hadn't spoken to his wife for at least a day after that. The memory gave him a peculiar feeling, a kind of wistfulness for something, although he wasn't sure what. He didn't miss those days, his teenage years, when he felt constantly undervalued, pushed aside, and discounted. But there was something there, some small warmth that he thought maybe he'd like to have again, although he hadn't the faintest idea of how to get it. Maybe, he thought, maybe I could just talk to Emily, make her see that I'm really in her corner. I always was, just not in the way she wanted. Harry Sterling, a galoot if ever there was one, what the hell is she doing with him? Jonathan thought about Harry's son, Dustin. What a pretentious name to give your child. But Ann Sterling, now there was a name. The name of a movie star.

His thoughts had distracted him from his purpose, so he left the yawning black maw in the ground and again moved along the path, his once nice shirt soggy and sticking to his back. The chirping tree frogs were so loud that he couldn't have heard a semi if it was roaring up the path behind him. It sounded like complaining, Jonathan thought, like millions of the little beasts were yelling at him to go home. Mentally he told them to go fuck themselves, then halted in midstride as the sight in front of him took his breath away. He saw what looked like a UFO landed in a clearing of the trees, a great black thing surrounded by lights, like something from a modern sci-fi blockbuster. "Holy shit," he said aloud. The sound stopped the chirping of the tree frogs, and the silence was worse than their screaming. It was suddenly so quiet that he could hear his own blood hissing in his ears, the pump-pump of it lurching through his temples and the sides of his neck, his heart beating his ribs. "Holy shit," he said again, mainly to hear something outside his body. For the first time in many years, the knowledge that he was absolutely alone discomfited him.

He walked slowly around the big building, his eyes adjusting to the relative brightness of the lights around the damn thing. He could see that they were fueled with solar panels and thought, Emily's been busy. How philanthropic, or maybe the old lady had paid her something. Although given the condition of the house, it was unlikely that she had much. Maybe she's one of those misers, he thought, buckets of money in a toilet tank or in the freezer, but all she buys with it are solar panels from her neighbors. He grinned to himself, relaxing as the strangeness of the setting began to wear off. The tree frogs were back at it now, one having started and given the rest of them courage when they saw that it wasn't smushed by a foot or tire or swallowed by a snake. He walked slowly around the odd, dark building till he found the door. The lights were all mounted high on poles, so what reached the deep carvings in the wood drew fine shadows around them, making them look as though they moved. Dancing doors, he thought; it sounds like a good name for a band.

He pulled the key from his pocket and fitted it into the incongruously modern-looking lock in the door. Although the building didn't really look old-fashioned. Rather, it looked other-fashioned, from no time that had ever existed or would ever exist. Bizarre. Insane, he thought, that's the word I'm looking for. And the lock looks so common, like what you'd find on the front door of a suburban split-level.

He turned the key and pushed the door open. He experienced a quickening of his circulation just as he had when the temple had first come into view. The darkness inside had a foggy, gray quality that the night itself lacked. He reached inside for a switch, wondering as he did so if the solar panels powered the inside wiring, and if there was enough juice stored up to light the place. He found what he was looking for just inside the door frame, a big box that jutted out from the wall, the unmistakable shape of a toggle switch on its face. He flipped it up, which took some effort; rust or dirt had caked around it. Nothing happened, but he thought with some alarm, Maybe I've just put my hand in some sort of insect nest encrusted around the switch. He pulled his hand back quickly; for a moment he had the sensation that something was crawling on it, but he held it in front of his face, turning it so that the light from the poles fell directly on his palm. He turned his hand over and over, looked up and down his arm, turning his entire body this way and that. Nothing walked on him, nothing was burrowing in his shirt. He pulled the handkerchief out of his pocket and wiped his hands. His mother had had him tested for every allergy known to modern medicine when he was a young teenager; the doctors had pronounced his immune system perfectly normal, able to distinguish genuine threats to his health from relatively benign intruders like pollen and bee venom. Nevertheless, the prospect of a spider bite or scorpion sting didn't appeal at all. He found contact with insects generally repellent, and it certainly didn't take a shrink to understand why. How could I ever live in Florida? he thought. There are more bugs than oxygen molecules.

The old lady had warned him that parts of the floor were missing, so he went in only as far as the outside light reached. He smelled damp and mildew, heard some sort of liquid trickling and thought that the roof must leak, and that some rainwater must have been trapped between the roof proper and the ceiling during the last storm. He imagined tar-paper reservoirs of buggy, tea-colored water under the roof tiles dripping mosquito larvae and worse onto his head. Onto Emily's head, too, since she works here all the time, and then he thought, So she's sunk to this. She works in this hellhole. He wondered what she used for light.

He took a small, careful step even as he pulled the flashlight out of a pocket with his right hand, the handkerchief still wadded in his left. He thought, I wish Miss Tokay was my grandmother, then turned the flashlight on, and something happened that he couldn't have explained to anyone if he was ever to have had the chance. The room exploded into view, all in black and white, no color, although there was an impression of lavender, like you see in faded old photographs that have been tinted improbable faint shades, the years hammering them into almost nothing. There was a smell, too, ozone and melted rubber, and a sound, *zing*, quick and then gone. He had an instant of recognition, of some deep memory stirred; he'd seen this thing in action before, he'd seen this light, smelled this smell. But the memory evaporated as quickly as it had come and did him no good at all. He jumped and screamed and then felt his footing disintegrate, as though he was standing on nothing; he could hear wood creak and separate with a series of small groans in the same moment that the hellish flash went out. He had the sensation of falling, the quality of which was so nightmarish and bizarre that he wasn't even afraid, couldn't grasp the reality of what was happening enough to be afraid, couldn't understand any piece of what his senses were trying to tell him. Complete blackness and free fall, a feeling that was almost of joy, of immense fun. Then he hit water, that he could tell at once, and it was so cold that he couldn't breathe, which was just as well as it went over his head and he went down and down and down, and it was so dark he couldn't tell where up was at all, even though he was sure his eyes were open since they felt like they had frozen solid.

His arms and legs began to move in spasms, kicking and waving through what felt like liquid ice. His head finally broke free from the water, and he breathed in great gulps of thick, wet air. But he still couldn't see anything except velvet black. He treaded water, one shoe gone into outer space for all he knew, the flashlight or whatever it was gone as well, as was his father's handkerchief. As he felt the cold start to eat him up, he realized what had happened, or part of it. He'd fallen into one of those sinkholes, and he thought, The old lady, the motherfucking old lady did this to me, she gave me the goddamned motherfucking key. She's dead, she has no idea how dead she is; I'll kill her myself and won't care if anyone knows it, she's a goddamned walking corpse.

59

THE WHEEL
OF FORTUNE

REVERSED

Luck goes this way and that.
You'll get what you deserve

Harry talked to Dusty again in the room
while watching Maggie spread the Tarot
cards out on the big bed. Her hands
started shaking, and he cut the conversation short. "What's wrong?"

"I wouldn't let her do a reading for
me. Not for a long time now. I was going
to the library, and I told her that if she
didn't stop drinking, it was going to kill
her. All she said was 'Something else'll
get me long before that.' I got so mad at
her and just left her, sitting in Miss
Tokay's living room with her cards. She was right. Oh God, Harry. If
I hadn't left, maybe everything would have been all right."

"And maybe you'd be dead," he said, hugging her. "It's my fault a
lot more than it's yours. I opened my big fat mouth to Gillian De-
Graff. That's why Jonathan came down to Florida in the first place
and found you." He let her cry for a while. His cell phone rang; she
made him answer it. It was Miss Tokay.

. . .

He knew he had to keep moving, so he began to swim, carefully propelling himself in what he thought was a constant direction, to try to reach the limestone wall. He'd left the temple door open, and now he could see tiny threads of light from above, although he was horrified by how far away they were; they looked as far away as the stars. He estimated that in reality it was thirty feet, maybe more, the faint light caressing ragged, sharp planks forming the giant hole way, way above him.

He blinked to warm his frozen eyes and swam through water that smelled like moldy bread, and there were things in it, things he bumped against, lily pads or small pieces of wood, he hoped, although there was no way to know for sure. The water had a film on it, too, thick and greasy, and he could feel it clinging to his chin and his hair; some got in his mouth, and it tasted of rot so he spit it out; his whole body shuddered with revulsion and what he feared was encroaching hypothermia. It's summer, he thought. I'm in Florida. People swim in these filthy holes for fun. I'm freezing, but I won't freeze to death. I'm alive, I'm healthy, I'm strong, I'm not injured. I can swim.

He bumped against the side of the sink and patted the torn chunks of limestone, feeling shards crumble and cut his hands. There were indentations in the rock, but they were all wet and as slippery as if they'd been coated with oil. Algae, he thought, and some sort of bug, unused to being disturbed by anything as large as a human hand, chittered and ran across his fingers. He yelped and splashed away.

He took another gulp of the greasy, thick water, choked and gagged, treaded water, moved his arms, and thought, I have to conserve my strength, I've got to keep moving but I can't wear myself out. He had a vague memory of his father talking about work in terms of kilocalories, Emily gently correcting him on one point or another, and his hatred of her flared into a determination to live, to get out of this nightmare if only so he could kill her with his bare hands. Emily and the insane old lady and Harry the big galoot and his precious son and anyone else connected to them, who'd ever even smiled at them.

His eyes were starting to adjust again; even in this deep blackness, the light from above was enough to begin to see dim gray patterns in the rock around him. He thought again of Emily, remembered her telling him about experiments involving infinitesimal amounts of light shooting through tiny slits in paper barriers. "Light acts as a wave or a particle, depending on what question you ask it," she had said, as if she was revealing something wonderful to him. He hadn't understood then how you could have so little light, a beam consisting of one photon at a time, something she said you could even see if you had a dark-adapted eye. He thought, My eyes are as dark-adapted as you can get, and he wondered if that was what he was seeing, one goddamned motherfucking particle of light, taking its goddamned time wafting down to him. He could hear her correcting him. "It won't take any time at all. It'll move at the speed of light." Haha, he thought. "I'm going to kill you, you know," he said aloud and was terrified by the sound of his voice, so faint, so weak, so hoarse. He sounded like a dying monster.

Now in the light from the few photons that had made their way into the hole, he could see something largish and dark pushed against the side of the sink farthest from him; it looked like a log, and for a moment he wondered if sinkholes had alligators in them and in his terror he felt his bladder let go, which was awful but warmed the water directly around him, which felt horribly good. Then the knowledge came to him from somewhere in his underappreciated brain, alligators were cold-blooded, they wouldn't want to live in a place like this, and sinkholes were fed by underground streams and rainwater; alligators didn't live in underground caves and rivers, he was safe, he wasn't about to be food, thank God, thank God.

His relief threatened to weaken him, so he made himself move to the big log. He thought, It must be a fallen tree, rotten maybe, but something that will float, that I can rest on. Maybe I'll get lucky and it'll be stuck to the side, maybe even give me some purchase out of the water. He reached it, his feet still doing most of the work of keeping him afloat because he didn't want to thrust his weight onto the log and be disappointed. He reached out an icy hand and touched it. It felt soft and unpleasant, but as if it had some solidity under the squishiness; it didn't move much, just bobbed a little in the wake he'd made. It was attached in some way to the rocks, caught on something. It appeared to be a small rotting tree, a few small branches protruding from it, one of which fell off as he searched the surface of the log for a place to get a better grip. He found a narrow spot above the waterline that he could get his arms around, and he lifted himself slightly, his shoulders coming out of the water into the warm air. The smell of the water and the rotting log was getting worse. I'll never eat seafood again, he thought. Not anything that once lived in water.

"She said she was fine and not to worry," Harry said. "She was just checking on us, to make sure that everything had gone well today."

"That was awfully sweet of her," Maggie said.

There was a sound from above, a long way away, a faint sound, a door creaking, footsteps, the light from the hole so far above him growing stronger. He started so hard he almost lost his grip, but he pulled himself up higher, trying to make a sound, trying to yell for help. Finally he managed a sound, a croak that he feared wasn't loud enough, but then the light brightened further and his happiness was

boundless. He found his voice again and managed to yell, "Help me!
Help me!" It sounded as though he'd been crying, as though he was
begging for something. He could see the silhouette of a head over
the rim of the hole, indistinct in the weird light, impossible to tell
anything about it. The light pooled around the head, making a halo;
an angel, Jonathan thought, and his relief was such that he would
have laughed if he'd had the strength.

The beam of a flashlight, a real one, shone down on him, blinding him for a moment, but then the light seemed to call to itself, although it could only have been a reflection, some eerie property of
the beam bending in the bottomless water; it looked as if a ball of
light of incredible beauty was coming down to him. He felt like
praying when it seemed to come together with its mate, its reflection appearing to come from the water itself, and the image and the
reflection seemed to merge somewhere in the warm air above him,
giving birth to sparks that fell around him like rain. He blinked to
get his eyes to work properly, and that was when he saw that the log
was in fact a corpse, an empty and ruined head inches from his own.
The branches were arms, one now knocked loose into the frigid
water; he was gripping the greasy and raddled torso, and he
screamed and screamed as he lurched away from the horrible thing.
He screamed some more, and then the light went away altogether,
taking the angel with it.

60

DEATH

Everything dies.
Everything is born

Their flight to Jacksonville was direct; Harry had left his car at the airport, so he planned to drive back to Stoweville as soon as they'd collected their bags. Maggie said, "Is anyone renting your beach house this week?"

"I don't know. Probably. Why? You want to spend some time there?" He thought about it for a moment, liking the idea.

"I'd love to, but that's not why I asked." She looked uncharacteristically sheepish. Harry cocked an eyebrow at her, and she said, "I put some stuff there."

"What? What stuff? When? How?"

"I still had the keys from when Josie and the girls and I were there before."

Harry waited.

"Josie had a feeling that Jon was planning something. Well, not a feeling, exactly. You know."

"She saw it in the cards."

She nodded, not looking at him. "I knew he was going to be after me one way or another anyway as soon as I found out he was in town." She looked at him. "I borrowed your storeroom."

"For some stuff."

"Uh-huh. I was there between renters, so no one saw me go in."

"What stuff, Maggie?"

"A lot of paper. Notebooks. Of mine. And some other stuff. Prototypes."

"Prototypes?" He forced himself to lower his voice. "Of what?" Oh God, he thought. The stun gun. He lowered his voice some more. "Not more weapons?"

She looked startled. "Oh no. Nothing like that. A hair dryer that I was working on for Miss Baby. It's energy efficient."

"Okay. What else?"

"Some components of a car engine that will run on water. Another one that uses cooking oil. A card shuffler for a big deck, like Tarot cards. A few extra solar panels. Lightbulbs. A battery you can recharge with body heat. Stuff like that."

"Oh," said Harry. "It's all at the beach house?"

"Yes. Locked up in your pantry. I thought maybe we could get it out. Your car's not big enough, though. We'll need to rent a truck."

"Oh, Jesus," Harry said.

They found a U-Haul dealership that had a trailer Maggie decided was of sufficient size and made arrangements to drop it off in Stoweville when they returned home. They had to wait an hour for the man behind the counter to install a hitch on the back of Harry's car.

"I'll pay you back," Maggie said, patting her pocket where she'd stashed the check that Gillian DeGraff had couriered to their room early that morning.

"It's okay," he said. "I know you're good for it."

Harry called the beach house before they left the U-Haul dealer and spoke to irritated renters. They were put out that their vacation was being interrupted by a visit from the owner. "Too bad," he said to Maggie after hanging up. "Goddamned Yankees think they own the world."

When they got to the house, the sun was falling into the west and the heat had peaked for the day. The only tenant there was a fat man with a thick Brooklyn accent; his wife and children were down at the beach. He let them in with the air of one whose fun has been seriously disrupted. Harry and Maggie ignored him after a few attempts at pleasantness and went to the pantry.

Harry opened the door with his key and found the little room crammed with mismatched cardboard boxes and large black garbage bags. The bags might have held bodies for all they weighed and for the odd angles made by whatever was in them. The boxes were heavy, too; she told him they held notebooks.

"There must be dozens of them. What's in them?"

"Notes."

"What kind of notes?"

"For designs. Some calculations. Schematics. You know."

"When did you do all this?"

"Over the past few years."

Harry thought, So much for Dan Polti's theory that physicists burn out before thirty. Her mind was still on fire.

They pulled into the oyster-shell driveway at noon, the trailer bouncing and hitching on the uneven surface. Before they'd reached the front door of the double-wide, Miss Baby came running across the yard to where they stood with their suitcases in hand.

"I'll ask how things in Pennsylvania went in a minute." She looked at Maggie's black eye, then at Harry. "Although I will ask right now if you're responsible for that."

Harry said, "Not in the way you mean."

"It was Fay, Miss Baby. I told you about her." Maggie put down her case. "She wasn't too happy to see me."

Miss Baby nodded. "She thought you were dead, and didn't like to be contradicted." She patted Maggie's cheek and, after ascertaining that nothing else was bruised or broken, said, "Miss Tokay's missing."

"For how long?" Harry asked.

"I don't know exactly. I went over there this morning to check on her. No sign of her anywhere. All her stuff's there, as far as I can tell. The thing that's got me concerned is that her shawl was lying on the sofa like she'd just tossed it off."

"I've never seen her without it," Maggie said, looking worried.

"Me neither," Miss Baby said.

Harry asked, "Have you called anyone? Her niece? The police?"

Miss Baby gave him a look. "Of course I called Gretchen. She claims to know nothing about it. Miss Tokay threw her and Hugh out day before last. Evidently there were some nasty words spoken, and they haven't talked to her since. Hugh is way too interested, of course. I didn't want to call the sheriff just yet. His people aren't exactly our good friends about now. There's a strange car parked behind her house, too. A rental car, looks like."

Harry said, "Jonathan must have a rental, but I don't know what make or color. Do you?" he asked Maggie. She shook her head.

Miss Baby said, "There's no sign of him either. You'd think if he abducted her, he'd take his car." She made a visor of her hand and looked through the trees toward Miss Tokay's house. "I got a few folks walking around on her property to see if she's out there somewhere. But there's an awful lot of land. I checked both sinks, hollered down into the old temple. No answer."

Maggie said, "Oh God, if she fell in, she's dead for sure."

"Maybe she was pushed," Harry said. Maggie and Miss Baby

looked at each other in horror. He went on, "We have to call the sheriff. He's got the manpower to do a proper search." He put his suitcase down on the grass and pulled out his cell phone. The dispatcher didn't sound terribly interested but said that they'd send someone out shortly. Harry put the phone back in his pocket and said, "I'd like to take a look inside the old temple again. If I were her, that's where I'd want to hide. We'd better get a flashlight." He looked at Maggie. "A real one."

61

ACE OF
WANDS

*A new undertaking,
grand, ambitious, and noble*

Serge had never seen Harry look so fit. He looks younger, too, he thought; he looks happy. They were meeting for lunch at Crane's, even though Harry swore that the food wasn't as good since Maggie stopped working there. But he said that she insisted they still patronize the place. One reason was out of loyalty to Calvin Crane; another was that she had trouble tolerating the fluorescent lights of most other Stoweville restaurants.

Serge asked, "How many times have Kimble's people gone diving in the sinks now?"

"Three times into Temple Sink. It's a lot easier to see in Tokay Sink, so one dive was enough to know that she wasn't in there. Of course, if her body got sucked into one of the underground caves, they'll probably never find her."

"You don't think the Sky People came and got her?"

"No, but I'm less inclined to roll my eyes about it than I once was. We live in a bizarre universe."

"It can be a pitiless one, too," Serge said. "Can you imagine Jon Ziegart's last hours? Floating around with a rotting corpse before drowning? Amelia's had more than a few nightmares about it."

"So has Maggie," Harry said. "So have I, for that matter."

"Have they identified the other body? There's been nothing in the paper."

Harry shook his head. "I doubt they'll ever be able to make a positive ID. Maggie thinks that it's Warner Lefland, Miss Tokay's old suitor."

"Do you think the old lady murdered him?"

"I have no idea, and neither does anyone else. There's not enough soft tissue left to be too specific about his death, and the sheriff's people aren't telling us much anyway. But I gather there's some doubt about whether or not he drowned. He almost certainly didn't die in Temple Sink. It didn't even exist when he disappeared."

"You can't mean what I think you mean."

"I'm not sure what I mean. But it's possible that she kept him in her house for a long time before his body wound up in the sink."

"Dead?"

Harry nodded. "Maybe."

"Yeesh."

They studied their menus for a while in silence. Shawntelle brought two glasses of water and plunked them on the table, spilling just a little. "Sorry it took so long," she said. She took their order, then said, "You say hey to Maggie, okay?"

"Will do." As she shuffled off, Harry added, "Hay is for horses."

"Still a snob," Serge said.

"I'm not a snob, I'm discerning. Also complicated."

"Hmm. So what else has been going on? You've been hard to reach for the last three weeks."

"I got some lousy news. I told you about Dusty's homeless friend, right?" Serge nodded. "Kimble made a call. The boy's body was found in a canal. He was identified by a social worker. I'm hoping that there will be some forensics to connect his murder to the man Quick. Unfortunately, that's unlikely."

"Will Dusty have to give evidence? If Quick gets prosecuted?"

"Probably not. Enough people saw Jake and Quick together, so I doubt they'll need him. I haven't decided whether or not to tell him, assuming I have the option to keep it from him."

"You're on your own. I have no idea what the right thing to do is."

Shawntelle brought them each a cup of soup. Serge tasted his and said, "The soup seems the same."

"Maggie never made that."

"Oh." He took another spoonful. "I know you've been meeting with Amos Harper. He, of course, won't tell me anything. But Amelia's dying to know why you're monopolizing a lawyer who specializes in trusts and estates."

Harry said, "Miss Tokay saw Amos a few weeks before she disappeared. She deeded her land and house to Maggie and Miss Baby."

"She *what*?"

"Hugh Covington, the nephew-in-law, is madder than hell, but Miss Tokay was meticulous. She even had Amos bring in a shrink to do a psych evaluation on her so that she could be declared compos mentis, and everything's properly witnessed, so there's not much her nephew-in-law can do about it. It will be a while before the legal mess is cleared up, but at least Hugh can't get the bulldozers in there in the meantime."

"I bet he's having a shitfit."

"You ain't just a-bumpin' your gums." Serge grimaced at this, but Harry just laughed at him. "Sorry. A Miss Baby-ism. Anyway, that's the main thing I wanted to talk to you about today, although you're ultimately going to have to deal directly with Maggie. Amos is helping her set up a foundation. She's got some seed money that we got out of the folks at Cantwell."

"That you extorted out of them, you mean."

"Whatever. That'll be a start, but she's also going to tie a few of her patents to it, which should keep it in funds for a while."

"Patents for what?"

"All kinds of things." He looked up again. "Beautiful fluorescent bulbs. Windmills. You wouldn't believe all the other stuff she's been building in the Purple Lady's garage. The big-ticket items are probably the solar panels. She first worked on them at Cantwell, and Charlie filed the patent in his name, and the university's. She's made substantial improvements over the years, but there could be some trouble from them. But Amos knows something about patent law. He can smell money."

"Like any good attorney. So what's the foundation for?"

"Environmental issues. That's where you come in."

"I'm flattered. Also, I'm not cheap. We're thinking about having kids. They'll need shoes. Good ones."

Harry smiled. "Good luck with that. I'd say name your price, but I'm not your advocate."

Shawntelle came back with sandwiches. After she left, Serge said, "Frank Milford's slobbering all over himself to get her on the faculty, you know."

"She needs time for her main project. They're dickering now about how to work that out within the demands of a faculty position." Harry took a bite of his sandwich, making sure to swallow before he spoke again. He frowned at it, then said, "She's going to build the big tower."

"The Tesla thing?"

"Uh-huh. She's talking to some folks in the biology department about the impact on migratory patterns of birds and other local wildlife and so on. Harper's already filed the patent for the receivers."

"So everyone with one of those would get their electricity for free?"

"Yep. Within a hundred-and-fifty-mile radius. And with satellite uplinks, a lot further."

"Who's going to pay for it?"

"People will have to buy their own receivers. Amos has already been in touch with a company outside Atlanta that will probably be willing to mass-produce them. The foundation will pay for the tower and transmission, at least initially. It'll be cheap enough to generate the power itself. For now, it's simply philanthropy. We're hoping it'll be easier to find other funding once the environmental implications become clear." He smiled again. "Close your mouth, Sergei."

"Do you think it'll work? My God, that would really piss off anyone with stock in power companies. But doesn't she have a foundation to run? Or will that be your job?"

"God, no. I'm writing a book on sexism in the sciences. You'd be amazed at what still goes on. Cantwell's not going to look too good."

"I thought you'd agreed not to eviscerate them in print."

"No. I only agreed not to accuse anyone of murder without evidence. Anyway, running the foundation will be up to Miss Baby."

"The hairdresser?" Serge's voice had raised an octave or two, and several fellow diners looked their way.

"She's got a head on her shoulders, especially for finance."

"My God." Serge looked at his sandwich, still intact. He'd been too distracted to eat a mouthful. "Harry," he said carefully, "you realize the danger she's going to be in. She's going to be bucking the most powerful financial interests in the world. Others have tried. A lot of them have been ruined. More than a few have disappeared."

"That's why we need as much public scrutiny as possible. I've got phone calls in to every major news organization in the country, and quite a few outside of it. You need to contact as many attorneys as you can, especially those with any background in patent law, environmental law, and civil liberties. We need to prepare an information packet and get it out ASAP, on the Internet, on TV, everywhere."

"So it can't be buried."

"So there's less point in trying to discredit Maggie again. Or in killing her." For the first time, Serge could see the fear behind Harry's smile. The weight of their conversation was trickling slowly into his understanding, like groundwater through limestone, and as the pool grew, Serge started to feel some fear himself. Harry was saying, "This is partly Dusty's idea. Like in Lord of the Rings. Make alliances, appeal to everyone's mutual interests. Amass an army of lawyers, journalists, bloggers, activists, politicians, scientists, teachers, whoever, against the forces of greed and waste and darkness." He looked more than fit now. He looked dangerous.

"Jesus Christ," Serge said.

"Something like that," Harry agreed.

Epilogue

The sun was so hot it made you dizzy if you stayed out in it too long. She had on her floppy straw hat, which helped a little, but she knew she'd have to get into the shade soon or her skin would ache with burning. She was almost done with the planting anyway, fall mums aligned like yellow and purple soldiers in tiered planters placed on each step of the shrine. It had been rebuilt and repainted; new lights hung all around, powered by a discreet solar cell placed just behind the enormous heart, fragrant with new enamel. Miss Baby walked down the long driveway, bringing the last flat of flowers from the porch. Charlotte followed, staggering with Miss Tokay's old metal watering can; it was full and sloshing, too heavy for her skinny arms. Tamara came after her with some tools, a child's trowel and a miniature grass rake. The girl's mouth was a gleaming mass of silver; when she smiled in the sunlight, it hurt your eyes to look.

She heard Harry's car; she'd memorized the sound the way you do any glad and eagerly awaited thing. She turned; the top of the little convertible was down, and she could see him and his son, both wearing baseball caps. They waved as the car slowed to pull into the driveway. She waved back with a gloved hand, distracted by the green and blue and orange that crackled off them, and the gleaming points of light that pulsed through it all like the phosphorescence of the sea on a sandy beach. She'd told him many times now that she loved him, no longer waiting for a question. He hadn't had a drink for months; still, he had joined AA and went to his meetings. So far, the craving hadn't overtaken him, and according to the cards, they were safe, at least for the time being.

Harry hopped out of the car and handed her one more plant, a small rosebush in a metal pot. "Is this what you wanted?" he asked. She nodded as Dusty looked up at the shrine and said, "Whoa. It looks awesome, Maggie."

"That's Dr. Roth to you," Harry said. Dusty punched him in the upper arm and Harry proceeded to punch him back. She looked at them with curiosity; what was it like to feel that loving aggression, the lovely ferocity of these men? It appeared to her as throbbing packages of energy that passed between them, teardrop-shaped and moving like leaves in wind. It was so beautiful she couldn't speak.

She placed the rosebush on the ground by the foot of the shrine; Harry had found it at her request. She was going to plant it on Josie's grave; roses had always been Josie's favorite flowers, although she hadn't had a garden just for beauty in the last years of her life. Maggie watched as a single bee found a bloom, circling and swooping down to a soft petal, resting for a moment before it burrowed into the flower's heart. She crouched down to watch it, close up at last, not afraid of it at all.

ABOUT THE AUTHOR

LILA SHAARA is the author of *Every Secret Thing*. She lives in western Pennsylvania with her family.